ADOLPHUS, A TALE

&

THE SLAVE SON

The abandoned Perseverance Estate house, Diego Martin, Trinidad

ADOLPHUS, A TALE

(Anonymous)

THE SLAVE SON

by Mrs William Noy Wilkins

Edited by
Lise Winer

With annotations and an introduction by

Bridget Brereton, Rhonda Cobham,
Mary Rimmer, Karen Sánchez-Eppler and Lise Winer

Caribbean Heritage Series, Volume II

University of the West Indies Press
Barbados ● Jamaica ● Trinidad and Tobago

University of the West Indies Press
1A Aqueduct Flats   Mona
Kingston 7   Jamaica

07 06 05 04 03   5 4 3 2 1

CATALOGUING IN PUBLICATION DATA

Adolphus, a tale / (Anonymous); & The slave son / by Mrs William
Noy Wilkins; edited by Lise Winer with annotations and introduction by
Bridget Brereton . . . [et al.]

p. cm. – (Caribbean heritage series; v.2)

Adolphus, a tale serialized in Trinidadian newspapers in 1853.
The slave son first published: London: Chapman and Hall, 1854.

Includes bibliographical references.

ISBN: 976-640-133-0

1. Slavery in literature. 2. Trinidadian fiction. 3. Historical fiction,
Trinidadian. I. Wilkins, William Noy, Mrs. II. Winer, Lise. III. Brereton,
Bridget, 1946–. IV. The slave son. V. Caribbean heritage series; v.2

PR9272.A1A3 2003   810.972983

Cover illustration: The abandoned Perseverance Estate house,
Diego Martin, Trinidad. Photograph by Hans E.A. Boos.
Set in Sabon 10.5/14.5x2
Cover design by ProDesign Ltd.
Book design by Robert Harris, Jamaica.
Printed in Canada.

Contents

Acknowledgements

We acknowledge with pleasure the patience, generosity, scholarship and acumen of many people who assisted in explanation, translation and identification. Any errors of commission or omission are, of course, the editor's responsibility.

Philip Baker
Yasmin Baksh Comeau (National Herbarium, Trinidad and Tobago)
Hans E.A. Boos
Margaret de Castro
Ichiro Fujinaga and Ian Knopke, Faculty of Music, McGill University
Maricruz García-Rejón
Joe Rao (Hayden Planetarium, New York)
John V. Singler (New York University)
Michael Toussaint (University of the West Indies, Trinidad and Tobago)
Earl Wilson

The editor is grateful to the National Endowment for the Humanities (United States) for a Summer Stipend grant in 1994 to work on this project.

We would also like to express our appreciation to Pansy Benn (Arawak Press, Jamaica), who shepherded this series through the acceptance process at the University of the West Indies Press, and to the staff at the University of the West Indies Press.

CONTRIBUTORS

Lise Winer is Associate Professor in the Faculty of Education, McGill University, Montreal, Canada. She is the author of *Trinidad and Tobago: Varieties of English Around the World, Dictionary of the English/Creole of Trinidad and Tobago* (in progress), and articles on Caribbean language, literature and culture in *Dictionaries, English World-Wide, Journal of Pidgin and Creole Languages, Language in Society, Language Problems & Language Planning, New West Indian Guide,* and various anthologies.

Bridget Brereton is Professor of History at the St Augustine campus of the University of the West Indies, Trinidad and Tobago. Her major books include *A History of Modern Trinidad, Race Relations in Colonial Trinidad,* and *Law, Justice and Empire,* as well as articles on gender and history in the Caribbean.

Rhonda Cobham is Professor of English and Black Studies at Amherst College, Amherst, United States. She has edited special issues of *Research in African Literatures* and the *Massachusetts Review,* as well as *Watchers and Seekers: An Anthology of Writing by Black Women in Britain.* Her essays on Caribbean and African authors and postcolonial theory have appeared in *Callaloo, Transition, RAL* and critical anthologies.

Mary Rimmer is Professor of English at the University of New Brunswick, Fredericton, Canada. Her publications include an edition of

Thomas Hardy's *Desperate Remedies* and articles on Thomas Hardy, Margaret Laurence and Nino Ricci.

Karen Sánchez-Eppler is Professor of American Studies and English at Amherst College, Amherst, United States. She is the author of *Touching Liberty: Abolition, Feminism and the Politics of the Body*, and is completing a book on childhood in nineteenth-century America. Her essays on nineteenth-century American culture have appeared in *Representations, American Quarterly, American Literary History, English Literary History* and critical anthologies.

Introduction

The Historical Corpus

In his pioneering study of "the West Indian novel",[1] Kenneth Ramchand ([1970] 1983) accepts George Lamming's definition: "the novel written by the West Indian about the West Indian reality" (p. 3). That is, he considers for inclusion all literary works that

> have a West Indian setting and contain fictional characters and situations whose social correlates are immediately recognizable as West Indian. The books have all been written in the twentieth century; and their native West Indian authors include descendants of Europeans, descendants of African slaves, descendants of indentured labourers from India, and various mixtures from these. (Ramchand [1970] 1983, 3)

However, stipulating that the books "have all been written in the twentieth century" by "native West Indian authors" arbitrarily cuts off novels which fulfil the other requirements, and which can prove crucial to understanding the development of later works.

The present Caribbean Heritage series of historic republications comprises four Trinidadian novels published between 1838 and 1907.

---

1. "West Indies" and "West Indian" are the terms most often used traditionally to refer to both the anglophone Caribbean – that is, former British colonies whose official (and therefore literary) language is English – and also to the entire region – that is, both the islands of the Caribbean Sea and many of the countries on the bordering mainland, such as Guyana. Recently, the term "Caribbean" has been used more frequently in this manner. Both terms are used in these senses throughout the introduction and notes to this series.

(Several additional works were "rediscovered" but excluded from this series; see details in E.L. Joseph's *Warner Arundell* [(1838) 2001, xiv].) These virtually unknown works constitute the roots of a much longer and deeper local literary tradition and foundation in Trinidad – and the anglophone Caribbean – than hitherto realized.

- E.L. Joseph's *Warner Arundell, the Adventures of a Creole* (London: Saunders and Otley, 1838) is the earliest novel we know of set at least partly in Trinidad, and it is a good candidate for the first Caribbean novel in English. E.L. Joseph came to Trinidad from England as a young man; he is well known for his *History of Trinidad,* which appeared the same year as the novel, and which demonstrates an intimate knowledge of the island. The novel takes place in a number of Caribbean settings, primarily Grenada, Trinidad, Antigua and St Kitts, as well as the Spanish Main (Venezuela and Colombia). In the story, Warner Arundell, a white creole of British descent, is born in Grenada and brought up in Antigua and Trinidad. He is defrauded by lawyers, studies law in Venezuela and medicine in England, then goes to seek his fortune. After many adventures, he is reunited with the coloured branch of his family and with his Spanish lady love.

- *Adolphus, A Tale* (Anonymous) was serialized in the *Trinidadian* newspaper, from 1 January to 20 April 1853. Given its viewpoints, it was probably written by a Trinidadian of mixed race (see below), thus making it the first Trinidadian – and possibly Caribbean – novel by a presumably non-white writer born and raised in Trinidad (see discussion below) and the first novel set almost totally in Trinidad. In the story, Adolphus, the son of an enslaved black woman raped by a white man, is raised by a kindly Spanish-Trinidadian padre. Adolphus grows into a handsome, well-educated, noble character. He falls in love with Antonia Romelia, a beautiful mixed-race woman. She is kidnapped by the villain DeGuerinon, a cruel slave owner who appears to be white. Helped by Cudjoe, one of DeGuerinon's slaves, Adolphus and his friend Ernest rescue Antonia, wounding her captor. As Antonia is restored to her family, her mother dies in her arms. Adolphus and Ernest flee to Venezuela until it is safe to return, and Adolphus and Antonia are free to marry.

- Mrs [Marcella Fanny] William Noy Wilkins, author of *The Slave Son* (London: Chapman and Hall, 1854), was a white woman of Irish birth, but who evidently spent some years living in Trinidad (see below). The heroine of the novel, Laurine, is a mixed-race freed slave who is working to earn enough money to buy the freedom of her mother, Madelaine, an enslaved black woman owned by St Hilaire Cardon. Laurine loves Belfond, a mixed-race slave who has escaped from (his father) Cardon's estate, but she refuses to run away with him or to use stolen money to buy her mother's freedom. Belfond becomes involved in a conspiracy with his uncle, the African obeahman Daddy Fanty, to poison Cardon and his family. There are extensive scenes of brutal estate life under slavery; Mr Dorset, the white owner of a neighbouring estate, tries to treat his slaves more humanely. Belfond is recaptured by Cardon; Mrs Dorset and Laurine plead for him. A slave uprising leaves Cardon dead. Belfond and Laurine escape to freedom in Venezuela.

- In Stephen N. Cobham's *Rupert Gray, A Study in Black and White* (Port of Spain: Mirror Printing, 1907), the hero, Rupert Gray, is a well-educated black accountant, of noble character, who works for Mr Serle, a white businessman who thinks highly of him. When Serle's daughter Gwendolyn returns from England, she and Rupert fall in love. Gwendolyn's friend Dr Florence Badenock comes to visit. A jealous black co-worker, Jacob Clarke, starts a poison-pen campaign against Rupert and alerts Serle to the affair. When Serle finds out, he attacks Rupert and refuses to forgive his daughter. Rupert goes to England under the patronage of a white English lady. Gwendolyn falls into a decline, her father drinks himself to death and Gwendolyn finally dies also. When Rupert returns, as a lawyer, to Trinidad, he is contacted by Florence, and a court trial over the Serle estate ensues. In a dramatic courtroom scene, it is revealed that Gwendolyn is still alive. Helped by her faithful maid, Edith, she had fled to recuperate in Scotland with Florence. Rupert and Gwendolyn are married, have children and live happily – though shunned by "society" – ever after.

Social context is a particularly important aspect of Caribbean literature (McWatt 1985). The novels in this series have a strong political and social impetus. Several speak out against slavery at a time when it was already abolished in Trinidad but still legal in the United States; Mrs Wilkins cites this explicitly as a reason for writing *The Slave Son* in 1854. All of the novels support more rights for the disenfranchised mixed-race and sometimes for the black segments of the population.

The novels also share an underlying thematic continuity with the non-class-based "social consciousness" of later Caribbean literature. As Ramchand explains:

West Indian novelists apply themselves with unusual urgency and unanimity to an analysis and interpretation of their society's ills, including the social and economic deprivation of the majority; the pervasive consciousness of race and colour . . . the lack of a history to be proud of; and the absence of traditional or settled values . . . this social consciousness is not class-consciousness. This is one point at which the West Indian writer naturally departs from the nineteenth-century English novel with which he is most familiar . . . Most West Indian novelists write about the whole society . . . the chaos . . . the open possibilities of their society . . . along with an interest in the previously neglected person. ([1970] 1983, 4)

Trinidad's Literary Roots

When did a literary tradition "begin" in Trinidad? Ramchand does not mention Trinidadian literature earlier than the 1934 publication of Alfred Mendes's *Pitch Lake*. In a later work exploring the origins of the "literary awakening" that occurred in Trinidad during the 1930s, Reinhard Sander (1988, 7) states that "until the late 1920s the literary scene in Trinidad, by contrast [to Jamaica], seems to have produced nothing very remarkable". He quotes Anson Gonzalez (1972), that there was "the occasional work of fiction"; however, Gonzalez himself had seen almost none of these (Gonzalez, personal communication, 1990). Similarly, J.R. Hooker notes that

> Until the 1950s, when Trinidad's literary talent began to astonish the English public, the island produced very little literature. Between Cobham and Naipaul there is only C.L.R. James. There was a small body of fiction preceding the 1907 appearance of *Rupert Gray*. All had grave weaknesses, mostly involving the melodramatic use of two-dimensional characters, but generally they used local settings and hung their plots on actual issues. (1975, 127–28)

The "Trinidad Awakening" is now considered to have begun in 1927, with the publication of C.L.R. James's short story "La Divina Pastora". Writers such as C.L.R. James, Alfred H. Mendes, C.A. Thomasos, Percival Maynard and Katherine Archibald published short fiction in magazines such as *Trinidad* and its successor the *Beacon*, and they experimented with various language registers in their narratives and dialogue; the *Beacon*'s editorials campaigned for the use of more realistic themes, settings and language in local stories. In his introduction to *From Trinidad*, an anthology of writing culled from these journals, Sander points out that "what distinguishes the writers and intellectuals who were involved in the publication of *Trinidad* and *The Beacon* from [other earlier West Indian writers] is primarily their appearance as a group, which fostered the exchange of views and theoretical discussions and prevented creative loneliness and frustration" (1978, 2).

However, it would be a mistake to read this absence of a record of earlier group activity as a sign of complete literary stagnation. It now appears that literature in Trinidad was not totally asleep throughout the nineteenth and early twentieth centuries. The earliest novel in the present series predates James's 1927 story by eighty-nine years and Mendes's novel *Pitch Lake* by ninety-six years; the last of the series novels was published only twenty years before the former and twenty-seven before the latter. That the novels were published over a span of time – 1838, 1853, 1854, 1907 – rather than during only one short time period supports a picture of a longer and deeper literary tradition than has been posited previously.

There is at present no way of knowing how much direct influence these novels had on writers, at the time or later. Certainly *Warner Arundell* was publicly reviewed at the time of its first appearance, and *Adolphus* was serialized in a well-known newspaper. Though it is likely that some copies of the published books were available, there were probably never very many around, given the scarcity (and sometimes incomplete condition) of known surviving copies today. Nevertheless, these novels manifest the same social, cultural and literary impulses, orientations and concerns that have been considered archetypally West Indian, both historically and currently, and are an integral part of Trinidadian and Caribbean literary traditions. Recognition of the deeper literary roots of these traditions should strengthen, rather than weaken, this view of thematic and stylistic continuity. The awakening did not arise without warning; the same impetus that drove the first works of literature only lay "sleeping" until conditions arose in the 1930s that *re*awakened it.

The Social Context of Trinidad

Both *Adolphus* and *The Slave Son* are set in the period of Trinidad's history which saw the last two decades of slavery, between 1812 and 1834, a period dominated by the governorship of Sir Ralph Woodford (1813–28), who also appears in E.L. Joseph's *Warner Arundell*. Starting with the Registration Order in Council of 1812, attempts were made by the British government to "ameliorate" the conditions of the enslaved people, with important new laws enacted in 1824 and 1831, culminating in the Imperial Act of Emancipation (1833) which came into effect in August 1834. At the same time, Trinidad's large "free coloured" group agitated for legal equality with whites, gaining substantial concessions by 1829 (Brereton 1981, 52–75).[2]

---

2. In Caribbean historiography, the term "free coloureds" is used to denote persons in slave society who were legally free but were not "white". Many, including nearly all the better-off and the political leaders, were mixed race, often light complexioned. Some were of mainly or wholly African descent and the term "free blacks" is sometimes used to distinguish this group. We use the term "free coloureds" in this introductory essay in preference to the US term "freedmen/women".

During this period the island's population was small but diverse. No accurate censuses were taken before emancipation, but the total population was estimated at 37,980 in 1813 and 42,250 in 1825. Whites, mainly of French, Spanish, Corsican, Irish and English origin, numbered around 3,000 or about 8 per cent of the total. The free coloureds – everyone, except the aboriginals, who was neither "white" nor enslaved – were very numerous, estimated at 8,102 or 21 per cent of the total in 1813 and 14,983 or 35 per cent in 1825. In other words, they greatly outnumbered the whites. Enslaved persons, some born in Africa, many born in other Caribbean islands (especially Grenada and Martinique), others locally born, were estimated at 23,230 in 1825, about 55 per cent of the total population. Trinidad was thus far from being a classic slave colony with the enslaved constituting 80 per cent or 90 per cent of the total population. A small, rapidly dwindling population of indigenous Amerindians was estimated at 727, or under 2 per cent of the total, in 1825 (Campbell 1992, 58; John 1988, 40).

The Free Coloureds

The situation of the free coloureds is central to the plot of *Adolphus*, and to a lesser extent of *The Slave Son*. Trinidad had an exceptionally large free coloured group which, as just noted, greatly outnumbered the whites and constituted over one-third of the total population in 1825, making the island unique in the British Caribbean. Many free coloureds had come to Trinidad in the 1780s and 1790s from Grenada and the French Caribbean, attracted by the promises of free land grants, citizenship and access to public posts contained in Spain's Cédula de Pobulación (1783). Others came from the British Caribbean after Trinidad was captured by Britain in 1797. Many free coloureds became landowners and slave owners, especially those who settled in the country around San Fernando in the district called the Naparimas, in the south of the island. Others settled in or around Port of Spain as store-keepers, artisans or small estate owners. The Cédula offered propertied free coloureds a secure place in Trinidad's society and economy; when the British took over, a clause in the Articles of Capitulation (1797) seemed to promise that this would continue under the new regime. As Carl Campbell writes, the Cédula and Article 12 of the capitulation agreement were the "two charters" girding the special position of Trinidad's free coloureds (1992, 52–83, 84–126).

After the British conquest, however, the position of the free coloureds gradually worsened. Most had originated from the French Caribbean and were suspected by the authorities of "republican" sympathies; no one forgot that the great slave rebellion in Ste Domingue (Haiti) had been preceded by a free coloured rising, or that a "French free coloured" leader, Julien Fédon, had led the anti-British revolt in Grenada in 1795 (an important event at the beginning of *Warner Arundell*). In Trinidad, unlike in, for example, Jamaica or Barbados, the local authorities and whites in general probably feared the free coloureds more than the slaves. These concerns lay behind the various forms of controls and discrimination against the free coloured community under the military governors between 1797 and 1813, and continued during the first ten years of Woodford's regime (1813–23) (Campbell 1992, 52–83, 127–82).

Nonetheless, Trinidad's free coloureds never faced some of the forms of discrimination known elsewhere in the Caribbean. There were no legal limits on their ownership of land, slaves or businesses, no special taxes against them, no prohibitions from practising any trade or profession. Marriages with whites were not barred in law, though they were certainly discouraged; free coloureds received free land grants from both the Spanish and British Crowns between 1784 and 1812. The free coloureds had two major grievances during the period in which *Adolphus* and *The Slave Son* are set. First, propertied coloured men were not allowed to serve as officers in the militia nor to hold posts in the civil service, privileges a few had enjoyed in the last years of Spanish rule (1784–97). (Political issues important elsewhere, notably the right to vote for and sit in the elected assembly, and to serve on juries, held no relevance in Trinidad, which lacked both an assembly and a jury system [Campbell 1992, 61–64].)

Second, the free coloureds complained of social and symbolic discrimination and humiliation. There were special curfews and regulations requiring them – but not whites – to carry lighted torches on the streets of Port of Spain at night; public places were segregated; respectable men and women were denied courtesy titles of address by whites; white men often treated all coloured women, regardless of marital status or class position, with contempt or discourtesy. The indignation felt by educated and prosperous free coloureds was brilliantly captured in Jean-Baptiste Philippe's famous 1824 treatise, *A Free Mulatto*. In a striking passage, Philippe complains of a situation which forms the central plot of *Adolphus:*

> Is it to be borne, I ask; that one particular set . . . should enjoy the privilege of triumphing with impunity over the honours of the mothers, wives, daughters and sisters of another class; should enjoy the right of robbing an aged father of his only child, and bowing down his hoary hairs with sorrow to the grave? . . . I have seen it, my Lord, I myself have seen it; a fond parent deprived of the solace of her infirmities, and of the prop of her age, of her only joy . . . Such a mother, aged and infirm, have I seen bereft of her daughter . . . by the blandishments of a villain. (Philippe [1824] 1987, 169–70)

Although security concerns about their loyalty to Britain waned with the end of the Napoleonic War in 1815, Governor Woodford soon came to be seen as the worst enemy of the free coloureds. He encouraged or directly instituted new forms of discrimination and social degradation against them; he insulted them by his own strongly prejudiced attitudes towards them and by the example he set to officials and whites in general in their interactions with them. This is the social and political milieu in which *Adolphus* is set. Taking advantage of the British government's new interest in slave amelioration, and under the leadership of Philippe, who was a doctor from the island's most prominent coloured landowning family, the free coloureds began a campaign for legal equality. Of course, they went over Woodford's head to the Colonial Office (Philippe's famous appeal was addressed to the secretary of state). In 1826 many of the offensive laws or regulations were repealed on orders from London; in 1829 an Order in Council provided for legal equality. It remained for the coloured leadership, both before and after slave emancipation, to agitate for a fair share of public offices and for an end to non-legal discrimination (Campbell 1992, 183–274; Philippe [1824] 1987, *passim.*).

The Enslaved People

African slavery was critical to Trinidad's social and economic development for a comparatively short period, as the island only began its career as a plantation economy in the 1780s and slavery was abolished in the 1830s. Moreover, Trinidad was never a classic slave society with a huge majority of enslaved persons. When the British took over in 1797 there were only some 10,000 slaves, constituting about 54 per cent of the total population; by 1825 there were about 23,230 slaves, who made up about 55 per cent of the total. The slave population was sparse – about eleven slaves per square mile in 1834 – and average slave holdings were far smaller than in most other British Caribbean islands (Brereton 1981, 47–51; Higman 1984, 41, 104–5).

Nevertheless, slavery was a crucial formative institution in the development of Trinidad's society, and the majority of persons living in the island during the period in which *Adolphus* and *The Slave Son* are set were enslaved. Because the arrival of captured Africans only began in the 1790s, Trinidad's enslaved population included significant numbers of people born in Africa well into the 1820s or 1830s (the British abolished their slave trade in 1806–7). In 1813, 54 per cent of Trinidad's slaves had been born in Africa, the largest single group being Igbo, Ibibio and Moco people from the Bight of Biafra. The famous "Koromantines" (Koromantyns) from the Gold Coast constituted only 8 per cent of the Africans in Trinidad in 1813. The "creole" slaves – those born in the Caribbean – included a significant proportion who had been born in other French and British Caribbean islands. Most enslaved persons in Trinidad at this period spoke French Creole (a creole language with mostly French-derived lexicon, and called "Patois" in Trinidad); many spoke different West African languages; some, especially the migrants from British islands, spoke an English-related creole. Those slaves owned by French or Spanish planters were generally baptized into the Catholic faith, but African beliefs and religious practices – indiscriminately labelled "obeah" by the whites – remained strong (Higman 1984, 122–32; John 1988, 5, 40; Brereton 1981, 47–51).

Trinidadian whites, especially those of French descent (the "French Creoles"), argued that slavery in their island was "mild and paternal", because of the influence of liberal Spanish laws and traditions, and because most French and Spanish planters lived closely with "their people" on small or medium-sized estates.[3] This French Creole view of slavery has persisted to the present, but professional historians have been consistently sceptical. The establishment of new estates (plantations) in the 1780s, 1790s and early 1800s caused massive slave mortality in the harsh conditions of a "frontier" colony; the relative scarcity of enslaved labourers in Trinidad encouraged a severe work regime, especially on the sugar estates. The British authorities, taking over in 1797, increased both the number of hours worked by estate slaves and the level of corporal punishment permissible. Death rates were appallingly high, and Trinidad showed consistently negative rates of natural increase between 1813 and 1834. In 1813, the expectation of life, at birth, for an estate slave was about seventeen years; the infant mortality rate – the number of deaths in the first year of life – was between 365 and 370 per 1,000 live births. Over half of Trinidadian slaves born alive died before their fifth birthday. In short, there is no hard evidence to suggest that Trinidad's estate slaves fared any better than their counterparts elsewhere. Campbell is correct to conclude that the island experienced "a somewhat harsh" slave regime and that it was not a "better" place to be enslaved in – though it probably was a better place for a free coloured person (Campbell 1992, 79–82; Higman 1984, 200–201, 310–11; John 1988, 162–63; compare de Verteuil 1987, 92–94).

Despite these hard conditions, there was no major slave rebellion in Trinidad during its relatively short experience of slavery, from the 1780s to the 1830s. Resistance was an ever-present threat, however, haunting all slave owners, especially the French Creoles who could never forget the great rising in Haiti. "Conspiracies" and "plots" – real or imagined – were discovered from time to time and one, in December 1805, saw four leaders executed and several others mutilated, flogged or banished. Running away – marronage – was endemic. Indeed, Barry Higman has shown that the largest proportion of "maroon" slaves identified in the initial registration exercise was to be found in Trinidad; in 1813, just under one percent of the island's slaves were officially recorded as run-

---

3. See Anthony de Verteuil's *Great Estates of Trinidad* (2000).

aways. A high incidence of marronage continued throughout the "amelioration" period (1824–34); in 1827–28, for instance, over five hundred slaves were punished for "absconding". Runaways might try to merge into Port of Spain's large free coloured and free black populations; others attempted escape by boat to nearby Venezuela (though, as discussed below, forms of slavery existed there up to 1854). Moreover, Trinidad had extensive forested areas well into the 1830s, providing refuges for groups of maroons, especially in the northern and central ranges of mountains. Though Trinidad did not have large, well-organized maroon communities on the scale of Jamaica or Suriname, there certainly were maroon "camps" or settlements in the remoter mountainous and forested areas. These were regarded as a standing menace, because they might become magnets for estate slaves. During the period after the British slave trade was abolished (1807–34), when labourers were especially valuable, maroon hunting expeditions ("marooning parties")[4] were common. Planters turned these brutal expeditions into a kind of sporting occasion; the hunted quarry, when captured, faced severe punishment – though death or mutilation was generally ruled out because of a slave's economic value (Higman 1984, 387–92; Brereton 1981, 47–51; de Verteuil 1987, n.p.).

St Hilaire Bégorrat

A form of resistance especially feared by the French Creoles was poisoning: the use by slaves, often African "obeahmen/women", of traditional techniques in order to poison livestock, fellow slaves and whites. While deliberate poisoning as an act of resistance or revenge must indeed have occurred, many "suspicious" deaths were probably caused by gastro-

---

4. This term came to be used for picnics and excursions. As E.L. Joseph states in "The Maroon Party: A West-Indian Sketch" (reprinted as the appendix to the edition of his *Warner Arundell* in this series): "It was formerly the custom in Jamaica to make parties of pleasure, whose object was a ramble into the woods to visit the mountainous residence of the maroons. These parties took, during their stay, what in England is called *'gipsey-meals,'* and reposed a day or two amongst the maroon villages, subsequently the word 'maroon-party' was used to designate any party of persons joining in making rough pedestrian excursions into the woods, or to other retired places for recreation" ([1838] 2001, 504).

enteritis and similar diseases which were extremely common and often fatal in a matter of hours. In Martinique, spectacular "poison trials" had been staged since the eighteenth century, and it was particularly the Martinique-born French Creoles who brought to Trinidad the poisoning hysteria and the approved methods of dealing with the perpetrators. None was more prominent than St Hilaire Bégorrat (1759–1851),[5] the model for St Hilaire Cardon in *The Slave Son* (de Verteuil 1987, 1–125).

Born in Martinique in 1759 to a non-noble but prosperous family, Bégorrat emigrated to Trinidad in 1784, lured by the promises of the Spanish Cédula issued the previous year. He created sugar and coffee estates in the Diego Martin valley, west of Port of Spain, which was virgin forest in the 1780s. He quickly emerged as the leading "expert" on slave management generally and poisoning in particular. With the British conquest, he became Governor Thomas Picton's chief ally, deferred to on all matters related to slavery. He served as a member of the Port of Spain Illustrious Cabildo (city council) under both Spanish and British administrations; in 1801 he became alcalde of the first election (an elected judge). In 1801, and again in 1803–4, he dominated special poison tribunals à la Martinique to deal with two alleged mass poisonings; these tribunals ordered horrific executions (one man was burnt alive in 1801) and savage punishments.

Between 1797 and 1813, Bégorrat was the leading man on the island, with immense influence over the British governors. As a slave owner in Diego Martin (and elsewhere) he was ruthless, but thoroughly familiar with his slaves' African-French Creole culture, widely feared, a feudal lord of the valley. Oral traditions maintain that he was deeply involved in illegal importations of slaves from other Caribbean islands, landing them at remote coastal locations, smuggling them up to the caves on his main property and selling them at huge profits in labour-scarce Trinidad, scenes recalled in *The Slave Son*. Bégorrat was at the height of his power between 1797 and 1813; Woodford then shut him out of formal political office, but Bégorrat continued to be an influential defender of slavery and of French Creole interests for the rest of his long life. No doubt

---

5. His name is spelled both Bégorrat and Begorrat. His biographer, Anthony de Verteuil (a direct descendant), uses the latter spelling.

his death in 1851 at the age of ninety-two revived memories of his life and prompted Wilkins to model her villain on Bégorrat (de Verteuil 1987, 1–125).

Trinidad in the Early 1850s

Both *Adolphus* and *The Slave Son* were published, and presumably written, in the first half of the 1850s. Wilkins's novel responded largely, she states, to developments in the American anti-slavery movement and the appearance of *Uncle Tom's Cabin* (Stowe [1852] 1981). The anonymous author of *Adolphus*, almost certainly a mixed-race Trinidadian, was probably motivated to write his novella at least in part by the situation of his people in the post-emancipation years.[6]

At the time of final emancipation in 1838, Trinidad's population was estimated at 36,655, of which some 12,000 were free coloureds or free blacks and 20,656 were ex-slaves. The first formal census, in 1851, recorded a population of about 68,000; no racial breakdown was given, and the free/slave distinction had, of course, disappeared (Wood 1968, 44; Brereton 1979, 158).

After emancipation, mixed-race Trinidadians – the former free coloureds – tried to build upon the grant of legal equality (1829) and the subsequent abolition of slavery by struggling for a greater share of public posts and prestigious appointments such as justices of the peace and stipendiary magistrates. Some of their leaders agitated for an elected assembly to replace the wholly nominated Council established in 1831, hoping, of course, that they would be among the men elected, as was the case in Jamaica up to 1865. The Colonial Office rejected all requests for an elected assembly, and educated mixed-race men, by mid-century, resented their virtual exclusion from government and law making in the colony. An even greater grievance was social discrimination – countless slights meted out to coloured "ladies and gentlemen" by whites – and exclusion from the more lucrative or prestigious posts in the public serv-

---

6. It is, of course, possible that the author of *Adolphus* was a woman. The odds favour a male, however, and we have thus used "he" and "his" in preference to "he/she". (See discussion of this author's identity below.)

ice. In 1848, for instance, only one mixed-race man held any kind of senior public post, and his position – superintendent of the leper establishment – was hardly a plum. Under Lord Harris, governor between 1846 and 1854, a small clique of whites, often related to each other, dominated government and the public service (dubbed the "Harristocracy" by its critics). Educated mixed-race men felt they had much to bear in the 1840s and 1850s. A few dabbled in "radical" politics and were suspected of inciting, or at least sympathizing with, a riot in Port of Spain involving several thousand creoles who were protesting the practice of shaving debtors' heads in jail (Campbell 1992, 315–22; Wood 1968, 42–43, 247–62, 175).

The author of *Adolphus*, probably sharing in this complex of grievances, no doubt saw the utility of locating his novella in the period when discrimination against coloureds was open and blatant, not covert and subtle as in the early 1850s. He therefore chose to set his work in the first years of Woodford's regime, a full generation earlier – but sufficiently close in time that many living in the early 1850s had first-hand memories.

We have not been able to identify with certainty the author of *Adolphus*. One possibility we considered for author is Michael Maxwell Philip, the mixed-race lawyer (1829–88) who later became solicitor-general of Trinidad. He published a full-length novel, *Emmanuel Appadocca*, in London in 1854; some of its themes resonate with those of *Adolphus*. Philip was in Britain from 1851 to 1855, where he wrote his novel, but he had served as a reporter for the *Trinidadian* while he lived in the island from 1849 to 1851. On the other hand, as a law student in Britain he acted as the London correspondent for a rival paper, the *Free Press*, which was edited by a close friend of his; if, therefore, he had wished to have his novella serialized in a newspaper back home in 1853, one might have expected him to choose the *Free Press*, not the *Trinidadian*. In any case, differences in style – literary and linguistic – have persuaded us that Philip was probably not the author of *Adolphus* (Cudjoe 1999, 59–86, 104–24; Philip [1854] 1997).

G.N. Dessources and the *Trinidadian*

We believe the author of *Adolphus* was either George Numa Dessources – proprietor and editor of the *Trinidadian* – or one of his close associates. Dessources was probably born in "Santo Domingo" – presumably Ste Domingue, later Haiti – and came to Trinidad in the early 1800s. A mixed-race person whose first language was probably French, perhaps educated in France, he was from a landowning family based in southern Trinidad. He belonged to a group of prosperous, educated, free coloured families long established in the Naparimas and important in the public life of the district and its main town, San Fernando. His family, like most in this group, was probably hard hit by the post-1846 depression in the sugar industry. Dessources became a bitter critic of the British government, the crown colony system in Trinidad, the attempts to "anglicize" the society at the expense of French-speaking Roman Catholics like himself, and what he saw as rampant discrimination against educated nonwhites. He established the *Trinidadian* in June 1848 as his major vehicle to promote his views and champion the cause of the island's blacks and coloureds (Toussaint 2001; Brereton 1979, 86–89; Thomas-Bailey 2001).

The *Trinidadian* soon acquired a reputation for being a "radical", anti-white, anti-government paper. According to a hostile critic, C.W. Day, it was "a very low paper, the organ of the negroes, edited by a coloured man"; Day claimed it was the "object of the coloured people, and of their organ, the 'Trinidadian', to make it appear to those at home [Britain], that 'the badge of a coloured skin' alone causes their proscription" (Day 1852, 2: 75, 89). Certainly, under Dessources, the paper – which published editorials and letters in both French and English – consistently criticized the Harris government and upheld the interests of the "foreign", Catholic, mixed-race group to which he belonged. In general, moreover, the paper tried to defend the creole working class, the ex-slaves, against policies considered inimical to them, such as state-aided Indian immigration. The *Trinidadian* also promoted a kind of race consciousness, for instance by supporting annual celebrations of August First, Emancipation Day. One 1849 editorial stressed that August First should be sacred, not only to ex-slaves but also to former free coloureds who had suffered under a system of "proscription" which could only have been destroyed when slavery itself was ended (Toussaint 2000, 182–91; Toussaint 2001; Brereton 1983, 71–72). Such "proscription" is the central theme of *Adolphus*.

It seems clear that Dessources wrote all the editorials in the *Trinidadian*, except when he was in Venezuela. He may well have been the author of *Adolphus*. On the other hand, we know he was in Venezuela during the weeks that *Adolphus* was serialized (January to April 1853), though of course he may have completed the novella before leaving Trinidad in December 1852. If Dessources was not the author, we feel sure it was one of his associates, such as G.L. Savary, who edited the paper during his absence from the island (Toussaint 2000, 182–91).

Venezuela and Trinidad

The idea that Venezuela was a potential refuge for hunted slaves and persecuted free coloureds in Trinidad looms large both in *The Slave Son* and especially in *Adolphus*.[7] This strengthens our conclusion that Dessources or one of his associates wrote the novella, for he was an ardent proponent of Trinidadian emigration to Venezuela and actually led an ill-fated colonizing expedition there in 1853–54.

Research by Michael Toussaint has shown that Venezuela had been an important escape destination for slaves and free coloureds since the 1780s or 1790s, and even after emancipation, it retained a reputation as a place for new beginnings. It was always relatively easy to get to the Guyana province of Venezuela by boat from the southern or western coasts of Trinidad. This province, distant from Caracas, was sparsely populated during the nineteenth century. Runaway slaves tried to reach Venezuela up to 1838, and some free coloureds left Trinidad to take advantage of the fairly relaxed race relations enjoyed by the *pardo* (mixed-race) group there. Others fought in the War of Independence and stayed on. In the 1840s and 1850s, men like Dessources – disillusioned with life in a British colony which discriminated against "foreign", non-

---

7. Venezuela also figures significantly in E.L. Joseph's *Warner Arundell* ([1838] 2001) as a theatre of operation for those fleeing (or just leaving) Trinidad.

white people – saw Venezuela as an attractive destination for Trinidad's coloureds and blacks (Toussaint 2001).

But the attraction of Venezuela as a refuge or place of settlement was compromised by its complicated history of slave emancipation. Simón Bolívar, the Liberator, declared the abolition of slavery in 1816, making good on earlier promises of freedom to all who fought for the "Patriots". But the Congress of Angostura reversed this declaration in 1819, and in 1821 the Cúcuta Slave Laws reinstated slavery, albeit in a modified form. Children born after 1821 to slave mothers were technically free (*manumisos*) but had to serve their mothers' owners for eighteen years, then come under an "apprenticeship" under a local *junta*. Those already born in 1821 were to become *aprendizajes* (apprentices) who would be "redeemed" by a gradual system of manumission over a fairly long period. Subsequent laws made these conditions more onerous for both categories of persons. Venezuelan slavery was never as harsh as on the Caribbean plantations, and the *aprendizajes* were paid nominal wages, but the fact remained that neither *manumisos* nor *aprendizajes* were free. It was not until 1854, sixteen years after emancipation in Trinidad, that full freedom was finally enacted (Lombardi 1971).

One can easily understand why runaway Trinidadian slaves would have tried their luck in Venezuela: they were escaping a harsh regime to one which was generally easier, and in the sparsely settled expanses of eastern Venezuela, their chances of avoiding re-enslavement altogether were probably reasonably good. But why would freed persons, after 1838, wish to go to a country where slavery (however modified) still existed? And why might Dessources, a self-appointed champion of blacks and enemy of slavery, encourage emigration there in the early 1850s?

It is Toussaint's view that Dessources probably lacked precise information about Venezuela's complicated, sometimes contradictory, system of modified slavery as it existed in the early 1850s; certainly, little was published in his own paper or in any other in the island. In general, he writes, "what little might have been known about slavery on the Main seemed overshadowed by notions of open space. Venezuela was the new El Dorado" – for gold was discovered there in 1849. Toussaint also notes that the existence of slavery in Venezuela up to 1854 was potentially dangerous to black, but not to mixed-race, emigrants. The latter would easily have fitted into Venezuela's large *pardo* group, free and often quite prosperous. And though many black Trinidadians did take part in the 1849 gold rush, most of Dessources's group of emigrants were mixed-race persons like himself (Toussaint 2000, 114–56; Toussaint 2001).

In any case, from 1849 on, Dessources used the *Trinidadian* to encourage emigration to Venezuela. He linked his disaffection with the Crown Colony regime and its policies to a romantic notion of Venezuela as a land of infinite promise where mixed-race Trinidadians could flourish and prosper. Though the discovery of gold was clearly a factor, his was chiefly a political and racial agenda: non-white people, discriminated against and kept down by British rule, could be truly free, and economically secure, in a new land where *pardos* probably formed the majority. The fact that some Venezuelans, mostly black, were still more or less unfree up to 1854 seemed of little moment. (In a delicious irony, Dessources wrote that Trinidadians going there would be protected from enslavement by their British citizenship!) His view of Venezuela, as well as his sense of alienation at home, was well expressed in a speech given in San Fernando just before he left Trinidad:

> Emigrate we must, because we are that class of men without history, to whom providence had given the world for a home, wandering sons of an unhappy race . . . I shall go forth into a distant land, thereon to pitch the tent of our colonization, the cradle of our nationality . . . Happy will I be if indeed I succeed in procuring for our unfortunate brethren in an hospitable land, a wise liberty, a shelter, fertile soil, fruitful labour, a brighter horizon, in a word the possibility of happiness. (Toussaint 2000, 210)

Dessources persuaded over seven hundred Trinidadians – dubbed the "Numancians" after his middle name – to emigrate in 1852–53. However, due partly to mismanagement, partly to hostility in Caracas to the prospect of "black" colonists, the venture failed, and by early 1854 most had returned. Trinidadians continued, however, to go to Venezuela as individual emigrants for the rest of the century (Toussaint 2000, 173–216; Toussaint 2001).

Uncle Tom's Cabin, Frederick Douglass and *The Slave Son*

Harriet Beecher Stowe

In her introduction, Marcella Wilkins claims that she began *The Slave Son* in the late 1840s, but was only moved to finish and publish it in response to the unprecedented success of Harriet Beecher Stowe's novel *Uncle Tom's Cabin* ([1852] 1981). Stowe's novel was not only a best-selling work of American fiction by a good margin – selling an extraordinary three hundred thousand copies in its first year alone at a time when most novels were issued in runs of less than five thousand – but was even more successful in Britain. When Stowe toured the British Isles in 1853, *Uncle Tom's Cabin* had already sold three times as many copies in the United Kingdom as it had in the United States and was being widely celebrated there as the first great flowering of a truly American literature (Hedrick 1994, 233–34). For Wilkins to position her novel in relation to Stowe's is thus savvy marketing, but it also speaks to the complex relations that link British – including British colonial – and American anti-slavery literature.

There is a clear tension in Wilkins's introduction between claims of precedence and fears of belatedness: she began writing the novel before Stowe's only to be published afterwards, just as the earlier success of British abolition made that nation both a world leader in anti-slavery work and a realm where the anti-slavery struggle seemed no longer applicable. American abolitionists had been empowered throughout the 1840s by the British model and British money, but by the 1850s abolitionist sentiments had become more widespread and urgent in the United States and consequently more fragmented and autonomous; there was both less consensus about what the proper route to emancipation might be, and less clarity about the pertinence of the British Caribbean example. Wilkins's claim that her novel might "equally well" be "transferred . . . to any other slave country" clearly has Stowe's country in mind, as it voices the desire that prior experience could become a ground of authority, rather than a mark that she is too late.

As an author of an anti-slavery novel, Wilkins's position is markedly different from that of Stowe. Harriet Beecher Stowe was the daughter of a prominent family of New England ministers and teachers; thus she was born into a moderately reformist intellectual elite. Before she wrote *Uncle Tom's Cabin*, most of Stowe's writing had been centred on regional sketches and domestic lore, and was generally published in such regional and family journals as *Western Monthly Magazine* and *Godey's Lady's Book*. Stowe's personal knowledge of slavery was quite limited. She had never joined an anti-slavery society before her novel made her the foremost spokesperson for abolition. While living in Cincinnati, Ohio, she had witnessed slavery in neighbouring states, but such observations were distant, not intimate. Her own homes – both as a girl and as a woman – included black household servants, and one of the servants she hired in Cincinnati had been a slave in Kentucky. Her knowledge of black people was thus largely derived from the dependencies and loyalties of domestic service, as viewed from the perspective of a woman who considered herself a kind and capable mistress (Hedrick 1994, 110, 120–21). The black characters that emerged from such knowledge appear loaded with the virtues desired in servants: honest, loving, pious and with a childlike dependency. George Fredrickson has labelled this philanthropic but paternalistic image of African Americans "romantic racialism", giving Uncle Tom as the paradigmatic example (Fredrickson 1971, 97–129). "Of all races of the earth," Stowe writes in celebration of Tom's undaunted faith, "none have received the Gospel with such eager docility as the African. The principle of reliance and unquestioning faith, which is its foundation, is more a native element in this race than in any other" ([1852] 1981, 559).

Wilkins begins her novel by claiming a quite different ground of knowledge. To assert in her dedication that her book does not represent "slave saints and martyrs, of whom we hear so much" is a barb directed at Uncle Tom (p. 95). Instead, she describes herself as having spent her childhood in a plantation milieu which made it natural to view slaves "in the light of a species of cattle" whose "immorality" could be more or less taken for granted (p. 99). While Stowe's central tactic with Uncle Tom was to make slavery's inhumanity visible through its contrast to the Christ-like morality of her martyred hero, Wilkins's is to depict slavery as inherently dehumanizing, "deadening of every virtue" in the slave (p. 95). If for Stowe the "native element" of faith is proof that slaves deserve and will rightly use freedom, for Wilkins the horror of slavery is centred in the way that it dissolves and perverts Christian and domestic virtues. Commenting on the mixture of celebration and mourning that surrounds the deathbed of the enslaved Koromantyn king, Anamoa – the only scene of slave religious fervour in her novel – Wilkins is quick to remind her readers that "it was not the triumph of Christ they spoke of, nor the glory of the coming kingdom of Heaven . . . – they were heathens" (p. 266). Wilkins suggests that promises of Christian mercy are expressed in these deathbed rites "wrapped in the African superstition", but the ability to recognize these marks of grace attests her own faith, not that of the dying slave.

This notion that slavery strips slaves of all moral capacity runs largely counter to the predominant strategies in US anti-slavery works of fiction, which generally seek to show slaves worthy of emancipation, even if such writing, like *Uncle Tom's Cabin* itself, remains ambivalent about the capacity of freed slaves to live as full members of a republic. Accounts of the moral decay wrought by slavery can be found in US abolitionist writing, but almost exclusively in the anti-slavery arguments of African Americans. For example, David Walker's *Appeal to the Coloured Citizens of the World* ([1831] 1995), arguably the most radical of US anti-slavery writing, is scathing in its account of the "wretched, degraded and abject" condition of the "Coloured People of these United States" (p. i). His demand for the abolition of slavery is as much an appeal to his fellow "coloured citizens" to cast off such subjection and the ignorance, servility and deceitfulness that accompany it. The abjection and the erosion of moral character bred by slavery, Walker insists, makes slaves complicit in their own oppression. He upbraids the "coloured people" for "courting favor with and telling news and lies to our *natural enemies* against each other – aiding them to keep their hellish chains of slavery upon us" (p. 11). Clearly Wilkins's writing has none of this bitter, revolutionary anger, but it does share Walker's sense that the damage done by slavery dehumanizes the slave, and so threatens to undermine the humanizing project of – as Stowe put it in her original subtitle for *Uncle Tom's Cabin* – "making a thing into a man" (Fisher 1985, 99–104).

Wilkins's recognition of saintly slave characters as "more poetical than real" also shares some characteristics with US pro-slavery writing (p. 95). The Southern press's campaign against Stowe as unfeminine and inaccurate insisted that her depictions of slaves drew not on actual encounters with slavery, but rather from her own personal imaginings; the domestic and Christian passion she produced for these slave characters had no origin beyond her own feelings. As one Southern critic expressed it, Stowe had merely "translated herself in fancy to the cotton fields of the South as a slave, and then interrogated herself as to how she felt" (Young 1999, 35). If the political power of *Uncle Tom's Cabin* derived in large part from its capacity to make white audiences identify with the sufferings of its slave protagonists, such critiques marked this identification as a fundamentally solipsistic phenomenon. Instead of identification, plantation novels tended to represent slaves as alien beings without a moral or rational core; such creatures were unsuited to autonomy. In these pro-slavery novels, Southern authors present attributions of nobility, honesty or piety in slaves as naive northern fantasies. So, for example, Caroline Lee Hentz's *The Planter's Northern Bride,* also first published in 1854, depicts a Massachusetts woman's conversion to the virtues of the "peculiar institution" as she comes to recognize the dishonesty and incompetence of the family's slaves, and the benefits they receive from her planter husband's firm but benevolent control. Her initial sympathy for these slaves, depicted as ill-founded and dangerous, is understood as a product of regional ignorance, in need of novelistic correction. Hentz hoped that her novel would provide such lessons for northern readers.

The Dorsets are similar figures for Wilkins, their English – rather than New England – scruples marking their difference from the slave owners around them, and enabling them to mediate the scenes of plantation life for English readers. They differ from Hentz's "northern bride", however, in that they learn about the brutality of slavery rather than its "justness". Yet Wilkins's suspicions about the immorality of those raised as slaves keep her from representing "our good friends", as she calls the Dorsets, as critics of the slave system as a whole rather than simply recoiling from its excesses (p. 323). They continue as slave holders, attempting to "civilize the savages" (p. 173) with wheelbarrows, Bible study and sewing lessons: "On slaves that were African born they invariably succeeded in making some impression, but on Negroes born as slaves in the Colony, never; these were all hardened, cunning, and corrupt" (p. 323). Moreover, without the whip to enforce labour, their estate's yield is always bad, though after emancipation the loyalty of those African slaves serves the Dorsets well: they are "not so poor", one boasts, selling fruits and vegetables to help support her old masters, "while they have got friends like us" (p. 324). The Dorsets' economic and philanthropic failures suggest the impossibility of even the kind and just doing any good within the slave system. Wilkins's depiction of the Dorsets reveals the credulous incompetence of English perspectives on slavery – a critique that rebounds on her English readers.

The distinction Wilkins makes between "African born" slaves and those "raised as slaves" is absent from the vast majority of anti-slavery writing in the United States. There is some romantic predilection for African royalty among the stories published in abolitionist gift-books like *The Liberty Bell,* but for the most part nineteenth-century accounts of slavery in the United States reflect the historical reality that these plantations were largely worked by American-born slaves. The attention Wilkins pays to tribal differences, and her imaginings of African lore, give this novel a more exotic ethnographic feel than that found in US fiction, but also enmesh her in the kind of racial stereotyping that in other ways her novel deplores. "The present driver belongs to the Mandingo nation, a sly, cowardly, treacherous race, made ten times worse by being reduced to slavery," Wilkins asserts; and then as if to acknowledge the gratuitous nature of her own racial characterizations she admits that "this by the way, it has nothing particular to do with my story" (p. 200). Such exoticizing pushes against strategies of sympathetic identification, and Wilkins frequently comments on the impossibility of knowing what these Africans feel. When Anamoa recognizes his princess daughter in the new cargo of slaves brought to Cardon's estate, Wilkins wonders:

What were his feelings? Were they as keen, as bitter, as those of a white man placed under similar circumstances? Indeed I cannot say: the higher reasoning of the white man might render his feelings more continually tormenting, the deeper passions of the Negro might render his the keener, – perhaps yes, perhaps no; but this is certain – nature was there within him, degraded, injured nature, and the old man wept long and bitterly as he pressed his child to his breast. (pp. 196–97)

This questioning inconclusiveness – "perhaps yes, perhaps no" – appears in marked contrast to Stowe's strategies when narrating a similar scene, for Stowe presumes to know exactly what her slave father feels, just as she claims to know the feelings of her readers. Here is Tom weeping as he readies himself to be sold away from his children:

> Great tears fell through his fingers on the floor; just such tears, sir, as you dropped into the coffin where lay your first born son; such tears, woman, as you shed when you heard the sighs of your dying babe. For sir he was a man, – and you are but another man. And woman, though dressed in silk and jewels, you are but a woman, and, in life's great straits and mighty griefs, ye feel but one sorrow! (p. 91)

The "certain" sameness Wilkins calls "nature" is far more equivocal – more racially biased perhaps, but also more conscious of difference – than the easy appropriations of otherness that Stowe locates in that "one sorrow".

Stowe's "one sorrow" is essentially parental, distilled from her own grief at the death of her son Charley in 1849; parents' – especially mothers' – love for their children becomes her vocabulary for expressing the humanity of slaves and the possibility of sympathizing with their sufferings. Even more than Tom's Christian faith, maternal bonds provide Stowe's most potent ground for identification with the experiences of slavery: "If it were *your* Harry, mother, or your Willie that were going to be torn from you by a brutal trader," she asks her imagined readers, "how fast could *you* walk?" (p. 105). In contrast, Wilkins's portrait of Madelaine, the slave mother, offers not identification, but rather the novel's strongest example of the brutalizing effects of slavery, and the naivety of saintly portraits of slaves. Wilkins explains that Madelaine "had fallen to the condition of a brute; her maternal instinct, if indeed such had ever existed with her, had vanished" (p. 133). Maternal instinct lies at the very heart of Stowe's politics of sentimental recruitment; to imagine that for the slave mother this feeling was capable of vanishing – or worse, to believe that such maternal instinct may not have "ever existed" – would be to dismantle drastically the emotional economy of her novel, and hence to void its political efficacy.

But although Wilkins's attitude towards slave character is thus virtually antithetical to Stowe's, she finds Stowe's novelistic strategy of sympathetic identification compelling, and she employs this narrative technique in her depiction of a different element of the slave family. Recoiling from the slave mother, Wilkins locates her sympathetic feeling in the "mixed-race" characters of Belfond, the "slave son" of her title, and in Madelaine's freed daughter, Laurine. As with Stowe's depictions of the slave mother, Wilkins understands that familial allegiances are capable of making racial others appear familiar – family ties connect these characters to the human family (Fisher 1985). It is this familial logic that causes Wilkins to deviate from the motives of righteous resistance and the desire for freedom that generally mark Belfond's character to depict him as wishing to save his cruel master/father. Wilkins's investment in "the heart's natural pleadings" of a son's allegiance to his father, leaves Belfond mourning his master's death, bereaved of "one whom he would have loved had he been permitted" even though virtually nothing in the novel marks Cardon as loveable (p. 318). Similarly, Laurine, who remembers "the passionate love her mistress had borne for [her] child" (p. 133) adopts these free white models of familial love in her loyalty to and care for Madelaine. In imitating the affection that links her white owners, Laurine self-consciously learns the emotional patterns that Stowe would insist are universal. In adopting these ways of loving, Laurine reverses the relation of mother and daughter, and links the generalized "we" of author and reader with the moral and affective position of the novel's heroine:

> It is so ordained that the object we help becomes dear to us, and the more trouble we take, so also the greater love do we bestow. Laurine felt this; her automaton mother became dear to her exactly in proportion to her helplessness; she longed to be with her or to have a home for her. (p. 135)

In learning to love from her white owners, the freed Laurine becomes available for the reader's love and sympathetic identification, and even enables us to care about her otherwise unsympathetic "automaton mother". "Madelaine as a slave knew nothing of sorrow; Laurine, free, became thoughtful and sad" (p. 134); there is not, as there is for Stowe, one sorrow which links slave and free, though the mixed-race daughter does provide an emotional bridge between the suffering slave and the abolitionist reader.

Nearly two-thirds of the way through the novel, Wilkins seems to repent of the harshness of her portrait of Madelaine, sensing something unsatisfying about giving her heroine so unsympathetic and unattractive a mother, and she allows Madelaine to be one of the narrators of the personal histories told during a night of storytelling in the slave huts. These stories (chapters 16–18) are largely tangential to the plot of the novel. In her introduction, Wilkins notes that her initial work on *The Slave Son* had resulted in "detached pieces" which she had only later woven into "one consecutive story" (p. 99). The legendary invasion of the ants is clearly one of these original detached pieces. It is in many ways the best writing in this novel – certainly the most lively and engaging. In giving this story to Madelaine, Wilkins presents her as courageous, resourceful and trusting, and hence an appropriate mother for Laurine. Madelaine's story repeats a central motif of the personal narratives told by the Princess Talima and Quaco: white people cannot be trusted, their apparent friendship will end in betrayal and slavery. In the story of losing her freedom in the move from Grenada to Trinidad, in the sale of her husband, in the tale of how her young son is forced to flog her, "Madelaine shows", as the chapter title promises, "that she has had much to embitter her life". "'What should I care about Laurine for?' " Madelaine asks at the end of the chapter, "'I don't care at all, *for notin' nor nobody.*' And, relapsing into the wild half-idiocy usual to her, poor old Madelaine flung herself back against the wall, and gave a wide gaping laugh at her own folly in youth, to have ever cared for anything" (p. 257). But the invasion of the ants is a legend vested in both folly and caring. In it the young Madelaine is rewarded by the governor and, like Joseph dispensing grain in Egypt, she becomes keeper of a storehouse full of sweet potatoes, holding famine and catastrophe at bay. This is not a personal story, and it does not "show" the causes of Madelaine's bitterness; rather, it revels in the fecundity of the islands and the pleasures of exaggeration and storytelling. Instead of sympathy for "poor old Madelaine" or identification with her, Wilkins allows the joy and power of legend to redeem Madelaine. She is valued not as "mother" but as the source of myth. At the novel's end she must die, because, emptied of her humanity by slavery, she is never redeemable for Wilkins as an individual character, and so she cannot participate in her daughter's escape. Her only value lies in the impersonal virtues of storytelling and myth.

Frederick Douglass

Wilkins explains in the introduction how her long "sympathy" for "mixed-race", "free coloured" Trinidadians, and her hatred of the discrimination and "prejudice of caste that keeps the people degraded", motivate her writing (pp. 99–100). The heroine and hero of her novel, Laurine and the "slave son" Belfond, are just such characters. Wilkins's most eloquent polemics are addressed to this topic, yet interestingly the novel's plot has virtually no bearing on issues of racial prejudice. At the very beginning of the novel Laurine's mistreatment by white customers and the prejudice that Belfond encounters as he and several "rich Mulattoes" (p. 146) join the buyers on the slave ship do demonstrate such abuses. But while such prejudice may be "the barrier to real freedom" that most disturbs Wilkins in 1854 – with slavery long abolished in Trinidad – it is not the "barrier" that most concerns even Laurine and Belfond; for them, as certainly for all the other black and coloured characters in the novel, the obstacle to freedom is slavery. The novel's plot revolves around issues of emancipation, rebellion and escape – not around the injustices wrought by racial prejudice. In the wake of Stowe's success, slavery, it seems, makes the story; for Caribbean and British readers, however, it is prejudice that makes that story still relevant.

> It is the blight which remains when the simoom has passed, quite as deadly and as poisonous, and at this day holds influence as fully and forcibly in the free northern states of America as in the south. I need only refer to the circumstance of Douglas [*sic*] being horsewhipped for walking between two white ladies to prove this. (p. 101)

Significantly, in a novel where poison proves the most potent means of slave resistance, poison also provides a metaphor for racial prejudice (see discussion above).

The mention of Frederick Douglass's provocative promenades through New York suggests another set of connections between Wilkins's novel and US abolitionists. Like Stowe, Douglass marked the publication of his first anti-slavery book, *Narrative of the Life of Frederick Douglass, an American Slave* ([1845] 1993), by a tour of Britain. The circumstances were, of course, quite different. The 1845 publication of Douglass's *Narrative* by the Boston anti-slavery office publicized the evils of slavery, but it also increased Douglass's notoriety and visibility as a fugitive. Touring Britain provided Douglass with protection from the threat of recapture. An enormous success on the British circuit, Douglass was able by 1847 to return to the States with his freedom purchased by British friends and with enough money to launch his own newspaper, the *North Star.*

While in England he was befriended by Julia Griffith and her sister Eliza Griffith. In a piece titled "Colorphobia in New York" that he published in the *North Star* in May of 1849, Douglass described how the sisters "allowed themselves to take his arm, and to walk many times up and down Broadway . . . Such an open, glaring outrage upon *pure American* tastes had never before been perpetrated." Douglass then argues that the best way to eradicate racial prejudice "is to act as though it did not exist, and to associate with their fellow creatures irrespective of all complexional differences. We have marked out this path for ourselves and we mean to pursue it at all hazards" (Foner 1950–55, 1: 385–87). The hazards proved brutally real; during one such stroll in the Battery, Douglass was attacked and beaten (McFeely 1991, 165). Moreover, these public displays of intimacy between white women and black men scandalized abolitionists as well as racists, and Douglass's relation to Julia Griffith remained a source of tension within the movement (McFeely 1991, 162–64; Martin 1984, 40–44). Many American observers felt that inappropriate sexual dynamics suffused Douglass's British tour: John Estlin commented in a letter to his fellow abolitionist Samuel May Jr, "you can hardly imagine how he is noticed, better, I may say, by ladies; some of them really a little exceed the bounds of propriety, or delicacy" (Martin

1984, 43). (It is tempting to imagine Wilkins among this crowd of adu-
latory English women.) As with the New York promenades, such charges
of sexual impropriety reveal more about American anxieties than they do
about the behaviour of Douglass and his admirers; still it is indisputable
that Douglass was an extraordinarily charismatic and thrilling speaker.
In his 1845 preface to the *Narrative of the Life of Frederick Douglass*,
William Lloyd Garrison describes first hearing Douglass speak at an
1841 anti-slavery convention in Nantucket. "I shall never forget his first
speech at the convention," Garrison wrote,

> I think I never hated slavery so intensely as at that moment . . . There stood
> one, in physical proportion and stature commanding and exact – in intellect
> richly endowed – in natural eloquence a prodigy – in soul manifestly "created
> but little lower than the angels" – yet a slave, ay, a fugitive slave, – trembling
> for his safety. (p. 23)

Wilkins's portrait of her hero Belfond has many counterparts in anti-
slavery fiction, including George Harris, the fugitive mulatto of *Uncle
Tom's Cabin* who "made his declaration of independence" and fought
off slave traders with "sublime heroism . . . boldness and determination" (pp. 298–99). But clearly one important source for Belfond is
not a fictional character, but Frederick Douglass himself. Belfond not
only shares Douglass's heroic stature, mixed-race heritage and impres-
sive eloquence, but many of the details of Wilkins's description closely
echo Douglass's *Narrative* and the autobiographical accounts of slavery that characterized his lectures in Britain between 1845 and 1847.
For example, in Belfond's first appearance in the novel he argues with
Laurine about the morality of stealing from his master (pp. 126–28),
a practice that Douglass famously asserted in his *Narrative* to be "legitimate" (p. 58).

Such speculations on questions of morality, rich evidence of moral
consciousness and intellectual engagement, is what so struck Garrison
upon first hearing Douglass, and it is both the centre of Wilkins's portrait of Belfond and what differentiates him from other slaves. "In relating his adventures," Wilkins writes of her hero, "unlike his darker
comrades, he did not tell all that had passed in his mind. He knew their
understandings, unawakened to anything above the little affairs of their

brute condition, could never comprehend the tumults of his own struggling heart, or the strange feelings which had grown in him" (p. 258).
Wilkins's rendition of her hero's singularity portrays him, and the suffering of mixed-race characters more generally, as the horror of a white
mind imprisoned within blackness. In this account, what makes Belfond
different from his "darker comrades" is a quality of thought and consciousness that Wilkins presumes is shared by her white readers but that
remains incomprehensible to Belfond's black audience. "I have often
been bluntly and sometimes rudely asked," Douglass remarked in his
last, 1892, version of his autobiography *Life and Times of Frederick
Douglass*, "Whether I consider myself more African than Caucasian, or
the reverse? Whether I derive my intelligence from my father, or from my
mother, from my white, or from my black blood?" (1996, 317). To
Douglass himself, of course, such questions and the racial essentialism
that underlies them were absurd. In his *Narrative* he dismissed the question of whether or not "my master was my father" with the observation
that such speculations are "of but little consequence" when "the children
of slave women shall in all cases follow the condition of their mothers"
– noting how race and condition are made less by parentage than by
laws, and by the conjoined motives of profit and pleasure ([1855] 1993,
32). In his 1852 speech "What to the Slave Is the Fourth of July?"
Douglass sarcastically played on audience responses to his racially mixed
heritage: "I leave, therefore, the great deeds of your fathers to other gentlemen whose claim to have been regularly descended will be less likely
to be disputed than mine!" (1996, 114). Douglass's comments on his
parentage thus strive to disrupt racist assumptions that would make his
intellect and consciousness appear – like Belfond's – a white inheritance,
the result of being a "slave son". But these comments also make clear
that Douglass knew how white father and black mother mattered to his
audience, and suggest that he may well have appealed to Wilkins precisely in these equivocal terms.

For Douglass, the source of his difference is fundamentally a question of conditions, and particularly of access to education. Here Wilkins's
novel again recalls Douglass's *Narrative*. Belfond's "tumults" of consciousness she explains as stemming from his learning to read and write.
As he accompanies his young master to university in France, he siphons

information and skills from his master's lessons – till "the poor Mulatto was in reality the cleverer, and by far the better educated" of the two; Belfond comes to recognize "knowledge" as the source of "the tremendous power which the white man holds over the black race" (p. 261). In his *Narrative,* Douglass similarly cites lack of literacy as the means of "the white man's power to enslave the black man" and therefore literacy as "the pathway from slavery to freedom" (p. 48). For him, as for Belfond, it is not any particular cruelty, but rather knowledge and the consciousness it brings, that make slavery unbearable:

> my learning to read had already come, to torment and sting my soul to unutterable anguish. As I writhed under it, I would at times feel that learning to read had been a curse rather than a blessing . . . In moments of agony, I envied my fellow-slaves their stupidity. I often wished myself a beast. I preferred the condition of the meanest reptile to my own. Anything, no matter what, to get rid of thinking! It was this everlasting thinking of my condition that tormented me. (p. 52)

In this remarkable passage, Douglass's capacity to depict the psychic anguish of slavery poses a stark challenge to his readers. Reading should make you think, and thinking should make slavery intolerable. Douglass offers his readers no choice: abolish slavery or mark yourself as beast, reptile, or stupid slave. Slavery, for individual or for nation, can only be acceptable, Douglass implies, to those willing "to get rid of thinking". Here consciousness becomes a mark not of Douglass's specialness, or of a "white inheritance", but the very grounds of freedom.

By the 1850s the antithetical relation between reading and slavery had become a commonplace of the abolitionist press and a significant motivating force in the production of abolitionist writing. But such equations remained painfully problematic for the now popular genre of the slave narrative. For Douglass, the success of his *Narrative,* and his role on the abolitionist lecture circuit as the best embodiment of slavery, proved increasingly uncomfortable. As Henry Louis Gates Jr has noted, Douglass quickly came to serve as "the representative colored man of the United States" in part because he was "the most presentable", his very intellect and eloquence turned into objects for display (1988, 129). But Douglass desired a greater role in abolitionist strategy and theory than the position of "representative colored man" or the narrative range of personal testimony would allow. Douglass's break with Garrison and his assumption of the editorship of his own separate newspaper, by 1851 titled simply *Frederick Douglass's Paper*, made it much easier for him to disregard expectations for personal testimony and to experiment with a variety of genres of non-personal writing. Along with his many provocative and brilliant lectures and essays of the early 1850s, Douglass also tried his hand at fiction writing.

Carla Peterson has recognized a general shift during the 1850s from autobiography to fiction as the dominant genre of African American writing, seeing it as a means of navigating the limitations posed by "essentialized notions of black selfhood" (1993, 579). The recent authentication of Hannah Crafts's novel *The Bondwoman's Narrative* ([*c*.1855–60] 2002) – apparently written shortly after Crafts's escape from North Carolina – further demonstrates the rising dominance of this genre, and the desire to find a way of "telling slavery" that expands beyond the personal revelations of the slave narrative.

Douglass published a section of his novella, *The Heroic Slave*, in the March 1853 issue of *Frederick Douglass's Paper*, and the entire novella was published in the gift-book *Autographs for Freedom* that Julie Griffith compiled as a fund-raiser for the 1853 holiday season. Although *Autographs for Freedom* was initially published in Boston, Griffith used her British anti-slavery connections to put out an English edition as well, enabling this anthology to do good business on both sides of the Atlantic (Foner 1950–55, 1: 89–90). There is no hard evidence of Wilkins's familiarity with *The Heroic Slave*, but it seems highly likely that while Stowe's popularity and 1853 trip to England may have prompted Wilkins to complete and publish *The Slave Son*, the details of her novel – and in particular the portrait of her title character – seem far more significantly similar to Douglass's own 1853 novella. In his heroic slave, Douglass has created a fictional character derived far less from the historic Madison Washington, whose successful slave mutiny on the *Creole* provides the climax of the novella's plot, than from the role he himself had come to play on the abolitionist circuit.

As a narrative, *The Heroic Slave* is told primarily through the experiences of a white northerner, Mr Listwell, who is moved to abolitionist sympathies precisely by hearing Washington speak. In the figure of Listwell, and the fictional portrait it offers of Douglass's audience, Douglass recasts the sentimental strategies of identification that Stowe deployed in *Uncle Tom's Cabin* into something wrought by the black speaker's – rather than the white writer's – word. For like Belfond, and like Douglass, the speaker and writer – not the slave Frederick portrayed in *Narrative* – Washington's nobility is immediately marked by his bearing and his language. "I forgot his blackness in the dignity of his manner and the eloquence of his speech," Douglass has the mate of the *Creole* say of Washington (1996, 161), "I felt myself in the presence of a superior man" (1996, 163). Like the mate, Wilkins notes the affront to slavery and racial prejudice in such evident superiority:

> [Belfond's] proud dark eyes were full of meaning, his bearing was dignified and such indeed as would have challenged respect had he been a white man, but this, in one of his outcast race, testified to a rebellious spirit, and consequently portrayed an insult to every white man who looked upon him. (p. 152)

Like Listwell, Wilkins presents herself as a white person who can look upon such evident superiority and be not insulted but inspired.

Mrs Wilkins and the Irish Question

Our current knowledge about Marcella Fanny Noy Wilkins, apart from her own statements in *The Slave Son*, comes from her two applications for financial assistance to the Royal Literary Fund, in 1858 and 1884.[8] She was born Marcella Fanny Nugent[9] in Dublin, on 5 March 1816. If we can accept her account – in the introduction to the novel – of an

---

8. *Archives of the Royal Literary Fund 1790–1918* (London: World Microfilms Publication, 1982). The records for Wilkins are found in File 1476 (Reel No. 56).

9. She may have been related to Maria Nugent, the wife of General George Nugent, governor of Jamaica 1801–5. Her famous journal of her years in Jamaica is a rich source on the social history of that island, and reveals her as a sharp, perceptive observer, sympathetic to the free coloureds and not without concern for the plight of the slaves. (See *Lady Nugent's Journal of Her Residence in Jamaica from 1801 to 1805* [1966] 2002.)

upbringing on an estate in Trinidad, it seems likely that her family moved to the West Indies when she was very young.[10]

Marcella Fanny Nugent married a painter, William Noy Wilkins,[11] though it is difficult to say whether she met him in Trinidad (or elsewhere in the West Indies) and left for England with him or met him in England. In any case, at the time of her 1858 application to the Royal Literary Fund, some five years after the publication of *The Slave Son*, they were living in Manchester with two children, a son of nine and a daughter of five years old. She applied for a grant because her husband was "incapacitated by physical and mental infirmity" and she had been advised by physicians to "remove her husband . . . to a distance from his

---

10. A possible link may lie with John Nugent, an Irishman appointed by Governor Picton to the first Council of Advice in 1801 along with St Hilaire Bégorrat, John Nihell, the chief judge, and John Black, slave-trader and merchant. Nugent must have been a substantial proprietor at that time. (He may well have been a "capitulant", that is, having arrived before 1797; the Mallet Map of 1798 lists a Nugent as owning land in Santa Cruz and Naparima.) John Nugent may therefore have been one of the (mostly Roman Catholic) Irish arriving alongside the French in the 1780s and 1790s, taking up grants under the Cédula. In mid-1803, when several pro-Picton members were dismissed from the Council by Picton's enemy Colonel William Fullarton, Nugent was kept, perhaps because he was on leave in England at the time. However, when Lieutenant-Governor General Hislop reconstituted the Council later in 1803, Nugent was not reappointed. (He gave evidence, in London, on behalf of Picton in the famous trials of the ex-governor for the torture of Louisa Calderon.) In 1804, Nugent was in serious debt, owing six thousand pounds sterling, a very large sum, and was "financially embarrassed in later years". He is listed as one who had property destroyed in the great Port of Spain fire of 1808. Most interesting is an advertisement in the *Trinidad Courant* of 31 December 1817 (quoted in de Verteuil 1986, 13): "Mrs Nugent respectfully informs the public that she would feel grateful to be entrusted with the care of a few young ladies to instruct them in French and English, Arithmetic, etc. . . . Her reduced circumstances renders [*sic*] it indispensably necessary that she should exercise her abilities for the support of herself and her child during her stay in this Island. 93 Queen Street." This Mrs Nugent may have been John Nugent's widow, and the child Marcella Fanny, born in Dublin in March 1816. Or this Mrs Nugent might have been married to a son (or nephew) of the John Nugent described above, and her child his granddaughter (or great-niece). See Anthony de Verteuil's *Sylvester Devenish and the Irish in Nineteenth Century Trinidad* (1986, 12–14) and James Millette's *The Genesis of Crown Colony Government: Trinidad, 1783–1810* (1970, 154, 198, 209, 221).

11. In Wilkins's letter of 1 June 1858, to the Council of the Royal Literary Fund, she writes: "My husband Mr William Noy Wilkins, is known as a landscape painter, his works have appeared in the Exhibitions of the Royal Academy, the British Institution, the Society of British Artists, the Royal Hibernian Academy, and the Manchester Academy . . . In 1857 Mr Wilkins published his 'Letters on Connaisseurship'."

[professional] pursuits & domestic troubles". He later went to Australia, and his wife lost contact with him.[12] Mrs Wilkins and her children, like many other people of limited means, went to the Continent, where it was possible to live "respectably" at a much cheaper rate. They apparently lived in Brussels on the income from some property in Ireland left by her mother, although that property was later lost completely. Of the two children, according to her second application to the Royal Literary Fund in 1884, the son became an "engineer" in South Africa, and the daughter, Elizabeth, was intending to pursue a career in music, though hampered by ill health.

Apart from her novel, Wilkins did a variety of writing in newspapers, including articles on natural history and literature, and "leading articles" (editorials) in Brussels newspapers.[13] As of this writing, we know only that she was still alive in 1884.

Not surprisingly, given her Irish background, Wilkins makes several references in *The Slave Son* to Irish history, in particular to eighteenth-century Irish penal laws and the popular protests they brought in their wake. In 1688 Prince William of Orange and his wife Mary were invited to take the British throne by Protestants who objected to the succession of the Catholic James II; as a Protestant daughter of James II, Mary could claim to inherit the throne. William and Mary's army encountered very little opposition in England, so little that the accession of William and Mary is often called the "Bloodless" or "Glorious" Revolution. In

---

12. In her 1884 application to the Royal Literary Fund, Wilkins responds to a question on marital status with "Have been married, but do not know if my husband is living or not."

13. Of those referred to on her application forms, we have been able to locate "The Poetry of Brentford" (*Athenaeum,* 20 November 1847, 1196); and "Our Enemies Abroad and at Home" (*Dublin University Magazine,* June 1855, 742–48). We have been unable as yet to locate others mentioned (it is not certain that the places and dates of publication as listed are correct): "The Latest Wonder in Antwerp *Maison Plantin*" (*Argosy,* 1882); "A Wreath on the Grave of Mrs Jameson" (*Argosy*); "Ill Luck: A West Indian Story" (*Chambers Edinboro,* 1851); "A curious people" (*Argosy,* 1883); "Essay on the [. . .] of the Biblical Deluge" (Brussels); and "Essay on the Traces Found in Certain Plants — Marking Prehistoric Care & Cultivation by an Unknown People" (Report of the Congress of the Search for the Origin of the American Indians, Brussels, 1879). On the 1858 application form, Wilkins notes, "At the present time I am engaged on a work on the condition of the factory girls", but there is no longer any reference to this on the later application form.

Ireland, however, where many Irish Catholics supported James II, the struggle was protracted and far from bloodless, ending only in 1691 and followed by a series of penal laws intended to destroy Catholic social and economic power. These restricted Catholic activity in everything from ownership of landed property – and even horses – to participation in civil life and education. Some Irish Catholics had held a substantial amount of wealth, land and power before the penal laws, but afterwards the balance of social and political power shifted sharply: the post-1691 order is known as the "Protestant Ascendancy". At times, class loyalties turned out to be stronger than religious or political allegiances, prompting some Protestant families to hold land in trust for dispossessed Catholic heirs; many Catholics indeed converted in order to escape the prohibitions. But overall, the effect was to remove anyone who was openly Catholic from public life and to some extent even from society. Many sons of the Irish Catholic aristocracy left Ireland altogether. Wilkins herself was more likely Protestant than Catholic; her inheritance of land in Ireland supports that conclusion, as do her occasionally inaccurate references to Catholic religious observances (for example, vespers, note for p. 110).

The penal laws created enormous popular resentment, even among poorer people who were less materially affected by them. Some found an outlet in the eighteenth- and nineteenth-century agrarian protest movement known as "Whiteboyism", which opposed the enclosure of common land, high rents and payments of tithes to the Established (Protestant) Church of Ireland. Really a series of movements for which Whiteboyism became a generic term, this involved a number of separate secret societies whose members tore down fences, hedges and walls, maimed cattle, and terrorized the countryside. Society members were usually sworn to secrecy, with violent punishments for those who broke the oath. Though the actual level of violence was relatively low, the movement provoked fears of insurrection and assassination.

Together with *The Slave Son*'s references to Irish affairs, what little we know about her suggests that Wilkins had connections, if not sympathies, with the Irish "patriot" or "rebel" movement of the late eighteenth and early nineteenth centuries, inspired in part by the French Revolution and aimed at the establishment of an independent Irish republic. She was, for instance, a friend of Anna Jameson (née Murphy), whose father supported the Patriots, and who seems to have left Ireland with his family in order to avoid arrest. In her introduction, Wilkins also thanks John Patten, "the philanthropic Librarian of the Royal Dublin Society" (p. 104), who earlier in his life was arrested for "treasonable practices" in the wake of Robert Emmet's rebellion (1803), one of the patriot uprisings; Patten was connected to Emmet by marriage. Though as an absentee landlord herself for a considerable part of her life, Wilkins to some extent stood for precisely the sort of expatriate exploitation of Ireland that the Patriots opposed, she may well have had lingering sympathies for the movement.

Like Wilkins, abolitionists in the United States found the similarities between the condition of the Irish and that of the slave a source of complexity and contradiction; it remains one of the most fruitful areas for investigating the interactions of race and class in the United States. In general, the easy expression of anti-Catholic sentiments and anti-Irish prejudice amongst the northern, middle-class Protestant reformers, who made up the bulk of anti-slavery forces in the United States, surprises and disgusts contemporary readers. How could it be that people so opposed to racial prejudice and exploitation would themselves participate in ethnic and classist versions of these wrongs? Still, as the famines of the 1840s brought ever more penniless Irish immigrants to northern US cities, and affluent northern families began to employ – and deplore – Irish labourers and domestic servants, the Irish came to seem a significant threat to the American home and American cultural norms. In an article she wrote on "The Trials of a Housekeeper" for *Godey's Lady's Book* in 1839, a fairly young and apolitical Harriet Beecher Stowe complains of servants – and especially of immigrant "help" – her only happy example "a tidy, efficient-trained English girl". Stowe concludes this early essay with the question "What shall we do? Shall we go for slavery, or shall we give up houses, have no furniture to take care of, keep merely a bag of meal, a porridge-pot, and a pudding stick, and sit in our tent door in real patriarchal independence? What shall we do?" (p. 6). A decade later Stowe would be far less willing to jest about slavery as a solution to the difficulties of household help, or, for that matter to laugh at the idea of "patriarchal independence". But the notion that the nation's homes had to choose between slavery and Irish "slovenliness" was not hers alone.

For many northerners it seemed hardly a choice at all. African Americans were often referred to as "smoked Irish", while the Irish were denigrated as "niggers turned inside out" (Ignatiev 1995, 41). In northern cities, Irish immigrants and African Americans tended to live in the same poor neighbourhoods and compete for the same ill-paying jobs. There is much evidence for the development of close cultural ties and personal intimacy between these oppressed groups throughout the 1840s and 1850s.[14] But as anti-slavery feeling grew, and grew more respectable, many Irish came to feel this sympathy for the slave as a threat – an alliance between a white Republican elite and black slaves that disregarded the needs of northern white labourers. The charge that agitation against slavery in the South served to mask the exploitative conditions of free labour in the North contains a great deal of truth (Roediger 1991, 133–63). As Ignatiev has shown, in New York City anti-black racism in politics and the police force became a potent means for Irish immigrants to mark their difference from the blacks among whom they worked and lived, and so try to claim for themselves the prerogatives of whiteness (1995, 162–64). Such patterns would culminate a decade later in the New York City draft riots of 1863, where working-class sentiment against the Civil War draft began by targeting federal buildings but soon turned to attack black residents, with the Irish being the most prominent instigators of this racial violence (Bernstein 1990).

Douglass began his tour of the British Isles in Ireland, and he wrote Garrison that the Irish peasantry live "in much the same degradation as the American slaves . . . I see much here to remind me of my former condition" (Foner 1950–55, 1: 191). As late as 1872 Douglass was still describing himself as "something of an Irishman as well as a negro", suggesting how deeply his time in Ireland had affected his enlarged sense of the politics of oppression – helping him to turn a personal history into a far more general critique (Giles 2001, 799). Yet even for Douglass the antagonism between Irish and African Americans in the United States

---

14. Michael Ignatiev's *How the Irish Became White* (1995, 40–47) mentions sexual contact, shared lodging-houses, churches, dance halls and minstrel shows, friendships, and even an Irish-Black jailbreak attempt.

made a coalition seem impossible at home. In an 1853 speech in New York City on "The Present Condition and Future Prospects of the Negro People" Douglass comments that

> The Irish people, warmhearted, generous, and sympathizing with the oppressed everywhere when they stand on their own green island, are instantly taught on arriving in this Christian country to hate and despise colored people. They are taught to believe that we eat the bread which of right belongs to them. The cruel lie is told the Irish that our adversity is essential to their prosperity. (Foner 1950–55, 2: 249)

Clearly, empowered whites are the source of the "cruel lie" that pits racial and class oppression against each other. But though Douglass remains sympathetic to the plight of the Irish immigrant, he recognizes that slavery, racial prejudice and class exploitation, however similar they may be in form and cause, have been configured within the United States as competing claims.

Unsurprisingly, during the 1840s and 1850s, US pro-slavery writers proved the most willing to write about the abuses of northern labour practices. For example, in his novel *Cannibals All! Or Slaves without Masters* ([1857] 1960), George Fitzhugh famously argues that without the privileges and protections offered by "the patriarchal institution" northern labourers were "slaves without the rights of slaves" (p. 17). In *The Slave Son,* comparisons with English exploitation of the Irish peasantry are similarly offered by Cardon as a defence of slavery and a proof of English hypocrisy. It is Cardon who brings up the Irish in the course of arguments with Dorset, primarily to excuse West Indian slavery by noting that British anti-slavery activists were overlooking similar – and indeed worse – abuses much closer to home. Cardon's motive seems less indignation about the state of the Irish than the desire to deflect Dorset's criticism of the plantation system. As a Catholic, Cardon may well have sympathized with Irish Catholics, who in their own country were oppressed by laws that made it impossible for them to live normal lives. To some extent, however, the contexts of the Irish references in *The Slave Son* undermine their radicalism. For example, Cardon's reference to Whiteboyism, in the context of what he calls the "murdering work" of "obeah" on his estate, makes that sympathy problematic: if the Irish response to oppression has been to form secret societies like the Whiteboys, it seems logical to assume that other oppressed populations, such as his own slaves, would band together to do the same. His political beliefs appear to eat away at the ground on which he is standing, though he refuses to – or cannot – recognize it.

Interestingly, Dorset never rebuts these arguments, so that while their force as a defence of slavery may be overwhelmed by other scenes in Wilkins's novel – and by Cardon's obvious bad faith – the charge of symmetry between Caribbean slavery and British colonialism in Ireland remains uncontested. In terms of British policy in 1854, the novel's arguments against Irish oppression – both dispossession in Ireland and labour conditions in England – are perhaps more relevant than any critique the novel may offer of slavery itself.

Adolphus, The Slave Son and Literary Genres

To modern readers, *Adolphus* and *The Slave Son* (especially the former) may seem one-dimensional, particularly when it comes to the characterization of the heroines. But it is important to see these two works in their literary context. Both novels draw on the late-eighteenth-century British Gothic genre, and in Gothic fiction – as in the nineteenth-century melodrama that followed and borrowed from it – the heroine's helplessness is integral to the overall effect. Passive heroines abound in eighteenth- and nineteenth-century British fiction in any case, but the Gothic heroine's passivity is especially marked: she exists primarily to be threatened by the villain who, like DeGuerinon, imprisons her and threatens her with sexual violation. Gothic novelists set their plots in historical eras (especially medieval ones) and/or exotic locations such as Italy, because to their English-speaking audiences such settings provided a realistic context for fantasies of power, corruption and subjection. In *Adolphus* and *The Slave Son*, estate houses replace sinister Gothic dungeons, castles and monastic houses, but the effect is much the same, because a slave owner, like a Gothic villain, exerts a considerable degree of power over slaves and free coloureds.

Adolphus and *The Slave Son* are also both protest novels, focused primarily on making points about racism and slavery, and protest literature tends to have luridly violent villains, handsome and brave heroes, and heroines whose virtue is surpassed only by their helplessness. This is especially true of the protest melodramas that may well be models for both of these works. Melodrama, the dominant dramatic genre of the mid-nineteenth century, presents "a world of justice where after intense struggle and torment good triumphs over and punishes evil, and virtue receives tangible material rewards" (Booth 1965, 14). Wilkins manages to make this formula the vehicle for more complex fictional effects in *The Slave Son*, suggesting capacities for violence and dishonesty in Belfond as well as allowing us to see Cardon's point of view at times; this greater complexity accords with her desire to break with the tradition of sentimental anti-slavery fiction and to underline the corrupting influences of slavery on both owner and slave.[15] *Adolphus*, on the other hand, remains more clearly a melodramatic protest narrative: hero Adolphus is wholly admirable from start to finish, and villain DeGuerinon wholly contemptible.

The melodramatic overtones of *Adolphus* in particular suggest that it might have been written with performance in mind. Written for a popular newspaper, it might have been read out loud to those who could not read; such a setting could account for its rather declamatory discourse, as in Adolphus's very formal proposal to Antonia:

If I have offended you, speak, and henceforth deep repentance shall ever be my lot; and let me bid to hope who now encircles me with her deceitful dreams to hide for ever from me her unattainable pleasures. If it be the contrary, as I sincerely believe and trust . . . declare it to me, and my constant prayers shall be to render you as happy as you deserve, and thank my Creator for having granted me such a blessed lot among mankind. (p. 22)

---

15. Wilkins herself seems to have felt that this was the most important moral point of *The Slave Son*. In her letter supporting her second petition to the Royal Literary Fund in 1884, she states: "And I think, that in my little book the '*Slave Son*' I have shown that the real evil of slavery does not consist in the unrewarded work of the slave, but in the *irresponsible* & therefore degrading power of the slave-holder himself who is situated to abuse it."

When read silently, these words sound stilted; the dominance of realist fiction for over two centuries, and especially the plain-style realism of the twentieth century, has conditioned us to expect conversational rather than declamatory idiom in fictional dialogue. Read aloud, however, or imagined as part of a speech (especially given the rather formal public-speaking style of the mid-nineteenth century), this apparently over-wrought speech seems less "wrong", and the same could be argued of the narrator's frequent asides, such as the comment on Adolphus and Antonia's mutual glance just before the proposal: "Oh! the silent eloquence of the eye – who can describe it!" (p. 20).

"The Past Is the Parent of the Present"

The preface to *Adolphus* raises the issue of digging up the past, and foresees a hostile reception for the work: "Many voices will no doubt be raised against us, as endeavouring to arouse feelings which are supposed dead, and to revive things which some would have entirely erased from memory's tablets" (p. 5). The preface counters this with the argument that the past "is a source of lessons pregnant with utility" because the present grows out of the past. Though the assumption seems to be that the past is worse than the present, the author also sees it as an example, expressing the somewhat cryptic hope that the novel's exploration of past evils may teach the "coloured people" of the present "that they have only to exert themselves in the same manner as did their fathers to clear from their sight whatever causes of complaint by which they may be surrounded". Similarly, for *The Slave Son,* Wilkins declares her purpose to be not so much to support the "civil emancipation" of American slaves "as to invite supporters for its completion in the social advancement of the coloured race" (p. 101). More explicitly than the author of *Adolphus,* she notes that the end of slavery in the British Empire, "where . . . one half the population was beggared to emancipate the other", has done little to end racism: "prejudice against the emancipated race influences the local authorities, just as much as at the period of our story" (p. 101). For the British Empire as for the United States, she insists, political emancipation is worthless unless accompanied by social emancipation.

One means towards that emancipation is the appropriation of the literary and cultural past of the oppressor. Especially for mixed-race characters who have no secure place in their society, an education in Europe, or in European literature and culture, can be a potent source of symbolic power. True, that power is clearly linked to the oppressive past which defines their social disadvantage, but it can be possessed more easily than material forms of power such as land, money or political position. Adolphus and Belfond are at least as well educated as the powerful whites they oppose. The novels use a well-worn narrative convention here: the heroes' worth is at odds with their circumstances, and their "natural gentility" will eventually triumph, no matter how many sordid materialists try to push them down to their "proper" station. But to apply that convention to the racially charged context of nineteenth-century Trinidad is necessarily to change it, and to call the "naturalness" of gentle birth into question. The authors go beyond the obvious injustice of racism to query its fundamental assumption that colour defines nature. Any oppressed person who can successfully appropriate the cultural heritage of the oppressors can use it to challenge their claims to "natural" dominance. One element of the past can thus be used to neutralize the other – or, to put it another way, the cultural past allows characters to exchange an oppressive "parent" for an empowering one.

Although by focusing on mixed-race characters *Adolphus* and *The Slave Son* may capitulate to the notion that white blood is needed to fit people for full citizenship, the same device also problematizes the notion of an essential racial identity. *Adolphus,* for instance, makes it obvious that parentage, the very concept invoked in its preface, is fraught with contradiction and conflict. To return to the preface after reading the novel is to be struck by that choice of the word "parent", surely significant in a novel where fatherhood rarely appears in a positive light. The author does go on to speak of "fathers", but the first choice of "parent" suggests an uneasiness with "father" and its connotations.

In *The Slave Son,* the situation is a little more complicated. Wilkins clearly believes in essential racial characteristics to some extent, and places particular value on people of mixed blood, or "people of caste", because their birth "secretly but surely involves the grafting of European intellect on the warm strong feelings of Africa" (p. 132). But she also sees slavery as a pernicious influence on both the oppressors and the oppressed. The very "grafting" process does further damage – not because sexual relations between races are inherently bad, but because in the context of slavery they nearly always involve a series of oppressive, sinful acts, made worse by the failure of society to censure or even to see them. Such acts produce a demonic parody of parenting, in which fathers are owners and offspring a sort of "cattle".

The title *The Slave Son* draws attention to the contradictory and damaging place, or rather lack of place, that first-generation mixed-race children inhabit. Born into slavery, the "slave-son" Belfond, and the heroine, his beloved Laurine, are brought up seeing their parentage as an irresolvable problem. The narrator remarks of Laurine, "She had never inquired for her father, – no child of caste ever does" (p. 132). The narrator, however, makes her paternity plain, noting with pointed irony that her owner, Mr Perrin, has fathered "a great many children of caste" and sells them once they have "been grown", making "a great deal of money by raising human crops" (p. 131). Belfond is in much the same position; he does know who his father is, and his marked resemblance to him, as well as to the legitimate son whose personal attendant he is, makes his parentage plain, but at the same time invisible, to everyone. Nor are things much easier on the maternal side: Madelaine, Laurine's mother, is indifferent to her, and looks upon her "as an alien with whom she [has] nothing to do" (p. 133); her experience as a slave has led her to see even her love for her lost husband and their dead children as folly and sickness, which has now passed away and left her caring *"for notin' nor nobody"* (p. 257), not even herself. The clear implication is that Laurine has been conceived through rape, an act the more easily carried out because Madelaine is stunned by her grief at losing husband and children. And Belfond's mother, though she does love her son and his father, is flogged to death by her master/lover's new wife, jealous of her husband's former lover. The past, in other words, "parents" the present with a vengeance in this novel.

In *Adolphus,* it is specifically fathers who are demonic: there are hardly any good fathers in the novel except for the aged Mr Romelia, the heroine Antonia's father. However, though honourable, Romelia is physically very weak, his principal act being to die under the various oppressions of the villain DeGuerinon. Adolphus's experience of parental love is much bleaker: his grandmother, Agilai, is raped by her master, who has just sold her husband; she dies after bearing a child, Rosa. The grandfather cannot resist profiting from this transaction, as her uncle Jimbo puts it: "[Rosa] grew up, she was handsome; and her father, her Christian father sold her!" (p. 16). Rosa's new master has bought her solely to be his mistress; after he rapes and otherwise abuses her, she runs away, dying in her turn shortly after giving birth to Adolphus, who is thus fathered and grandfathered by acts of violence. Otherwise he has no parents at all apart from his surrogate father, Padre Gonzalvez, who adopts him just as he will later protect Antonia in the wake of her parents' death. The villain DeGuerinon, himself born of a similar master/slave relationship, is also mis-fathered, though more subtly: his father, having no other son, makes him his heir but also virtually deletes the black side of his son's racial heritage. Moreover, his overindulgence renders his son good for little but extravagant spending and the exploitation of others. The spending eventually trips him up: his estate falls into the hands of creditors and his racial identity, no longer "veiled with silver" (p. 80) suddenly becomes visible; one of his first responses to his financial reverses is to offer his mother to his creditors.

The problematic figure of the parent in *Adolphus* and *The Slave Son* makes it clear that the parental relationship of past to present can never be an easy or simple one: to return to the preface to *Adolphus*, looking backward seems to reveal fewer fathers who have exerted themselves to throw off injustice than fathers who have perpetrated it. (Mothers are less violent, but largely helpless, and tend to figure most prominently in their dying moments.) Although Anamoa in *The Slave Son* is depicted in a positive light – he shows real affection for his recently arrived daughter Talima – when he attempts to protect her from Bretton's rudeness, he cannot: he gains nothing but the flogging that hastens his own death. Similarly, although Quaco's father too has been a good one, setting his son the example of sacrificial loyalty – dying on the slave ship in Anamoa's service – ultimately he can protect neither his son nor his king, who both end up enslaved. Almost the only father who acts to any beneficial effect in either book is Padre Gonzalvez, whose fatherhood is only spiritual. The suggestion is that slavery and the slave trade destroy parent-child bonds and make benevolent parenting at best ineffectual.

If the problematic nature of biological heritage makes the fluid patrimony of culture more attractive in both books, cultural tradition is still marked by the pervasive influence of slavery and social prejudice. Adolphus, in the course of his education, seizes on Roman history as a narrative which can ennoble him; if his society brands him a "bastard", and forces him to think of himself as the son of a "villain" and a "prostitute" (p. 20), in reading Roman history he can be fired by a different sort of narrative, from which he takes "enriching lessons of patriotism" (p. 19), as the narrator puts it. This more abstract kind of parentage proves, however, to be nearly as troubled as its biological counterpart. Patriotism, especially as drawn from classical models, may seem an untainted and prestigious heroic tradition, allowing Adolphus to claim motherland and fatherland without reference to his personal past, but what country can he claim as his own? Any European country his father and grandfather might have come from is tainted by its associations with slavery, and Trinidad itself, as Ernest points out, is "a shore which slavery and oppression daily stain with the blood of your fellow-creatures" (pp. 72–73). True, Adolphus never wavers in his desire to return to Trinidad, but that determination may have more to do with his love for Antonia than his love for Trinidad as a country.

Nature, Gardens, Gender

Both the novels under discussion here invoke nature to some degree as a source of spiritual strength and as an index of character. In *Adolphus*, Antonia Romelia's lush, loved and well-tended garden, with "its neatly gravelled walk, its bed of choicest flowers" and the "uncommon taste" (p. 8) which directs it, stands in obvious contrast to DeGuerinon's neglected garden and contempt for horticulture: "the pleasures of nursing a tender plant, the sublime thoughts which spontaneously rise from the heart at the contemplation of a flower garden, that scene where nature assumes the form of a lowly enchantress and fills the heart with rapture – to him it was all 'useless trash' " (p. 49). In *Adolphus,* nature is something to be tamed and controlled: the benevolent order of Antonia's garden reflects not only her delight in nature but also her civilized character. Antonia's plants are almost all imported from Europe, and the use of classical terms such as "Flora's temple" (p. 8) to describe her garden underlines the extent to which she regulates nature according to traditional European aesthetic principles.

In *The Slave Son*, the nature invoked is wilder, and closer to the one defined by the Romantic movement in late eighteenth- and early nineteenth-century Europe. Wilkins's nature figures as refuge, spiritual inspiration and alternative parent; interestingly, even St Hilaire Cardon has fleeting access to it (see below). The more complex use of the nature motif matches the more complicated characterizations in *The Slave Son*, where hero, heroine and villain each have a degree of integrity, though their moral codes and political stances are at odds. Laurine is perhaps the closest to a stereotype: a slave to the age of thirteen, brought up with hardly a parent to speak of, she nevertheless grows up a paragon of virtue. "From Laurine's earliest childhood," we are told, "the characteristic feature of her disposition was devotion" (p. 130). Treated kindly by her mistress and by the child whose attendant she is, and finally freed at that child's dying request, she gains with her freedom "new life, new spirit, new thoughts, new powers and self-respect" (p. 132). The rather improbable ease of all this may be explained by Wilkins's tendency to present Laurine as an emanation of nature: freed, she feels "like a bird escaped from a cage, not knowing what to do with herself, but bewildered with the joy" (p. 132). Predictably, she at first uses her freedom to spend whole days in the woods, "gathering flowers, picking berries, and watching the birds" (p. 132), only slipping into her mother's hut after dark to sleep. Interestingly, Laurine's contacts with nature are not marked by epiphanic moments of communion with nature, as the men's tend to be, but seem simply an inevitable part of her life.

Laurine moves out of the woods when her innate "devotion", finding itself without an object, constructs one out of her mother, whose love she has never had; without knowing Madelaine's history, she sees that slavery has "annihilated all power of thought, care, will, even self-preservation" in her mother, and that Madelaine stands "more in need of her child's aid, than the child of her mother's" (p. 133). At this point she begins to cultivate her mother's garden patch, to earn money to support her mother (who habitually eats or wastes most of her weekly food ration at once and then goes hungry) and finally to save money towards buying her mother's freedom. Yet although she thus moves back into a social environment, she still acts largely according to nature; the narrator comments on the sacrifice of her labour and of her "youthful, sociable inclinations, unpretendingly, unostentatiously, and almost unconsciously offered up on the shrine of filial affection" (p. 135). She is "naturally gifted" (p. 120) in arts which also connect her to nature: dancing and singing, gathering flowers and arranging them into the bouquets she sells, and writing songs – songs whose lyrics focus on the birds, the woods and the freedom of the "wide savannas" (p. 123).

The gap between Laurine's "almost unconscious" reactions and those of Belfond and other men certainly owes something to gender. The abolitionist cause in the United States and in Great Britain was clearly – though not unproblematically – linked to the emancipation of women; many of the same people worked for both causes, and on similar philosophical grounds. In calling for social as well as civil emancipation in her introduction to *The Slave Son*, Wilkins sees the distinction as part of a gendered division of labour: "The political emancipation of the coloured race is a deed for the men; their social emancipation is an heroic act worthy of the American ladies" (p. 103). The implication is that, like Laurine, women "naturally" possess the "benevolence" and "independence" necessary to make social emancipation a reality. There are, however, several women who suggest otherwise. Mrs Cardon is one; though she takes some interest in the hospital for sick slaves, and is even pitied by the gossips in chapter 1 as "a martyr to her servants" (p. 114), she reacts with angry jealousy to the presence of Belfond's mother on the estate, and banishes her rival to the fields to be flogged and die. The gossips, too, with their admiring discussion of one Madame Hinde's slave management, suggest that women's benevolence, as Wilkins sees it, has distinct limits. Madame Hinde, despite her "excellent heart" and kindness to strangers, "manage[s] her Negroes" (p. 113) by flogging them herself, so severely that they cannot function for days afterwards.

Predictably, then, Wilkins makes Belfond's childhood very different from Laurine's. Brought up like her as a slave and personal attendant to his white half-sibling, he reacts not with devotion but with "all those vices which slavery burns into the soul of man", including "falsehood, flattery and theft" (p. 259). His intelligence only makes him more adept than most at these vices until his young master/brother is sent to Europe to further his education, with Belfond as his attendant. The journey ends up giving Belfond a much better education than his hapless sibling, who concentrates instead on riotous living. Belfond becomes fascinated by the "power of reading" (p. 260); he learns to read, attends lectures, studies and reaches the conclusion that "knowledge" gives white men power over black. For Belfond, escape from slavery (as a state of mind) comes not through nature but through literacy and travel. Nonetheless, the process is incomplete, leaving him still partially "blighted" by slavery, and by the "constantly repeated words of scorn and contempt [which] wither up the best and dearest feelings of man" (p. 261). Possessing "devotion" much as Laurine does – to Wilkins, apparently, this is an innate racial as well as a gendered characteristic, though more likely to be submerged in men – unlike her he cannot see religion except as a "dim, confused, incomprehensible page" (p. 261). He thus becomes a runaway and a renegade, joining and organizing a group of runaway slaves in the mountains of Trinidad; he is also able to live in nature as few others in *The Slave Son* are. Even Laurine, despite her days there, is less at home in the forest, always coming back to her mother's hut to sleep, and gathering flowers or cultivating plants to sell rather than living entirely in the wild. Belfond, by contrast, builds a house for Laurine entirely of forest materials, "thatched with leaves of . . . forest palm, the walls and doorway of cocoa-nut basket-work, and the windows . . . trellised with liana fibres" (p. 124). He even adds a garden, using the existing trees and forest plants he has gathered: "Whenever I found a pretty plant, I brought it there to adorn the place for you, from the large changeable rose to the great cactus, and the modest little *four-o'clock*" (p. 124). He teaches the maroon colony to survive in the mountains; he swims easily to land when Cardon throws him overboard; and he even escapes the wily Higgins, whose skill in negotiating the forest is almost as great as his own, and who has weapons and dogs.

In addition to using natural materials and moving freely through natural environments, Belfond is responsive to nature's influence, which is here, as in *Adolphus,* a soothing and ennobling one. At one point, for instance, though disgusted with himself and upset by Laurine's refusal to flee with him, he is still moved by the sight of a beautiful bay: "his features relaxed from their stern expression; for here he had often walked with Laurine at sunset, when the golden streaks of light shot along the stream" (p. 142). This passage makes an interesting contrast to the garden scenes in *Adolphus*. For one thing, it focuses on uncultivated scenery – "a clear rivulet, which, after meandering through the forest, as if formed solely to give life and coolness to its beautiful shades, here flowed calmly into the sea" – (p. 142) and on local vegetation – "the palm-tops . . . the crimson flower of the wild shacshac and the broad disc of the prickly pear" (p. 142) – rather than on domesticated and imported flowers. Belfond resembles a Byronic hero rather than an eighteenth-century gentleman enjoying his garden. Like Byron's Manfred or Childe Harold, he is rebellious, defying moral codes (in his case the prohibition on theft), and he broods ominously over the sea: "at times [he] would stop suddenly and fix his eyes upon the sea, although in reality he saw not its billowy surface, but only the troubled visions of his own mind" (p. 142). Significantly, nature is only able to act on him at this point through Laurine: the scene subdues "the world and its hopes" in his mind, but does so by evoking memories of her "carolling blithely to the flowers she gathered" (p. 143). The effect is also merely temporary, for when Belfond's reverie is interrupted by Quaco, he reverts to his plan to break with Laurine and leave for Venezuela without her.

In Belfond's next encounter with nature, however, he no longer needs an intermediary. Having already decided, somewhat grudgingly, that he will not help Daddy Fanty poison his half-brother, he comes to Nature, to "her eternal hymn of harmony" (p. 226), and to the Moon, whose light is "like a spirit of peace . . . hushing to rest all angry sounds, even in the heart of man" (p. 226). This lulling by a gendered, perhaps even maternal, Nature, aptly presided over by a feminine Moon, is apparently effective enough to undo more of the blighting effects of slavery on his psyche, because he will soon extend love to his father, even after Cardon imprisons him to await execution.

Cardon, too, is blighted by slavery, except that his vices are those of the master, who simply cannot see his slaves as anything but cattle, cannot acknowledge his illegitimate child, and yet is haunted by the knowledge that Daddy Fanty will find a way to destroy him. Consumed by seemingly perpetual rage, Cardon dies in a slave insurrection – precisely what his savage floggings were designed to prevent. He is caught in a dilemma, for he needs both living slaves and the sense that he can put any of them to death if he sees fit, and the two needs prove incompatible: the new slaves he buys are rebellious, and his punishments kill some slaves and provoke others to overt and covert acts of violent resistance. He himself does have a brief encounter with nature at the end of an argument with Dorset about whether the poor Irish are worse off than slaves in Trinidad, but like Belfond's early response, it seems second-hand, dependent on Dorset. Cardon first swears at an overhanging branch of the orange tree which he runs into as they ride, but then, as Dorset collects the oranges, eats some, and lapses into a delighted survey of the wild nature around him, even Cardon seems soothed, and is "content to smoke his cigar without offering to interrupt the contemplations of his more romantic friend" (p. 180). He soon spurns this glimpse of content, however, just as he will spurn Belfond's filial attempt to save his life, and the moment of peace shatters as the sound of the slaves' protest song starts the argument going once again.

Nature in *The Slave Son* does have its evil as well as its regenerative sides. Daddy Fanty uses his knowledge of herbs and plants to produce poisons, and the vegetation around his cave could be read as a dark parody of Belfond and Laurine's favourite places, or Antonia's peaceful garden; the way to it is guarded by "a dense thicket of nux-vomica, palma-christi, the branched calaloo, poisonous shrubs of the cockroach-apple, and many other noxious bushes" (p. 203). The narrator explicitly contrasts this with other natural environments: "Nature, so beautiful and enchanting elsewhere on the mountains, here assumed a most repulsive aspect" (p. 203). Whether Fanty has deliberately cultivated this poisonous grove or chosen to live next to it so as to have easy access to the tools of his trade, the description suggests that nature can turn or be turned to evil as well as good: its moral and spiritual significance is not innate, but a human construct.

For Belfond and Laurine, however, Nature proves a beneficent surrogate parent after their violent losses of, respectively, a father and a mother. Belfond says of Trinidad, "God might have chosen you for

Eden" (p. 320), and their departure from the island is presided over by natural forces which seem almost Edenic in their natural beauty: the moonlight dances on the water, and the breeze and surf join in "the hymn of nature's joy, the mingled song of sea and forest" (p. 321). In Genesis, Adam and Eve's departure is a consequence of their fall, and they leave Eden for a harsh and hostile world; Belfond and Laurine seem rather to leave the fallen world behind. If Trinidad has been "spoiled, corrupted, poisoned by the white man" (p. 321), they themselves appear to be entering an unfallen state of oneness with nature, an impression confirmed by their disappearance from the narrative at this point. We know they are headed for Venezuela, but we know nothing of their future lives there, since the final chapter – at least the one we have – focuses entirely on the fate of those who remain behind.

Adolphus, The Slave Son and the Caribbean Literary Tradition

The authors of *The Slave Son* and *Adolphus* describe their stories as historical novels. Since their focus is on the period shortly before emancipation, which was within the living memory of most of their first readers, this claim may seem curious. But both authors argue that the legacy of several centuries of slavery overshadows social relations in their present. Wilkins maintains that she could "equally well have transferred [her story] to any other slave country, and to a more recent period, for the same causes are ever followed by like effects" (p. 99). Conversely, by setting his novel before emancipation, the anonymous author of *Adolphus* leaves himself free to concentrate on the historical roots of discrimination against the free coloured population without having to deflect arguments that emancipation had ameliorated the worst of the social ills against which he inveighs.

Although both novels mount vigorous attacks on the legacy of slavery, neither novel makes the lives of slaves its only – or its main – focus. In fact, it is possible to read *Adolphus* and barely register that legal slavery still exists, as practically all the story's main characters are free people of colour. *The Slave Son* takes place on a estate, so we are allowed to observe many more aspects of life under slavery. But Wilkins is explicit about wanting to use her novel "not so much to take rank among the champions of civil emancipation . . . as to invite support for the social advancement of the coloured race" (p. 101). Accordingly, her two main characters are nominally free: Belfond is a runaway and Laurine has been manumitted by her dying mistress. Moreover, both Belfond and Laurine are of mixed race. The institution of slavery certainly defines every aspect of these characters' lives, but in the main plots of both novels, the vicissitudes of the slaves take second place to the tribulations of free people of colour.

In this respect, the Trinidadian stories differ from nineteenth-century North American narratives that focus on protagonists of African descent. Novels like *Uncle Tom's Cabin* dwell on the day-to-day experiences of enslaved people of all stations and complexions. Personal narratives, like those by Frederick Douglass or Harriet Jacobs, although they focus on mixed-race characters as well as on characters who buy or steal themselves out of slavery, rarely invoke racial caste to make a separate case for civil liberties for free people of colour.[16] Particularly in those personal narratives, the free person's stated motive for speaking is to give voice to the sufferings of his or her kinfolk, still silenced by slavery. Even when racial mixture or superior erudition makes them seem more socially privileged than field slaves, these spokespersons for the race are loath to revel in caste distinctions. (One may note, for instance, Frederick Douglass's dismay, after being reunited with his half brother late in life, at the degree to which the accidents of birth and freedom had separated their lives.)[17] And when caste does become salient in literary representations of race, the mulatta figure's end is inevitably tragic.

---

16. The American literary convention of playing down caste should not be taken as evidence that caste distinctions were not also rife among Americans of African descent. Apart from the notorious aristocracies of skin in Louisiana, which, it could be argued, were part of a social milieu closer to that of the Caribbean than to the rest of North America, there were well established free communities of colour in Virginia, as well as smaller communities elsewhere, in which shade and status played a significant role. For a full discussion of this phenomenon see Ira Berlin's *Slaves Without Masters* (1974).

17. For a discussion of this reunion, and of Douglass's children's horrified response to their southern cousins, see David W. Blight's *Frederick Douglass' Civil War* (1989, 196–97).

Not so her fictional Caribbean counterpart. All the mixed-race lovers in the Trinidadian stories live happily ever after, and that outcome is never really in question. Their relationships are for the most part endogamous, so they do not provide the main source of narrative tension. The salient distinctions here are between slave and free, not black and white. They are played out, for example, when Adolphus and his free coloured friend, Ernest, interact with the slave, Cudjoe. The social gulf between Cudjoe and the well-educated young men makes it difficult for the black slave to distinguish between brown and white masters, except that the brown masters treat him with greater *noblesse oblige*.[18] Indeed, when Ernest demurs at Cudjoe referring to him as a "country buckra", Cudjoe points out that "[i]n dis country ya, once you lily bit white, you gat money, you gie grog to drink, you is buckra" (p. 47). In a parallel scene in *The Slave Son*, Belfond successfully passes himself off as a slave owner when he attempts to buy the African princess, Talima. He is later unmasked, not because he does not *look* the part – he is one of several mixed-race buyers present – but because he refuses to assume the air of craven obsequiousness demanded of free coloureds in the presence of whites.

Both *Adolphus* and *The Slave Son*, therefore, turn on this central contradiction – that people of colour, although in some instances as wealthy as whites and, in others, better educated, nevertheless found themselves denied the social prestige of white men. But, since prestige was predominantly a function of white power over blacks and of claims of racial superiority, the free coloureds' claim to white privilege in these novels often depends on the authors' ability to demonstrate that such individuals were superior to enslaved or darker complected blacks. In choosing to focus on the couples Adolphus and Antonia, and Laurine and Belfond, the novelists engage our sympathies for relatively cultivated protago-

---

18. Here, too, literary conventions should be distinguished from common knowledge. In the ideological debates of the time, brown masters and mistresses often were castigated for being more cruel to their slaves and/or servants than whites. *Warner Arundell* offers examples of this claim in its narrator's comments on the mixed-race mistress who cheats Warner out of his inheritance. The author of *Adolphus* is deliberately inverting that stereotype here, when he allows Cudjoe to single out brown masters as superior to white ones. Conversely, the fact that the dastardly white master, DeGuerinon, turns out to be of mixed race may be a backhanded gesture towards the prevailing stereotype.

nists, whose refined sensibilities differ markedly from the more robust passions of the slave couple Quaco and Talima who, in turn, are distinguished from ordinary creole slaves because they are African born and therefore knew freedom before being enslaved.

America was still a slave society in the 1850s, when Douglass, Jacobs and Stowe were writing, whereas, as Wilkins points out in her introduction, Trinidad had been a slave-plantation society only from the closing decades of the eighteenth century, shortly before it fell into the hands of the British, to the 1830s, when slavery was abolished. Moreover, both Wilkins and the author of *Adolphus* look back on the regime of Chacon, the last Spanish governor of the island, as a golden age, during which free people of colour enjoyed many civil liberties. Perhaps these historical peculiarities account for the differences between the narrative conventions in the early Trinidadian stories, as compared to the American ones, but it is also the case that very few Caribbean historical novels today deal directly with slavery, and that almost all those that do, end up in some way focusing upon caste – the ascription of status on the grounds of birth, class, and sometimes ethnicity – rather than race.

The historical event most frequently depicted by Caribbean writers is the Haitian Revolution. But in C.L.R. James's play *The Black Jacobins* (1976), Edouard Glissant's *Monsieur Toussaint* (1981), Alejo Carpentier's *El reino de este Mundo* (1969) and Derek Walcott's *Haitian Trilogy* (2002), the emphasis is on life during and after the revolution, and on the distinctions of caste that quickly emerged between the masses and their new brown and black leaders. H.G. De Lisser, the most prolific author of historical romances in the anglophone Caribbean, develops an explicitly racist version of this theme. In novels like *Revenge* (1919), *Psyche* (1952) and *Morgan's Daughter* (1953), all of which deal with historical moments when blacks resisted oppression, De Lisser dismisses the events he fictionalizes as the irrational outbursts of primitive blacks, manipulated by cunning whites or envious mulattos. De Lisser himself was light-skinned, a journalist who aligned himself culturally and politically with the most conservative white elements in early twentieth-century Jamaica, so it is hardly surprising that his novels indulge such stereotypes. But the fact that he successfully cultivated "white" social status, despite his obvious pigmentation, speaks to the complexity of racial categories in the

Caribbean, as well as to the salience of the anxieties that surface in the work of other Caribbean writers when they address the distinctions that separate their educated, mostly brown, protagonists from the black masses. Read thus, both *Adolphus* and *The Slave Son* are precursors to twentieth-century Caribbean caste romances like Claude McKay's *Banana Bottom* (1933), V.S. Reid's *New Day* (1949), George Lamming's *Season of Adventure* (1979), Earl Lovelace's *Salt* (1996), Walcott's *Omeros* (1990) and Erna Brodber's *Myal* (1988). All confront the desire of the "better" class of educated non-whites to transcend the divide between black and brown, educated and illiterate, without sacrificing the social privileges they have aggrandized through education, racial mixing, and cultural refinement. The resolutions of such plots rarely hinge on the romantic union across class lines of an individual man and woman, as is the convention in European romances. Rather, the caste romance seeks a political union between the leader and the masses, or a cultural union of the intellectual with the folk.[19]

Caste privilege in this context, therefore, is seldom simply about racial mixture. In both of the early Caribbean novels reprinted in this volume, good breeding in the genealogical sense is superseded by its figurative equivalent: the cultivation of the virtues of erudition, refinement, and intellectual independence associated with the European Enlightenment. Belfond rises to heroic status on account of his exposure to French Enlightenment philosophy when he goes to Paris as his white half-brother's valet. Adolphus is educated by the Catholic Church, a symbol in newly British Trinidad of a more humane European tradition than the harsher brand of Protestant colonialism introduced after Chacon's sur-render. Laurine and Antonia, quintessential Rousseauan ingenues, culti-vate their refined sensibilities by communing with nature in their idealized gardens and by performing acts of charity.[20] Thus, the protag-onists in both novels absorb all the highest virtues of Enlightenment cul-

---

19. Doris Sommer in *Foundational Fictions* (1991) makes a related claim for the genre of romance in early Latin American nationalist fiction although, in the Latin American case, the two categories united by the device of romance are the European and the Native American.

20. For Jean-Jacques Rousseau's description of education of the ideal woman, destined to be the partner of his model young man, see *Emile* ([1762] 1970).

ture without being tainted by its vices. Although Belfond's white half-brother dies before the beginning of the action in Wilkins's story, the (mixed-race) author of *Adolphus* makes sure to emphasize the distinction between biological and cultural good breeding by pointing out the contrast between Adolphus and his nemesis, the dastardly DeGuerinon, whose European education confirms in him only the most brutal characteristics of the slave-holding class. Both men are the sons of slave mothers and white fathers. However, DeGuerinon is exposed as "truly" black when his fortunes fail and his superficial gentility falters, while Adolphus's high-flown rhetoric, his refined sense of honour, his distress with his illegitimacy and his exquisite sensibility with respect to Antonia's affections epitomize the gentility we ascribe to the heroes of eighteenth- and nineteenth-century European sentimental novels, with the important distinction that, while foundlings in the European novels are rescued from obscurity by the revelation that they are indeed of noble and legitimate birth, our mixed-race heroes can scarcely claim legitimacy through the rapists of their mothers. When their noble blood outs, therefore, it is the cultural connection to specific aspects of Europe, rather than the biological link to their white fathers, that stains the sheets blue.

Such claims are repeated in the work of almost every Caribbean novelist of the twentieth century, although not all of them are as baldly patronizing in making them as the narrator of *Adolphus,* who endorses Cudjoe's assertion that free coloureds are as deserving of status as whites with the comment: "Had Cudjoe always spoken so truly, or prophesied as correctly, he would have been indeed a wonderful being; but as from the rock there often springs the prettiest flower, so from a degraded mind there are often emitted those sparks of truth which the most refined cannot but admire" (p. 47). C.L.R. James, whose novel *Minty Alley* ([1935] 1971) uses the hero's sentimental education through contact with the urban poor to confirm his intrinsic superiority to them, has reflected that his own education was facilitated by the good fortune of his having imbibed the ideals of social justice and personal liberty through his reading of the Western canon before he encountered their corruption in actual European societies (James [1963] 1983). For Walcott, from the oft-quoted line from his poem "A Far Cry from Africa", about refusing to choose between "this Africa and the English tongue I love" (1969, 18), to the epic poem *Omeros,* the burden and gift of mulatto privilege have been central themes in his poetry. Like Wilkins and the author of *Adolphus,* Walcott is adamant that social oppression inevitably brutalizes its victims, and in "What the Twilight Says" he reminds those who would romanticize the folk and forswear all attachment to colonial erudition that "the last thing which the poor needed was the idealization of their poverty" (1970, 19). However, Walcott is explicit about the contradictions inherent in his caste privilege. In the concluding cantos of *Omeros,* he remains exhilarated by the access his colonial education has given him to the most invigorating aspects of the European cultural tradition, even as he reiterates his anxiety that his use of the folk to create art remains inherently exploitative.

Other Caribbean writers have attempted to resolve these contradictions. Although both the natural parents of McKay's heroine, Bita, in *Banana Bottom* are black, Bita's education, like that of Adolphus, is the happy accident that follows an unhappy rape. First, through the missionaries, who educate her in England, and then through Squire Gensir, who introduces her on her return to Jamaica (as Belfond is introduced in France) to those aspects of Enlightenment philosophy that challenge the colonial status quo most directly, Bita is bred up to embody the civilized virtues of gentility, erudition and open-mindedness. McKay bridges the gulf between this paragon of caste privilege and the uneducated masses by marrying Bita off to her father's drayman, Jubban. But, in a simultaneous gesture of affiliation with and erasure of whiteness, Bita takes Squire Gensir's entire library with her into her marital home, once her mentor is safely dead.[21]

More recent Caribbean writers have begun to challenge the reduction of the differences between Europe and the Caribbean to a dichotomy between erudition and open-mindedness on the one hand and brutish ignorance on the other. Both Lovelace in *Salt* and Brodber in *Myal* critique the assumption that education and "good breeding" are intrinsi-

---

21. In fairness to McKay, it should be noted that he is fully cognizant of the implications of his plot and he struggles to deflect precisely the interpretation advanced here. For a fuller discussion of the anxieties surrounding caste privilege in his novel, see Rhonda Cobham's "Jekyll and Claude: The Erotics of Patronage in Claude McKay's *Banana Bottom*" (2000).

cally ennobling, and they question more explicitly than their nineteenth-century precursors any wholesale endorsement of Enlightenment values. In a plot reminiscent of that of *Banana Bottom,* Brodber reconfigures McKay's contradictions by questioning the relevance of both white and black cultural values to the advancement of modern Caribbean societies. Thus, Ella O'Grady's accomplishments are neither promoted as signs of inherent virtue nor excoriated as evidence of mixed-race exclusivity. Rather, they are valued only to the extent that they contribute to the greater good of the entire community. The same is true of Maydene Brassington's missionary zeal, Mass Levi's Protestant work ethic and Mass Cyrus's traditional healing arts.[22] In *Salt,* Lovelace redirects the plot at the point where the intellectual aspirations of some of his central characters begin to set up a moral distinction between those who have been granted access to education and those who have not. By giving over the novel's narrative authority to the voice of the community, and by following the positive and negative consequences of the education of individual protagonists over time, *Salt* challenges the equation by which erudition and good breeding – the badges of caste privilege – have come to be the virtues most anxiously defended by post-emancipation Caribbean elites.[23]

Some of the awkwardnesses of the narrator's language in *Adolphus* may be a consequence of the tension of the author's desire to maintain affiliation with the best that Europe represents, even as he espouses the goal of social justice for both free coloureds and enslaved Africans. Compared to the authentic representation of colloquial speech in Wilkins's *Slave Son,* much of the dialogue among the free people of colour in *Adolphus* seems stilted. Its coloured gentlemen sound for all the world like minor luminaries in a second-rate sentimental novel (although see discussion above on the possible mitigation of such a judgement).

---

22. For a discussion of the way in which, "[r]ecovered from narratives of villainy, marginality, exceptionalism, sentimentality, pathos, and racial equivalence alike . . . the mulatto in *Myal* becomes emblematic of Jamaica's tangled ancestry", see chapter 5 of Shalini Puri's *The Caribbean Postcolonial* (2003).

23. In Roy Heath's Guyana trilogy — *From the Heat of the Day* (1979), *Genetha* (1981a) and *One Generation* (1981b) — the characters' desperate striving for caste respectability under crippling social and personal constraints leads to a host of disasters.

Indeed, the coarser language of the novel's villains is much more vigorous and engaging than that of its heroes, who seem to spend a great deal of their time sighing. One is reminded of Patrick Chamoiseau's *Texaco* in which characters like the autodidact Ti-Cirique speak what the novel's English translators term "mulatto French" – "a laminated language spoken by the dictionary and by books from France. 'More French than that of the French' . . . [A language that] simplifies, overlooks, disregards Martiniquan Creole and its reality, in order to achieve correct speech" (1998, 394). But as late as the 1940s, similar forms of elocutionary excess in Standard English were *de rigeur* among the writers who belonged to the Jamaica Poetry League. The formal speech patterns of educated non-white elites in the anglophone Caribbean only ceased to be dominated by such traits after the political changes of the 1960s and 1970s, and the influence of American mass culture made colloquial speech in all contexts more acceptable. Even today, dramatic productions such as the Jamaican pantomime or the plays of the Sistren Theatre Collective still elicit laughter by parodying the stilted diction of "high brown" characters.[24] The audience's amused recognition confirms the enduring presence of linguistic markers of caste in today's Caribbean society.

It would be a mistake, however, to relegate the two nineteenth-century novels reproduced here to the status of mere cautionary tales, significant only because later Caribbean writing has moved beyond their limitations. In several important respects these novels offer us a view of Caribbean society rarely glimpsed in later works set wholly or in part before emancipation. When twentieth-century novelists, like Edgar Mittelholzer, in his *Kaywana* trilogy of the 1950s, or Dionne Brand, in *At the Full and Change of the Moon* (1999), root their plots in pre-emancipation events, they need do no more than sketch stylized tableaux of tormented slaves and cruel slave owners on conventionally rural plantations, in order to motivate the entire panoply of human desire that drives their multi-generational sagas. But both *Adolphus* and *The Slave Son* allow us the space to imagine a more complex set of interactions between

---

24. See also, for example, the diction of Mistress Myrtella Lee, an increasingly sympathetic character in Olive Senior's story "Real Old Time T'ing" (1986).

slaves and free coloureds, slaves and maroons, urban and rural slaves, free coloureds and working-class whites, as well as among whites of different classes and political persuasions. Perhaps only Chamoiseau's *Texaco* (1998), in its dissection of the social intricacies of Martiniquan society in the late nineteenth and early twentieth centuries, matches the combined achievement of these two nineteenth-century novels.

Indeed, the uncanny resonances between *Texaco* and *The Slave Son* deserve much more consideration than is possible here. For a start, the plot of *The Slave Son* demonstrates a claim that Chamoiseau's narrator makes explicit: that the condition of slavery circumscribed the meaning of freedom for all classes and races in Caribbean societies. Laurine's liminal existence as a free person on St Hilaire Cardon's estate, for example, parallels Esternome's "savannah freedom" in *Texaco*. In both cases, personal liberty is automatically constrained by the boundaries of the plantation, beyond which the manumitted remain vulnerable to surveillance and insult. Even the maroons, lionized today in the popular imagination as heroic figures who flourished beyond the reach of the plantation, are depicted as subject to a complex range of accommodations with slaves, freed blacks and even with whites.[25]

Adolphus is given by his maroon uncle to a Catholic priest so that he will not grow up a heathen nor have to endure the hardships of life in a community constantly on the run. Powerful, solitary pariahs – like Esternome's mysterious father in *Texaco,* or Daddy Fanty in *The Slave Son* – maintain their quasi-independent status on the periphery of the plantation by manipulating the dependence of both blacks and whites on their magical powers. Personal liberty seems least compromised in urban settings, with their colourful melée of wealthy coloureds, freed blacks, and slaves for hire. However, for the black revellers in *Adolphus* whom DeGuerinon attacks, as well as for Adolphus himself, the city's cosmopolitan *laissez-faire* never quite stabilizes the nervous equilibrium between freedom and terror. Whatever their station, therefore, free coloureds remain intimately dependent on slaves for protection and suc-

---

25. For a discussion of the range of meanings associated with the trope of marronage in modern Caribbean fiction see Barbara Lalla's *Defining Jamaican Fiction: Marronage and the Discourse of Survival* (1996).

cour.[26] In *Texaco,* Esternome's infatuation with Ninon brings him back each night to her slave hut. DeGuerinon's slaves provide Adolphus with the information and cover he needs to rescue his fiancée. When Belfond is finally captured, after hiding on his former owner's estate, he is saved from death by a slave insurrection. The paradoxical limits of freedom within the confines of slavery help explain why both of the nineteenth-century novels republished here invoke Venezuela as a refuge for free coloureds (see discussion above). That move is less a tribute to the mainland's more progressive policies than a lament against the island's limitations. Like Esternome's unsuccessful retreat to the hills in *Texaco,* Guinea John's fateful decision to fly back to Africa in *Salt,* or Marie Ursule's failed resolve to poison all her progeny in *At the Full and Change of the Moon,* the *deus ex machina* of escape to Venezuela names a desire for a symbolic space beyond the shadow of slavery – a shadow that even death may not, in the end, outrun.

Adolphus and *The Slave Son* also offer myriad examples of the diminished social capital of free coloureds in a society where whites are valued because they are free and blacks are valued because they are slaves. The mixed-race men who board the illegal slaver in Wilkins's novel can bid on its wares, but no one skips a beat when one of their number falls overboard, whereas a valuable slave in danger of drowning is worth paying a white sailor to save. And even though Antonia's father in *Adolphus* is a free man of some substance, he has no rights in civil court to challenge the actions of the white man who kidnaps his daughter. One aspect of this anomaly that finds only faint echoes in modern Caribbean writing is the complex relationship between lower-class whites and free people of colour. Both *Adolphus* and *The Slave Son* introduce white characters who compete with black characters as story tellers, workers, and villains. The white sailor, Higgins, who volunteers to dive overboard to rescue a drowning slave, is also the character who hunts down Belfond, and who bargains with Daddy Fanty for magical potions. In

---

26. For a historical study that makes a similar claim, see Hilary Beckles's *Black Rebellion in Barbados* (1987). Beckles argues that, although Barbados had a well-established, fairly prosperous free coloured population by the nineteenth century, at various crucial junctures, free coloureds joined or led outbreaks of civil disobedience in the years leading up to emancipation.

Adolphus, the captain of the ship taking the coloured gentlemen to Venezuela calls on a white sailor to tell stories to divert the fugitives' gloom. The social status of the white characters places them in a situation between slave and free that mirrors and reverses that of the free coloured population. Clearly members of the servant class in a way that many free coloureds were not, they nonetheless can claim the privileges of race in their dealings with slaves and masters in many situations. The author of *Adolphus* uses these distinctions to bolster the class status of his coloured protagonists, whereas the author of *The Slave Son* uses them to dramatize the regrettable perversions of proper social hierarchy among whites that the system of slavery fosters. Thus, Wilkins's narrator notes with distress that the sailor Higgins is "freely admitted into the society of persons who, if in Europe, would hardly have allowed him to sweep their stables" (p. 304).

The disappearance of white lower-class characters in Caribbean fiction follows the trajectory of social change in most Caribbean societies, where, by the mid-twentieth century, people of colour had begun to take over many of the roles formerly reserved for lower-status whites, without really redefining the relationships such roles reproduced. The nineteenth-century novels republished here allow us to excavate the discursive origins of many of the literary conventions associated with these roles. In *Texaco,* Esternome's first employer, the itinerant white carpenter who is addicted to the flesh of black women, is a rare latter-day example of this type of lower-class white character, more ubiquitous in early-twentieth-century novels. Some of the rogue overseers in De Lisser's historical novels, and the sailors who rape the mulatress Lucille in *New Day,* also belong in this category. Like the overseer in *The Slave Son* who lusts after Laurine, and the white sailor who dabbles in obeah, the inferior caste of these characters usually is signalled by their sexual predilection for black women and their recourse to "black magic". The white overseer in De Lisser's *Revenge* incites the Morant Bay Rebellion (in De Lisser's version of events), in order to spite a planter he suspects of diverting the affections of the black woman with whom he is obsessed. The plantation mistress in De Lisser's *The White Witch of Rose Hall* (1929) loses all pedigree when she succumbs to her fascination with obeah. These white characters' attraction to all that is deemed irrational and lascivious in blackness inverts the association of free coloured protagonists with all that is considered virtuous and ennobling in whiteness. It is worth noting that heroic mulattos in the early novels rarely are fathered by such low-brow types, nor are their high-status white fathers, however cruel, usually portrayed in naked pursuit of black women, or as susceptible to obeah, despite the incontrovertible evidence that such pursuit occurred.

Over time, the qualities associated with this class of whites in Caribbean fiction have been subsumed into the spectrum of characteristics ascribed to brown middlemen. Thus, whereas in *The Slave Son*, a noble mulatto character is contrasted with a venal lower-class white, in *Adolphus*, those opposing characteristics are distributed between Adolphus, a brown man of noble character, and DeGuerinon, a brown man of low character who passes for white. De Lisser puts an ironic spin on this trope in *Under the Sun* (1937), in which a respectable, mixed-race Jamaican man marries a lower-class English woman so as to improve his social standing back home, only to be upstaged completely when she uses her race to gain an entrée into Jamaican high society and abandons him. In Alfred Mendes's *Pitch Lake* ([1934] 1984), the low-brow white protagonist's anxieties about not being able to live up to the cultural norms of whiteness lead him to murder his black mistress (although the novel does not contrast him explicitly with a brown character of greater refinement). By the time Lamming's *In the Castle of My Skin* appeared in 1953, such lower-class white characters had all but disappeared, their characteristics reassigned to brown middlemen like the overseer on the Creighton estate, whose predatory behaviour towards those he refers to as "my people" is first contrasted to, then aligned with, that of the emergent class of educated black and brown elites, represented by the school teacher, Mr Slime.

One curious final parallel between *Texaco* and *The Slave Son* bears noting here. Both novels include cautionary tales about black women so depraved by the physical, emotional and sexual abuse to which they have been subjected that they lose all sense of themselves as human, despite the best efforts of their children to emancipate and rehabilitate them. Esternome, in *Texaco*, leaves the plantation in order to purchase his mother's freedom, but she dies during a slave revolt at the side of the white people who tortured her lover to death. The other slaves describe to Esternome how they found his mother "by the side of the Lady. Dead without wounds. Her heart had simply let go of life and sunk lower than the eyelids, far below our fates" (p. 104). Laurine's mother, Madelaine, in *The Slave Son* also relinquishes her humanity long before she is trampled to death by Don Duro's horse in the midst of another slave insurrection.

In the chapter devoted to her life, Madelaine recounts three stories that are staples of the oral repertoire of slaves and their descendants throughout the New World.[27] The first is the story of her capture, which revolves around an African community's betrayal by white men it formerly had trusted. The versions of this story which Michael Gomez cites include such standard tropes as exchanges of cloth (usually red); the laying of a trail – of goods, sugar or brightly coloured objects – to lure Africans, especially children, to the seashore; and a ritual evocation of Africa through prelapsarian imagery. These stories fly in the face of fact, since they elide the role played by the African middlemen who captured most of the slaves, or purchased them as prisoners of war from other Africans. And, indeed, in Wilkins's novel, the African slave Talima, her father, Anamoa, and her lover, Quaco, all end up in Trinidad as a consequence of such intra-African intrigue. But Gomez argues that stories like Madelaine's are part of the creolization process, by which enslaved Africans, by inventing an originary myth of innocence betrayed to account for their presence in the New World and the shared nature of their suffering, were able to forge a new identity that transcended ethnic and linguistic boundaries. From this perspective,

> [t]he development of an initial capture account that points the finger exclusively at the European and excludes any mention of his African counterpart . . . marks an important stage in the emergence of the African American aggregate identity and signals the fording of a major divide in the journey from ethnicity to race as the principal determinant of collective self perception. (p. 207)

---

27. For a discussion of the significance of the shared characteristics of African American myths of capture see Michael Gomez's *Exchanging Our Country Marks* (1998, especially 198–214).

Caribbean literary references to a mythical Africa are never quite as utopian as those in African American novels – witness, for instance, Kamau Brathwaite's poignant rendering, in the "Masks" section of *The Arrivants* trilogy (1973), of the qualified welcome and mutual distrust that the New World Negro must negotiate on his return to the motherland. Nevertheless, the myth of origins enunciated in Madelaine's story is pervasive enough that contemporary readers are likely to be brought up short by the stories in Caryl Phillips's *Higher Ground* (1990) that challenge this racial memory, depicting Africans who work for European slave traders as well as repatriated former slaves who struggle unsuccessfully to "civilize" their African brethren.

Madelaine's second story, about the plague of ants, has similar pedigree. The plague represents and undermines the idea of slavery as a total institution by comparing and ultimately subjecting it to a natural cataclysm. Like slavery itself, the plague of ants invades every space and relationship within society. It affects the production of food and cash crops; it infests the bedrooms and public spaces inhabited by slaves and slave owners; it tortures everyone it touches, by depriving them of the basic physical necessities of sleep, food and freedom from pain. The suffering is ameliorated by the courage and creativity of a single slave – in this case, by Madelaine's discovery that the ants will not eat sweet potatoes, which prompts the governor's promise to emancipate her. But it takes another natural cataclysm, a hurricane, to end the plague, just as it would take a social cataclysm – not just an isolated act of personal generosity – to make Madelaine's freedom an enduring reality.

Like the myth of capture, versions of this commentary on the meaning of slavery crop up in a variety of folk legends that have made their way into the Caribbean literary tradition. Brathwaite in *The Arrivants* and Chamoiseau in *Texaco* both make use of oral traditions surrounding the explosion of Mont Pelée in 1902, which obliterated the town of St Pierre and produced a cloud of ash so dense that it blocked out the sun over islands as far south as Barbados for several days.[28] In both soci-

---

28. In a footnote in *Barabajan Poems* Brathwaite points out that it is possible that the Barbadian oral tradition probably conflates the Soufrière eruption of 1812 and the Pelée eruption of 1902 (1994, 305). But this does not affect the symbolic significance attached to both events.

eties, that act of God quickly took on apocalyptic significance in the popular imagination which the authors exploit to fashion symbols of extremity and powerlessness. In *Barabajan Poems,* Brathwaite recounts his astonishment at finding the volcanic eruption of St Vincent's Mount Soufrière in 1812 used in almost the same way in a poem called *Barbadoes,* published by M.J. Chapman in 1833, and comments "when I read it & then read what *I* wrote a century later without then even *knowing* of Chapman, you will begin to see what I mean by tradition – about culture being what filters and fuses in/to you from yr landscape people happenings mysteries fossils histories time" (1994, 86). The ubiquity of such tropes suggests that they too are part of an incipient creole mythography that reads slavery and the social conditions it has created as a species of natural disaster whose horrendous consequences can only be mitigated by divine intervention.

Wilkins draws on several other stories from the oral tradition to convey the texture of the slaves' response to the extremity of their condition. These include Madelaine's story of eating earth as a symbol of despair (which we encounter again in Eric Walrond's *Tropic Death* [1926]); St Hilaire Cardon's story of slaves choosing to die, rather than to reveal the source of the poisons used to destroy their masters and even each other (which Brand and Chamoiseau also invoke in novels already cited); and many iterations of trickster stories about slaves whose humanity saved their masters' lives, or slaves whose cunning procured their freedom, all of which draw on stock properties of the oral repertoire. Wilkins may not have credited the full symbolic import of these stories but, because she transcribes them so faithfully, readers of her novel are granted access to a world view that takes us well beyond her stated interest in the lives of free coloureds.

In her third story, Madelaine chooses to be human rather than to be free when she agrees to continue after her emancipation in the service of her master so that she can legally marry her slave lover Paul and raise an intact family of free children. Her Faustian bargain backfires as, one by one, her husband and children die or are dispersed because of the limits slavery imposes on her nominal freedom. Left, finally, with only her mixed-race daughter Laurine, a child she cannot love because she represents the profound diminishment of rape, Madelaine chooses to curse

God and die a living death, refusing all social responsibility as an act of revenge against those who have deprived her freedom of meaning. As she challenges her listeners: "What am I? – I am not my own slave. I am my master's slave. Then let him take care of me, let him feed me, let him clothe me. I don't care at all *for notin' nor nobody*" (p. 257).

Madelaine's double negatives recall the discursive style of Jamaica Kincaid's *Autobiography of My Mother* (1996), in which the narrator registers a similarly extreme renunciation of social obligations through her stylistic and philosophical negation of negation. Wilkins reads Madelaine's refusal to accommodate to the limitations placed on her humanity as a form of blasphemy because, in so doing, she arrogates to herself the power of life and death; however, in Kincaid's hands, ultimate loss becomes the basis of a new world order in which personal freedom is no longer beholden to the social ties manufactured to maintain an unjust system.[29] Kincaid's Xuela loses her mother before she is born, so she is never vulnerable in the ways that Madelaine becomes to the loss of family or the illusion of a compromised freedom. Her survival is a terrible triumph of the power of refusal, but Kincaid explicitly distances it from the survival of the race since Xuela refuses to bear children. Edwidge Danticat takes negation in a different direction in *The Farming of Bones* (1998). Although Amabelle, the survivor of genocide who narrates this story, is similarly bereft of both parents and children, her story – unlike Xuela's – joins a chorus of testimonials offered by other survivors. Like Madelaine and Xuela, these storytellers hardly seem aware of their audience, as if the impetus to speak is more compelling than their need for anyone to hear.

The work done by these cautionary tales and their terminally blighted tellers in these three very different novels suggests that all three writers are drawing upon an oral tradition in which rituals of abjection, like the penitent's testimony in the context of religious conversion, become new rallying points from which to assert the right to a human existence in communities cleansed of evil. Madelaine herself remains beyond redemp-

---

29. For a discussion of the symbolic significance of Xuela's negations, see Rhonda Cobham's " 'Mwen na rien, msieu': Jamaica Kincaid and the Problem of Creole Gnosis" (2002).

tion, but her story motivates Laurine to work for her mother's freedom and towards the possibility of renewal and reconciliation. Xuela's terrible divinity establishes her as a transcendent symbol of destruction and creativity – of life emerging from death. For the survivors of genocide in Danticat's novel, the act of bearing witness has a therapeutic effect. Although all the storytellers are permanently scarred, Amabelle, at least, is able to begin to craft new possibilities of beauty out of her deformities.

In a novel as replete with comedic resolutions as *The Slave Son*, Madelaine's failed attempt at creating a microcosm of human dignity in the midst of inhumanity introduces a tragic undertow into the flow of the narrative. Writing at only a nominal distance from the death throes of the entire institution of slavery, Wilkins is well positioned to appreciate the enormity of the social challenges that still awaited Caribbean societies. Her optimism about the possibilities for further reform is buttressed by her having witnessed abolition. But she is too close to the harrowing events attendant on both slavery and abolition to discount the violence and personal ruin that accompany both enforced stasis and radical change. This may explain why Laurine's black mother, Madelaine, is united symbolically in death with the planter St Hilaire Cardon. Both meet their deaths because they refuse the protection of their mixed-race children. In Wilkins's moral universe, their deaths are inevitable if post-emancipation society is to move beyond the limitations of white arrogance and black revenge. That utopian ideal animates the novel's postscript about the benevolent planter couple, the Dorsets, who are generously supported after Emancipation by the very slaves who instigated the destruction of property during the insurrection. For the Irish-born author of *The Slave Son*, who had experienced private loss as well as political discrimination in her own country, the kind of personal accountability and respect for others that underpins true freedom cannot be expected or demanded within an unjust system. As Belfond declares at the end of the novel, when he finally abandons his atheism: "All I wanted was to feel myself something in this great, beautiful world – something responsible to God . . . The very spirit of rebellion I exhibited, my disgust and discontent, were but so many proofs of my worship of the Supreme" (p. 320).

By comparison with *The Slave Son*'s epic sweep, the concerns in *Adolphus* seem local, even banal. And yet they articulate the very human dilemmas that the first generation of free people of all colours in Trinidad after slavery had to address. Unlike the mixed-race lovers at the end of *The Slave Son,* who ride off into the Venezuelan sunset, Adolphus plans to returns to Trinidad to consummate his romance and to struggle for civil rights for his own class in his own birthplace. That struggle continues in the work of Caribbean writers such as Lovelace and Brodber, who have chosen not to follow the path of so many of the region's most talented writers into exile. Their focus on the quotidian – their attention to the petty challenges of survival in everyday life – does not lend itself to epic resolutions. The work these authors produce remains accountable to local aspirations to create stable civil communities, in situations where dramatic refusals of all European influence may be a luxury the society can ill afford. Taken together, these nineteenth-century novels delineate the two major fronts along which Caribbean writers in the twentieth century have staked their claims: on the one hand, like Wilkins in *The Slave Son,* they have mounted a radical attack from the margins on the institutions at the centre of the former colonial empire. From another vantage point, like the author of *Adolphus,* they continue to defend the incremental changes and modest accommodations on which post-emancipation societies must build their futures.

Notes on Editorial Procedures

The most striking aspect of *Adolphus* from an editorial point of view is its obvious incompleteness. The story simply stops at a point where the reader would expect at least one final chapter in which the hero (eventually) returns to live with the heroine (happily ever after). However, thorough searches of the *Trinidadian* have not turned up any further chapters. (Available issues constitute an apparently complete run during, and for some time after, the appearance of the serialization.) It seems likely that the author simply tired of the tale, or had other pressing demands to meet. A further possible problem for *Adolphus* was the apparent omission of chapter 14. In the original publication, the current chapter 14 was chapter 15, and so on; however, examination of the newspaper and the continuity of the text itself indicate that this involves a numbering error, rather than a missing chapter (see note to p. 71).

In the original publication of *Adolphus*, some of the chapters lacked titles. We have added plausible titles to the remaining chapters for the convenience of the reader, as follows: chapter 6, "The White Mulatto"; chapter 7, "Abduction"; chapter 8, "Agitated Minds"; chapter 9, "Cudjoe"; chapter 11, "The Arrest"; and chapter 15, "The Letter". In the original publication of *The Slave Son*, some of the chapter titles as listed in the table of contents are slightly different in the actual text; these discrepancies have been left alone.

Original footnotes in *Adolphus* are included on the relevant pages; the author's original symbols have, however, been replaced by continuous numbers. For both novels, all items in the text that have been annotated by the editorial team in the annotative endnotes are identified by the superscript symbol †; annotations are arranged consecutively according to text page number, at the end of the text of each novel.

Consistent author's spellings now considered variant or obsolete – for example, "hussey" (hussy), "staid" (stayed) and "transcendant" (transcendent) in *Adolphus*; "dulness" (dullness), "accidently" (accidentally), "infuriate" (infuriated), "secresy" (secrecy), "trowsers" (trousers), "vilain" (villain), "waggon" (wagon) in *Slave Son* – have been left as in the original, with any comments in the annotations. Where variant spellings or capitalizations appear to be idiosyncratic, with no supporting instances of usage, they have been corrected to standard usage, as the following: from *Slave Son*, "Santissima"/"Santissimo" → "Santísima"/"Santísimo" (chapters 1 and 21); "boistorousness" → "boisterousness" (chapter 9); "tenour" → "tenor" (chapter 11); and from *Adolphus*, "jessamin" → "jesamin", "blind fold", "blind-folded" → "blindfold", "blindfolded", "bretheren" → "brethren" (chapter 3); "gate way" → "gateway" (chapter 5); "cooly" → "coolly" (chapter 7); "graveyard" → "graveyard" (chapter 10); "comerades" → "comrades", "paralized" → "paralised" (chapter 12); "christian resignation" → "Christian resignation", and "crusifix" → "crucifix" (chapter 13). In *Adolphus*, the name rendered as "Gonsalves", "Gonzalvez" and "Gonsalvez" has been regularized to "Gonzalvez", and the instances of "padré" have been changed to "padre". Variant or archaic constructions, for example "eat to table" (more commonly, "eat at table") (*Adolphus*, chapter 2), have been noted in the annotations.

A few obvious errors have been corrected: "had never completely recovered her little girl's death" → ". . . recovered from . . .", and "the old man ate as though he not broken fast for three days" → ". . . he had not broken . . ." (*Slave Son*, chapter 24); "he had better had it substituted" → "he had better have it substituted" (*Adolphus*, chapter 6); "there she laid in all the appearance of death" → ". . . lay . . ." (*Adolphus*, chapter 7); "He was however spared the pangs of uncertainty state" → ". . . uncertainty's state" (*Adolphus*, chapter 10); "When she opened her eyes, she gazed around, none stood near her – Adolphus has departed" → ". . . had departed", and "he left the office open" → "he left the office" (*Adolphus*, chapter 11).

Adolphus, A Tale

First published in the *Trinidadian*

1 January through 20 April 1853

Contents

Adolphus, A Tale

Preface

In submitting to the public the present tale, we deem it necessary to offer a few words in order to point out its object. Many voices will no doubt be raised against us, as endeavouring to arouse feelings which are supposed dead, and to revive things which some would have entirely erased from memory's tablets; but, we reply, to create disagreeable feelings is not our aim. The pages of history, which unfold to us the barbarities of past ages, are not intended to throw us back into barbarism; on the contrary, it is by reading and meditating upon the evils of the past, that we find the most enrichening lessons of wisdom. The past is the parent of the present, and to whom can the youthful turn for instruction with more sanguine hopes of success, than to a father whose mind is ripened by age and experience? Therefore it is we disclaim any desire to arouse bitter feelings; all we wish is, that the past, however disgraceful it may appear to one party, and however painful to another, be not entirely buried in forgetfulness, because it is a source of lessons pregnant with utility. Hence it was we devoted a few moments of leisure to the production of the following chapters, and, under the veil of fiction, we painted in as true colours as our abilities could admit, a picture of the past state of colonial society. Our principal object is to shew the contrast between the present position of the coloured people and that in which they stood formerly, that they may see the better the great step that colonial society has made in advance; and to learn that they have only to exert themselves in the same manner as did their fathers to clear from their sight whatever causes of complaint by which they may be surrounded. That the same may be received in the like spirit as that in which it is offered; that it may prove amusing and interesting to all, and offensive to none, are the only rewards hoped for by

THE WRITER.

CHAPTER I.

The Romelia Family

It was in the year 181–, when slavery with its lengthy tail of many evils, raged through the length and breadth of the West India Colonies; when cowardly oppression in every shape triumphantly domineered; when the badge of a white skin was considered superior to wisdom or virtue; when the barriers of colonial prejudice were raised against the march of progress, that Mr. and Mrs. Romelia landed on the shores of Trinidad. They were previously inhabitants of the island of Grenada. For more than 30 years they had lived together in the holy bonds of matrimony. They were of African descent; they formed part of that small portion of their class of society to whom the pleasures and advantages of Education, of Religion, were at that time known; and although exposed to the numerous vexations and disadvantages under which their entire class suffered, yet, by a virtuous course of life, a meek resignation, supported only by those consolations which true religion alone affords, they toiled assiduously amidst all the difficulties which surrounded them, and as the reward of their industry and frugality they, after many struggles, acquired sufficient means to enable them to pass the rest of their days in such peace and comfort as their position in colonial society could admit.

At that time the island of Trinidad was fast rising in some importance; numerous inhabitants of the neighbouring colonies flocked to its shores, among those were Mr. Romelia and family. Many were the inducements† which the people of the sister Colonies had for seeking a home in Trinidad; besides the fertility of the soil, the salubrity of its climate, stood one great consideration which tempted many like Mr. Romelia to seek an asylum in Trinidad, namely, the provision which the benevolent and philanthropic Chacon[1] had made, at the capitulation[†] of the colony, for the proper treatment of the coloured people by the English government; alas, at that time the suffering class, possessing no public organ, could neither send forth nor yet receive any thing like correct information, and the dominant class caused these favourable reports to be circulated in the other Colonies for the purpose of inducing immigrants to come and settle; for at that time as at the present, Trinidad had the same difficulties under which she at present labours, that is, want of sufficient population. Therefore, on arriving in this country, what was the surprise of Romelia and those like him to find, that slavery with his sword of fire ruled more tyrannically than in any other part; and that a coloured skin was held inferior to a soul black with corruption and sin, if that soul was only cased within a white body, and that the fatherly provision of Chacon was trodden under foot, and only used for the cowardly purpose of increasing the number of victims constantly offered in sacrifice to the Moloch[†] of prejudice.

However the step was taken, and to make the best of a bad affair, he resolved upon seeking what he desired in retirement, for that purpose he travelled over several parts of the island and at last decided upon purchasing a small cocoa plantation in the quarter of St. Joseph[†] in the neighbourhood of the old village of that name. The spot Romelia selected for his dwelling was on one of those lonely spots on the left of the road leading to the village. A few months after he had taken possession of his property the small estate shewed a most picturesque scene; a new and neatly constructed cottage stood on one of those little eminences which like so many amphitheatres stand at the foot of the northern range of hills; as it were in conformity with a plan much delighted in by the inhabitants of the districts, in front of the cottage stood a large arbour covered with the luxuriant vines of the granadilla.[†] The granadilla is one of the principal fruits which afford comfort in the tropics, not only does its gentle shade invite to repose during the heat of some sunny day, but the fragrance of its flowers added to its agreeable taste, render it one of the indispensables of rural life. On another side laid a flower garden; its

---

1. The last Spanish Governor.[†]

neatly gravelled walk, its bed of choicest flowers, shewed that uncommon taste directed every thing therein. This was the garden of Antonia, the only daughter of the Romelias. In it was to be found all that is most varied and most beautiful in Flora's temple.[†] Around the palings were dahlias, like blushing beauties dressed in a hundred colours, hanging down their heads before the coxcomb breezes which insolently attempted to ruffle their petals; whilst the jesamins and tube roses mingling together their fragrance embalmed for yards around the atmosphere; and the butterfly flower almost seemed to invite its living brother to frolic in the air; the roses with open faces proudly held up their graceful heads as if claiming admiration as queens of the fields; the sunflower, with its many rays expanding around, reflected with great lustre the brilliancy of the orb of day; whilst the myrtle, ever green, ever unfaded, sweet emblem of eternal love, stood in the midst.[†] Taken all in all, the entire scene was highly interesting; extravagance shewed not its gauderies there, but it stood in all the beauty of simplicity; the home of retirement, of comfort, and of love.

CHAPTER II.

Antonia

The only daughter of Mr. and Mrs. Romelia, was one of those singular cases which are met with in life, and which come within our ideality of perfection. Although an only child, she had not been allowed all those indulgences which form the spoilt-child; or even, if she had been indulged in such, the superior construction of her mind would never have been overcome. From certain motives,[†] schools, except of a certain stamp, were altogether discountenanced by the authorities, or at least not encouraged, hence fathers who would not have their children vegetate in ignorance, had also to perform the duties of instructor. Thus it was Antonia was instructed at home by her father and mother; she possessed in an eminent degree that vivacity of intellect which is peculiar to the youths of the tropics. The aptitude with which she learned, the rapidity with which she mastered all the lessons given her, gave unbounded satisfaction to her teachers; but arrived at a certain stage, she encountered many difficulties in pursuing her studies from want of books; however she still persevered. At the time of her family's arrival in Trinidad she was seventeen. Her very appearance strikes the stranger with admiration; in her seem combined all the graces of beauty, added to that modest fascination which intelligence and worth ever attract. Her colour was of that light Italian *brunette*[†] which commands admiration throughout the world; her hair of a glossy black floated gracefully in a profusion of curls around her spotless and well formed neck, and contrasted most beautifully with her high and well organized forehead; her eyes black, large and soft, were surmounted by arched eye-brows which seemed to have engaged the compass and pencil of some renowned artist of Nature's school; from her well-formed features there appeared to radiate the strength of a soul which virtue had chosen for one of her sacred sanctuaries, and in which she sits with arms extended to keep at bay the foul designs of temptation; in one word, she was a true personification of "a bright intelligence from heaven".[†]

See her now in her favourite garden; every shrub receives her attention, wherever she passes she leaves behind her the footsteps of order. See her near her aged father, with her delicate fingers playing with his silvery locks, and by her sweet smiles banishing "dull care"[†] from the old man's thoughts; she is all innocence; she is all saintly. See her in the humble cabins of her poor black neighbours; listen to the simple lessons she gives to the children who stand around her; harken to her word of advice to the poor ignorant mother, her gentle admonitions; there she represents a most perfect study to the artist who would picture Charity.

To have such a child was the greatest pride of the aged couple; at evenings when they eat to table;[†] her pleasant conversation, which borrowed so much strength and beauty from her well-stored mind, was their chief delight. She was not only their pride, but their hope. In the moments of heavy trials, when injustice with felt-shod tread would enter their door, it was Antonia's sweet smile of innocence which poured the soothing balm of consolation into their bleeding hearts. Upon her they looked as one given them from on High, to dry their tears in the hours of suffering, and to soothe their pillows at the moment of dissolution. Oh! parents, the winter of whose days is cheered by such a sun, how blessed are you; how gladsome, how satisfactory to behold thus before you the child you love, you solicitude;[†] how thankful ought you not to be to Him who alone giveth such gifts, and how much more faith do you not feel in his divine precepts when you have before you the truth of the words of his bard, "Train up a child in the way it should go"![†]

Her parents had not long been residents in Trinidad, ere her benevolent spirit gained her the love and admiration of the poor of the neighbourhood, her virtues and many acquirements; the esteems of the good and aged; and principally of Padre Gonzalvez, the curate of St. Joseph. The more this venerable prelate became acquainted with the interesting daughter of the Romelias, the more he delighted in her company; such was the unostentatious richness of her mind, such the sincerity of her piety, he threw open to her his entire library, and there the lovely student found that for which she had long thirsted.

CHAPTER III.

Padre Gonzalvez

As in all countries where the minds of men are still surrounded by the darkness of ignorance, or brutalised by the existence of the horrible system of slavery, the priests exercised quite an undue influence in the West India Colonies. Whether they were selected in Europe expressly for the mission which they had to perform in these Colonies, or whether their benevolence and consciousness were paralised from inhaling the atmosphere of slave-cursed countries, yet certain it is, they performed their duties in a manner which it is truly painful for a Christian to think of. In the midst of such a corrupt set, how gratifying must it not have been, how consoling to the inhabitants of the parish of St. Joseph, to find in their curate, Padre Gonzalvez, one in every respect the opposite to the generality of his brethren in order. He was one of those who take up the sacred gown of priesthood, not as a profession, but as a duty which they owe to their Creator and their fellow-men; to elevate the soul, and not to abase it; to edify the beauties of Religion, and not to stain them by the foul hands of uncharitableness. For many years Padre Gonzalvez had officiated in the same quarter, he was in the island previous to the Capitulation; and was acquainted with the humane manner in which the slaves were treated by their Spanish masters; he knew, further, the privileges which were allowed the coloured inhabitants, he had seen them holding high ranks as officers in the militia; he had known them to fill civil offices with advantage to their country and honour to themselves; his grief was therefore great when he saw the change which had taken place after the cession of the island to British Rule. His sympathy was excited for the poor slaves; his indignation was kindled at the humiliation of the free coloured people. Therefore, he was much disliked, and sometimes even persecuted by those in power; but the support which he met from the old Spanish settlers who were the principal proprietors in the quarter, and the veneration in which he was held by the slaves and the coloured people around, made the authorities afraid to interfere with him.

Thus he continued his divine mission, ministering to the wants and comforts of the poor; constantly visiting the estates and imparting words of consolation to the poor suffering bonds-men.

About 20 years previous to the events which form the subject of this tale, Padre Gonzalvez was one night in his private chapel engaged in prayer and silent meditation. The clock had struck ten, when the door opened, and his servant announced that a person outside desired to see him. The padre instantly walked towards the door, and there saw a negro, wretchedly clad, with a glittering cutlass[†] in his hand.

"Padre," said the negro, "I have been sent to request you will come and minister to a dying person."

"'Tis well, my son. Is the distance great?"

"No, sir," he replied.

"Domingo," said the priest to his servant, who stood by; "my hat and cloak; get yours, and come with me."

It was one of those dreary nights of the month of August, so well known in the West Indies. A thick black cloud covered the face of the heavens; the thunder was heard to growl at a distance, and vivid flashes of forked lightening at intervals cut through the air; everything indicated a coming storm. The priest, however, did not hesitate; he ordered the negro to lead the way, and they set out. Soon the leader left the road and walked into a trace;[†] the priest and Domingo continued to follow. For more than half-an-hour the party continued the route in silence.

The guide led them through dark and unfrequented paths, till the Padre, fatigued, turned round and enquired, "how much farther is the place?"

"A few more steps, sir, and we are there," replied the negro. So saying, he turned from the road, and commenced descending a small hill almost overgrown with brushwood, the padre and Domingo following.

They soon found themselves in the midst of a wood; the guide stopped, a shrill whistle was heard, and before the priest could enquire into the meaning of this, he was seized by a pair of powerful arms. In an instant he was blindfolded, and a voice whispered in his ears, "fear nothing, you are a good man." With that he was lifted into a hammock, and soon felt himself in rapid motion. In that manner he was carried for about an hour, not a word was said, except by the fearful Domingo, who, at every moment, enquired, "whither are you going with my master?" and he only received for answer, "fear nothing." — At last the party halted, the priest was raised out of the hammock and placed on his feet; the bandage was removed from his eyes, and he stood in the midst of a wretched hut. No one stood near him. In one corner blazed a bright fire; around the dwelling were guns and cutlasses hanging; several quarters of smoked lappes[†] and quencos[†] adorned the sides; the skins of snakes and other reptiles hung about in profusion and formed the ornamental portion of this hovel. The padre gazed around for a moment in surprise, but still, no one came; he soon, however, collected himself, and perceived that he was in a camp of "runaway negroes."[†] An old woman now appeared; she seemed overcome with grief, and was giving relief to her burdened heart by shedding a flood of tears. She beckoned in the priest, who followed her into another part of the hut; a small lamp made in a broken bottle shed a dim light over the place, and gave a ghastly appearance to everything around. In that room was a scene of death. On a bed of straw there laid a woman going through the last act of life's great drama. The padre here saw that he had not been deceived; he approached the bed, and the woman, opening her eyes, she saw him and said rather inaudibly — "Ah! Padre, you have come in time."

"Blessed be the Lord for that, my child," replied the sacred man.

"Padre, I desired to see you before dying, to request one favour, that is . . . that is," . . . and the tears flowed fast from her. She stopped . . . a heavy sigh broke from her swollen heart; the effort was too great for her emaciated frame, and she fainted. The priest stood over her in the greatest anxiety; he longed to hear her request; but fearing she should not recover, he commenced administering to her the last sacraments which the Roman Catholic Church accords to her departing children.

During the time the sacrament was going on, she recovered herself and understood the priest. With the aid of the old woman who knelt by, she crossed herself and seemed to accompany the minister with great fervour. The sacrament being over, he asked her,

"Now, my child, what was your request?"

"My child," she replied, "my child . . . take him . . . suffer him not to grow in this place in sin . . . do grant . . . grant this."

"I will — I promise!" exclaimed the padre; but before he could say more, she swooned again. This time strong convulsions ensued, — and pressing the arm of the child who laid near her, she expired.

Oh, mothers! think how bitter would have been the last moments of this forlorn creature, had they not been relieved by the consoling promise of this charitable man! Ah! with how much more peace of mind can you meet death — you who leave the world in the conviction that your offspring shall not be outcasts of the earth!

The moment the mother had expired, Padre Gonzalvez ordered the woman to remove the child from the bed, which was done. A murmur was heard outside; the priest stepped out, and he saw eight negroes partially naked with cutlasses in their hands. At the sight of the priest they fell on their knees; except one, a tall athletic man; his bare arm shewed that he was of uncommon strength. This was *Jimbo,* the leader of the "runaway slaves."

"Padre," he said, kneeling, "I have come to beg your pardon for having brought you to such a place, but you see there was necessity for it."

"I have no forgiveness to grant you; on the contrary, I owe you thanks for having put me in the way of doing a good deed. But no more of that," continued the man of God; "why do you lead such a life?"

"Padre, because I love freedom, and hate the white men; here I have freedom, and I do not see the whites!"

"But it is not Christian, my son, to hate your fellow men."

"They are not my fellow men," replied the negro, with eyes that flashed fire; "no, they cannot be! Padre," he continued, as he drew himself to his full height and majestically pointed to the apartment where laid the yet warm corpse; "in that room is the dead body of my niece, the blood of my sister's blood. I and my sister Agilai were taken from Africa; we were Foulahs,† we saw our aged mother sent on board of one vessel, and we were sent to *another*; it was the last we saw of her; we thought our young hearts would not have borne the shock; but we unfortunately lived, we were brought here — we grew, — my sister lived with a young man on the estate as her husband, they loved each other and thought then they were happy. Our master conceived a passion for her; the villain, to gratify his lust, *sold her husband,* and forced her to be his wife. The girl now dead in that room was the fruit of that connection. My poor sister did not live long after the birth of that child; she died broken hearted. I took care of the child, she grew up; she was handsome; and her father, her Christian father sold her!" The negro stopped, his bosom heaved, he clenched his fist, and ground his teeth with rage, "Well, she was sold; her new master bought her to be his mistress — the ill treatment of whom she could not endure — she ran away! Poor girl, she wandered about the woods for two days, until I met her, quite accidentally. She was heart-broken — she said she had not long to live — asked for you . . . you know the rest" . . . and the tears gushed from the negro's eyes, but he dashed them away, and cried, "no, this is no time for tears — I must study revenge!"

The storm had abated — day was approaching. The padre arranged that the body should be buried early in the morning. At six a grave was prepared near to the hut, and the body, wrapped up in an old blanket, was laid in its last resting place; the priest read the service; and the grave closed over the unfortunate Rosa. The hardened negroes stood around, and as the priest turned from the grave, he saw them all in tears.

Preparations then commenced for the padre's departure. A hammock was slung across a large stick; Jimbo advanced, and respectfully bowing his head, said — "Father, pardon, but I must blindfold you; 'tis not desirable that you see through what road you go from this place. I and my friends love you, padre; we believe you to be a good man, but we have all sworn never to trust a white skin."

"Very well," replied the curate; "do with me as you please. I trust you — but the child!"

"Shall follow you, sir," replied Jimbo.

"But, Jimbo—"

"Trust to my word, sir; I love this child also, and do you think I would allow him to remain here and die from want?"

The priest believed Jimbo, and allowing himself to be blindfolded, was soon on the road. Arrived at a certain spot, he was put down, his bandage removed; he was shewn the road; the child was placed in the arms of Domingo, and the padre, followed by his servant with the child, went home. That child was Adolphus.

CHAPTER IV.

Adolphus

Time, with rapid strides, soon flew over many years, and Adolphus, under the paternal care of Padre Gonzalvez, grew; every possible care was bestowed on his Education by the Priest himself, and the progress of the pupil was more than compensating to the tutor. In a short time his proficiency was great. At the time we introduce him to our readers, he is a young man of twenty; he is of the middle stature; fair, hair black, rather curly;[†] his eyes large, shedding over his fine figure the rays of an intelligent mind; his deportment graceful and noble; his voice sonorous, yet soft and agreeable; on his brow he bore the impress of nature's nobility. Notwithstanding the prejudice which existed at the time against all persons of his class, yet Adolphus, partly from the influence of Padre Gonzalvez's friends, and greatly from his own enterprising genius, was appointed assistant clerk of the Commandant[2†] of St. Joseph; his assiduity at his duties; his acquaintance with the three languages,[3] so indispensable in Trinidad, soon gained him the esteem of his superiors in office, and he in a short time became principal clerk. He was the first of his stamp that ever attained so high an office under the English Government in this colony! After repeated enquiries, he at last succeeded in learning from Padre Gonzalvez the secret of his birth; that was to him often a source of bitter reflections.

---

2. Names formerly given to the Magistrates.

3. English, French and Spanish.

The close intimacy which existed between Padre Gonzalvez and the Romelia family, led Adolphus to become acquainted with them. From the first day he had seen Antonia, he felt an uncommon interest in her; her conversation so rich at all time; the innumerable resources of her mind, her perfect acquaintance with History and the Classics, led Adolphus to find in her a "kindred spirit." From that time a sentiment, as yet unknown to him, began to creep over him; to him, methinks there was in his heart a blank, who, or what, was to fill up that blank he either did not know, or persuaded himself to ignore; his studies were not so interesting as heretofore; his favourite *History of Rome,*[†] from which he often imbibed some of those enrichening lessons of patriotism with which that work abounds, was neglected; to him the conversation of Antonia was sufficient; in her words he found a library from which he fancied more could be learned than all the books ever printed; poor youth, he loved; yet he tried to deceive himself; Antonia also felt the influence of that subtle passion.

Previous to her acquaintance with Adolphus, in her own estimation, she was happy, the gentle stream of her life was only ruffled when a cloud hung over her father's brow; but that the sweet zephyr of her smiles soon cleared. But now she felt the want of a *certain something*; there was something wanting to make her enjoy her ideality of happiness; what was it she could not tell; yet, whenever Adolphus was near her, it appeared that object was found; whenever he was away, again 'twas missing; "ah! and is this love," she sighed, as she one day sat alone in her chamber; "how happy they who love!" Day by day the sentiment which filled those two bosoms became more fired, and well it was, no youth was more fit to love, no woman more worthy of being loved.

Adolphus one evening, with quick and agitated steps, was walking to and fro in his chamber; suddenly he stopped; a deep sigh escaped from his overflowing heart. "Yes," he exclaimed, "I love Antonia; I feel that without her no pleasures, no joys can attend my days henceforth. But —," and he paused . . . "Oh! the bitter thought! does she think as I do; will she sympathise with me, will she reciprocate my affections, will she listen to my words? — no, whenever I am near her she always appears so cool, so collected; and I so agitated, so pensive, so lost to myself; no, no, it cannot be, she loves me not, — but, sweet angelic soul, she will pity me, she will forgive my presumption . . . But her parents; to conform with the rules of society they will ask who am I? they will enquire into my parentage! who was my father, — who was my mother? Alas! the first was a villain, the latter was a prostitute, and I . . . I am a bastard!" At these words he stamped his foot on the floor; his hand grasped his broad forehead which seemed ready to burst from the agitated state of his mind . . . "No," he resumed, "I am not, cannot be, a fit companion for their daughter."

Ah! society, how pervert! Thou hidest vices, accidents thou exposeth; what has the innocent child committed that he should suffer for the sins of his father?

Poor youth, in such soliloquies was he wont to vent his feelings when in the solitude of his chamber, his nights were restless, this acted upon his frame; his face began to appear pale, he was nervous. Some days after the evening above described, he one afternoon visited the Romelias. On entering the door, he found Antonia alone.

"Ah! Mr. Adolphus," she said, with a smile, "you are welcome; 'tis now some days we have been deprived the pleasure of seeing you."

"Call you that a pleasure, Miss Romelia, when you see me?"

"Well, my dear papa says so; mamma also; and I am sure, I think they are right. . . ."

"Miss Romelia," replied Adolphus, with a sigh, "your mind is fertile in producing compliments."

"Pardon me; but indeed it is not the case; I never speak otherwise than what I think."

Adolphus sighed heavily and answered not. Antonia fixed her large dark eyes on him, and saw the unusual paleness of his cheeks, and his downcast looks, and timidly enquired, "Have you been ill Mr. Adolphus?" "No, no," he answered; and raising his head, his eyes met Antonia's. There was in that glance more than words can tell. Oh! the silent eloquence of the eye — who can describe it!

Mr. Romelia here entered; he was delighted upon seeing Adolphus; he shook him cordially by the hand; and soon they were engaged in conversation: the conversation turned upon several subjects. At last Antonia, who had left the hall returned from her chamber, and, placing her hands around her father's neck, said, smiling,

"Oh! dear papa, you and Mr. Adolphus always get into such a passion when you talk about these pestering politics. I wish you would never talk about such matters; let us go rather into my garden, it is cooler there than it is here; you and Mr. Adolphus can converse; and at the same time you can aid me in arranging some plants."

"Dear Antonia, I am tired, go with Mr. Adolphus, he will accompany you. Won't you Adolphe,[†] my love?"

"With great pleasure, if Miss Antonia desires it."

"Come then," said Antonia, as she skipped out of the house, Adolphus following. Then, arm in arm, they bent their steps to the garden, almost strangers to one another, and as to the mode of disclosing the secret thoughts of their hearts.

As they passed along, the jesamins seemed to send forth their sweet perfumes with greater profusion than usual; the roses to hide themselves among their leaves before the blushing cheeks of Antonia.

During the while Adolphus considered this a most excellent opportunity to declare his sentiments to Antonia; yet he knew not how to do it, until turning, as if in deep meditation, he gazed on the myrtle, and, turning to Antonia, said, "These leaves are ever green . . . they are not like the roses whose perfection is but momentary, whose beauty is witnessed by the rising sun, and which fades to nothingness ere he sets; nor yet do they, like other leaves, wither and fall to pieces after the showers of the heavens. They ought, therefore, to be the emblem of fidelity, for they are ever the same . . . Think you not so, Miss Romelia."

"I am almost inclined to believe so myself: however, it is my favourite, and I care it[†] more than any other plant in the garden."

"I am indeed happy to think that you coincide with me in opinion, and since the myrtle be your favourite and also the emblem of fidelity, henceforth I shall ever wear it next my heart, for I admire fidelity wherever found. Fidelity is indeed so precious an object, that he must truly be blind to every virtue who does not cherish it."

And, in saying this, he plucked two small branches, one he placed on his vest, and the other he handed to Antonia.

"Assent, and ever wear this," he said; "let it be the model of your life, and ever remember that the custom was taught you by him who shall ever be faithful to you."

"In what," said Antonia, apparently surprised.

"In all the vicissitudes of life," he answered. Antonia blushed and was silent.

"Ha! Antonia," continued Adolphus, "forgive I pray you the blunt manner in which I have disclosed that which I could no longer conceal; to the honest heart 'tis hard to restrain its true feelings — say, is it not so. If I have offended you, speak, and henceforth deep repentance shall ever be my lot; and let me bid to hope who now encircles me with her deceitful dreams to hide for ever from me her unattainable pleasures. If it be the contrary, as I sincerely believe and trust . . . declare it to me, and my constant prayers shall be to render you as happy as you deserve; and to thank my Creator for having granted me such a blessed lot among mankind . . . For to love you, Antonia, and to be beloved by you, is indeed earthly bliss. — Speak; think you not so. Your eyes — the mirrors of your soul — which you now fasten to the ground, and tremble to raise, seem to speak the word which your lips are too faint to express. Your blushing cheeks, your playful ringlets, seem to waive the blissful seal, and foretell that you love me, Antonia, as much as life . . . life . . . what is life? . . . as much as your God."

Antonia started and again hung down her head in silence, "do not blaspheme," she said; and again dropt her head. "I do not blaspheme," continued Adolphus; "the time and place you might no doubt think unbecoming for such a disclosure, but where could I more properly disclose my affections for you than in this happy retreat, where, to witness my vows, stands the pride of creation, and he who made them thus . . ."

Still Antonia was silent; the blood rushed to and from her cheeks in such rapid succession that she could not find words.

"Why thus silent, Antonia?" continued Adolphus, whilst he took her hand, which firmly grasped the myrtle, "why not relieve me from that awful state of suspense in which I am now placed? Ah! did you but know the tortures of uncertainty, did you but know the pangs which rend the heart of him who awaits the moment which is to decide his fate? Ah! you would relieve me of my fearful anguish . . . Still silent . . . are those glowing lips sealed by offended pride? or does mischievous Cupid make use of them as an artifice to torment me . . . Still you answer me not . . . then do I know my fate. Antonia loves me not." And he dropped her hand which he held. "Then am I truly the forsaken, without father, mother, friend or kindred; I'm now doomed to behold my guardian angel precipitately flying from me, and leaving me to undergo the torments of the fiends of hell. Antonia hates me; why then was I born? Sun! thou whom the morning birds welcome with tuneful notes, and shepherds greet with joyful hearts, thrice cursed wert thou on the day that Adolphus was first ushered into this base and deceitful world — thrice cursed wert thou!"

"Stay!" cried Antonia, who now lifted her head, her eyes in tears, and fixed them on Adolphus in an imploring manner. "Why curse that day which to me, was the most joyful that creation ever saw. That sun which shone on the birth of him; whose slave I now am, for whom I live, for whom I would die. Ah! cruel, cruel Adolphus;" and she fell in his arms.

Adolphus was struck with amazement, he fancied himself in a dream, he could not believe it was Antonia who was in his arms. He gazed on her whilst her head rested on his shoulder, and the light breeze made her curls to play around his neck. Then pressing her to his heart, he exclaimed, "Forgive me, Antonia, forgive my unbecoming words, you yourself, although like myself as yet a stranger to the mystic powers of love, know too well its capricious nature."

"Rather pardon and pity my ignorance," replied Antonia, "for having so long kept you in suspense, for long ere this I should have said, I love you, Adolphus."

"Mysterious powers! is it possible that for me such felicity was reserved on earth; is this the world which sages scorn and stern philosophy rejects with contempt; let them preach, let them remonstrate, to me 'tis the seat of bliss. Bear record, ye flowers and shrubs that now enchant the air with your sweet perfumes; ye witnesses of our first promises; ye angels, who now play about the Heavens, attest that henceforth, my life, my all is devoted to my dearest Antonia. And may the divine Author of all blessings inspire me with strength and vigour in leading her to happiness."

And at that moment their lips unconsciously met, and the first kiss of love, that yet unrivalled gem, the secret powers of which all have failed to describe, passed between them. It was the seal of future trials.

CHAPTER V.

A Night in Port of Spain, or
Common Occurrences

Let us now leave for a while the new lovers to bask in the sunshine of the first days of love; let us leave the retired quarter of St. Joseph, with its romantic hills, whose faces are intersected here with luxuriant vegetation, there with a sterile spot; in all forming the enclosures of the delightful valley of Maracas;[†] and take a peep into the *then* rising capital, Port of Spain. Some of the ruins of the fire of 1805[†] are yet visible; the new houses are next, covered with red tiles; buildings are springing up in every quarter; the stately trees which now adorn Marine Square[†] were then mere saplings; the beautiful — but neglected and ill managed — Brunswick Square,[†] under the solicitous care of Woodford,[†] was then rising into existence; everything indicated a city in its infancy. The streets thronged with dandies, who, with narrow tailed coats and short waistcoats, swordbelt, pantaloons, — all *à l'anglaise,*[†] fancied themselves actually strutting up and down the most fashionable squares of London or the Boulevards of Paris. But enough of outward appearances; let us raise one or two curtains, and enquire into the "Common Occurrences" which passed in this youthful city.

It is evening; the bell of the Catholic Church has struck 8; every free coloured man or slave found in the streets at that hour stands a good chance of being accommodated with *free lodging* by those ever-polite gentlemen then called *aguazils*;[†] but which refined taste and civilization now style Police Constables; as the proscribed classes form the major part of the population, of course the streets are almost deserted. But, stop . . . something sounds like music; let us approach . . . yes . . . it is a violin, accompanied by a guitar, a tambourine, and a triangle; the sound is not altogether such as would "soothe the savage breast,"[†] yet it affords amusement; there is dancing going on.

In the street, near the house, are four persons; from appearance they are Europeans. They seem engaged in some conversation: let us approach and listen.

"I say, Dull," enquired a young looking man named DeGuerinon (of whom more hereafter), "what's going on there?"

"Oh! ah! it's that old mulatte[†] Navetto, who is, I suppose, treating his smutty[†] friends to a hop or jig, or some such trash."

"D—— it, how I'd like just to go up there and break up the dance, merely for a spree."

"No! no!" cried the others; "leave the poor brutes alone!"

"Now, by G——d, we must go," persisted DeGuerinon; "come, Dull, you are the alcade,[†] you can pretend to ask whether they have got permission to disturb the public peace in this manner; and that will be an excellent passport for finding our way up stairs. — Come now, come gentlemen, come along. There must be fine girls there, and we'll have first rate fun — come, come."

These words had the desired effect; soon the whole company, four in number, walked into the gateway leading to the ball-room; when they came to the door a few servants who stood by scampered away in all directions to make way for them. Such was the terror, if we may use the term, which even the appearance of the white man had on the poor slaves. The four *gentlemen* neither knocked at the door nor asked for admission, but *sans gene*[†] walked coolly into the apartment where dancing was going on. At their sight the music stopped, the dancers remained like statues, and the host, old Navetto, a fine looking old man, who, with the exception of his dark complexion, was a perfect portrait of the "real old English gentleman," came, and making a bow, such as those of his class usually made to the potent whites, asked, "will you, gentlemen, be pleased to tell your humble servant what is your desire?"

"Well," replied Dull, who now played the part of chief actor, "we have come to see whether you have permission from one of the alcades for keeping such a d——d noise."

"We have permission, sir; we would not dare to act contrary to the wise laws of our country."

"All right then, since you have permission; but we must have a jig with those fine girls you have there."

"Gentlemen," the old man answered, "I am afraid I cannot grant this; those ladies you see there are the wives, sisters, and daughters of my guests; and I do not think they will like to dance with you."

"Hell!" exclaimed DeGuerinon, "we will make them dance!" And with that bounced into the room and cried out, "Come, strike up, musicians, or noise makers, and let us have a reel;" and walking up to a young lady, said, "will you have a dance, dear?" The young lady shuddered with indignation, and a youth who stood by had already lifted his hand to strike the insulter, but he was stopped by old Navetto behind, who cried out; "Remember, 'tis treason to strike a white man, *under any* circumstance (!!!)" A noise ensued, threats and curses rang through the room as the civilised Europeans offered all sorts of insult to the persons of the ballroom; all the men began to lead away their wives and daughters, and in a few moments the room was left to the aggressors alone. Enraged at having been treated in what they considered an *uncouth* and *uncivilised* manner, they found their revenge in breaking a few shades with their sticks, upsetting the tables, chairs, &c. To all this there was no resistance offered, — of course not; to resist or strike a white man was a crime to be wiped off *only* by imprisonment with hard labour or banishment;— to lay a complaint against him before the Chief Alcade de Bario† was a calumny, and the calumniator was kicked out of court.

After having satisfied all their bacchanalian propensities, the four worthy Europeans left the house and repaired to the residence of John Dull, one of themselves; there they remained; it was near midnight, the brandy and water commenced to circulate.

Their indignation at the *insults* they had received knew no bounds.

"By Heaven!" cried DeGuerinon — "A happy idea has just occurred to me."

"What is it? What is it?"

"Well," he resumed, "we must make those fellows pay for their insolence of this night."

"How will you do it?" said Dull.

"Why, this way; there is a mulatto now in gaol, who will no doubt be whipped for having been impudent to one of his superiors; those fellows are all furious at the idea; this is known at Government House; thus, we have only to concoct a placard — threatening fire and blood to all the whites if that prisoner be whipped. This placard we will affix to this house, it being the house of an Alcade, and mark well, if we only keep the secret it will bring down the whole weight of Sir R——'s power upon them."

"Capital!" they all exclaimed, "a d——d good plan."

"Come," said John Dull; "at it, at once; here, Poly — you d——d nigger, some pen, ink, and paper."

The materials were brought; and Dull, throwing the pen to DeGuerinon, said, "write, I shall dictate; I know the style of those fellows; let us have it à la Des Saline.[†] Write '*Fire and blood! whites, take notice! that if any free man is put in the tread mill,[†] this house shall be burnt down, and every other house like this.*' "

Having finished their demoniacal deed, the party retired to their respective houses. Next morning a crowd was seen near Dull's residence; every body was reading the placard attentively; the pale faces of many around told how much the libel was believed to be truth; throughout the town nothing was spoken of the whole day but the placard; orders were given to hold the troops in readiness; a coloured man was avoided more than before. The dreams of the mighty whites were nothing else but scenes of San Domingo.[†] Such are the phantoms which guilty consciences can conjure up. However the scheme had the desired effect. The day following the placard, the following proclamation was issued from Government House:—

TRINIDAD.

Government House, 28th May, 1823.

NOTICE OF GOVERNMENT.

R.J.W.

Whereas some daring and evil-minded persons affixed on the door of the store of J.. S.., Esq. Alcade in Ordinary of the Second Election,[†] on the morning of Sunday, the 25th instant, a paper writing, threatening to burn the town of Port of Spain, if a free person was put in the treadmill;

A reward of *two hundred and fifty pounds* currency is hereby offered to any person or persons who shall or may discover the writer; or the person who affixed the same; so that he or they may be convicted thereof.

The said sum to be paid out of the public treasury, immediately upon the conviction of either of the said persons; and, should the discovery be made by a slave, he shall be entitled to his manumission, upon conviction, as aforesaid.

By his Excellency's command, &c.

CHAPTER VI.

The White Mulatto

Jean de Lopelli Pierre Paul DeGuerinon — (the colonial aristocracy delighted in long names) — was the same individual who performed such an active part in the last chapter. He was the son of an old Corsican immigrant,[†] who, by great industry and frugality, added to the protection which his class always met in these parts, soon rose from the mire of indigence to the summit of opulence. His mother was to him unknown. From very early childhood he had been sent to Europe, where he consequently grew as ignorant of his parentage as of every thing else. But, as facts had it, he was one of those extraordinarily stupid animals so commonly met with in the West India Colonies and vulgarly known as "white mulattos."[4] In Europe he was placed in the best of Colleges; he studied, or rather was placed under the ablest professors; yet such was the dullness of his intellects that they actually refused to take cognisance of the most ordinary rudiments of any art or science. The only thing for which the youthful DeGuerinon shewed any taste was the love of dress. He studied most closely and minutely all the fashions of the day. Thus after having remained in England until he had attained manhood, he received from his father a letter directing him to repare[†] to Trinidad; the letter also contained further instructions that as his hair was *rather curly*[†] he had better have it substituted[†] by a glossy wig if he wished to occupy any position in the colonial aristocracy; and also on his arrival in

---

4. That is, a set of men who, from some blind infatuation, actually fancy themselves that which they are not, and in the "good old days" of prejudice, were foremost among the oppressors of their own class.

Trinidad to say that he was a native of Europe, the nephew, and not the son of the old DeGuerinon, and in his conversation to borrow a little of the Corsican *twang*.[†] Being thus instructed he arrived in Trinidad.

On his arrival his father was overjoyed at seeing him, and failed not to encourage him in all the licentious habits which would render him a gallant of the day; his acquaintance was courted by the greatest, who saw not the dark tinge of his complexion, because it was overspread by a white veil of dollars. His father, however, soon after his arrival died, and he, believing his fortune sufficient to enable him to lead an indolent life, resolved on giving up all the business of his father, which, had he possessed judgment of conducting, would have increased his riches; but ignorance pointed to him the easier course to ruin and that he followed.

In the bought smiles of harlots and midnight revels he spent his days and nights. Senseless of the softer passions which often check the lewdness of men, he felt no obstacles in his way, and gave unbridled speed to his debauchery.

Such was the character of him who at first sight of Antonia feigned to love her, and swore that she would be his.

Having had many friends in the quarter of St. Joseph, DeGuerinon was a frequent visitor of that place, he had often met Antonia on the road; and was highly taken up with her beauty; he used to gaze upon her, but never could he find in her countenance one mark of encouragement or approbation. But he was not to be discouraged; from the moment he had seen Antonia he had marked her out for one of the victims of his libidinous soul. To attain that end he was determined to use every artifice and make any sacrifice. He knew the road was open. He was reputed to be a European, and of course the laws protected him, his person was inviolable! After one of his excursions he one day met a black woman on the road.

"Woman," he said, "who is it lives in that house?"

"A gentleman dem call Mr. Romelia massa!"

"Aw . . . and, aw . . . what sort of people are they, and . . . aw . . .[†] do you think I can gain admittance there?"

"Me no saby, massa. Mr. Romelia and he wife da be bery good people, dem give charity to poor niggers, but me no tink dem like white folks and me tink dem know you."[†]

"Ah! I suppose they must have heard of me. What a cursed pity it is to be popular, that my name is so much hawked about the country, but if I can only succeed to get in I shall soon convince them to the contrary of what they have heard.

"Oh! by the bye, do you know of any young man who visits the house, for I might no doubt be introduced by him as a friend. Tell me, do you know of any!"

"Yes, massa, there be one Mr. Adolphus."

"Adolphus, — oh, ho! that blackguard of a clerk of the peace, the scoundrel, he knows me, and hates me also, and so there is no chance of success with him. No other?"

"No, massa."

"Well, chance is dull; but . . . aw . . . tell me my good woman, of what disposition is the girl?"

"She da be a bery good soul, she na go to church aften."[†]

"Never mind that, think you she would love me?"

"Massa, poor nigga no saby."[†]

"Do you think there is any chance of getting her to live with me as my wife?"

"Ah! massa, me da sartin sure she no go do dat; dem is folks fou get married you dem no like a wee poor nigga, en beside she da go to church to aften fou dat."[†]

"This is the very same thing that I have heard from every one with whom I have spoken concerning this girl . . . but aw . . . as some people say virtue often gives way to gold."

"Me no tink da be de case wid she massa, cos dem got money demself."[†]

"Well, we'll see. So good morning my good woman, I thank you for your kind informations," and throwing a dollar to the woman, he rode away, swearing on that very day to gain the affections of Antonia or to make her his by force. He was soon in the town of Port of Spain, when he communicated his passions for Antonia to several of his friends by whose counsel he devised one of the most diabolical deeds that ever man could have conceived.

CHAPTER VII.

Abduction

"Have you heard, dear mamma," said Antonia to her mother, "that our poor neighbour Maria is very ill?"

"I have, my child, and it is even supposed she will not outlive this illness. I would willingly go and read for her, as I was asked this afternoon, but I feel so sick myself."

"Well I can go, dear mamma."

"Very well, my child, go at once, and do not remain late."

Antonia walked into her chamber, and having taken a prayer book from her table, came out, kissed her mother, and departed. The house of Maria was at no great distance. It was towards six, the sun had just set beneath the western horizon, and there yet remained his rich retinue, dressed in their gold and purple attire, gently following the ruler of day through his endless journey.

Antonia arrived at the house of the sick person, and there performed the duties of reading the prayers for the sick and imparting words of consolation to the sufferer. Towards seven it was almost dark, the moon had just commenced to peep over the high hills which stand to the east of St. Joseph, and here and there one of its silvery beams pierced the thick foliage of the surrounding trees, and gave to all around that majestic and imposing appearance which nothing but nature can assume.

At that hour Antonia left the house of the sick person; many offers were made to accompany her, but she gently declined, as her home was near by, and she had often before passed the same track; and she preferred, no doubt, to go alone on this occasion to feast her soul upon the enchanting scene around her. With her mind thus occupied, Antonia was bending her way towards her home — her steps were guided by that firmness which is the fruit of innocence — when suddenly a figure appeared before her, — she started, and cried, "Who are you?"

"One who wishes to speak to you for a moment," was the reply of the stranger.

"Perhaps you mistake the person, sir," said Antonia, still trembling with fear.

"I have not, indeed, — are you not Miss Antonia Romelia?"

"I am, sir; if you would say anything to me why not come to my father's house, which is near by?"

"What I have to say had better be said here, Miss Antonia. I am Mr. DeGuerinon, one of whom you have no doubt heard, and who has long felt for you the most ardent passion, but denied of every chance of disclosing to you my sentiments, I sought this stratagem."

Antonia remained silent from astonishment, but recovering herself, walked up to DeGuerinon and said, "Sir, I pray you make way, and let me pass."

"You shall not pass until I have your answer."

"I have no answer to give, sir," said Antonia, with an agitated voice; "give way, I pray you."

"No, no, think not to escape me so easily," and raising his voice, cried "Here, Dingberry!"[†] At this she was suddenly seized by a person, who lifted her from the ground, whilst a voice exclaimed "you are mine." She screamed and swooned. None heard her scream, her faint voice was re-echoed by the woods, which innocently mocked the unfortunate child. Senseless, she was placed in a carriage, which instantly drove off and never stopped until it arrived at the gate of DeGuerinon's dwelling, which was in the capital. Still unconscious of her situation, she was lifted from the carriage into the house as a gentle lamb borne to the slaughter; on being brought into the hall she was laid on a rich couch, such as those on which indolent princes lounge and waste in idleness the precious hours which might be used in promoting the well being of their subjects. Whilst there she lay in all the appearance of death, and DeGuerinon, watching over her with the greatest anxiety to hear her speak, a servant entered and handed him a note; on opening it, he found that he was at that moment compelled to leave the house on a most pressing engagement. He stamped, and throwing his eyes around the room as if seeking for resolution, at length he decided, and ordering an old slave, Selina by name, in whom he confided, to watch over Antonia, he walked to the door; again he returned with hasty steps to her side; again he moved towards the door, and with a countenance reddened with rage, he reluctantly left the house. At his departure all was mournfully silent; the old slave pitied this one of the numerous victims of the lewdness of her master, and earnestly wished for her deliverance from the shame and disgrace that awaited her. Whilst the old woman sat by her side and watched her with pitying looks, Antonia opened her eyes and gazed around, and again closed them, whilst her feeble voice sent forth that word which is the first that mortals breathe, the first which Nature first places in the mouth of the babe whilst yet in its cradle, "*mother.*" But, alas, that tender one was not within reach of her voice. She who had caressed her in childhood and smoothed her pillow in sickness, answered not to her call; but instead of that mother; numerous servants ran around her and presented to her phials of such odoriferous scents as would have suited the handkerchief of the proudest Sultana, and such creams as the palate of the proudest prince would not scorn to envy; but all she rejected with a slight push of the hand, none seemed to afford such consolation or remedial effect, as the tender and consoling words of a mother! Shortly after she however perfectly recovered herself, and the senses having returned to their forsaken seats, instead of viewing the neat and humbly furnished hall of her father or the simple and innocent fittings of her own chamber, she found herself in the midst of a large and fashionable drawing room reclining on a mahogany couch overlaid with the richest scarlet; around her she beheld all the pomps of worldly grandeur, nothing but the richest crystals and rarest of *porcelains* struck her eyes; the floor was covered with mats of the richest of India's production; from the ceiling, of snow white, was appended a large candelabra of the purest crystal, with lights which made the room as bright as the sun does an open field. Servants stood around, ready to obey all her mandates.

On beholding these things, astonishment was at first printed on her countenance; she believed herself in a dream, but soon was deceived and found that it was indeed too sad reality. Then came to her almost distracted mind the moment in which she had left the house of her old friends, the scene on the road, and casting another glance around her, she enquired,

"Where am I? whose house is this? when was I brought here? . . . by whom?"

None answered, but all the servants retired and left her, save Selina — who stood weeping by her side.

Again she spoke, and in a louder voice, whilst the tears ran down her cheeks, and her sobs rendered her voice scarcely audible.

"What will my mother think of me? she will call me ungrateful — alas! I am innocent . . . oh! my mother — my father . . . Adolphus . . . and he also shall call me unfaithful! Ah! horrible and distracting thought, more terrible by far than a thousand deaths!" And she searched for her sprig of myrtle which she always wore in her hair from the day that Adolphus had first declared it the emblem of fidelity, but it was gone — and she fell on the couch and wept — the tears ran through her fingers like molten lead.

Whenever overtaken by the storms of misfortune and adversity, there is ever to be met an interposing spirit which casts always its protective wings over the innocent. That angel is Sympathy. Antonia, at this critical moment, whilst plunged in the lowest depth of sorrow, cast her eyes towards a corner of the hall, and there beholding Selina in tears, she exclaimed,

"Even in this place, which to me represents the horrors of vice, doth pity find a habitation. Ah, Sympathy, ever welcome messenger of Heaven, to how much advantage might not thy presence be used!"

Then rising from the couch and advancing towards the old woman, she addressed her.

"Tell me, good mother, what place is this? who brought me here? Can you not save me?"

The old woman answered not.

"Are you not a mother? Have you not a child? . . . your appearance answers in the affirmative. Think, then, of the afflictions which would rend your breast at an unexpected separation from an only child, and also the shame, the disgrace which it would bring on your aged head, were that child like me doomed! Save! oh save me . . . an unknown spirit whispers to me, 'tis in your power . . . not only to save me, but to save an aged father and mother from falling into untimely graves, — say, will you — can you not release me?"

Selina, unable to speak, mournfully shook her head.

"If in you, I can find no succour, in whom within this habitation must I then seek it? I have friends who, to effect my rescue, would brave the tempest and all the powers of earth . . . but alas, they know not where to find me."

"My young mistress," answered the old woman, "what can I do? — alas, nothing — however much I may be willing to serve you . . . my situation renders it impossible."

Antonia's head fell on her breast, — despair had already commenced the foundation of its destructive empire, when suddenly a happy idea occurred to her, and hope bade her to cheer; and pulling from her bosom an "*oraison*,"[†] which she always wore about her, she tore a blank piece from it, and with a little pencil cased in gold which Adolphus had presented to her but the night previous, she hastily wrote the following:

"*Adolphus,*

"Brought by force to a place of which I know nothing, I am apparently a prisoner . . . and with strong reason to believe myself not in safety. 'Tis in thy power to save: haste, therefore, to the rescue of thy

"ANTONIA."

"Here, mother," she said, "have this but conveyed to the place, directed by some in whom confidence can be placed, and I might yet be saved without your being compromised."

"My little mistress," answered the old slave, "I will use all my efforts to serve you; but your letter cannot be sent before the morning, and then I am afraid it will be too late."

"It is never too late to aid the sufferer; so your mission is good, and heaven shall protect you."

These words were scarcely uttered . . . the note was yet in Selina's hand. DeGuerinon entered in a dreadful state of irritation . . . With a terrible curse he ordered the old woman to retire, and then advancing towards Antonia, who stood trembling by a chair which was her chief support at the instant, his looks softened, and he addressed her.

"Well, my girl, how do you like your new dwelling, eh? I suppose you find it strange, it isn't that old rattle-trap of a hut in which you lived up in that cut-throat-valley of St. Joseph . . . and why do you not speak?"

Antonia, lost in astonishment, neither moved nor spoke but fixed her eyes on him, and instantly recollected in his bloated features the person who had so impudently gazed at her on the road some days previous — she trembled violently —

"Ho! ho! why do you shake, eh? — Do not be afraid my little hussey! you are not quite in hell — neither am I the devil altogether — but you are at home, and aw — with your sweetheart or husband, which ever you might be pleased to call me, you have only to make yourself at home and ask for whatever you want, and have it at your will if Old Nick himself must be called here to manufacture it for you."

These words shocked Antonia, to whose ears they were entirely new — unable any longer to bear herself up she fell on her knees, and said,

"Since I have but to express my wishes to have them gratified, please restore me to the bosom of my family; let me see my parents who must be suffering at my absence, and I shall have reason to believe you the most magnanimous of men."

"Oh, ho! very fine words, all these very sentimental indeed, my little pet; but aw — I had too much trouble in bringing you here to let you off so easily. Do not be afraid, you'll soon see your mother."

"Then, for what purpose was I brought hither?" asked Antonia; "What are your intentions towards me?"

"The very best, my little love, only to make you my wife and companion you see, and of course the partaker of my fortune — only this — and that can easily be done, and the fact is, aw — it must be done."

"What!" answered Antonia, with indignation at the loose manner in which DeGuerinon had spoken, "What can give you such authority over me? Such power you can only possess were it given by some higher authority or my own consent. Have I ever known you? have I ever consented to be your wife? how then must I be such?"

"Stop! stop! don't be in such a fret now! take things coolly as I do."

"Think you," continued Antonia, who now stood erect and firm, "think you that you will be allowed to carry your evil deeds to that extent which you imagine? Is the majesty of the laws so much fallen as to deny protection to the helpless and innocent?"

"Pooh! pooh! talk about laws, eh! you are a pretty hussey of a lawyer, ha! ha! laws, my dear child, were made for slaves, and aw — petty fellows. But we *whites* (!) do not bother our brains about them. In this country you see, my child, it is all money — money can make the stiff laws to bend — and make you love me too."

"I am resigned to the worst — for, know, that whatever power you may possess over the life of an unprotected female, you can have none whatever over her chastity; that impregnable fortress for the gift of which, we have to thank but Him who is the giver of all great good. That chastity, sir, is like the light within the crystal shade which, as darker grows the scene which surround it, the brighter are the rays it emits."

"Ha! ha! I admire courage, and from all appearance you seem to have pluck — for that very reason, I love you the more by G——d. But, as I said before, be cool and reflect on the good which you will do to yourself by loving me. Now, you know it is of no use to squall, you are mine you know, and no one dares claim you from me, since we are married."

"Married, sir, when? where? or by whom? what minister of the church or law officiated on the occasion, pray tell me for I am ignorant?"

"Ha! ha! ha! really my dear Antonia — (do not start, I suppose you never thought I knew your name), we men of the world never bother our heads, about either ministers, persons, or churches, or laws, or such trash, we have but to imagine a thing, and to us it is law and everything else you choose."

Antonia, who during the dialogue had observed that the great ignorance of DeGuerinon, did not allow him to listen to any reason, nor yet to feel her bold rebukes, thought the only means to gain over him would be by the most humble entreaties, and she addressed him,

"To reason, sir, you seem a total stranger, and to mercy much more so. Therefore, to expect pity from you would be vain. If reason then, sir, within your senses be denied admittance, let mercy at least occupy for an instant a slight portion. Without my knowledge or approbation was I taken from the home of my parents and brought hither. You ask me to love you and stoop to your desires, how can you expect such things; you seem inflexible, but is pity unknown to you? would you be so hardened as not to feel its dictates? go seek in the most barbaric states where the rays of civilization have never yet penetrated the shadows of ignorance, or melted the dark mist of superstition. Go search the breast of the boldest outlaw, and pity, you will find, holds there a seat, why then do you not for an instant open your heart for its reception, even if it be but for this night. Oh listen — listen to its dictates. Since for me you entertain such affections as those which you have expressed, let indulgence, the constant companion of love, at least display its powers. I pray, I entreat you, but grant me time to consider, and the results might be beneficial to both. What is ever the result of all affairs transacted in the moment of hurry and without reflection? do they not always prove fatal to those engaged? Therefore again I conjure you to grant me time to commune with my mind, that I might be the more able to obey your commands."

These words were said with an expression so confident and so imploring that the flinty heart of DeGuerinon itself could not withstand their effect. He gazed on her; she was on her knees — her eyes fixed on the floor, she stood as the innocent convict that awaits the fatal blow of the executioner until DeGuerinon addressing her, said,

"It is true, time can do great things. I knew a lovely lady — (something like yourself) who at first could not bear my sight, yet with time she became so fond of me that nothing on earth could make her leave me, and the same might be the case with you. So I shall leave you to consider until to-morrow at eight in the evening, when I expect to meet you with your countenance beaming with love; all for me. So good night, you shall have all you require."

And he retired.

Taking up his hat he left the room. A moment after Selina entered and led Antonia into a chamber, and promised to pass the night with her. Immediately as they entered the clock struck twelve. Antonia fell on her knees and commenced to pray.

CHAPTER VIII.

Agitated Minds

Having now left Antonia a disconsolate prisoner in the house of the infamous DeGuerinon, let us now return to the scene where she was always the "life and soul." It is her parents' dwelling. On a chair near the door sits the corpulent old Romelia, enjoying, quite "à l'Espagnol,"[†] his highly flavoured "long tom";[†] within a few yards of him sits Adolphus, apparently engaged in conversation with the old man, but with his mind roaming over some distant plains where imagination is the chief action, and representing naught else but scenes of heavenly prayers, unalloyed happiness, — in short, every ideality of perfect bliss. Near the centre table is Mrs. Romelia, busily engaged mending the clothes of some orphans under her care. The village clock struck 8. Mrs. Romelia started.

"How, already eight! and Antonia not yet returned! She promised to return soon. Mr. Adolphus, would you not favour us by going to meet her? The road is rather lonely at this hour."

Adolphus readily assented, and left the house. To have been despatched on such a mission, was to him a source of joy incomparable. Oh! how little is necessary to upset a lover, — one look sets him in flames, one whisper turns him to a babe; one ray of hope makes of him an enthusiast — a thousand reasons cannot make him a sober man!

On Adolphus fled over the road with a light and cheerful heart; in a few minutes he was at the house where he expected to have met Antonia. But, reader, judge of his astonishment — picture for a moment the thousand expressions which, like sparks of electricity, flew from his countenance, when the words, like so many minute-guns,[†] fell on his ears, that "Antonia had left two hours ago with the intention of returning to her home." He was surprised, and knew not what to say, nor yet what to think. He paused, he mused, and could not conceive what could have become of her. It was in vain he reflected, in vain he conjectured. In haste he walked away, as one distracted, — he knew not whither he went. Of all he met he enquired, but none could give him information — until at last, giving away to the mad caprices of an agitated mind, he imagined she had eloped with some secret lover whose suit she entertained whilst she perfidiously smiled on him. At this he instantly resolved to return to the cottage and declare the unsuccessfulness of his search, and the perfection of Antonia, invecting, at the same time, the most fearful imprecations on her head and that of her imagined paramour, cursing her entire sex as vile deceivers, and calling them by no other name but as vile instruments of torture, sent from the furthest abyss of hell to aid, as it were, in accomplishing the wretchedness of the world, whilst now and then a consoling idea would intrude upon him and say, "Antonia is still faithful," but soon it would again depart and leave him again in abject misery and despondency. Oh! Imagination — what a conjurer.

In that state he entered the house, and declared, with tears in his eyes, the sad result of his search. At this the aged couple knew not what to say; a silent pause ensued — but at last, giving unbounden way to their grief at the loss of their only child, they saw the gates of the world about to be closed on them. Adolphus himself could not restrain his grief, for without Antonia what was life to him! — to him what was fortune? — what was the world? — the entire creation presented no other like her! Yet he bore this stroke of misfortune with more firmness than did the aged parents. Youth lent him courage, and Hope still fluttered around him. Never before was happiness so quickly changed into distress.

"If," cried Mrs. Romelia, "of her own free will she has forsaken us, may she be as easily forgiven from above as I now forgive her, and may she live to repent of her folly . . . But alas! that repentance will come too late — too late to give me any consolation; for I feel that I shall then be in the dark grave."

"Why despair," said Mr. Romelia, in that voice which denotes an afflicted heart struggling to ride over the pains, whilst the tears trickled down his furrowed cheeks; "have you not faith in him who protecteth the innocent and defenceless! — for I am persuaded, and indeed too much so, that our child has committed nothing which might bring disgrace either on herself or upon her parents, — she might yet be returned to us. Therefore, speak not of Death; already too dismal and distressing is the scene to admit of his ghastly name; but rather let us pray, and the coming day might bring tidings of our child."

The old man clapped his hands to his face, and bent his head to his knees; and Adolphus, although himself lost in despair, advanced near the disconsolate mother, and assured her that no part of the land would be left unexplored until her child was found.

But to her these words brought no comfort. For a while she was perfectly silent; then heaving a deep groan, she fell from her chair — Adolphus, who stood near, caught her in his arms, and with the aid of Mr. Romelia, bore her to her bed; the servants were called in, and all sorts of restorants were immediately applied to her. A physician was sent for, but the disease baffled all their efforts — it was beyond the powers of physics[†] — it was mental.

Adolphus on that night went not to his home, but remained, together with Mr. Romelia and the servants of the house, watching with the greatest anxiety over the suffering mother.

CHAPTER IX.

Cudjoe

The morning dawned over the cottage of the Romelias; such a morning was never before witnessed there. Anxiety was painted on every countenance; Mr. Romelia, with a dejected air, was pacing up and down the gallery, — the neighbours all running in and out the house in the greatest state of consternation,— the arrival of the physician and the Padre Gonzalvez,[†]— the different little groups of servants and neighbours who stood in different parts of the yard, some weeping, others in great excitement — all combined to form at once a confused and melancholic scene. The fit into which Mrs. Romelia had fallen the night previous, instead of leaving her, seemed at every moment to take a firmer hold upon its victim.

A little way from the house Adolphus stood alone, leaning against a tree, his head reclining on his hand. Poor youth! could he have been reflecting? No; there are moments in life when, notwithstanding every effort to raise the reflecting organs of the minds, all exertions prove vain; in vain we attempt to raise them; but every effort tends only to sink them lower, so ponderous are the claws of grief! In that state, incapable of forming any plan, of devising any scheme, of conjecturing any means, — deprived as it were of all the superior attributes which belong to man; the question hung before Adolphus in fiery letters, "How or where to find Antonia!" In that sad and pitiable state he was, when, suddenly, he was raised from his lethargic state by the voice of a person who addressed him,

"Massa, you sabby read?"[†]

Adolphus raised his head and saw before him a negro with a note in his hand.

"Yes, my friend," he replied, "I can; can I be of service to you?"

"Wa, yes, suppose you lek you sabby help poor Cudjoe, suppose you no lek, well you sabby do t'oder ting. Look me got one paper ya, me no want no baddy see em, but me na go shew you. Now, bougois,[5] tell me da who dis yer for,"[†] and he placed the note in the hand of Adolphus.

Like the mariner cast away upon a solitary rock in some distant part, who beholds the white sail of some friendly ship rising from the horizon; like the wandering huntsman surrounded by beasts of prey, who sees at last his companions arrive to his rescue, — like the traveller lost in a forest, who, after miles of wanderings, overcome by fatigue, beholds from afar the glimmer of a light of some friendly cottage, — so felt Adolphus at that moment: his heart, till then, overcome by cruel anguish, and fettered in the dark dungeons of grief, at one bounce shattered its chains, broke from its confines, when the letter which he held in his hand glittered with the too well known handwriting of Antonia. Without a word to the negro he tore open the letter, but old Cudjoe held his hand and cried.

"Tay dey, mass; heigh! da wha you da do? — do, fou Gar-a-mighty sake, gie me my paper and lay me go."[†]

"This letter is for me, my friend," replied Adolphus; and regardless of the negro's opposition, he opened it and read the contents. At first he stood paralised — "What . . . how . . . a prisoner," he muttered . . . "an unknown house."

"Tell me, my friend," inquired Adolphus, in the greatest excitement, "Where are you from? When did you receive this letter? Who gave it to you?"

Cudjoe eyed Adolphus with that look peculiar to the suspicious negro, and asked,

"You sartain sure, massa, da paper da fou you? You know paper saby talk, may be dis one tell lie."[†]

"No, my friend, it tells no lie, it is for me; but, who gave it to you?'

"Ol Selina gie em to me."[†]

"Who is old Selina?" inquired Adolphus.

---

5. A term applied by negroes to their superiors.

"My massa nigger,"[†] replied the negro, with that round about manner of answering questions.

"Who is your master, then?" impatiently asked Adolphus.

"Mass DeGuerinon."

"Was any lady in the house when you left?"

"Yes, massa, one purty lilly gal, what got nice hair pan he head."[†]

"How did she get there?"

"Last night, mass DeGuerinon he tell Dingberry and mysel and two oder niggas fou come wid he, a wee fallou him; when he come little bit lower down yonder dey, he make a wee get in de bush; and when the lily gal pass, he talk wid she — she want fight him — he call a-wee, we come, and Dingberry (da bad flatterer nigger) he take de gal and put na carriage, and massa take em na house fou he na town, Oh! poor lilly ting," (continued Cudjoe, assuming a pathetic tone) "sence las night she da cry, she da cry so; and she gie old Selina dis ya paper; Selina now she gie me, and tell me bring em na de sem place whey a-wee take de gal, and me ge em to one gemmen dem call mass Dolphus."[†]

Adolphus had to exercise all his strength of mind to be able to hear out the recital of Cudjoe; and when the negro finished, he burst out:

"Ha! DeGuerinon, perfidious wretch, you shall feel me! . . . I thank you my friend for your kind information; do but wait here for a moment, and I soon shall be with you again;" and, placing a coin in the negro's hand, he ran to inform Mr. Romelia of what he had heard.

On hearing the news, the old man cried, "Oh! I knew it; I knew my child had committed nothing wrong nor dishonourable; but where she now is, her life, her honour, is in peril; therefore, we must be prompt to her rescue. Had we not better see the commandant?"

"What will the commandant do for us?" replied Adolphus. "Know you not yourself, Mr. Romelia, in such cases — aye, in no case — there is no redress for us. If we seek the aid of the law it will only be exposing ourselves to the laughter, the ridicule of these merciless villains! Is it not our fate, our cursed fate, to see our homes dishonoured, our sisters and daughters prostituted without our daring even to seek redress! But, oh! I will not seek redress at the hands of any bastard tribunal, but I myself will take it; I will shew them that offended honour scorns even their justice!"

"You are right, Adolphus, my son; but be calm, 'tis the best weapon in a moment like this. As you say there is no law, no justice for us, we must take it into our own hands."

"You must not come with me, sir; a life so precious as yours must not be risked. Rather stay here and attend to your suffering wife. I have a friend in whom I can rely; — we will to the rescue of Antonia."

"Well," replied the old man, "since you will not have me go with you, I'd remain; but, let me caution you, be careful, be prudent; you know that this DeGuerinon passes for one of the privileged class; therefore, be cautious. You had better also arm yourself;" and the old man ran into his chamber and brought out a brace of pistols and a sword.

Adolphus took up the pistols, examined them, declared them good, and said, "Well, I take the pistols; the sword will be useless." The pistols were branded on the barrels '*Romelia.*'

"Farewell, then, I go," said Adolphus, extending his hands to Romelia. The old man pressed them, whilst he gave the youth his blessing.

As Adolphus stepped out of the door he saw Cudjoe, who was waiting for him. "Come, my friend," he said. "Are you obliged to return to your master's immediately?"

"No, massa; Massa DeGuerinon love flagy he poor niggus too much, and me tink whilst me out o' de way me go take de bush at once."[†]

"Well, come with me Cudjoe, and if you serve me well you shall be free;" and Adolphus took to the road followed by Cudjoe.

On they walked for a while, and having crossed a small track they entered a large and commodious house.

This was the dwelling of Ernest, the friend and companion of Adolphus, who, having become sole heir to a large fortune, lived by himself. On entering, Adolphus addressed Ernest:— "I need your assistance this day, Ernest."

"For what purpose?"

"Antonia my friend — she whom you alone know that I love, — she is in danger, and must be rescued."

"Antonia! Is it not rumoured that she has eloped with some youth; it was the first thing struck my ears this morning?"

"'Tis false, by Heavens," cried Adolphus; "as false as rumour." Rumour — that cursed indefatigable worker of mischief, of wretchedness, Pegasus of calumny,[†] principal destroyer of all social intercourse, tormenting nettle of all domestic life, on its poisoned tongue the name of Antonia had already been borne throughout the quarter.

"But stay, Adolphus, at first I believed it not myself. I know the scandalousness of public rumour. Have I myself not suffered from its shameful calumnies; has my peace of mind not been often distracted by it; has it not often made me pray for death; and do you think, my friend, that I would believe its reports. Adolphus, I knew Antonia before you, and she would never be guilty of the offence imputed to her. But since you know where she is, tell me, and I'll accompany you, and, if it be at the cost of life, we shall rescue her."

Adolphus, so much touched by the affection of his friend, knew not how to thank him, nor yet to answer a word; but pointing to Cudjoe, who stood by the door, he said: "This friend will give you all the information you require, I cannot speak of this."

Ernest then advanced toward the slave, and requested of him to seat himself — asked of him to relate the circumstance, which Cudjoe did in a very short and explicit manner; after which they proceeded on the manner of entering the house and rescuing Antonia. On that point Cudjoe assured Ernest not to make himself uneasy as he would be certain of success. Cudjoe then described the house and the plans which had been contrived between himself and Selina, but added, nothing must be done before dark.

During the lengthened conversation which took place between Cudjoe and Ernest, Adolphus, in the greatest agitation, paced up and down the room. The moment he had perceived that the conversation was terminated he was for starting at the instant; but both Cudjoe and Ernest refused to comply, as it would be useless to proceed on such an undertaking before dark. It was now about mid day, and the hour of five was appointed for the departure; then came into the mind of Adolphus the torments of suspense — every minute seemed to him an hour, every hour to have no end. Before the place where he was seated stood a time piece, his eyes he kept fixed on it, and he imagined that the 'hands' moved not. Then to despair he would yield himself, and fancy that the appointed hour would never arrive.

During the time that Adolphus was suffering Ernest conversed with Cudjoe, and carefully imprinted in his memory every circumstance; and when he was convinced that the entrance of the place could be easily and safely got, he called on his servant for a meal, which was immediately placed on table, and Cudjoe was asked to table. Surprised at such a request, the poor fellow knew not what to answer, indeed he almost fancied himself mistaken; but when he was a second time requested he was convinced; and for the first time in his life poor Cudjoe set down to a table together with what he considered buckras; and, unable to suppress his feelings, he said with a sigh:— "Well! well! country buckra good for true. Hay! da whar you go see one poor nigger lika Cudjoe sit dong pon table na town."[†]

"I am not a buckra[†] my friend," answered Ernest coldly, "that you can see yourself, therefore think not to flatter me with so blind a compliment — if I may term it a compliment."

"Da who say you no buckra; s'pose you no bin one, whar but you gat purty house and land, and purty trousers lika what you gat. In dis country ya once you lily bit white, you gat money, you gie grog[†] to drink, you is buckra, dem no look pan you kin, dem look pan you packet and de grag what you gie dem, dats all. Look pan my massa, de hangman, he ent no more white man dan my poor grandfader what dead dey in Africa, but he da pass, and gat plenty lika him too, and dere always will be."[†]

Had Cudjoe always spoken so truly, or prophesied as correctly, he would have been indeed a wonderful being; but as from the rock there often springs the prettiest flowers, so from a degraded mind there are often emitted those sparks of truth which the most refined cannot but admire. The meal being over, the rest of the afternoon was spent in preparation, as Cudjoe advised, to be ready for resistance, because there were no means of getting out Antonia but by force, and if DeGuerinon and his friends happened to be in the house there would be hard fight. The clock having struck five, Adolphus, Ernest, and Cudjoe left the house, each armed with a pair of loaded pistols.

CHAPTER X.

The Rescue — Death

Along the fine broad road leading to the delightful valley of St. Ann's, where now stand several cottages remarkable not only for the beauty and advantages of their situation, but for the neatness and taste of their construction, — about that part where the Queen's Park[†] with its level of green, its numerous herds of cattle seen strolling over the turf, or lolling under the protecting shade of some motherly tree, or basking in the warmth of a noonday sun, — where the bold hills of Maraval and those of St. Ann's[†] stand as it were like ramparts fitted up to protect the verdant plain from the rude intrusion of fitful weather, — near to that spot stood the house of DeGuerinon. It was a low house; it stood a little way to the right of the road; it was large and capacious; in front was a flower garden, which seemed to have been once the favourite of some fond owner, but now it was neglected, the fences broken, the gravelled walks overgrown with rank weeds. To the low and vulgar mind of DeGuerinon, the pleasures of nursing a tender plant, the reflections, the sublime thoughts which spontaneously rise from the heart at the contemplation of a flower garden, that scene where nature assumes the form of a lovely enchantress and fills the heart with rapture, — to him it was all "useless trash." Next to the garden was a wicket-gate, which led through an avenue of small trees to a side door by which the servants generally went into the house.

It was towards seven; the night was perfectly dark; the stars were concealed beneath a thick mass of clouds; three men stood in the avenue concealing themselves under the still darker trees — those were

Adolphus, Ernest, and Cudjoe. Adolphus, with all the rashness of a lover, was for entering at once the house; but Cudjoe and Ernest, who had already prepared their plans, held him back. They had not long stood there when the sound of an approaching coach startled them.

"Da massa gig,"† whispered Cudjoe, "stoop down, stoop down."

They accordingly stooped beneath the trees, and the carriage rolled and passed them quite unobserved. A while after this Cudjoe said, "Now the time is commin — aint got no company day in de house wid massa, get ready mass Ernest," and he whistled two long shrill notes.

Faithful to the call a tall figure was soon seen moving towards them; it was a woman — that woman was Selina.

"Is that you, Cudjoe?" she inquired.

"Yes, da he sel,"† answered the negro.

"Who is with you Cudjoe?" continued Selina.

"Two gemmen — Mass Dolphus be one."†

"Yes, I am one, my good woman," said Adolphus. "Is Miss Antonia still in this house?"

"Stay," whispered Selina, "speak not thus loudly — she is still in the house."

"Can you not lead her out? Say I am here waiting for her."

"No, I cannot; she is in slumber and this evening before the master went out he made me lock the door quietly, and he took the key with him; but he has just come home, and the moment he goes to the chamber you must take her by force . . . come with me, follow me," . . . and saying this she led gently the way, followed first by Cudjoe, and then Ernest and Adolphus. They went towards the house; arrived at the door Selina whispered, "Softly, softly," and she led them through the house and placed them in a chamber next to that in which Antonia was locked up a prisoner.

Here description must yield the pen, and imagination picture to itself the state of Adolphus, when but a partition of thin cedar boards† barred him from his Antonia, whom he knew to be in danger. How often were not his hands lifted to break through that frail barrier, but the *sang froid* of Ernest, and the correct suggestions of the shrewd Cudjoe, kept him back. He was however spared the pangs of uncertainty's state for long; for soon the door of the next chamber was heard to open, and the voice of DeGuerinon rose with the words —

"Well, my dear Antonia, how do you feel this evening?"

Every drop of blood in the veins of Adolphus at that moment boiled; he trembled, but Ernest had him by the arm, and Cudjoe whispered, "Wait, massa, wait lily bit."[†]

DeGuerinon, however, fancying himself safe in his own house, and at liberty to carry out his diabolical purpose, continued taunting the unfortunate Antonia.

"Why, my girl — whoy, aw, — it's strange, it seems the time I allowed you for reflection has produced no good. Have you not yet made up your mind to love me? — why do you cry? Come now, come, hussey, do be gracious," and he drew a chair near the one on which she sat, and attempted to pass his arm around her neck, but a timely push from Antonia nearly laid him sprawling on the floor.

The fire of his offended pride was kindled, but assuming a tone of *plaisanterie,* he said, "Surely, my love, this is all joke: you are merely, aw . . . shewing me a bit of your strength — come now, let us make friends — come give me a kiss," — and he again approached her, but Antonia, rising from the chair in which she sat, drew up her person and said in a voice hoarse from crying, yet with firm dignity.

"Away from me, sir, if you please!"

Those few words for a moment quailed the relentless man. There is something so eloquent in the words of a virtuous woman that the most unfeeling heart bends before their mighty power. But to DeGuerinon it was the evanescence of a moment, and he ran to Antonia to embrace her. Seeing that everything now depended upon force, Antonia prepared herself for a conflict, and cried,

"Approach me not, sir, — approach me not, at your peril — Oh, God! oh, God! where is Adolphus!"

"Ha! ha! ha! Adolphus, who the devil is Adolphus? Come now, girl, none of your nonsense; come, you know, you are my wife, — now it's no use, give me a kiss." And he laid hold of her, Antonia, possessing great strength struggled vigorously. Whilst struggling suddenly the door flew open, and a voice was heard, "Let go, villain!" accompanied by the flash and report of a pistol, DeGuerinon fell — Antonia shrieked. Adolphus then throwing down his pistol, ran to her. In a moment she was in his arms, and he cried, "Fear nothing — 'tis I, 'tis I, Adolphus!" The report of the pistol, the shrieks of Antonia, the noise made by Adolphus and Ernest on entering the room, created an alarm, and the footsteps of servants were heard running into the house. By this time Adolphus, bearing the almost lifeless form of Antonia in his arms, followed by Ernest and Cudjoe, were at the gate, where a carry-all,[†] which Ernest had ordered his servant to provide, was in waiting. They all embarked, and in a few minutes were several miles from the place where the infamous DeGuerinon, under the auspices of an unchristian state of society, had projected the schema of ruining the honour of an unprotected maid, and bringing to untimely graves the hoary heads of a doting father and a loving mother! But life is but a passage with a few level parts and many ragged ones; we pass from one stone to another, and often when we think we have left the worst part behind, we meet with the largest pool; so it was with Antonia. The carry-all drove up to the door — it was near nine.

The cottage which at evenings presented but scenes of joy, wherein contentment dwelt, and happiness was the portion of each inmate, was, on this night, the scene of desolation. None stood in the hall for the joy and laughter of preceding evenings; — the silence of the graveyard reigned, — that silence was at intervals interrupted by the whispering of prayers which came from the chamber, in which Mrs. Romelia was breathing her last. Her husband was leaning over her, watching every gasp which escaped her. At the foot of the bed was Padre Gonzalvez, repeating the Litany of Saints, to which the *ora pro nobis*[†] was responded in a low murmur by the servants and neighbours of the sufferers.

At that moment, hand in hand with her preserver, Antonia entered the house. At the door she expected to have been welcomed by the smiles and caresses of her parents — that night she thought to have drowned her past grief in spending a peaceful night in the bosom of her beloved parents. But, alas! what was her disappointment, what was her amazement, when on entering the house none stood there to greet her. It was then Adolphus remembered the state in which he had left Mrs. Romelia in the morning, and he whispered to Antonia — "Your mother is ill."

"My mother!" exclaimed Antonia, as she ran towards the chamber and rushed into the midst of those who were there assembled. At her sight all were struck with astonishment.

"Antonia!" cried all with one voice. Her aged father folded her in his arms, and pressed her to his bosom.

"My child! my child! thou art saved! — blessed be the Lord!" he cried, "but, alas! thou hast arrived but in time to receive the dying blessing of thy poor mother;" and taking her by the hand, he led her to the side of the bed, where laid her expiring mother!

Daughters! you who have assisted at the bedside of a dying mother — you whose painful duty it has been at the fearful hour of dissolution to watch every heave of the bosom, expecting every breath to be the last — oh, picture to yourselves the feelings of Antonia. But a little more than twenty-four hours had elapsed since she had left that mother in health, in good spirits — now she stood beside her, gazing on her departure from time to eternity! Unable to give utterance to her sorrow, — unable to bear the pangs which rent her heart, she stood and gazed on her mother, — then suddenly bursting into a flood of tears, she said —

"Ah, mother, why not open your eyes, and look on your child! Behold her again at your side — your own, your Antonia! She has escaped from the snares which were laid for her . . . and now returns to solicit your blessing . . . would you at this moment forsake her, and leave her in this world without another friend like you, to guide her in the ways of truth? — No, no, I cannot, cannot believe it . . . Do but speak and bless her, that she might feel happy. Oh, God! be merciful, and spare my mother. What other in her stead can be offered me? — None, none can be like her! Oh, Heaven! listen to my prayer: already too heavy has been thy chastisement of my sins; they are stronger than I can bear, and would you now augment them! Oh, list to the supplication of a child, and spare her mother!" and she fell on her knees and sobbed heavily.

Adolphus, who stood near her in tears, also knelt by her, — deep silence prevailed on all around, and tears flowed plentifully from this heart-rending scene. The dying mother, who, from the moment she had fallen into the fit, had not spoken, now opened her eyes, which instantly fell on Antonia, and Adolphus, who both on their bended knees stood nearer her than any other. A smile lighted her countenance — life at that moment seemed anxious to obtain the sway, but death had already counted upon her to form part of his multitudinous army; then raising her hands, which Antonia quickly supported, she extended them and placed them on the heads of Antonia and Adolphus; she said, in a hollow and feeble voice, "Now I shall die contented . . . be happy . . . and . . . in all things . . . remember Him to whom I go — farewell — I now fly! . . ."

Romelia, who knelt at a little distance from them, ran up to catch also some words of consolation from his old and faithful companion, but he arrived too late. At the moment she had uttered those words she fainted in the arms of her daughter, and as gently as if going into a slumber, resigned her spirit into the hands of her maker. Antonia still gazed on her mother — she pressed her lips to hers, but they were cold.

How imposing, how solemn, how sublime is the death of a true Christian! What a noble lesson! How pregnant with useful subjects of contemplation! Yes, 'tis such scenes that bring the wayward soul to its right path, that disarm death of its terror, that open the portals and for a moment display to our view the transcendant bliss of eternity, and that prompt the heart spontaneously to exclaim, with the Apostle —

"Oh! Death, where is thy sting!"[†]

CHAPTER XI.

The Arrest

"Poor is the friendless master of a world;
A world in return for a friend is gain." — Young.[†]

On the morning following the death, whilst preparations were being made for performing the last offices due to the dead, Adolphus stood in the garden with Antonia, trying to assuage her grief by engaging her in conversation. It was on the very spot where they had first made known to each other the sentiments which glowed in their bosoms; little did they expect that those very shrubs, those very flowers which had been witnesses to their first and tenderest promises, would on that day have borne testimony to their parting vows. There they stood, unconscious of the storm which was gathering around them, as Ernest and Cudjoe ran up almost breathless. Ernest seized Adolphus (who, till then, was ignorant of the cause of their visit) by the arm and said — "Adolphus, your rashness of last night has been the cause of your ruin."

"What rashness?" inquired Adolphus.

"Do you recollect the pistol that you dropped at the house of DeGuerinon?"

"What of it?"

"On the barrel was stamped the name of Romelia, and from that they have found our track. DeGuerinon is not dead, he is but slightly wounded — and the Police is in search of us."

"What is to be done?" enquired Adolphus.

"Fly of course, precipitately," replied Ernest.

"Where to?"

"Beyond the seas. I know of a vessel which leaves this port this night for the neighbouring continent, and in her we must leave. I have already despatched a friend to make necessary arrangements. We can make our way through the woods, — a boat will be in waiting for us on the Caroni,[†] thence we sail to Chacachacare,[†] where the vessel will call for us."

Adolphus could answer no more, but stood aghast.

"These," cried Ernest, "are not moments to be lost in thoughts, for they are far more precious than life; — if lost, disgrace and dishonour must inevitably be our lot. Therefore we must not think, but act."

"And must I leave my country, . . . my friends — my Antonia?"

"Adolphus," replied Ernest, assuming a tone of severity, "to serve you I have involved myself in one of the most serious affairs that ever man was in. For I do consider my life in danger every moment that I breathe the air of this cursed place. If therefore this country, which so much oppresses and scorns your entire class, be dearer to you than life; if to you those friends who, with folded arms, would gaze on your misfortunes be dearer to you than your honour; if you would not have it to live to render your Antonia happy at some future day — stay; — for my part I leave at this instant; the faithful Cudjoe accompanies me."

"And shall I," said Adolphus, "not do likewise? shall I whom you accompanied in necessity, now forsake you in adversity? No, my dear Earnest," grasping the hand of his friend, "at a moment like this, Death alone shall sever us. But I pray you, Ernest, grant me but a moment, one single moment, and I will follow you."

"Granted! I know you wish to speak in private with Antonia; — love hates to part: to its uncalculating spirit hours are but seconds; — therefore be brief — all is ready for the voyage. I go a little way and shall soon be with you. I have already been to Padre Gonzalvez and related all to him, your trunk is now being packed, be easy about everything." Saying this he darted away, followed by Cudjoe.

Adolphus stood immoveable on the spot where they had left him. To him this was the most terrible moment he had ever felt in life. Whilst he thus stood, Antonia, who had walked a little way at the approach of

Ernest and Cudjoe now came up to him. His bosom was writhing with the terrible idea of parting; his lofty spirit was emaciated. Then observing Antonia, he took her by the hand, with his eyes swimming in tears, and his voice trembling, but with a presence of mind which seldom accompanies many on such occasions, he addressed her:— "Antonia, one of the heaviest calamities which ever befall mankind has this day befallen you — a mother whom you love has fallen a victim to the evil designs of a villain, and to the utter disregard which is paid by the laws, by the rancours of that prejudice which is the bane of our country, and you have cause to mourn; but be patient in your afflictions, and bear with the fortitude of a Christian the pangs of adversity. Let these words be imprinted on your heart . . . they are the parting advice of Adolphus."

"Parting?"

"Aye, Antonia, it is our cursed fate to part, and we must part; recollect you, at the moment of my entering the chamber wherein you were imprisoned — the report of a pistol? Well, that shot proved fatal — not to him who received the wound, for to such a wretch such an easy death would have been too merciful, too humane. He still lives, but, as I hope, to share later a more deserving fate, and meet a less honourable death. But it was fatal to us in causing our separation. Ah! Antonia, 'tis cruel, cruel; to part! But fate has decreed it . . . and from you I must go. But promise me, Antonia, — ah! pour this soothing balm into my wounded heart, — promise never to forget your Adolphus!"

And he folded her in his arms, and pressed her to his bosom, the tears streaming down the cheeks of both. After a moment in this position, Antonia lifted up her eyes and fixed them on Adolphus, who was blinded with tears, she said,

"And must we part, Adolphus?"

"We must. I would fain stay with you, but disgrace — death — the gallows!"

"Ah! speak no more; — since it be so, since that life, which I value much above mine be in danger, let us resign ourselves to the will of him who will never suffer us to perish, though painful it might be. But Adolphus, my only friend, my preserver, my only hope, in indelible letters, on every page of the book of memory shall thy name be written, night and day shall I think of thee, shall I pray for thy safety."

"And I vow, Antonia, —"

"Ah! do not vow — I know, my Adolphus, thou art faithful." At this moment they perceived Ernest and Cudjoe running to the spot where they stood with all speed. At their sight Adolphus pressed his lips to Antonia — their tears mingled together, and one long and fervent kiss announced the terrible moment of separation . . . Antonia, unable to support herself, was still borne in the arm of Adolphus, of whom she enquired,

"When shall we meet, Adolphus?"

"Alas, my dear Antonia, fate alone shall decide!"

"Where?"

He pressed her hand, and in a voice choking with emotion; answered "perhaps . . . in heaven!"

Whilst as yet in that position Ernest came up and seized Adolphus by the arm. "Come on, imprudent youth!" he vehemently cried, whilst he dragged him away. Antonia, loosened from him, staggered, but was supported by Cudjoe, who assisted her to reach a tree, and there left her, and precipitately followed them. Adolphus turned, saw her, and made an effort to run to her assistance, but the united strength of Ernest and Cudjoe detained him. She was faint and almost senseless. When she opened her eyes, she gazed around, none stood near her — Adolphus had departed.[†]

Five minutes had not elapsed, Antonia was yet standing on the spot they had left her; she saw four constables of police entering the cottage. In those days the qualifications necessary for a police constable were not those which are required at this day: sobriety, humanity, and intelligence were not the qualifications for that office; it was sufficient to possess, as the most essential quality, a white skin — to be deprived of every principle of humanity, and to be, in short, in every respect one of the "real Yankee slave-catchers,"[†] — such were the men who performed the important functions of police constables. It was four such men who had just entered the once happy cottage of Romelia. Seeing them enter the house, Antonia instantly ran towards there, and as she entered, she found her father already in custody.

"Why am I arrested?" demanded the venerable man.

"You know as well as we do, you old blackguard," replied the chief of police; "we have a warrant to arrest every male in the house; and we must search further."

At this reply the old man, although overcome with grief, could not restrain his indignation and cried out at the pitch of his voice,

"I will not move hence until I know the reason why I am arrested."

"Secure him there, lads," said the chief to his assistants, with the utmost coolness and indifference, "whilst we search," and immediately the search commenced — every part of the dwelling was overturned, and lastly they entered the chamber wherein was laid the corpse of the deceased mother. The heartless men, if men they could be called, pulled about the corpse and treated it in the most brutal manner, all the while cracking all sorts of jokes.

During the search all the women of the neighbourhood flocked to the house, and found on their entrance the aged Romelia already fettered. He stood erect, yet unconscious of his accusation; his demeanour was majestic — in his countenance sat all the beauties of innocence, and with a moderate tone he addressed the chief.

"Say, friend, why am I arrested? Shew me the warrant. Tell me of what am I accused. Speak and I shall instantly follow."

"Since you pretend not to know, you shall learn later; — I cannot find any other rogues, but we will catch them bye and bye — in the meantime walk on."

It was not until he had heard these words that Romelia was convinced, of their determination to take him away, and casting his eyes towards the chamber in which was laid the corpse of his wife, he exclaimed, "Look, friend, in that chamber as you have yourselves seen is laid the corpse of her who was once my wife; in an hour hence she will be taken to her last place of rest . . . grant me but time, I entreat you, to follow her to her grave, where she will ever be hid from me, and I will then willingly follow you . . . to whatever place you lead me."

"No! no!" replied the chief, "we have other business to do besides seeing them bury an old black wretch — come on, you old thief."

"Do you refuse me this? Be pitiful. Are you not men, are you not husbands, have you not wives, have you not children, and will you refuse to let me perform the last and sad duties of a husband?"

Who is it that has ever witnessed the painful sight of a husband following to the grave the remains of a beloved wife, that has not felt his eyes moistened by a tear; who is it that will picture to himself the case of the unfortunate old Romelia, that will not shudder at the idea of such occurrences; yet, children of humanity, at one time such scenes were pompously displayed in Trinidad and other West India colonies; at this moment they are being acted in other places.[†]

The words of the unfortunate man had no effect on them, and one stern look from the chief, told to his subordinates their duty, who instantly dragged the innocent captive away.

Antonia clung to her father, she would have spoken, but grief gagged her . . . she could say nothing.

Padre Gonzalvez having heard of the arrival of police at the cottage instantly hurried there, and found his friend about to be taken to prison.

On beholding the padre he addressed him.

"Padre, I am now being led a prisoner, for what, I know not — my offence to me is yet unknown — farewell! — to your fatherly care I recommend my only child, my daughter . . . Look to her, since no other friend is left on earth but yourself and the young Adolphus. Farewell!" and perhaps, he would have said "for ever;" but the words died on his tongue, and pressing his lips to the burning brow of Antonia, he kissed her, he would have spoken to her, but the chief of police became impatient, and he brutally tore Antonia from him, whilst the others led him away, panting for breath.

CHAPTER XII.

The Voyage

The rising Sun of the morning after Adolphus had been borne by misfortune from all that was dearest to him on earth, found him pensively sitting on the deck of an English Schooner[†] bound to "La Guayra."[†] In this position he had stood from the moment he arrived on board of the vessel. His thoughts wandered far and wide — a thousand wild fancies distracted his mind, — now ghastly despair wielded its sceptre of lead over his mind, and wretchedness tore his heart assunder, — then would all relieving hope flash its brilliant and deceitful fires before his eyes, and appease a little the torments of affliction — now would the caprices and uncertainties of love spread their nettles over his heart; then would Faith assuage his suffering and bring him relief, — thus it was, his hours passed.

The wind blew a fresh gale, the Schooner steadily kept her course, all on board was merry — save Adolphus. Ernest sympathised with him . . . . Cudjoe was among the sailors, rejoicing at his escape from slavery, and the whole crew was kept in one continual state of merriment by the jovial discourses of an old sailor named Roughtide.

The captain, to whom the adventures which had brought the passengers on board was fully related by Ernest, pitied Adolphus, and tried every means in his power to render his passage as agreable[†] as possible, and seeing that nothing would console him, determined to divert him by some of the humourous stories of Roughtide.

After breakfast in which Adolphus took no part; the old humourist was called aft.

As prompt as the call, he was standing on the quarter deck, his hat in his hand . . . "Here we are, sir, as sound as a lobster."

"Now, old fellow," said the skipper, "this is the day on which you had promised to give us a narration of your adventures . . . are you ready?"

"Ready, sir, I am ever ready, as old Nick says, when a sinner knocks at the door."

"Well, take a seat and proceed."

"All right Captain," said the merry old sailor, making a very awkward bow. "But there is something which always forms the most important part of a story, and that's not here?" pretending to look about.

"What is that, pray?"

"Oh, Poets, you know, never begin any long story without previously invoking their muses, and of course, your honour, I cannot relate a very long fact without having first the aid of my inspiring Angel."

"Oh! I understand what you mean. Here, steward, hand old Roughtide a glass of grog, here . . . let it be stiff."

"Aye . . . as stiff as a marlingspike,[†] . . . but not as difficult to swallow."

The grog was handed him, which he instantly drank, and heaving a deep sigh to testify his approbation of the mixtures, he commenced —

"It was on board the Teresa, a brig[†] belonging to Liverpool,[†] which constantly traded to the West Indies, that I was second mate, some twenty years ago. After a passage of thirty-six days from home, we were on a fine morning standing off the lee of Jamaica, to which Island we were then bound; on that morning some dispute happening to arise between myself and the first mate, who never liked me, a scuffle ensued, and the result was, I pitched him overboard — and he disappeared as we thought forever, as we were then about four miles from land. The report soon ran around the ship that I had drowned the chief mate, and the captain, who then was in his cabin, hearing of this, immediately ran on deck. In vain I tried to defend myself by stating that it was not I who had drowned the mate, but it was salt water, but none paid any notice to my defence, and I was accordingly placed in irons, a situation by no means pleasant; well, I patiently suffered my punishment, but the only thing that truly grieved me was, — my grog was stopt; yet, notwithstanding, I bore it all patiently, and the weather being uncommonly calm, we never reached the port until two days after I was a prisoner. The moment the anchor was cast, and the harbourmaster had visited the ship as is usual, and the requisite declarations were made, I was quietly lowered by the tackle in the boat, as it were a barrel of flour with the head and the boat was rowed to the shore, and in an instant a crowd of darkies came running to the wharf to see what they considered a most extraordinary sight 'one buckra man wid him hand and foot tie.'† Well, sir, I was then lifted out of the boat by my brother sailors who had rowed me on shore, who in turns all pitied me, and at the same time gratefully thanked me for having rid the ship of a rascally chief mate. They then loosened my feet in order to enable me to walk to the Gaol. But no sooner had I stood on my legs than I perceived a person advancing towards us. At sight of him I bellowed out like a whale when struck on the flank, together with me the other sailors, all saw him, and we stood as if paralised, all trembling with fear, each thought he had seen a ghost. Whilst we were thus standing as mute and motionless as Quakers,† to the no small astonishment of the people around, the too well known voice of the chief mate struck our ears. 'Hellow! lads d'ye not know me?'

"At the sound of his voice each recovered himself, but I could not look him in the face, for I was almost convinced it was his ghost that had come either from heaven or hell, or the bottom of the sea, one or the other, to give evidence against me, and see me hung to his satisfaction. But these ideas were soon driven from my mind when he tapped me on the shoulder, saying 'Cheer up, old boy, it is not a ghost, but Bob Rogers himself.' He then ordered the fetters to be taken off my hands, leapt into the boat; we followed his example, every one, and rowed off to the ship; until then it was a mystery how he had come among us. On arriving alongside all who saw us was as equally surprised as we were on the landing place at seeing the mate at the helm of the boat — a shout of joy ran through the ship — not so much for the mate, but for me, as each had taken a last farewell of me but half an hour previous. The captain, as equally happy as the others, was at the gangway to receive us. Bob Rogers was the first to bounce on deck and receive his congratulations, as also those of the crew, and I who expected never more to have seen the old craft was the second to stand on deck; at that moment I felt a grateful sensation, like that of a lost child who finds his mother, but I had not time to play the philosopher, the crew ran round me, some embraced me, and three cheers for the first and second mate pealed through the air. Ha! there is nothing on earth like a sailor's welcome, 'tis at once plain, brief . . . but ah 'tis sincere. The first thing that Rogers did, after all the bustle of congratulations was over, was to give a perfect relation of the dispute which had happened between us, and clearly showed that he was the party who deserved to have been blamed and not I. 'Nothing like fair play,' cried every man on board the ship, and the captain then ordered an extra grog to be served round, — and three more cheers were given to the health of the gallant captain, mate, and second mate, I was merrier than any on board, and well might I have been for I had just escaped the chance of being elevated by means of a rope above my fellow creatures. The captain, as every one else, being anxious to hear how Rogers had so mysteriously escaped drowning asked of him to relate his adventures, to which he instantly complied. All hands were then piped[†] to the quarter deck,[†] and formed into a ring,— and the captain and Rogers sitting in the centre, he began his narration.

The Adventures of Bob Rogers.

" 'At the moment I had received the last and well applied clip from Roughtide, I felt myself overboard. I had not gone down eight fathoms in the water, than I fell in with a very bulky thing, which at the moment I could not well discern, I grasped it firmly round the body, the motion which I felt on holding it was so terrible that I thought it was an electric eel I had caught, but soon I felt myself above water, I breathed, and looked — I was a mile and a half from the ship, and on the back of a shark!'

" 'A shark!' cried everyone with surprise.

" 'Aye! a shark, — do not be surprised. I was too long on the fellow's back not to have known him. Well, to proceed, the moment I perceived that it was a shark, I determined not to let go, unless compelled so to do, away he started about a dozen times round about different ways as if inclined for sport, and after playing about for the whole day, now and then taking a dive for a few minutes, and afterwards scudding away on the surface of the water, at the rate of about fifteen knots an hour, whilst I held on as tight as any land lubber.

" 'The sun had just sunk into the water, and the fellow as if judging of my inclinations, steered directly for the shore, and when I had observed myself within a hundred yards from a fine beach on the western side of old Jamaica, I resolved for a bold stroke, and holding on his fin firmly with one hand, with the other I took over my knife which stood by my side in its scabbard, then passing it under the fellow, I gave him one gash from his mouth to his tail, he made a sudden leap which threw me off his back; the sea became like a pond of blood; I saw him no more, but swam as fast as I could to the shore, — on reaching the beach I was faint . . . I could not stand, I staggered and fell under a tree, where I slept until the following morning.

" 'On rising the next morning I perceived the sun was already high and the day much advanced, my bones ached me dreadfully, my eyes were sore, my joints all chafed by the sea, my throat was parched. I mustered all the strength I then could, walked a little way, where I found a little stream of water. I drank plentifully, and felt greatly relieved, then on my knees I fell and returned thanks to heaven for my providential escape . . . I was then returning to the same spot where I had slept during the night. I perceived a fishing boat passing, I hailed to them, they came, and a passage was given me to Kingstown,[†] where after remaining two days I met you my friends and comrades.'

"After he had related his adventures, everyone was silenced with amazement, until one more incredible than the rest, enquired whether it was positively a shark.

" 'Aye, that it was.' "

The captain, overjoyed at the wonderful escape of his favourite mate, again ordered the grog to be served round.

"Thus it was, captain," continued Roughtide, "that your poor old boy (meaning himself) was saved from his first and most serious scrape by a shark."

After Roughtide had terminated his story the captain ordered for him a glass of grog, which he drank, and making a bow, he left the quarter deck.

Adolphus, who had not spoken since he came on board the Schooner, was forced to smile, whilst the old sailor related his story . . . his mind became much diverted, after Roughtide had left to join his brother sailors at the forecastle, Adolphus conversed freely with his fellow passengers; and after a pleasant passage of four days, during which they were daily amused by the humourous stories of old Roughtide, the voluntary exiles landed on the free soil of Venezuela.[†]

CHAPTER XIII.

Fortitude. — A Court of Justice

On the fourth day following the death of her Mother, as also the imprisonment of her Father, Antonia, who had become an inmate of Padre Gonzalvez's house, was in the chamber allotted her, on her knees, before her crucifix, devoutly engaged in communion with her God. Whilst thus engaged, the door opened slowly, and the prelate entered. So much was her mind absorbed by her occupation, that she heard him not, — observing her thus, he would not interrupt her, but waited patiently by the door, observing with a secret pleasure the piety of the young penitent, — when she had risen, her countenance was calm and serene, and observing the venerable prelate learning against the door,

"Ha! pardon, Padre!" she cried, "I hope you have not been long waiting."

"Apologize not, my child; thou wert better employed than in conversing with a wretched sinner." A tear then trickled down his furrowed cheeks!

"What means that tear?" enquired Antonia, "can it be any ill tidings which you have for me, padre? . . . Is it of my poor father? . . . where is he? tell me is he well?"

"I have, indeed, tidings for thee, my child. — Antonia, I know thy fortitude, it is indeed great, and well thou mightest thank thy Creator for this gift . . . Thy trials in this life have been indeed severe — severer, I may say, than those which usually afflict those of thine age, — and thou hast borne them with a meekness and resignation which would have glorified a martyr. But though they have been strong and poignant, thy afflictions are yet not over, — adversity has given thee another and a severe stroke which I earnestly trust will be the last that thou shalt have to suffer on earth. Thou askedst just now of thy father, thou enquiredst whether he was well. — He is indeed well, — he now rests from the miseries of this profligate world — for he was last night snatched from the persecutions of inhumane men by an all merciful Creator."

Antonia, on hearing this, heaved a deep sigh and her head fell on her bosom, whilst she rested her frame weakened by grief, on her bedstead. She could shed no more tears; the spring of her heart seemed exhausted.

"My child, yield not thyself to despair, restrain those tears which, though ordered by weak nature, can avail thee no good. Nay! be patient, and bear without a murmur, the will of Him who is all great and wise. Look but in Him for consolation, for it is He who has thus afflicted thee, that He might test the sanctity of thy heart, and shew thee the frailties and deceptions of the world of which some make an Idol — and also that thou mightest taste, with far more delight, the sweets of the life to come. Learn to be submissive to His will, and let thy constant prayer be "Thy will, not mine, be done."

"I have learnt that," she replied, "and I still continue daily to learn its dear importance. For into His sacred hands I have already committed everything — but to be without a father, a mother, — ha! nature feels rebellious;[†] but I, —"

"Patience, my child; with Christian resignation, one must support the troubles of life."

At that moment the door bell rang — "I must leave thee for a while, my child, some one awaits me below stairs. Be patient, and a happy issue might spring from thy sufferings."

"Amen!" she responded, in a firm voice, — and the padre left the chamber and proceeded to the hall, where he met his old and intimate friend, Signor Farfero, a wealthy merchant of the town, who had called on him, and was also acquainted with old Romelia.

"I have called on you," said the Signor, after having saluted the padre, "to inform you of the death of your friend and neighbour, Mr. Romelia."

"Alas! my friend, the sad intelligence has already reached my ears, as also those of his only child, who is at present an inmate of this house."

"Poor child!" sighed the Signor; "how I pity her!"

"She is indeed worthy of your compassion. But, tell me, Farfero, you who reside in the town, tell me how did Romelia die — what were the circumstances attending his death?"

"Sad, indeed, were the circumstances . . . but you shall know them. On being brought into the Town on the day of his arrest, he was immediately taken to the office of the Chief Alcade, where he was placed in the criminals' dock, and there informed of an accusation that had been laid against him, and some other of his household, for forcibly entering the premises of Mr. DeGuerinon, with intention to rob and murder him."

"How false!" exclaimed the padre.

"And the proof of the charge was, that Mr. DeGuerinon was then under the care of a Surgeon† from the wounds he had received on that occasion, and also that a pistol, on which was inscribed the name of Romelia, had been found in the very chamber wherein the accuser was wounded. On hearing the accusation read, the aged man, whose frame was bent by sorrow, and the fatigue of a long journey, stood erect, and with a contemptuous smile on his lips, he said in a voice strengthened by innocence, —

" 'The accusation is false! the villain whose name stands in the warrant as my accuser, did try to rob my daughter, my only child of her honour, of her virtues, but she was rescued from his hellish designs by a friend whom I indeed regret I cannot compensate. The pistol, which stands as proof of my guilt, is indeed mine, I placed it into the hands of the valorous youth, who offered, at the peril of his life, to save my daughter — but they were never used for any base purpose, nor would I either use them myself, or allow them to be used in any dishonourable cause. I know not the residence of this DeGuerinon. I know him not at all, except by name. I have never robbed, nor have I ever' — He would have said more, but his voice faltered — offended honour, and indignation struck him dumb.

"Such is the contempt with which the sanctity of the law is treated — such are the effects which bigoted prejudice take on the minds of those who are entrusted with its administration, that justice to him whose misfortune it is to be the descent of afric's clime† is unattainable. This was fully illustrated during the trial of your old friend, for the moment he had finished speaking the Alcade with an air of austerity and contempt, addressed him thus:—

" 'It is very well for you to speak of honour, of having never robbed, and all such stuff, but the proofs against you are too clear to be denied and the simple evidence of Mr. DeGuerinon is more than sufficient to condemn you, much less the very pistol which you used in the murderous attempt, any evidence of such sons of niggers like yourself which might be brought in your defence, will not be received by me!'

"Then turning to his subordinate he said, — 'take this fellow to prison and have him well secured until the accuser be sufficiently recovered to appear in Court.'

"The unfortunate accused was then dragged in a most shameful and barbarous manner to the prison house. This morning DeGuerinon, being sufficiently recovered, appeared in Court and stated he was prepared with sufficient evidences to substantiate his charge. Malice, foul and black, was printed on his brow, and revenge, that first fruit of hell, was ripe in his soul, — his witnesses were four men whom no doubt his gold had taught to say any thing. The accused was then ordered to be brought before the Court, he was sent for and when on its rusty hinges the door of the cell wherein he was confined was turned — Alas! Romelia was no longer there — his noble spirit unable to bear the injustice of his fellow men, had taken its departure to that sacred sanctuary within whose doors are not admitted either dogged faced† prejudice or gnawing persecution. Romelia had departed, but a cold corpse was left, stretched on the pavement of the cell, — on his heart laid his right hand, in which was firmly grasped a small crucifix, testifying that he died in the faith of a future life of bliss. Such, Sir, was the lamentable end of a man who, in every sense of the term, deserved a better fate.

"This was announced to the Court; and DeGuerinon, struck with the terrifying powers of a guilty conscience, was unable to withhold himself, — he appeared frantic, he walked with hurried steps across the Court hall, his friends, who every one knew of the transaction, instantly dragged him away, lest he should betray himself, and the poor Romelia, without a prayer read over him, was buried among the deceased criminals!"

"*Requiescat in pace*"† ejaculated the priest. And the two friends stood in silence, whilst tears flowed plentifully from the padre.

CHAPTER XIV.

Venezuela

It was at the conclusion of the war of independence,[†] — the demons of hostility had entered their dens, and peace had begun to throw open its prospects of happiness to the Venezolanos, that Adolphus and his companions landed at LaGuayra. Their stay in that sea-port was but of short duration; for although the prudent Ernest had supplied himself with sufficient means to defray their expenses before leaving Trinidad, yet he felt the necessity of having immediate employment, in consequence of which he immediately resolved on going to Caracas.

*　*　*

Guides having been obtained, they set on the journey over the mountains which separate LaGuayra from the capital city, and after 10 hours' travelling, they entered the city.

Adolphus, although plunged in the deepest sorrow, could not withstand being struck with the contrast which presented itself to him. He had left a land where prejudice against colour had destroyed many of the social ties, — where the soil was daily watered with the tears of slaves, — and where none whatever of the descendants of Ham[†] could claim the rights of a man and a citizen. Another picture was now before him — all was free, all men were equal.[†] Joy reigned in every dwelling, — Liberty had given life to all; the father, instead of mourning for his son who had fallen in the last campaign, felt proud and joyous at knowing that his child had offered himself as a sacrifice at the shrine of Patriotism; the ten-

71

der spouses beheld with secret admiration the glorious scars which their husbands had brought home from the scenes of combat, as the fruits of their devotion to their country's cause; and throughout the environs the romantic sound of the *bandolas*† told to the stranger the mirth of the peasantry.

Adolphus could not behold the scene without emotion. He could no longer restrain his delight; and, rising from one of his deep reveries, he exclaimed — "What a change! How unlike an unfortunate and degraded country, is this land! Ah! Liberty, who can be so blind as not to admire thy grandeur! How sublime are thy lessons!!! Tell me, thou great goddess, shalt thou ever smile on poor Trinidad?"

Whilst he was thus musing, Ernest entered the hotel at which they lodged, and, finding Adolphus pensive, he addressed him:— "Adolphus! it grieves me to see you in this dejected state — you must shake off that dullness which hangs over your spirits. Recollect we are in a strange land, without employment or friends; it is true we have sufficient money to maintain ourselves for a long while: but money without employment or friends is like a turret without foundation. This is not the moment to yield yourself to the blind caprices of love, or to despair — we must act. What say you, have you any projects, any mode of life in view?"

"I have none."

"This is indeed sad; but did you not sometimes speak to me of Bolivar,† as an intimate friend of the Padre Gonzalvez?"†

At the name of the padre, Adolphus sighed. The dear remembrance of his home, which but a moment previous had wandered a little from him, again rushed back with all its force into his mind. But soon recovering himself, he replied, — "The padre often spoke to me of this great man, and he one day placed on my finger a ring, telling me at the moment — 'This ring was given me as a mark of esteem and gratitude by Bolivar for having once saved his life whilst we were together at a party of pleasure. Should fortune ever throw you in his path, you have but to shew it to him, and he shall be your friend.' What say you now, Ernest — if I present myself to him as the *protegé* of Padre Gonzalvez, and show him the ring in support of assertion?"

"The idea is excellent," said Ernest, "and the less time lost about this the better."

Adolphus, after having received some advice from Ernest, prepared himself to visit the President. On the following day he went; and after the usual formalities, were admitted into his presence. On entering the hall of reception, the frank and open countenance of the great patriot filled him with confidence.

"What would you have, young man?" inquired the President, in a most inviting tone.

"I am," replied Adolphus, "from the Island of Trinidad; and am come to present myself to you as the adopted son of Padre Gonzalvez."

"Gonzalvez! my oldest, my best of friends — he who was the constant companion and guide of my youth! It is long since I have not heard of him — tell me how he fares. Is he well?"

"When last I left him, Signor, he enjoyed all the blessings and comforts of health."

"It is well. You are his adopted son."

"I am, Signor."

"I now recollect," said the President, after a moment's reflection. "By the last letter I received of him, some years ago, he stated that he had adopted an orphan, to whom he had given a ring with which I presented him. Your name, if you please?"

"Adolphus — and here is the ring."

"'Tis the same; Adolphus!" and he seized the young man's hand. "You are thrice welcome to Venezuela; and since I may never have the pleasure of embracing my old friend and companion, let me at least embrace him whom he loves;" and he tenderly threw himself on the young man's neck.

"Now, Adolphus, my son — for such I may call you — tell me what brought you here? — what made you leave the old man, now that he most needs your company?"

"The tale is indeed sad, but I will tell."

"I am patient, Adolphus — relate and I will listen."

And Adolphus then minutely related to the President every circumstance attending his departure from Trinidad.

After Adolphus had concluded, Bolivar — that model of patriots, could not restrain his just indignation.

"Ought England not to blush! She that pretends to be the greatest and most magnanimous of Nations, to tolerate such things in any part of her dominions? And is that the land which Padre Gonzalvez so much cherishes!! I am astonished that he does not instantly forsake such a pernicious place, and come here to breathe the pure air of liberty. I shall write to him. Meanwhile, Adolphus, command me — in what can I be of service to you?"

"My stay with you Signor," replied Adolphus, "shall not be long. I have reasons which force me to return shortly to Trinidad at all hazards; therefore I need no employment here; but I have a faithful friend, who was the partner of all my adventures, and who would much like to make this his abode; could you be of any service to him, I would ever be your debtor."

"That I can readily do; as for you, it would be folly to think now of returning to Trinidad, at the peril of your life. If you are desirous of writing to the packet† do so, and I shall forward your letter by safe messengers; and should you wish for employment I can place you in my Secretary's office as an assistant."

"I am certainly under many obligations to you, Signor. My letters shall be ready in the morning."

"Well," said the President, "and you must also be at the office at six in the morning, as we have business of great haste and importance. I shall also think of your friend."

"Your orders shall be obeyed," and saluting the President, who shook him cordially by the hand, Adolphus left the hall of reception highly gratified at the President's generous behaviour towards him, and went directly to the hotel where they boarded, to inform Ernest of this gladsome intelligence.

After he had related to Ernest the result of his interview, he remarked, "All bids us be happy: we have the protection and friendship of the greatest; our good fortune is altogether singular. But Ernest I cannot long remain here — I cannot!"

"And what will you do?"

"Return to Trinidad."

"Truly, young man, your senses have certainly forsaken you. Would you leave a land of freedom to go again on a shore which slavery and oppression daily stain with the blood of your fellow creatures? Would you forsake the nectar of happiness, to go and drink the bitter dregs of misery? I know the reason which tries to bring about your ruin — it is that ridiculous Love which seeks to make you one of its foolish victims. Why not be like me, and scorn all women, and all the flimsy ideas of your wonderful passion as you call it?"

"Ha! Ernest, 'tis well for him to laugh at misfortune who himself never felt the weight of its ponderous claws."

"It is a misfortune in reality!! and thank Heaven I am clear of it; so, take my advice, Adolphus, and drive it away from your mind; it will do you no good my friend — what is the reason that I feel happy, although distant from my home and my friends — although my properties are left without any particular person to guard them — what is the reason that I admire all the beauties of novelty which surround us, and find delight in the liberty which all around us enjoy, whilst you are always dull, pensive, and appear even dejected? Truly, you astonish me; you whom I have so often heard sigh for liberty — you, who, within my hearing, have so often prayed for the sight of its resplendent light! Is that the way you treat that heavenly Goddess, now that you sit in her temple! Oh! fie! fie!"

"Ernest you injure me. You know yourself I love Liberty; indeed, I revere its sacred name. I find pleasure in looking on those who breathe its pure and limpid atmosphere. But, my friend, had you ever felt the pangs of separated love, you would surely speak otherwise."

"The pangs of separated love!" echoed Ernest, in a sarcastic tone. "Ha! ha! ha! it is true you are far away from her, but what of that; can you not write? Has the President himself not offered to forward your letters? Why then do you not write a parcel of stuff, such as generally fills love letters! and one day, before you die, you might doubtless see her, and suffer yourself to be linked to her if you choose — and I doubt not you will be soon as sick of united as separated love. But for my part, I would advise you to pitch love out of your brains — try and make the most you can out of the berth which the President has offered you — learn to be merry, and hope, like myself, to live and die an old bachelor."

"Your curious ideas, Ernest, really amuse me; in fact, they force me to laugh. But we have had enough of them, for this day at least. It is already late, and as I have letters to write I must retire to my bedroom."

"And so have I," exclaimed Ernest; "I must write to my old friend Ariosto, and make him my *chargé d'affaires*. So to your quarters, and I to mine."

The friends then parted. Adolphus entered his chamber to acquaint his adopted father and Antonia in what post he was.

Adolphus, in the profoundest sorrow and despair, heeded but little whither he was led; to him the present was insupportable, the future a dim and fathomless chaos. How different his situation from what it was but some days previous, — then he dwelt in the midst of hope, his career seemed bright, he saw but peace and happiness awaiting him in futurity. Now it was the reverse. Often when alone would he fall into a reverie, and imagine that Antonia was near him melting, by her warm and glowing lips, those mists of cares which hung over his brow, — he heard her sweet and musical voice, which often before had borne him, as if in a trance, from the world of cares to that of delight, — he felt her hand, warm with fire of her soul, pressing his, — and then would he try to fold her in his arm — and as quick as the vapours which are driven by the rising sun from the surface of the ocean, she disappeared!

How treacherous is Love! At the very moment that his disciples most need his aid, 'tis then he forms his greatest artifices to torture them; he bids defiance to Memory to erase from her tablets the pleasure of the past, in order to render the pangs of his victims the more terrible, — he bids hope to fly from them, and sends despair to prey on their minds. How happy must he be who can withstand the influence of that wonderful passion and brave its darts. But, then, what an uncommon being must he be? where must we seek for him that could shield himself from that which finds its way into every soul — whether it be in the most refined circles of civilized nations, or in the densest forest of the most barbarous climes. He must be indeed no child of nature who loves not; 'tis the earliest passion which invades the mind, the playful smiles which lighten the countenance of the babe whilst looking on the author of its days, testify but too well those feelings which his lips are too faint to express. In youth the frank and open attachments which are mutually formed are also evidences of its powers, but 'tis in manhood he firmly erects his temple — there he finds firm ground to raise his edifice, which is to last with the length of his days; thus man, from the very commencement, is partly consecrated to love, — in childhood he loves filially, in youth fraternally, in manhood connubially, and in old age paternally.

But let us now leave aside this mysterious passion, and follow our adventurers.

CHAPTER XV.

The Letter

Months had elapsed since Adolphus and Ernest had written to their friends in Trinidad, and as yet they had received no answers to their letters. Adolphus, at this time a clerk in the Secretary's office, was one day at his occupation. Bolivar entered the office and addressed him:

"My young friend! I have this day received letters from Trinidad, and among them is one from Padre Gonzalvez, which gives me such good accounts of your character and merits as to render you dear indeed to me. Here is a letter for you and another for your friend. I must now leave you — be at my residence this evening. I await you there." And he left the office.

Adolphus, with the greatest anxiety, tore the letter, which he knew was from the padre and inside was enclosed another. Such is the influence of passion over the lover that to him the health or wants of his dearest relatives are but secondary objects to those of the partakers of his affections. Adolphus, perceiving by the address that the enclosed was from Antonia, he instantly thrust the padre's letter into his pocket, and opened the other. It ran thus —

"Dearest Adolphus, — As an orphan I now write to you. Indeed, an orphan, for my father is no longer among the living. I am now an inmate of the house of Padre Gonzalvez, without any relative on earth, and without any in whom to place my hope, save my God and yourself. Daily on my knees do I thank that Providence who so mercifully led you from this land of persecution, and placed you beyond the reach of our enemies. He was indeed merciful: for had you staid, this day would I be without a father, and without you. And how then could I live? In such a state life would be a burthen, and death my constant prayer. You seem resolved to return here. You must for the present forbear; forbear! Adolphus, I conjure you by those affections which unite us. My tears disfigure the paper. On my bended knees I write my supplication, when forced, to advise the length of our separation. Though the pang be severe, yet would I not rather know that you live, and still cherish my memory, though distant from me, than have you near me, and see you persecuted and brought to an untimely grave, like unto my poor, poor father. No! no! stay. He who rules our destinies is wise. He has separated us, he has greatly afflicted us, and will he not reward our troubles? He will! I know too well he will.

Again, in your letter you ask me not to forget my promises. Adolphus, how can you be so weak? Think you that the sanctuary of my heart, where you alone are adored, shall ever be polluted by the idol of any other? No! there is but one who can rival thee — that is the grave; and until his order, I am forced to obey. I shall ever be thy

ANTONIA.

P.S. My best wishes to your friend Ernest. Farewell!"

"An orphan!" cried Adolphus, after having read the letter, and his tears flowed fast. "And must I not haste to console her? Yes, by Heaven! though the whole artillery of human thunders be levelled at me — though they be ranged around the horizon to launch at me their murderous forces. I shall have them. I must, I must see my Antonia . . . But she herself entreats me not to come. Yes, and on her knees with tearful eyes she writes. Heavens! my Antonia on her knees, and in tears, begging of me to desist from this adventure. Aye! Antonia I will obey. I am comforted, once more thou assurest me of thy fidelity. Ah! dearest dearest of friends! 'tis not I see we can never be severed. Though fate might place us at the two extremities of earth, never! never! shall our hearts be separated, for they are too fastly linked."

Whilst he was thus musing, Ernest entered the office, his eyes sparkling with delight.

"How, now, Adolphus, sad and in tears, after such gladsome intelligence?"

"Gladsome do you say? Pray what is there gladsome in this? There, take and read," and he handed Antonia's letter to Ernest. Ernest read quickly, and returning the letter said, "Strange she has not communicated the most essential; here, behold my letter. The villain DeGuerinon is ruined, beggared in fact, and is at present in prison."

"How! DeGuerinon, but eight months past so wealthy, so highly considered."

"Yes, DeGuerinon, but eight months not so wealthy, but so highly considered. I knew myself before we left Trinidad that his debts were more by far than he would ever be able to liquidate. Yes, Adolphus, his extravagance and debauchery have beggared him, and it is now that he can no longer supply with champagne his once dearest friends, now that he is no longer veiled with silver — that he is found out to be a mulatto; his birth is traced; his mother found out to be a slave, and no other than the old Selina, who was, according to my letter, the very first levy which he handed over to his creditors."

"Strange Antonia made no mention of all this in her letter."

"How, my dear Adolphus, could you expect her to mention anything of the sort? Do you not know yourself that you lovers are always blind and as often deaf to your own interests? But has the padre not written you?"

"Ah! I had entirely forgotten — I also received a letter from him; it is in my pocket."

"Ungrateful youth — is it thus you treat him who was more to you than a father?"

"Ah! pardon, pardon Ernest — no more reproaches I pray. I admit I am guilty of ingratitude."

The padre's letter was instantly opened, read, and every word that Ernest had said fully confirmed.

Adolphus (noble soul!) would not permit of his rejoicing over the sad, though deserving fate of his enemy — he pitied the wretch who had so basely and irremediably injured him. But suddenly a light beamed on his countenance, and, starting into one of his favourite apostrophes, exclaimed — "Trinidad! Sooner than I expected shall I revisit thy shores. Ha! Antonia, little did I expect again to embrace thee. What say you, Ernest, when do we sail?"

"Where to?" enquired Ernest, with his usual *sang froid*.

"Why to Trinidad," replied Adolphus.

"Oh! Be calm, my dear friend; I will never allow you to leave this abode of safety until we shall have heard further from Trinidad. For my part, if ever I again leave Venezuela, it will not be to return to Trinidad, though 'tis true I have friends, I have properties there, yet all these offer to me no enticement; I am very well situated here, highly esteemed by my employers. I have all the comforts that life can desire, and to complete my happiness, my dear Adolphus, I must now avow to you what I have ever concealed — I am in love!"

"Is it possible? And how, Ernest, could you have concealed this?"

"Easily, my dear friend; it is not he who sighs and sobs the most that loves the most faithfully."

"That is indeed true; but pray tell me the happy one who is to be the spouse of such a worthy youth?"

"The charming Josefitia, the youngest daughter of my employer. From the first day that I entered the store our eyes met — a strange feeling possessed itself of my heart; from that we have had many private conferences. She plighted her faith to me, and I vowed never to love any other than her; and I do feel within myself, Adolphus, that I shall ever be faithful to my vow."

"And her parents, Ernest, what say they?"

"To them it was made known last week — they instantly consented, and we are to be married in four months."

"And so, Ernest, you are a lover, and shortly to be a husband. I congratulate you on the happy change which has taken place in your life. How little you expected this when you swore to die an old bachelor?"

"It was always my conviction that none could be happier than an old bachelor; but now I find that he who would be truly happy must follow another tract in the expanded field of life."

ANNOTATIONS TO
Adolphus, A Tale

p. 6

† **Many were the inducements**: The Spanish Crown issued the Royal (Réal) Cédula
(also "Schedule") of 1783, offering free land, tax concessions and other privileges to Catholics who emigrated to Trinidad. Many "free coloured" families
from Grenada (like the Romelias), Martinique and Guadeloupe settled in
Trinidad as a result.

p. 7

† **Chacon**[1] [1]**The last Spanish Governor**: José Maria Chacon was the last of the
Spanish governors of Trinidad, serving 1784–97 and implementing the provisions of the Cédula.

† **capitulation**: The surrender of Trinidad to the British in 1797. Also the usual
name for the Articles of Capitulation, the treaty between the previous Spanish
colonial governor and the conquering British general in 1797, which included
a number of provisions such as the retention of Spanish civil law, the recognition of the free coloureds' rights and protection for the Roman Catholic faith.

† **Moloch**: The name of a Canaanite idol to whom children were sacrificed
(Leviticus 18:21), represented by the poet Milton as one of the devils. Hence,
any object to which horrible sacrifices are made.

† **the quarter of St. Joseph**: Chacon divided Trinidad into administrative districts
called "quarters", each under a local official or magistrate known as the
"commandant". St Joseph was the old Spanish capital of the island up to
1784, and is situated a few miles inland from the coast in the foothills of the
Northern Range of mountains.

† **granadilla**: *Passiflora quadrangularis,* a climbing plant and its large fruit; the
thick, white flesh and greyish jelly seed covering is used for making ices and
drinks. Also known as *barbadeen.*

p. 8

† **Flora's temple**: Flora is the Roman goddess of budding springtime, cereal, fruit
trees and flowers.

† **dahlias, jesamins, tube roses, butterfly flower, roses, sunflower, myrtle . . . in the midst**: Virtually all of these are imported plants. "Dahlias", native to Mexico, were introduced into Europe in 1789 and commonly cultivated in gardens for their large brightly coloured flowers. "Jesamins" refers to several local shrubs, especially *Nyctanthes arbor-tristis* and *Cestrum nocturnum*, with fragrant white flowers; "jesamin" and "jessamine" are older spellings of "jasmine"; the European *Jasmimum officinale* is the common or white jasmine of British literature. The "butterfly flower" cultivated here is probably *Schizanthus*, also known as "Angel Wings" or "Poor Man's Orchid", bearing orchid-like blooms in brilliant light pink, purple or scarlet with a golden centre. "Tube roses" (tuberoses) *Polianthes tuberosa*, native to the East Indies and cultivated widely in Europe at the time, have creamy white, funnel-shaped, very fragrant flowers and a tuberous root. Roses were widely cultivated in Europe; most of this period were very fragrant. "Sunflower" refers to any of the *Helianthus*, mostly native to North America, having conspicuous yellow flower-heads with a large seed disk and bright yellow rayed petals suggesting the sun; the flower turns so as to follow the course of the sun during the day. The common European myrtle, *Myrtus communis*, is a shrub with shiny evergreen leaves and white sweet-scented flowers; the myrtle was held sacred to Venus and used as an emblem of love.

p. 9

† **From certain motives**: In the period in which the novella is set (1813–28), the colonial authorities were reluctant to give permission to free coloureds – of mixed African-European heritage – to run schools; the children of the free coloureds would not have gained access to schools run by whites.

† **light Italian *brunette***: That is, "coffee-coloured", light brown, fair-skinned. The Romelias were "free-coloureds". "Brunette" in the nineteenth century referred to complexion at least as often as to dark hair colour.

p. 10

† **"a bright intelligence from heaven"**: Probably a paraphrase of Samuel Rogers, "Human Life" (1819). In this passage, from the section on childhood, a boy watches his mother with reverence: "Close by her side his silent homage given, / As to some pure intelligence from Heaven" (lines 208–9).

† **"dull care"**: "Begone, Dull Care" is the title of a well-known song from *Love and Wine,* a popular eighteenth-century cantata; it was frequently reprinted in songbooks such as *The London Songster, or Polite Musical Companion* (1767).

† **eat to table**: More commonly, "eat at table".

† **you solicitude**: In the original, "you solicitue"; this probable use of "solicitude" as a verb is idiosyncratic, but clearly means "care about; be anxious about".

† **the words of his bard, "Train up a child in the way it should go"**: A biblical quotation (Proverbs 22:6): "Train up a child in the way he should go: and

when he is old, he will not depart from it." The divine "bard" is Solomon, by tradition the writer of the Book of Proverbs.

p. 13

† **cutlass**: A long, wide-bladed cutting tool, used by swinging it to chop or swipe. (A "machete" rather than a sword-like implement.)

† **trace**: A narrow unpaved pathway, bigger than a track but much smaller than a roadway.

p. 14

† **lappes**: *Agouti paca,* the paca, is the largest rodent in Trinidad, and is hunted extensively for meat; also "lapa", "lappe" or "lap".

† **quencos**: *Tayassu tajacu,* the collared peccary, a kind of wild pig, hunted for its meat; now usually "quenk".

† **"runaway negroes"**: That is, escaped slaves who had formed camps or settlements in the deep forest, and generally known as "maroons" throughout the English Caribbean. There were apparently relatively few in deep forest areas of Trinidad, such as Brigand Hill. (See discussion in the introduction.)

p. 15

† **"I and my sister Agilai were taken from Africa; we were Foulahs."**: The Fula ethnic group extends from present-day Senegal and the Gambia as far east as Nigeria and Cameroun. This term continues to be used in Africa.

p. 18

† **fair, hair black, rather curly**: "Fair" at this time generally referred to complexion rather than hair colour (see note on "brunette" to p. 9). Adolphus, the son of a "mulatto" mother and a white father, was light-complexioned, but his curly black hair signalled his part-African ancestry.

† **Commandant² of St. Joseph ²Names formerly given to the Magistrates**: See note to p. 7.

p. 19

† *History of Rome*: The particular history referred to here is difficult to determine.

p. 21

† **Adolphe**: The French/Creole form of Adolphus, and thus affectionate.

† **care it**: Now obsolete, "care for; take care of".

p. 24

† **the delightful valley of Maracas**: The Maracas Valley is one of several valleys intersecting the Northern Range of mountains.

† **the fire of 1805**: Actually 1808, when much of the small town of Port of Spain, the island's capital since 1784, was burnt down.

† **Marine Square**: Established by Governor Sir Ralph Woodford in 1816, this was a long tree-bordered avenue on a line of reclaimed beach in the southernmost part of Port of Spain, which the Spaniards had called "Plaza de la Marina" or "Calle Marina". In 1962 the name was changed to "Independence Square", and in 1995 to "Brian Lara Promenade" after the Trinidadian cricketer.

† **Brunswick Square**: The principal open space in the city's heart, situated across from the Red House (Parliament), established in 1797. It was renamed Woodford Square in 1917.

† **Woodford**: Sir Ralph Woodford, governor of Trinidad 1813–28, was responsible for the rebuilding of Port of Spain after the devastating fire of 1808.

† *à la anglaise*: "in the English style" (Fr.)

† *aguazils*: Spanish term for policemen, police constables, used in Trinidad up to the 1840s; also "alguacils".

p. 25

† **"soothe the savage breast"**: A slightly altered quotation from the opening line of William Congreve's *The Mourning Bride* (1697). Almeria, the heroine, in mourning for her supposedly dead husband, laments her inability to be cheered by music, even though it "has charms to soothe a savage breast". This well-known phrase is often quoted to emphasize the redemptive effect of music, and was frequently used as the epigraph to song collections in the eighteenth and nineteenth centuries.

† **mulatte**: The French/Creole form of "mulatto".

† **smutty**: "Soiled, dirty, blackened, dusky"; a very derogatory term for dark-skinned people.

† **alcade**: A type of magistrate, city or county councillor; established under Spanish rule; usually "alcalde".

† *sans gene*: French *sans gêne*; that is, easily, without taking notice of others' reactions.

p. 26

† **Chief Alcade de Bario**: The "Alcalde de Barrio", the chief magistrate for the city; his counterpart in the rural districts was the Commandant of the Quarter.

p. 27

† **à la Des Saline**: Jean-Jacques Dessalines (1758–1806) was born a slave in Ste Domingue (Haiti) and became a leading general in the Haitian Revolution from 1791. He led the resistance in 1802–3 to Napoleon's attempt to re-establish slavery and regain control over the colony, and was known for his ruthlessness. After a fierce campaign marked by atrocities on both sides, the French forces were defeated; on 1 January 1804, Dessalines proclaimed the independence of Haiti. He ordered the annihilation of all Frenchmen still on the island. He proclaimed himself emperor later in 1804, but was assassinated in 1806.

† **tread mill**: A device for punishment, requiring the victim to climb up steps
around the periphery of a horizontal cylinder, thus making it revolve. It was
considered a "humane" alternative to flogging.

† **San Domingo**: Whites were haunted by fear of the Haitian Revolution, which
began in 1791 and followed closely after a suppressed rising by the free
coloureds of Ste Domingue (San Domingo, modern Haiti).

† **Alcade in Ordinary of the Second Election**: One of two magistrates who presided
over the courts.

p. 29

† **Corsican immigrant**: Among the French settlers who emigrated to Trinidad in
the late eighteenth century were several Corsicans; Corsica had recently
become part of France. The author's "white mulattos" suggests that De-
Guerinon was actually "coloured" but "passed" as a white French Creole.

† **repare**: Go, betake oneself, make one's way; a spelling now obsolete in favour of
"repair", and archaic at the time of writing.

† *rather curly*: A thinly veiled reference to DeGuerinon's mixed race ancestry.
Note that the same terms are used for Adolphus's hair (p. 18), but the italics
here draw attention to a crucial difference: DeGuerinon seeks to disguise his
mixed race; Adolphus does not.

† **he had better have it substituted**: In the original, "he had better had it substituted". The use of "substitute" meaning "replace; take the place of", is now
archaic.

p. 30

† *twang*: A distinctive manner of pronunciation or intonation differing from that
usual, or regarded as the standard, in a country, especially one associated with
a particular district or locality, for example, "an Irish twang".

† **"Aw . . . and, aw . . ."**: The peculiar and striking use of "aw" seen here is also
found (as "A—") in the gentlemanly villain Grandcourt in George Eliot's
1876 novel *Daniel Deronda* (pp. 383, 469, 658, 742). It suggests a foppish,
affected tone, and may derive from a contemporary stage convention. (See
Winer and Rimmer 1994.)

† **"Me no saby, massa. Mr. Romelia and he wife da be bery good people, dem give
charity to poor niggers, but me no tink dem like white folks and me tink dem
know you."**: "I don't know, massa. Mr. Romelia and his wife are very good
people, they give charity to poor negroes, but I don't think they like white
folks and I think they know you."

p. 31

† **"She da be a bery good soul, she na go to church aften."**: "She is a very good
soul, she goes to church often."

† **"Massa, poor nigga no saby."**: "Massa, [this] poor negro doesn't know."

† **"Ah! massa, me da sartin sure she no go do dat; dem is folks fou get married
you dem no like a wee poor nigga, en beside she da go to church to aften fou**

dat.": "Ah! massa, I am certain sure that she will not do that; they are people who get married, not like we poor negroes, and besides, she goes to church too often for that."

† **"Me no tink da be de case wid she massa, cos dem got money demself.":** "I don't think that is the case with her master, because they have money themselves."

p. 33

† **Dingberry:** This is surely an allusion to the slang term "dingleberry", a piece of excrement clinging to the hairs around an inadequately cleansed anus.

p. 36

† *oraison*: Usually a prayer for protection; here, a protective amulet.

p. 40

† **"à l'Espagnol":** That is, "in the Spanish style"; here this probably refers to a very relaxed manner.

† **highly flavoured "long tom":** A type of cigar.

p. 41

† **minute-guns:** The firing of a gun at intervals of a minute, used as a sign of mourning or distress.

p. 42

† **physician . . . physics:** "Physics" refers to knowledge of the human body, especially the theory of diseases and their treatment by the use of medicines and other non-surgical means. A "physician" was an authorized practitioner of medicine, graduated from a college of medicine and licensed by an appropriate board. The division between physicians and surgeons often overlapped in mixed practices, but see below (p. 69) where a surgeon is called for the gun-shot-wounded villain.

p. 43

† **Padre Gonzalvez:** In this instance only, the original newspaper version has "Abbé Gonzalvez".

† **"Massa, you sabby read?":** "Massa, do you know how to read?"

p. 44

† **"Wa, yes, suppose you lek you sabby help poor Cudjoe, suppose you no lek, well you sabby do t'oder ting. Look me got one paper ya, me no want no baddy see em, but me na go shew you. Now, bougois,[5] tell me da who dis yer for":** "Well, yes, suppose you want to, you know how to help poor Cudjoe; suppose you don't want to, well you know how to do the other thing. Look, I have a paper here, I don't want anyone to see it, but I'm going to show you. Now, sir, tell me who this is for."

† "Tay dey, mass; heigh! da wha you da do? — do, fou Gar-a-mighty sake, gie me my paper and lay me go.": "Stop that, massa, hey! What are you doing? Do, for God-almighty's sake, give me my paper and let me go."

† "You sartain sure, massa, da paper da fou you? You know paper saby talk, may be dis one tell lie.": "Are you certain sure, massa, that paper is for you? You know paper can talk, maybe this one tells a lie."

† "Ol Selina gie em to me.": "Old Selina gave it to me."

p. 45

† "My massa nigger": "My master's negro"; that is, another slave of the same owner.

† "Yes, massa, one purty lilly gal, what got nice hair pan he head.": "Yes, massa, a pretty little girl [young woman], who has got nice hair on her head."

† "Last night, mass DeGuerinon he tell Dingberry and mysel and two oder niggas fou come wid he, a wee fallou him; when he come little bit lower down yonder dey, he make a wee get in de bush; and when the lily gal pass, he talk wid she — she want fight him — he call a-wee, we come, and Dingberry (da bad flatterer nigger) he take de gal and put na carriage, and massa take em na house fou he na town, Oh! poor lilly ting . . . sence las night she da cry, she da cry so; and she gie old Selina dis ya paper; Selina now she gie me, and tell me bring em na de sem place whey a-wee take de gal, and me ge em to one gemmen dem call mass Dolphus.": "Last night, Massa DeGuerinon told Dingberry and myself and two other negroes to come with him, we follow him; when he came a little bit lower down yonder there, he made us get in the bush; and when the little girl [young woman] passes, he talked with her – she wanted to fight him – he called us, we came, and Dingberry (that bad flattering negro), he took the girl and put her in the carriage and Massa took her to his house in town. Oh! poor little thing . . . since last night she's been crying, she's been crying so much; and she gave old Selina this here paper; Selina now she gives it to me and tells me to bring it to the same place where we took the girl, and I should give it to a gentleman they call Massa Adolphus."

p. 46

† "No, massa; Massa DeGuerinon love flagy he poor niggus too much, and me tink whilst me out o' de way me go take de bush at once.": "No, massa, Massa DeGuerinon loves to flog his poor negroes too much, and I think that while I'm out of the way, I'll take to the bush at once."

p. 47

† Pegasus of calumny: In Greek mythology, Pegasus is a winged horse; the image is used here to indicate the speed with which lies travel.

p. 48

† "Well! well! country buckra good for true. Hay! da whar you go see one poor nigger lika Cudjoe sit dong pon table na town.": "Well, well! Country buckra

is really good. Hey! Where would you see a poor negro like Cudjoe sitting
down at a table in town."

† **buckra**: A white man; also "backra", "beke"; from Igbo *beké* "white man,
European".

† **grog**: Rum.

† **"Da who say you no buckra; s'pose you no bin one, whar but you gat purty
house and land, and purty trousers lika what you gat. In dis country ya
once you lily bit white, you gat money, you gie grog to drink, you is buckra,
dem no look pan you kin, dem look pan you packet and de grag what you
gie dem, dats all. Look pan my massa, de hangman, he ent no more wite
man dan my poor grandfader what dead dey in Africa, but he da pass, and
gat plenty lika him too, and dere always will be.":** "Who says you're not a
buckra; suppose you aren't one, but you have a nice house and land, and
nice trousers like what you have. In this country here, once you are a little
bit white, and you have money, you have grog [rum] to drink, you're a
buckra, they don't look at your skin, they look at your pocket and the grog
you give them, that's all. Look at my massa, the hangman, he isn't any more
a white man than my poor grandfather who died there in Africa, but he is
passing, and there are plenty like him too, and there always will be."

p. 49

† **Queen's Park**: A very large open flat savannah, about 200 acres (81 hectares) in
area, at the northern end of the city of Port of Spain; originally part of the
Paradise sugar estate, it was purchased from the Peschier family by Governor
Sir Ralph Woodford as a public park in 1816.

† **hills of Maraval and those of St. Ann's**: The Maraval and St Ann's valleys inter-
sect the Northern Range at its western end and are situated to the north of
Port of Spain.

p. 50

† **gig**: A light, open, two-wheeled carriage pulled by one horse.

† **"Yes, da he sel"**: "Yes, that is he himself."

† **"Two gemmen — Mass Dolphus be one."**: "Two gentlemen – Massa Adolphus
is one."

† **cedar boards**: *Cedrela odorata,* a large deciduous tree; the aromatic wood is used
for cigar boxes, houses and furniture.

p. 51

† **"Wait, massa, wait lily bit"**: "Wait, massa, wait a little bit."

p. 52

† **carry-all**: A light carriage for one horse, usually four-wheeled and capable of
holding several persons.

† **Litany of Saints, to which the *ora pro nobis* was responded**: The Litany of Saints
is a responsive form of prayer in which the priest or leader implores the help

and intercession of each saint; *ora pro nobis* (Latin "pray for us") is the con-
gregational response in each case.

p. 54

† **with the Apostle — "Oh! Death, where is thy sting!"**: A biblical quotation (1
Corinthians 15:55): "O death, where is thy sting? O grave, where is thy victory?" This part of Corinthians is often read at funerals; it asserts the victory
of Christ's resurrection over the powers of sin and death. St Paul, the writer of
this epistle, is responding to and correcting the "false doctrine" current
among some members of the church at Corinth, "that there is no resurrection
from the dead" (15:12).

p. 55

† **"Poor is the friendless master of a world; / A world in return for a friend is
gain." Young**: A slightly inaccurate quotation from Edward Young's nine-
book poem *The Complaint, or Night Thoughts on Life, Death and
Immortality* (1742–45): "Poor is the friendless master of a world; a world in
purchase for a friend is gain" (lines 572–73). As he mourns the deaths of
three relatives and reflects on life and death, Young's speaker produces many
such quotable epigrams.

p. 56

† **Caroni**: Trinidad's largest river, which reaches the coast some miles south of Port
of Spain.

† **Chacachacare**: An island about 13 miles (21 kilometres) west of Port of Spain,
the most westerly of the islands of the Bocas between Trinidad and Venezuela.
Around the turn of the nineteenth century it became a whaling station, and
later a leper colony. In the early nineteenth century, it was the point from
which the Venezuelan patriot, Santiago Mariño, invaded Güiria during the
Venezuelan War of Liberation (Anthony 1997, 115).

p. 58

† **Adolphus had departed**: In the original publication, this reads "Adolphus has
departed".

† **"real Yankee slave-catchers"**: In the southern states of the United States of
America, patrols of white men hunting for runaway slaves were infamous for
their brutality. There were also Americans from the free Northern ("Yankee")
states who caught fugitive slaves in order to collect the rewards offered for
them. ("Yankees", a term used within the United States of America only for
the northern states, is widely used elsewhere for anyone of that country.)

p. 60

† **at this moment, they are being acted in other places**: That is, specifically, in the
United States of America, where slavery still existed.

p. 61

† **Schooner**: A small seagoing vessel, fore- and aft-rigged, that is, with triangular
sails set parallel to the length of the vessel.

† **"La Guayra"**: A city on the north coast of Venezuela, directly across the
Serpent's Mouth (in the Gulf of Paria) from the south coast of Trinidad. Now
usually spelt "Güiria".

† **agreable**: An archaic variant spelling for "agreeable".

p. 62

† **marlingspike**: An iron tool, tapering to a point, used to separate strands of rope
in splicing; now usually "marlinspike".

† **brig**: A brig, or brigantine, is a two-masted, square-rigged ship, but carrying on
her mainmast a lower fore-and-aft sail.

† **Liverpool**: An important port on the west coast of England, in Lancashire; for
many years it was a centre of the slave trade.

p. 63

† **"one buckra man wid him hand and foot tie"**: "a white man with his hands and
feet tied".

† **as mute and motionless as Quakers**: Quakers, or members of the Society of
Friends, were proverbial for their sobriety, and the periods of silence characteristic of their services. The term "Quakers" was originally used derisively
because the leader of the religious group, George Fox, asked the members to
"tremble at the word of the Lord."

p. 64

† **all hands were then piped**: Various combinations of notes sounded on the
boatswain's pipe or whistle were used to regulate the movements of a ship's
crew – to pipe "all hands" is to summon the entire crew at once.

† **quarter deck**: The quarterdeck is the raised aft portion of a ship's deck, used
primarily by officers and cabin passengers. Announcements to the entire crew
generally took place from the quarterdeck, with all hands assembled just
below on the main deck, though here they apparently all end up on the
quarterdeck.

p. 65

† **Kingstown**: Kingston, the chief port of Jamaica.

p. 66

† **the free soil of Venezuela**: In fact, slavery was not finally ended in Venezuela
until 1854.

p. 68

† **nature feels rebellious**: In the original, "natures feels rebellious".

p. 69

† **Surgeon**: One who heals by manual or operative means, treating wounds, fractures, deformities or disorders by surgery. (See note on "physician" to p. 42.)

† **the descent of afric's clime**: That is, persons of African descent.

p. 70

† **dogged faced**: More commonly, "dog-faced".

† ***Resquiescat in pace***: *Requiescat in pace* "May he rest in peace", a Latin phrase from the Catholic burial service; customarily said when the name of a deceased person is mentioned.

p. 71

† **war of independence**: The struggles for the independence of Venezuela, and the other Spanish colonies of northern South America, from Spain, 1811–21.

† **descendants of Ham**: That is, Africans, by biblical tradition descended from Ham, one of the three sons of Noah.

† **all was free, all men were equal**: Slavery existed in Venezuela in a modified form up to 1854, but there was little discrimination against free non-whites, and slaves were a small minority of the population. (See discussion in the introduction.)

p. 72

† ***bandolas***: A small guitar-like stringed instrument, with four double strings and a flat back; of Spanish origin.

† **Bolivar**: Simón Bolívar, the Liberator, leader of the independence struggle in Venezuela, Colombia and Ecuador.

† **Padre Gonzalvez**: In this chapter only, the original newspaper version has "Padre Assebido" throughout.

p. 74

† **packet**: A "packet" or "packet-boat" carries packets of mail and government dispatches (as well as goods and passengers). Given the unusual state of affairs and uprisings, this packet may be more directly under the command of Bolívar's forces than a regular peacetime packet. "Writing to the packet" is an unusual construction in any case: "writing by the packet" would be more idiomatic. (See also the note on "mails" for *The Slave Son*, p. 167.)

THE SLAVE SON

by

Mrs. William Noy Wilkins

London:
Chapman and Hall, 193, Piccadilly.
1854

Printed by
John Edward Taylor, Little Queen Street,
Lincoln's Inn Fields.

DEDICATION.

MY DEAR MRS. JAMESON,[†]

I had some thought of dedicating this work to those ladies who have laboured courageously and unremittingly for the emancipation of the African race, and many distinguished and revered names occurred to my recollection: this would also have been in harmony with the intention of my tale. Yet if homage there be in a Dedication, I feel it ought surely to be rendered to her who has cheered and encouraged me through the difficulties which have beset my labours, — to her whose kind and generous sympathy throughout has been to me like a beacon in the midst of darkness.

To you therefore, my dear Mrs. Jameson, I beg to inscribe this little book, as the best expression of my respect and affection which I have to offer.

I have endeavoured to describe Slavery under a different phase from that which has hitherto come before the Public. The slave saints and martyrs, of whom we hear so much, I believe to be more poetical than real. I hold moreover, that, were it otherwise, and slavery produced many such, the system would be a good rather than an evil, or only of that kind of evil which pertains to physical suffering; but there lies hidden within it a deeper woe than this, — the debasement of the mind, the deadening of every virtue, the calling into action those weapons of defence which nature has given to the weak — cunning, deceit, treachery, and secret murder. Root out therefore, ye who call yourselves Christians, — root out and utterly destroy a state of things which is the occasion of such ruin!

All are born free and equal, whatever differences may afterwards arise, and all are equally placed here to tread a path which has Heaven for its goal. It therefore becomes a question which concerns, not the Negroes alone, but all nations, — Shall one half of mankind crush beneath the wheels of their gilded car the other half who humbly toil their way on foot? Or shall not the humbler half lay claim to space upon the road, that they, as well as their more fortunate brethren, may win the Heaven to which God invites them? Ay, truly they shall. The grey light is in the sky; the dawn will soon appear; the day is coming, when the wrongs of crushed humanity shall find a voice in every heart, and every Christian hand be stretched forth to help.

With esteem and affection,
I remain, dear Mrs. Jameson,
Yours,
MARCELLA FANNY WILKINS.

Contents

The Slave Son

———————

Introduction

The following pages were written about six years ago, but it was thought advisable to alter the narrative, then consisting of detached pieces, to one consecutive story; even then being little encouraged, as the subject of slavery had passed away from the public mind with the days of Wilberforce,[†] I threw it aside, until the appearance of Mrs. Stowe's work[†] removed the objection, and the cessation of family cares and the return of health enabled me to listen to the suggestion of my friends and submit the work to the Public.

For the sake of truth I have placed the scene of my story in the Colony, and at the period, in which the principal events took place. I might equally well have transferred it to any other slave country, and to any more recent period, for the same causes are ever followed by like effects.

I did not start in life however with any particular sympathy for the Negroes. There were no scenes of cruelty or oppression in our homestead to awaken my pity, — far otherwise; and while our domestics presented all those features of an enslaved people so repulsive to the free, I learned from the first to regard them, as the children of all slaveholders do, in the light of a species of cattle, — I do not mean because they were bought and sold, and their labour unrewarded, I mean something worse still, — I mean that neither their total dismissal of all the proprieties and decencies of life, nor their immorality, ever shocked my principles or affected my mind any more than the habits of the beasts of burden working with them; and yet the Negroes were always with us and about us, so also were the domestic animals belonging to the house. I record these facts the more willingly, as it may help to show the nature and extent of the influence which slavery holds over man.

But the mixed race, the coloured population, early enlisted my sympathy: first of all, through their innate abhorrence of slavery and constant struggle after freedom; and then, when free, through their constant, yet vain and impotent upheaving against the social weight which keeps them down as Pariahs. I speak of the prejudice of caste.[†] None but those who have lived in slave countries are aware of the cruel extent to which this prejudice is carried. I saw them longing for education where no school would admit them, — yearning after excellence where no right to excel was allowed them, — at the same time ready to kiss the feet of those who only made a show of teaching them on friendly terms, and never stopping to inquire whether this passing condescension was not for the sake of the money which they freely and generously gave. The devotion and gratitude of these poor creatures was too touching ever to forget; but a circumstance arose which fixed their wrongs indelibly in my mind.

There came to the Colony where we lived a young lady of colour from Europe, — a lady, I repeat the word. To a refinement of breeding which only belongs to the best society, she added accomplishments and manners of the first order; she was spoken of as a wonder. But soon it was understood that she would not receive gentlemen unless they presented themselves respectfully, and as they would to white ladies. Instantly society was in a ferment. Ladies who customarily made closet companions of coloured women whose life was an open acknowledgement of their degradation, were here all amazed at the impudent assumption of virtue by this coloured girl; and although crowds would gather at night opposite her window to hear her sing, in the daytime she was avoided as if struck with the plague. Those who met her in the street would turn back, or cross to the other side; and every invention was put in play to show her how completely she was thrust from the position she had dared to assume. I was then very young, scarcely better than a child, and just at that age when the heart is fresh and open to all the most generous feelings of our nature; and, romantic as it may seem, in my room that night I made a vow that it should be my one great task through life to raise the coloured race to social emancipation and respect. In my youthful enthusiasm I felt persuaded that my one little feeble voice would shame away prejudice from the millions of white people who entertained it; and I came to England full of my subject and elated with my hopes of doing good, in spite of the ridicule which was often thrown on my endeavours and remarks. Of course such illusions passed away with growing years and riper judgement, but I never once lost sight of my subject, even when the cares of life were thickening around me. I prepared a series of stories (of which the following is the first) calculated to show what these people are, and to create such an interest in their behalf as might lay the groundwork for their future rising; and I still hoped on through it all, that the time would come when I should have leisure and opportunity to finish what I had begun.

And the time is come, thanks to Mrs. Stowe! when my subject is no longer irrelevant to the topics of the day.

I present myself however not so much to take rank among the champions of civil emancipation (for they are numerous enough already), as to invite supporters for its completion in the social advancement of the coloured race; for slavery can never be said to be abolished where prejudice of caste keeps the people degraded. It is the blight which remains when the simoom† has passed, quite as deadly and as poisonous, and at this day holds influence as fully and forcibly in the free northern states of America as in the south. I need only refer to the circumstance of Douglas† being horsewhipped for walking between two white ladies† to prove this.

Nay, in the British Colonies, where eighteen years ago† one half of the population was beggared to emancipate the other, prejudice against the emancipated race influences even the local authorities, just as much as at the period of our story.

It was an easy matter for statesmen at the head of Government in England to pass, for their political and commercial ends, an Act for favouring a distant people who never come across their feelings either to annoy or perplex: but how comes it they have never directed their appointed governors to open the colonial offices and departments to the deserving and the capable among the coloured race? How comes it they have never given encouragement to place them on an equal footing with the white? Have they never once thought of doing this? It is really poor justice, — a mere mockery of a great deed, more boastful than real.

But it is different with the American statesmen. *They* are surrounded with coloured people in every relation of life, and they have to wrest from the very growth of their minds a prejudice of no common force, before they can give that heartfelt, earnest labour to emancipation which can alone obtain success. None can tell but those who have lived in slave countries what a hold it takes of the mind, and how far and wide its influence spreads throughout all the feelings and actions of life, till it forms part and parcel of one's very nature, like the creed we have learnt from our mothers; and often, when boasting of having risen superior to it, we find ourselves suddenly as much under its sway as ever.

This happened to myself. I had been already a few years in England, still full of my subject, — talking of it by day, dreaming of it by night, — when I went with some friends to a party. I had not been long seated when I saw entering the room a young man of colour. It was the first time in my life that I had seen a person of colour enter a room on equal terms with myself; and my surprise and discomfort were by no means diminished when the daughter of our hostess introduced him to me as partner for the next quadrille. If the footman had presented himself for that purpose I could not have been more startled, and had I met this gentleman of colour at Court it could not have saved him from the feeling of aversion and contempt with which I instinctively regarded him. This, no doubt, was very absurd, as the hue of his complexion was the only circumstance against him; but it illustrates the force of a prejudice which interferes with the social welfare of a whole race.

There is no more fatal extinguisher of genius, of talent, of worth, of all that is noble in the mind of man, than this general blackballing, — no surer means of crushing the mind, of fettering the intellect, of lowering the morals, than this scourging rod of prejudice, which indiscriminately condemns the coloured people to the condition of brute and Pariah. Read what the Irish were in the days of the penal laws,[†] and it will give some faint idea of what the coloured race at this day suffer, not by written law, but social custom; for nothing in England can.

It is true that this is a country of castes, but it is also true that the wall which encircles each may often be climbed, not only by casual visitors, but constantly by strangers who come for affiliation; and where the upper classes exercise their selecting power judiciously, it acts wholesomely, and imparts to the people a vigour of exertion which has the best effect upon their children and upon themselves. But for the coloured man there is no hope: the barrier which separates him from intellect, worth, honour, greatness, reaches high up to Heaven, far beyond his power of surmounting, and all that is left him is to sit down in its shade and mourn!

But what though it requires the powerful effort of a powerful mind, dictated by a still more powerful heart, to overcome a feeling which has rooted itself in our very nature, still I do not despair. The whole matter rests with the American ladies, and of all the women upon the earth there are none superior in independence of spirit and benevolence of heart. The political emancipation of the coloured race is a deed for the men; their social emancipation is an heroic act worthy of the American ladies, and I dare promise them a glorious reward. The coloured people, with their patrimonial heritage of intellect grafted on the warm strong temperament of their mothers, exhibit while yet children, all the elements of fire, imagination, and genius. What may not they henceforward become under genial influence and encouragement? The women of caste are modest in their demeanour, faithful to their homes, fond mothers, and true generous friends, and have a refinement of feeling which is astonishing in the low condition to which they are condemned.

In their physical constitution too they are an extremely interesting race. The French, whose research in science is greater than ours, have discovered an affinity between their various castes and those of the Asiatic families, particularly among the women. The Mulattoes,[†] born of white and black parents, bear a marked resemblance to the Copts or Egyptians, the people who first gave civilization to the world. The Terzerons,[†] born of the Mulattoes and whites, have the golden complexion, straight nose, and slender forms of the Persians, the most refined people of the East. The Quadroons,[†] born of the Terzerons and whites, have eyes like houris, regular features, and the languid expression of the Asiatic Turks, — many indeed with perfect faces like the Greeks and the Romans, who once bore sway over the nations of the earth in philosophy, science, and warfare. While closer again to the Negro, the caste called *Capre*,[†] sprung from the Mulattoes and blacks, show the rounded proportions and plump faces of the Hindoos.

I do not apprehend that the mixed race will ever form a nation apart. In these days of swift travelling and increasing interchange of thought, it is more likely that exclusive nationality has seen its best days, than that it should spring up anew with another people. But I look forward to a thorough equalization of races, which shall procure for all equal rights by written law, social law, and the law which comes from Christ; when man shall owe his greatness to his own striving, — to the exercise of the talents he has received from God, not to the hue of his complexion, or rather, I should say, to the complexion of his parents; and when the coloured man, taking place among his fellow-men on earth, may do credit to the generous and glorious nation[†] which has freed him. To quote the prophetic words of Burns, —

"And let us pray, that come it may, and come it will for a' that,
When man to man, through all the world, shall brothers be and a' that."[†]

I have done; and it only remains with me to say that I repudiate all personal responsibility with regard to the sentiments I have put in the mouth of my hero: I have drawn him such as I have seen him, — the type of his race, — and such as may be found in every slave country; and he speaks here as every slaveholder speaks when irritated by the observation of strangers or the reproaches of the abolitionists. I have only to add my grateful acknowledgements to Mrs. Jameson, whose large warm heart found place for sympathy with my subject and earnest encouragement for my labours in the very midst of her then pressing labours on Legendary Art;[†] and also to Mr. Patten, the philanthropic Librarian of the Royal Dublin Society,[†] a man whose liberal heart and mind will ever be admired by those who know him, and who, like myself, have derived their best ideas and happiest suggestions from the stores of his intellect. And having spoken thus much for myself and for those to whom I am indebted, I beg at once to introduce my Story.

CHAPTER I.

A Short Review of the History of Trinidad — And a Little Gossip

Of all the Colonies ever visited by the Abolitionists there is none where the slave was found so happy in his condition as in that most fertile and beautiful of the Antilles, the fair island of Trinidad. It lies southernmost and last of the band of isles called West Indies, and just in the delta of the magnificent Orinoco,[†] of whose shores, from its close resemblance to the mainland in point of geological formation and natural production, it is supposed to have once formed part, and to have only been rent therefrom by some comparatively recent convulsion of the earth. But fertile and lovely as is the isle, it was nevertheless the latest known and the latest cultivated of all the Colonies, for reasons I will explain, and which, with a short review of its history, may go far to account for the somewhat easy life which the Negroes enjoyed.

It had the honour of being named by Christopher Columbus himself, who discovered and visited it during his third voyage to the West. It was on a Sabbath-day he first caught the outline of its mountains, from which circumstance he dedicated this new land to the Santísima Trinidad, — Sunday being set apart by the Spaniards for the particular worship of the Trinity. And as the gale from the shore came loaded with perfume, and the opening vista disclosed, as he neared it, a richness and magnificence of vegetation hitherto unknown, he called it exultingly the Indian Paradise.

But his glowing descriptions were doomed to pass unheeded, for the great discoverer had fallen under the displeasure of Royalty, and the island was suffered to remain as wild and uncultivated as when first proclaimed a Spanish conquest,[†] till the year 1783, when by a romantic adventure it was suddenly brought into notice.

About this time Roume de St. Laurent,[†] a French inhabitant of Granada,[†] happening to visit its shores in quest of natural curiosities, he was struck with its aspect, — its grandeur, its fertility, its large and numerous rivers, and, above all, the advantage of its situation. He became enthusiastic; he imagined himself a rediscoverer of the colony, a benefactor of mankind, and forthwith taking passage to Spain, he succeeded so well in advocating his views with the Ministers, as to win from them that celebrated Royal Schedule[†] which soon after resounded throughout all Europe, inviting Catholics of every nation to establish themselves in the new colony, under promise of free trade, exemption from taxes, protection during five years from creditors left behind, and many other immunities equally encouraging and important.

Meanwhile St. Laurent was not idle, but continued visiting all the great commercial cities of Europe, rousing the indolent, interesting the speculative, holding forth golden prospects to the ruined, and so eloquently speaking on his subject, that in a short time were seen emigrants flocking from all quarters of the globe to this new land of promise: the Colony soon acquired a political and commercial importance equal to its geographical position.

Much of all this success was owing to its first Governor, Don José Chacon.[†] A wiser and more benevolent man, a truer Christian, was never chosen to hold that despotic power which is vested in the hands of a Spanish Governor. He carefully watched the carrying-out of every law which protected the slave, and more than this, he set the fashion of mercy and kindness towards them, which afterwards, even under British rule, never entirely disappeared from the Colony.

We are apt to revile the Spaniards. Let us take a glance at their laws, such as bear upon our subject: perhaps we may find something to admire, perhaps even to learn from. Chivalrous nation! Though feudal and despotic their government, they nevertheless framed their laws studiously to protect the friendless; thus were women, children, vassals, and slaves, all attended to, their various cases considered, and officers provided for their protection.

Among other privileges of the slaves they who from tyranny or other cause became discontented with their masters' service, were entitled to require a written pass, good for three days, wherein to seek another owner; they were also entitled by law to demand and obtain manumission on producing the sum of 500 piastres[†] purchase-money; and be it observed, that the murder of a slave, a circumstance mostly unnoticed in other colonies, was here punishable by law, and the perpetrator made liable to a fine of fifty dollars (£10) to Government, besides the full payment of his value to the owner.

But here, as elsewhere, that damning clause was in force, which denied to the slave the power of bearing witness against a white man in a court of law; and all this talk of protection would have been but a mockery, had not the religion of the land, which was formed for a system of feudality and acted ever in harmony with it, stepped in to correct the vices of its enactments. The priests, unable, by the nature of their vows, to hold any personal property or tie, and having consequently but little interest in upholding the slaveholder, easily and naturally acquired the privilege of interference, and became, by means of confession, arbitrators-general between master and slave, thus exercising a salutary check on that irresponsible power which in other colonies has so demoralizing an effect upon society.

The observance of at least thirty Saints' days, besides Sundays, was also in favour of the slave, who had a proportionate amount of time to himself; thus, those Negroes who were in any way inclined to industry might very well contrive to save, — a disposition favoured by Chacon, who benevolently appropriated several acres of Crown-land[†] for the sole use and profit of slaves working out their freedom.

But it was not to the slaves alone that Chacon extended his merciful protection: there were yet two more races over which he watched with equal care — the free mixed race, or Mulattoes, and the Indians. Of the former the number was at first very small, but they soon increased in proportion to the rest of the population; for these unhappy victims of persecution had also been induced by the Royal Schedule to leave their old abodes in quest of a new and happier home, whose Government consented to grant them protection in return for a stipulated portion of their wealth. This indeed was no new thing: arrangements of this sort were commonly practised in all the other French, English, and Spanish Colonies, where, in return for a considerable tribute, they received a very slender and capricious protection; here, on the contrary, when Chacon made the agreement he kept it, and under his protection they did not so deeply suffer from the disabilities to which, in common with the Negro, they were made subject.

The priests aided Chacon here too. Far from sharing the general prejudice against a tinge of African blood, they professed it a part of their ministry to level all ranks and conditions. They had all the dead buried within the same sacred enclosure, without excluding (as was the case in other colonies) slaves or Mulattoes; and permitted in their churches no pews or any kind of private seats, so that within the precincts of their temples the scene presented was one of perfect equality, the Negro, the Mulatto, and the Indian kneeling fearlessly by the side of the white man, praying to the same God and benefiting equally by the offices of the minister.

Thus discountenanced by the clergy, caste prejudice lost much of its evil effects, and the free Mulattoes also shared in the general prosperity of the island.

As for the Indians,[†] they only numbered a handful at first, having long before been sent to work in the mines, where they pined away in despair. Government however now considered they might be useful in the Colonies, and emissaries were accordingly sent to all parts of the adjoining continent, to bring over as many Indians as they could persuade, till in a few years their number in the island amounted to two thousand. It is true they were still sunk in heathenish superstition, and their habits, manners, virtues, and vices all partook of the savage life they had been accustomed to lead; yet, simple and inoffensive, they seldom intruded on the haunts of the white man.

As soon as they were tolerably settled in their new abodes, Government thought proper to burden them with a tax, which Chacon subsequently commuted to a weekly portion of labour on the high-roads then in progress, and he so contrived to time and soften their labours as to avoid inducing despair among them. They lived in scattered villages along the sea-shore or on the banks of rivers, very often in the most picturesque spot; and as each hamlet was formed, Government placed there a Regidor[†] and a missionary,[†] by whose influence the Indians gradually seemed to progress in civilization, as rapidly as their indolent nature and inherent love of savage life permitted.

The island now presented a mass of population congregated from almost every part of the globe, not even excepting China,[†] whence thirty families came to speculate in tea-planting; and as each day brought fresh importations of adventurers, all differing in habits, ideas, grades, and languages, confusion would soon have wrought its worst, but for the affability and wise behaviour of Chacon. He visited all, took an interest in the affairs of all, brought peace and harmony among the discordant masses, and dealt encouragement to their good endeavours; and it is even related that whenever he found a worthy individual too poor to improve on opportunities, he would generously help him with loans from his private resources.

This was the golden age of Trinidad. Its port became the mart for all merchandise going to and from the continent; wealth flowed in abundance to its coffers; and such, it is said, was the simple integrity of the inhabitants, that heavy bags of gold, sealed with the merchant's name who issued them, passed current among all grades of people, and were never either suspected or opened. It was common to see warehouses and shops cleared in an hour by a single purchaser, and a forest of ships from every trading nation of the earth brought life and business to its port.

But this was not to last always: war was proclaimed, the English fleet bombarded the town, and the good Chacon, left without sufficient means of defence, was forced to capitulate; for this he was ordered to be secured in chains, and sent home to his ungrateful king; and many a heart regretted him, and many a tear was shed, and many a child born years after was taught to bless his name as it rose on the lips.

The terms of capitulation were understood to secure to the inhabitants the continuance of Spanish law, the free exercise of the Catholic religion, and all the privileges granted by the Spanish Schedule, so that the Colonists still hoped that their prosperity would not be disturbed. But with British rule came taxes immediately, each one more burdensome than the last, and various enactments, among which, be it recorded, was one proclaiming that no Colonist should be empowered to purchase Crown-land unless he could show proofs of possessing eight slaves wherewith to cultivate it. Moreover the Crown-land appropriated by Chacon to the private use of the slaves was gradually withdrawn, and the laws which protected the Negroes were made, one by one, to give way to other statutes and a different order of things. The English Governors, unfortunately, were not men to soften matters, or to gain by comparison with the lost Chacon; and when to the arbitrary proclamations of the Home Government[†] were added a sensible impoverishing of the inhabitants, a falling-off in commercial relations, and lastly, and most vexatious of all to the Planters, serious threats to emancipate the slaves, it is not to be wondered that disaffection increased, and murmurs were heard in this island more loud and bitter than in any other of the West Indies. Secret emissaries, it was said, were even sent to America, to offer allegiance to that mighty nation; and it was indeed with despair in their hearts and hatred on their tongues that the inhabitants met an unsuccessful answer to their hopes; for the Americans, it was understood, would not consider it worth their while to interfere, unless the whole group of Colonies struck rebellion at once.

But, in the midst of all this ferment and discontent, the spirit of Chacon still prevailed. The Spanish laws, set aside as they were by arbitrary Councils of State and the partiality of the colonial employés, were still respected by the priests; and the slaves, even though their minds were unsettled, and the ties which bound them to their masters were fast loosening, yet their condition was easy. I refer in this more particularly, and I might almost say exclusively, to the Spaniards; for, to the shame of my brother Protestants be it said, they were the only slaveholders I ever saw who enforced the observance of religious service among their slaves and encouraged *the rites of marriage*. With them the Negro married woman bore a recognized title to respect; she had influence with her master's family, and privileges on the estates which were never accorded to the unmarried.

The Spaniard is indolent by nature; he has little ambition beyond the enjoyment of the hour, and his love of power is so mixed up with paternal care, that these become one in feeling as in action. What if, in the evening, after Vespers,[†] the Spanish master would call his slaves around him, and make each kneel down and kiss the rod; in the same tone would he not meet the morning greetings of his own children, by proudly holding out his hand for them to kiss? To both he dealt continual indulgence and mercy, and if in his fits of anger his actions often bordered on cruelty, still, as a matter of feeling, it was understood and submitted to, and the unoffending might still remain happy.

Not so with the money-loving races of Jews, English, and Dutch, and some of the French. Unchecked by their own free laws, unrestrained by the mandates of their own free religion, and swayed only by the ambition of fortune-making, the Negroes were with them worse than beasts of burden; souls were nothing, bodies were cattle-property; and the cold, hourly, continuous tyranny of these masters, who treated them like the cane-plants subjected to their mill, was such as to work its own destruction, even had emancipation never come to the aid of the oppressed. Something of this it is my purpose to show in the course of the following narrative.

Affairs were still in a state of considerable ferment in the year 1832, when, about midcrop-time,[†] several rich planters and some merchants from Port Spain[†] (capital of the island) were observed suddenly to leave their residences, to flock to a very obscure hamlet on the south-east coast,[†] where the country is wild, little cultivated, and less frequented. Of course each, as he arrived, offered some plausible excuse for his journey, — the curiosity of the villagers demanded it; but whatever was said, it seemed upon the whole to fall very far short of satisfying the gossips of the place, and the subject was thus discussed by a group of females returning one evening from Vespers; when, after the usual Spanish greeting of the hour, —

"You know," said one, after listening to all the various surmising, debating, examining, and wondering, "all this can betoken nothing but a visit from the Governor. His Excellency is a quiet Hidalgo,[†] liking to travel without much noise or fuss."

"Ave Maria!"[†] exclaimed another, struck with the grandeur of the event, "don't say that; for if the Governor comes here we shall certainly receive an invitation; and my *niñas* (daughters) have not a thing to appear in. It was but yesterday I was turning over our stock of flowers, fringes, and feathers: *bargame Dios!*[†] they all fell in powder as I touched them, — devoured, I tell you, by the white ants;[†] and the cockroaches have got to their laces; so what we are to do I don't know."

"Don't talk!" said a merchant's wife, "I have got some book-muslin[†] down here which I can sell you, and you can get Laurine to trim it. She has the prettiest way in the world of gumming down green leaves and flowers in all manner of patterns upon book-muslin. I recommend her as a workwoman. I assure you whenever there is a ball in Port Spain she is sent for expressly to help make the ladies' dresses; and through her taste your daughters will look beautiful."

"Or," observed another, "you can trim the muslin as the lady of our good Governor Chacon once did, — quilt it all over with fireflies within the squares."[†]

"*Sí, sí,* I remember my mother talking of that," interrupted the first speaker; "when the Señora sat down to converse the fireflies fell asleep and their lamps went out, so the dress looked as if spotted all over with black; but when the Señora but moved, or danced, or shook her dress, it was something to see the thousands of living diamonds which sparkled all over her dress: it was a clever device. Why don't you do the same, *caramba?*"[†]

"Because," replied the complaining lady, "this is crop-time, don't you know? and I have no spare hands to catch all the necessary flies."

"Well then," resumed the other, "I daresay I can lend you something, for my daughter is laid up, — she can't appear for many a day. Poor thing! her complexion is so fair and tender, like a *niña Inglesa.*[†] Just think, *mira!*[†] she sat at a window overlooking a cottage with a slated roof; the sun was shining on this roof, — mind, not on the window at which she sat, — and the glare of the roof caught her face, and the skin has actually peeled off like a mask. Ave Maria! but she is careless, the fair little creature. We brunettes don't suffer so much, you see; we are not like the fresh European ladies — obliged to shut ourselves up in dark rooms during the noon-tide heat, or to wear masks like some of those *Inglesas* when they only just put their nose out in the morning."

"That reminds me," observed Maria, a young lady with some pretensions to good looks, "I had better put on my gloves: I have let my hands grow so coarse and brown lately that I am ashamed of them, and just because it was too hot to cover them. I think my gloves must be in my bag;" and diving into the profundities of a black silk affair which hung from her arm, and which also contained her missal and pocket-handkerchief, she withdrew the gloves, and commenced pulling them on. The operation however was quickly cut short. "*Santos mios!*"[†] she screamed, as she convulsively capered about, and made efforts to pull off her glove, while a very respectable centipede, five inches long, crept from within the warm cavities of the glove, and coolly made its way up her arm.

And now behold the pocket-handkerchiefs, books, bags, parasols, sticks, all flourishing about in every direction! and, kindly belabouring the invaded arm, they soon brought down the intruder and put him for ever out of all pain and pleasure of this world. But it had set the company nervous. One fancied she felt a deadly scorpion down her back; another thought she felt a black spider on her knee, and under her arm she was sure there was something creeping, and without another word off she tore her sleeve and grasped at the offender, which proved this time to be nothing but a string, — a harmless bit of tape left to hang unused.

In the course of a few minutes tranquillity was restored, the ladies' nerves grew calm, and the conversation was resumed this time with many a tale of like rencontres: how one gentleman got bitten by a tarantula, and died two hours afterwards; how a friend's Negro was killed with a bite from a coral-snake; how a lady went to bed and found it occupied by a brood of boa-constrictors; and then one of the company laughed, and told how another had gone to mass with the edge of her bonnet presenting one continued fringe of long disgusting black millepedes; and audible symptoms of merriment were still going the round when a new comer came in sight, and brought back all their wandering thoughts to the point whence they started.

"*Bargame Dios!*" they one and all exclaimed, "there's Mr. Hinde; who would have thought to see him here? It must be that the Governor is coming."

"Do you know Madame Hinde?" inquired Doña Juana: "she is a fine woman, with such an excellent heart! Have you heard how she went to the sick stranger who was left ashore, they say, in the town of Port Spain, dying in a miserable room? Well, she took him to her house, had a doctor and a nurse, and tended him herself till he recovered: there's a good heart for you! And has she not a spirit too? Does she not manage her Negroes? *Caramba!* they are not impudent, I warrant you, in spite of all those horrid Orders in Council;[†] I tell you they jump and waltz about if she but holds up her little finger. Now there is her man-cook Achilles. *Ahí*, Señoras![†] the last time I was in Port Spain I saw her flogging that man herself with a cowskin[†] in the open yard: there's for you!"

"That must be some time ago," said the young Maria, "for town servants may not be flogged now, since that Order in Council."

"*Sencilla!*"[†] exclaimed Doña Juana, looking pitifully at her companion, "do you think Madame Hinde is to be baulked by Ministers or their servants? Not she! That man Achilles had the impudence to go out gossiping in the middle of cooking the dinner: that's what those Orders in Council bring, teaching the Negroes to rebel. Well, Señoras, Madame Hinde saw what was going on, and she waited. She expected seven guests that day, to whom she sent an apology, and a request for postponement of their visit; meantime the dinner-hour came, the bell was rung, and Achilles sends up the dishes raw, Señoras. So Madame Hinde calls up Achilles, — he had just eaten his own dinner, — and there she seats him and makes him eat up the whole dinner for seven, every bit, raw and burnt. In vain Achilles begged and prayed: there she was at his elbow, and he knew that if he but showed sign of resistance he would be sent off that instant to the estate, where of course his mistress could do anything she liked with him. Achilles, Señoras, was laid up ill for a week afterwards, and they were obliged to have a doctor to him; but I promise you it was a lesson: he won't forget that he is not to mind English Orders in Council more than his mistress."

"Bravo!" cried the company, "I like that. How different she is to her sister Angélique, Madame St. Hilaire Cardon! she is a fool, and a martyr to her servants."

"Ah, don't talk! I tell you she is broken-hearted since the death of her son."

"Poor thing! poor thing!" cried the commiserating ladies, "it is all the English people's doings, God help us! I hear all the Colonists say it is the way with them wherever they plant their sway. It is well for us we have such a man as St. Hilaire Cardon[†] himself; he is here, by the bye, — I saw him this morning."

"Indeed!" cried Maria, delighted, "then of course it is the Governor that is coming."

"*Sencilla, qué locura es esto!*"[†] snapped Doña Juana, "don't you know they don't speak? Don't you know the Governor is afraid of him, — that St. Hilaire is his sworn enemy, — that he writes in the newspapers against him and the Government? In short, he is the lash that keeps them all in order, those tyrants — *demonios*;[†] and he is the bravest, the cleverest, the richest, and most respected man in the Colony. You should see him as I have seen him when travelling on the high road: off goes every man's hat as he passes, his Lordship the Bishop's as well as the meanest Mulatto's. They could not do more to the Governor, and the Governor himself is afraid of him!"

Maria replied tartly that she had seen that doughty hero with an Englishman that morning, and she, for her part, did not like either Frenchmen or Englishmen: the Frenchmen were *traidores todos,*[†] and the Englishmen were *borrachones todos.*[†]

"Who says Englishmen are *borrachones todos?*" said a gruff voice behind them.

The suddenness of the question caused the ladies to start; some of them called out "Ave Maria!" then crossed their hands upon their bosoms and gasped; others elevated their voices to an angry pitch, and frowningly cried out, "Who is that?" but in another second they had all gathered round the speaker, with questions innumerable.

"Don Duro!" "Don Duro Harding!" "You too?" "Why all the world is coming here nowadays!" "What is the matter? What is going to be done in our little village?" "Is there a gold-mine discovered, and who discovered it, and whose is it?" "Or is the Governor coming? When will he come? Will he be here today? Will he stay long? Will he give a dance?"

To all this volley of interrogatories Don Duro made no reply: how could he, indeed, when he was not given time? He only thrust his hands into his pockets, and looked profound.

He was a dark little thin man, half Spaniard, half English, that is, his father was an Englishman and his mother a Spaniard, and he had all the long-headedness and reserve of the former mingled with the deep passion of the latter; but he knew how to dissemble at all times, and he owned a good place as manager of the Palm Grove,[†] then belonging to St. Hilaire Cardon.

"Come now," said the ladies, "you can tell us if you like; there must be something, or you would not have left the estate to come here today; now say, *de verdad, palabra de honor*,[†] what is it all about? What has brought Mr. Cardon down here? — at least you can tell us that."

"To look about him and see this part of the island, to be sure."

"Then what is that Englishman with him for?"

"Why, don't you know it is to show that new comer this part of the island that Mr. Cardon has accompanied him? Probably they will go all round the island; he is his friend, and may be his partner."

"*Bargame Dios!* but now I know why you took part with the English. *Hombre*,[†] you ought to be more attached to your mother's nation."

Don Duro turned his eyes upon the speaker with the slightest possible sign of displeasure.

But without noticing the look, or caring one straw, the lady took up the interrogatories with renewed vigour.

"Then what is Mr. Joseph Hinde here for?"

"He is come to visit his friends hereabouts."

"Well then, Don Juan Faxardo — he has no friends here — what is he come for?"

"Well, I will tell you: he wants to lay out some money in land; they say he can get land here cheap and productive."

"Hem!" said the ladies, "well then, what brings Don Lopez Mendoza?"

"Ask him," said Don Duro impatiently; "they are all most likely of the same party, and probably will go on board the same little vessel which will touch here today, and they may coast round the island in it."

"Oh," said the ladies, rather chap-fallen, "so there is no gold-mine after all, nor no Governor coming!"

"I shall go and ask Mr. Cardon myself," said Doña Juana, drawing herself up proudly after a moment's pause, "I can ask him anything I like. I knew him when his son was that high," she said, holding her hand some feet from the ground; "I knew the boy when he was sent to France for his education."

"*Ahí!*" interrupted Maria, "my father saw him there with his little valet behind, and, *bargame Dios!* I declare he said that there was so little difference between the two!"

"Listen to that! listen to that!" exclaimed Doña Juana, almost dancing with virtuous indignation; "Santa Maria! and are things come to this, that comparisons are drawn between master and slave? And even resemblances spoken of! Do you not know, for the matter of that, Niña Maria, that all men resemble one another in having legs, and arms, and noses, and mouths, and so on? but are we for that to be comparing Mulattoes with white men? Jesus Maria! but the world must be coming to an end. I never heard such things, — did you, Don Duro?"

To which the latter responded with a whistle long and clear, looking the while steadfastly anther way.

"I but hazarded the remark," urged Maria, quite conscience-stricken, "I meant no harm."

"*Sí, Señora,* but things should be said cautiously when the roads are full of Negroes, and one of them may be at this moment at your elbow, listening to your mad words, — sucking in ideas of rebellion thereby. Is it not enough to have the English *demonios* meddling with us, without our own young *locas* (madcaps) turning against us? Ask Don Duro there."

"*Muy de verdad, Señora,*"† observed the Manager, "sapiently, most truly spoken, a dangerous thing such speeches indeed!"

"And if we begin teaching Mulattoes to compare themselves to us, it is as much as to teach them to consider themselves equal to us," spoke the lady, with increasing warmth.

"My dear Doña Juana, consider — "

"Particularly in this case, where the Mulatto has turned out the most abominable *demonio, a vagamundo!*"†

"Doña Juana!" entreated the offender.

"A vile Mulatto, who showed so little gratitude to his dear young master as to run away from him in France too, leaving him without a valet, and, when the dear young man was dying, never to come back to receive pardon, but to keep like a wild beast in the woods, where every one knows he is at this moment! If I was Mr. Cardon, I would have the island scoured, I would! And I will tell him so, for I can say anything I like to him."

"Really," said the younger lady pettishly, "one can't say a word, I'm sure."

At this moment the party had reached the central part of the hamlet: they had loitered long, and the dews were too heavy to remain out, they separated therefore, some to go into their own homes, others to join more gossips, in order to discuss the all-absorbing subject of their curiosity, though with what success we shall not pretend to say just now. We must only crave permission to pass over that night, and lead our readers to the opening of that day on which most of the individuals here spoken of will begin gradually to figure.

CHAPTER II.

Lovers' Quarrel

The dawn was rising over the heights of Trinidad, and, in a sky fair and serene as that which spanned the valleys of Paradise, a few stray stars of the south were seen to sparkle brightly, even while yet the tints of Aurora were fading delicately and more delicately away before the morning breeze, which now arose soft, cool, and lusciously fragrant. The landscape, at this early hour, was still as though wrapped in sleep; the mountains were veiled in mist, through whose broken tissue occasionally shone the green of a highland midground, while the blue of more distant scenes, catching a reflection from the rosy dawn above, appeared to melt into the faintest lilac. As the light increased and the atmosphere warmed, the white vapours, which had rested so still over the ancient forests, now faded from the view, and the broad summits of the highland ridges appeared capped with lustrous gold, from which long streaks of rich colouring began to glide, softly though perceptibly, down to the highest points of the valleys beneath, where the barbs of the tall cocoa-nut glanced green and silvery, or where clusters of orange, tamarind,[†] and coral[†] mingled their tints with the bignonia[†] and locust.[†]

The scenery was richly tropical. Plantations of colonial produce chequered the view on all sides; young groves of cinnamon[†] on the heights, dark green fields of indigo[†] in the hollows; pleasant slopes, here reddened with the berries of the coffee, there white with snowy flakes bursting from the nuts of the cotton,[†] while yonder, gracefully winding round the base of the hills, might be traced the gorgeous coral-tree which shelters the tender chocolate-bush,[†] while in the plains vast sweeps of cane,[†] now bursting into bloom, shone in the slanting ray like sheets of waving gold shot over with silver and purple.

In front of these, and on the sea-shore, was a small hamlet, which we shall call Sant' Iago.[†] It was still quiet; not a soul was stirring, save in one cottage situated on the wharf, where, through the open shutters of its little front room, the inmates were seen moving backwards and forwards in a very busy manner. One, with broom in hand, seemed occupied in sweeping, while the other, after various arrangements, set a tray upon her head and tripped along to a neighbouring enclose, with that gay elastic step which tells of youth, innocence, and a happy mind. To hear her warbling in there among the flowers — for it was a garden she had entered — was like music of the birds, her voice was so clear, sweet, and silvery. Evidently the individual she sang to, dwelt somewhere in that huge forest-clad mountain which rose at a little distance to the back of the hamlet; for as the young girl returned from the garden with her tray all laden with flowers, her eyes often wandered in that direction, not with sadness however, but with a hopeful, joyous, trustful look of affection. View her near, you will find that she is a simple girl of caste, that is, one of those despised race of beings who bear in slave countries the appellation of Mulattoes. Nevertheless she has attractions of no mean description. Her eyes are large, dark, and lustrous, her hair silky, black, and wavy, and her small round nose and pouting mouth are by no means unpleasantly turned, particularly when moved by a soft dimpling smile, rich in its own innocent sweetness. Then her costume is such as greatly to enhance her southern beauty. A bright Madras shawl[†] twisted fantastically round her head, another thrown modestly over her shoulders, and a chintz skirt gathered in ample folds about the waist, so as to fall rather short in front, but let to sweep the ground behind, completed her costume, — the same which was adopted by all women of caste after they were prohibited by law the use of bonnet, shoes, stockings, long sleeves, or bodied skirt.[†] The white ladies of course affected to despise it as a garb of degradation, but the truth is, it far surpassed their own stiff fashions in graceful and picturesque arrangement. But Laurine was not only pretty, she was also naturally gifted: everything she touched bore the marks of ingenuity, from the embroidered pockets and plaited sleeves of her holiday costume, to the crisping and fashioning of the cakes[†] she sold. She was unquestionably the most graceful dancer in the whole island; and there are many yet living who remember the songs of Laurine's composing, and the inimitable sweetness with which she warbled the wild melodies of the Negroes. Yet she seldom joined the dance, was seldom seen with companions of her own age, and, although scarcely seventeen, she had the reputation of being a miser: at least she was censured for it by the uncharitable gossips of the neighbourhood, because the love of gain is so stigmatized by the Negroes, whose simple generous natures can never tolerate such a vice. Just look at her now, how busily she adjusts her flowers, forming them into bouquets! there is reseda and roses, pinks and myrtle, sweetbriar and English daisies,[†] with every other flower considered rare within the tropics; and there she goes now to arrange the blooming fruit and hot crisped cakes which an aged woman has brought in from some out-door place, probably one of those brick ovens of simple construction which are often seen attached to the buildings of a West Indian domicile.

"La Catalina," said the young girl, addressing herself to her companion, and using the Martinique patois,[†] which is spoken in all the Colonies, — a sort of mixture of French, Spanish, and Indian, — "I really think I am doing well; I have been reckoning my hoard, and I find I have nearly completed half the sum, — what do you think of that? Five hundred piastres is what the law binds me to: let me but offer that sum and Master Cardon can't refuse my mother's freedom! and so now I have only two hundred and fifty more piastres to make, and my mother is free. Thank God! Oh, Catalina, how happy I shall be to take her home to my little hut, wherever I have it, and to take care of her myself!"

"One, two, three reals,[†] these mangoes will fetch," murmured the other, who was a walking arithmetical table, — "five reals of rose-apples,[†] two of balatas,[†] and seven of sappodillas."[†]

The young girl did not seem to heed her reckoning, — she had already satisfied herself about the profits of all, and busying herself among her flowers, she continued to form them into bouquets, as she spoke aloud her thoughts.

"Yes, and when I brought my little offering of flowers to the altar of our chapel last evening, Padre Martino met me by the way. 'Ah, Laurine,' he said, 'this is all very well, but I fear you are what people say.' What is that, good Father? I asked. — 'Nothing but a little miser, my child;' and so I just whispered into the padre's ear what my motive was, and then the good priest blessed me, and bade me go on and prosper. Oh, now I am sure I shall succeed," and, with the same breath, she broke out into a little song of her own composing.[†]

Bis {
    And oft do I watch the gold-bird fly,
And, listening, catch its wild melody;
But never, sweet bird, would I prison thee;
Oh no, little bird, I love liberty!
So all the day long do I live merrily,
    Sing merrily, merrily, sing merrily,
    Oh! sing merrily, sing merrily.

Bis {
    And I love to look at the forest tree,
Where it stands afar in its majesty;
For I know that its boughs are the haunts of the free,
And it gives them a home for their sweet liberty;
So all the day long do I sing merrily,
    So merrily, merrily, sing merrily,
    Oh! sing merrily, sing merrily.

Bis {
And oft, on a fair and a sunshiny day,
To the wide savanas I roam far away,
To be with the birds and to feel I am free,
For this is my bliss, and the song of my glee;
And all the day long do I sing merrily,
So merrily, merrily, sing merrily,
Oh! sing merrily, sing merrily.

She had hardly finished these words, when she became aware of the presence of a third person, and she started as she recognized a young Mulatto, who, with his arms resting on the window-ledge, stood gazing in at her with intense admiration and delight. Smiling at her surprise, he entered the cottage, and, seating himself at once, he prepared himself to listen to the chiding of the damsel.

"Belfond! you here?" she exclaimed, with reproving eyes, — "in broad day, — the place full of white people! — your master himself here too! Oh, Belfond, what madness! you can have no real love for me, if you act so rashly; you must begone, indeed you must."

"Never fear," replied the youth, still speaking the patois of the Colony, but in terms so finely modulated and with such choice of expressions as to betray a romantic mind refined by a European education, — "don't be alarmed, Laurine, the white men are not abroad yet. But you say true," he said, assuming a more serious tone, "I must be on my guard, for what am I but a runaway — an outcast — an outlaw? suspected as a rebel — watched as a thief. Yes, I know they are on the look-out for me."

"Then why did you come? It is so rash!"

"I know it is; and I have braved all danger, Laurine, to come and plead my cause with you this morning."

"Hush!" said the young girl, holding up her finger as a warning, "don't you know you are never to speak of that till my mother is free; and oh, Belfond, La Catalina will tell you we have reckoned up just half the sum!" and as she spoke, her sweet face brightened as with the joy of a little child.

Belfond shook his head. "It will never do, Laurine; it will take too long to make up that other half, and the promised time will never come for me if you delay our union longer. It's of no use, I can't keep away from you, Laurine; I hover round this village day and night like one crazed. I shall be caught at last, I know. But come, Laurine, pack up your things, put up your money, and come; there is a good priest down yonder who will bind us together directly, without asking any questions, so do come, Laurine! It is such stuff, doing righteous where there is no righteousness recognized. I tell you we shall have a shorter, better way of making your mother free. You and I and La Catalina will pick her up our way, and we shall be as happy as kings."

Taken by surprise, Laurine opened wide her beautiful eyes, and fixed them on Belfond. "And where shall we live?" she asked, — "not in the trunk of a tree?"

"No, my bright star," said the youth, insinuatingly putting his arm about her, "I have a prettier place for you than the trunk of an old tree. Look out at the back there; do you see that mountain? Its forests look thick, don't they? Yet there, on the top, where no white man's foot has ever trod, I have cleared a space and built you an ajoupa,[†] Laurine, which the Governor's lady might envy." Laurine looked wonderingly in his face, as he continued, "I don't say it is covered with gold or lined with silver, but I think it is prettier. The roof is thatched with the leaves of our own forest palm,[†] the walls and doorway of cocoa-nut basket-work,[†] and the windows are trellised with liana[†] fibres, fine as lace, to keep out the vampires[†] and all ugly flies while you are asleep. Then it has its trees and its garden, — a large spreading tamarind on one side, beneath which you may sit in the evening, and sing to me some of your own pretty songs, and on the other side there is an ancient cotton-tree,[†] quite bare of its natural leaves, but covered all over with those fly-mocking flowers[†] which you are so fond of — it is quite a hanging-garden; then within the lowest fork is a large tuft of the fairy-fringe,[†] with its silvery and silky hairs all tipped with pink, and higher up is the blue-winged blossom[†] which hangs its garlands even to the ground, and hundreds of others that you will rejoice in. Wherever I found a pretty plant, I brought it there to adorn the place for you, from the large changeable rose[†] to the great cactus[†] and the modest little *four-o'clock,*[†] which will tell you the hour of the day."

Laurine stood entranced, and with a smile playing about her open lips, which gave fresh enthusiasm to her lover.

"And for provisions, Laurine, we have such abundance of them! you should just see our fields of maize[†] and purple cassava,[†] hedged all round with bushes of the Angola pea,[†] or wild fences overgrown with the climbing koosh-koosh[†] and sweet potato,[†] and all in bloom already; so that they will be ready for the game I shall bring home from the chase, before another moon comes round: meantime we have stores and stores of plantain[†] and cassava-bread[†] —"

"Who are *we*?" asked the young girl, turning round.

"Oh, did not I tell you? Why, there are about thirty brave fellows like myself, all enemies to slavery, who have settled with their wives up there, and built them green huts all round about yours, so that you shall live among them like a little queen."

"Oh, but," objected Laurine, "those terrible dark woods without any paths: suppose you were to lose yourself some of these days while at the chase, and never come home?"

"Oh, bah! no! — no fear of that! we foresters, we want no beaten track, we make paths for ourselves; we cut notches in the trees as we go, and mark them."

"But suppose you lost your hatchet, Belfond?"

"Well now, Laurine, suppose I did lose my hatchet; there are other signs for us, and he must be a stupid fellow who does not know that the roughest tree shows a smooth side to the south, and shape his course accordingly."

"Oh, but the bush-rangers,[†] — the bush-rangers!" cried Laurine, with a look of alarm.

"The bush-rangers! pah! let them come, we can give them a reception; but they won't come near us — we know how to detect them miles off; trust me for noting where the dried leaves are flattened by the tread; where the festooning liana has been snapped; where the overhanging branches have been roughly handled! Trust me too for hearing sounds at any distance; and when I put my ear to the ground, I can tell, even in the valleys below us, the creaking of a white man's shoe from the treacherous approach of a naked foot. It is only a little pleasant excitement for us. Oh, but a mountain life is a glorious thing! Come, Laurine; now, Laurine, make up your mind to make me happy at once."

La Catalina, who had been roused by the eager words of the young man, had gradually come round to where he was, and stood listening with all her might.

"And you too," continued the young man, looking at her, "you must come now at once, we can't do without you. It is such a busy, merry life up there! What do you suppose the women are doing now? why gathering up and melting down the fat of an aboma[†] we killed last night: the fat is for lamps, and they have already laid in a good store of wax of the wild bees for candles, so that we shan't want for light; then we have cut down heaps of the beebeewood[†] for tinder, and oh, such a pile of lianas, for twisting into ropes! Yesterday we felled a royal palm,[†] and the day's work for the women was to gather the sap to ferment for wine, to collect salt from the ashes, to make brooms from the leaves and matting with the bark, and by-and-by, when the vonvon beetle[†] has laid its grubs in the pith, our women will melt them and clarify them for butter. Always something pleasant to do! it is so delicious to do without white people! Say, Laurine, is it not charming? You yourself will be inventing some new plan every day: come, do come, Laurine, my angel, my bird, my star!"

"Indeed, my child," slowly put in La Catalina, "when the fruit is sold, I think we may go; there is one, two, three, four dozens —"

This passing allusion to the shop sent all those fine dreams vanishing into air, and brought Laurine back directly to her senses. She started: "Oh, Belfond! Oh, La Catalina! what a foolish girl I have been! Don't you know, Belfond, what a wicked thing it would be of me to make my mother a runaway?"

"What!" ejaculated the young man with surprise.

"Oh," replied the young girl, "don't think it: I am not finding fault with you, — indeed, indeed not; I daresay you were excusable in leaving your master; you have much to excuse you, I know. You had been in the white man's country, and you couldn't work again like a slave: yes, I understand that; still —"

"Still you think I am wrong?"

"No, I don't say that; at least I don't clearly know; at least my mother is different, and if she ran away to come with us, it would be stealing, you know — a horrible theft!" and in saying this, Laurine spoke from sincere conviction; for, in slave countries, it is not by law only that the fugitive slave is punished, but contempt and horror are everywhere inculcated by the white people against the culprit.

"Yes," continued Laurine, "stealing herself from her master is very wicked; Padre Martino told me so, and everybody says so, — it would be a great disgrace."

The young man threw back his head, and laughed long and loud, — so loud that Laurine, alarmed for his security, significantly imposed silence, and looked out at the door to see that there was no danger in the way; then, with an expression earnest and imploring, she entreated him not to treat the matter with levity, but to have patience a little, till she had earned the price of her mother's freedom fairly and honestly, as the law permitted.

"Well," said the young man, assuming his former gravity, "I had some misgivings about your scruples, and I have come prepared even for that; saying which, he unfastened the leathern belt which confined his waist, and he drew forth a large blue bag, which he placed jingling on the table: "There!" he exclaimed with an air of triumph.

Laurine looked in his face, not with her wonted simplicity, but with a keen searching eye, that went inquiring into his very soul.

La Catalina leaned her elbows upon the table, and bent over the bag, longing to reckon its contents, while Belfond still grasped the neck tight in his hand, in order to hold it upright for the inspection of both. "There!" he said, looking steadfastly at the bag, to avoid her eye, and pounding it down upon the table with emphasis, "there is enough money to buy twenty mothers; take it — take what you want, and buy your mother now — this day — this very hour — this minute, Laurine, if you don't wish to drive me mad."

Laurine placed her hand gently upon his shoulders, and gazed up intently into his eyes. "Where did you get it, Belfond?" she asked.

"Get it? Ha, ha, ha! get it? If you knew how I got it! so cleverly, Laurine! it was my master's last night — it is mine this morning."

"Only say you did not steal it," she said, her fingers grasping convulsively the arm she had touched.

"Well, what if I did? You know I am a slave," he said bitterly, "no good is expected of me, surely: what right have I to be honest? I only stole it from the man who would use the strength, the labour, the blood of his eldest child, to turn them to gold for his younger ones, — who would make a cowardly slave of his brown son, creeping and crawling before his fair son. You would not have me treat that man honestly, would you?"

"Belfond, dear Belfond," said Laurine, "it is not for us to judge others, or to be good only when we see others good; and other people's wickedness is no excuse for ours. Dear Belfond, I can't reason like you, but I know those little things, and this is stolen money, dearest, and I could not touch it, it would never prosper. Do take it back, put it where you found it, and let us be honest; be sure God will help us in another way."

The impetuous young man rose up, and indignant at the suggestion, "What! and are we to lie down like worms, and meanly say 'thank you' for all they rob us of — for what they do to us? Why, child, that money ought to be mine, and mine it shall be, were it only in payment of the long weary years of service I have given him. Why, look you here" (and he drew the maiden to the door), "do you see yonder, on the horizon, where the sun is just peeping from its couch in the sea, leaving behind it a part of its own brightness? Look well, you will see a spot darkening the light, — it may well be dark — it's a slave-ship. It is to meet it, and to bargain in the human cattle it brings, that so many white gentlemen are come down to this quiet place. The slave-trade is forbidden by law, and the creatures it brings are contraband goods; yet what matter? white men can always evade the law, for they protect and shelter one another. Suppose any coloured man were to inform against them, do you think he would be listened to? How would he be treated? Kicked out of the tribunal, I tell you, flogged — perhaps killed. Every one of those poor wretches in that ship has a home in Africa, and little ones many of them have left behind; but they are black, and of course it does not matter. Oh, Laurine, you are not safe, — even you! I know from good sources that the manager of the Palm Grove has been looking over the registry,[†] and is questioning your right to be free and if once they imagine to deprive you of the blessing of freedom, who can stand against them? What will you do then? Do you know, Laurine, what it is to be a slave? Have you ever thought of all you would be exposed to? Ah! even I, passionately as I worship you now, I should hate you, if once you were a slave. Why should I waste my precious affections upon the slave of another man? Cursed would be the day for you and for me which should see you a slave. See, Laurine," and he threw himself on his knees before her, "by the worship you give at the holy shrine of the Virgin, the protectress of maidens, Laurine, I conjure you keep me from crime, for I cannot answer for myself; don't condemn me any longer to the torture of seeing you, day after day, the standing butt of every white villain's jests, — I cannot punish their insolence. Say you will come; say so now," and he drew the young girl's hand passionately to his breast.

Laurine was weeping; her tears fell one after the other heavily down, — not indeed for the ills which her lover foretold to herself, but for the pain her conscience required her to inflict upon him.

"Belfond, don't ask me to do what is wrong," she sobbed; "I could not make a runaway of my mother; I could not use stolen money. God bless you, Belfond! The Holy Virgin protect us! but let us be honest."

He did not wait to hear more, but, dashing away the hand he was holding, he rose quickly and proudly to his feet, and as he seized his rejected present, his lips all blue and quivering with suppressed passion, — "That is not it, Laurine," he said, with a sarcastic, demoniac expression of his mouth, "but you love the white people, — you love to sell to them — you love to listen to their insulting jests — you prefer them to me, a poor hunted slave; farewell!" and ere the last word was uttered, he was already in the street.

La Catalina, in surprise, hurried to the door to look after him; she could not understand what was the matter all so suddenly; and Laurine flew to her room, where, throwing herself on her little tressel-bed,[†] she gave way to an agony of tears. This was the first quarrel she had ever had with her lover, and it was a serious one; not that his late robbery had at all altered her opinion; she had long known him to be, though scrupulously honest towards his own race, yet somewhat lax in his ideas of right and wrong towards the white people. But, like many a nobler damsel, his errors only attached her the more to him, and she fondly hoped that by her sole influence she might yet lead him back to what was right. "No matter," she said, as she endeavoured to comfort herself, "he will think better of all this by-and-by, and love me all the more for it. He is so hot! but when the fit is over, he will reflect upon it, and in his own good heart I shall find love greater than ever."

CHAPTER III.

Laurine

A word concerning this interesting girl. The picture is not overdrawn: to that quick sensibility and warmth of feeling which is common with those of their caste, she added a strong attachment to duty, or principle, such as she understood it to be. She was strictly just in all her dealings, and while her pleasant manner attracted customers from every quarter, she was never known to charge unfairly to either white or black.

It may be asked how it happened that the child of a poor slave had found money enough to set up a shop; or, further, as the children of slaves always follow the fortune of their mothers, how it happened that she was free. Something of her history will explain all this.

She was born on the Palm Grove estate, — not when it belonged to Mr. Cardon, for his possession was comparatively recent, but in the time of its first owner, Mr. Perrin. There were a great many children of caste born on this estate much about the same time, and, as they all bore a great resemblance to one another, scandal assigned them to one and the same father, even to the master himself; but as this has little to do with the tale in question, we shall pass it over, and proceed. Among all these children Laurine was considered to be the prettiest and the most engaging, and therefore was she chosen to play with and attend upon her mistress's only child, a sweet little girl of four or five years old. From Laurine's earliest childhood the characteristic feature of her disposition was that of devotion. Long before she knew what piety was, she reverenced authority in every form, and her heart was filled with affection for those who ministered to her kindly. Nothing could exceed her love for the little girl whom she was taught to call her mistress: she anticipated every wish the child could form, dispelled every gloom, made peace where there was crossness, and created interest out of the very spirit of dulness. Of course the little child became used to her, as they say; and when at a subsequent period it was decided to sell off the children that had been grown (for Mr. Perrin made a great deal of money by raising human crops), and Laurine was put down among the number to be sent away, little Eleanor Perrin filled the house with such loud and continued lamentations that their father was forced, for the sake of peace, to make the little slave an exception, and keep her as perpetual playfellow to his white child. This was not lost on Laurine, and her affection to her little mistress became greater than ever. Some time after, little Eleanor took ill of one of those terrible disorders common in the tropics; and now was Laurine's devotion appreciated. She attended upon her night and day — knew no fatigue of body or mind — was at the pillow at the slightest movement — made the room cheerful and pleasant as it was quiet and orderly, and if she ever left it for a moment it was only when her mistress watched the patient's sleep, and then she brought in the prettiest bouquets the garden could afford. But all the care in the world could not avail; the doctors were forced to acknowledge the uselessness of medicine, and the little life, which had so often given joy to the household, was now seen to ebb slowly and gradually away. In one of those lucid intervals which immediately precede death, little Eleanor fixed her eyes steadily upon her young slave. She did not thank her, she did not express affection, for she was never taught to think that either the one or the other was to be felt, but simply whispered a wish that Laurine should be freed. The little slave of course did not expect that this desire would be complied with, and when her dear little lady was gone, whom she was accustomed to care for and to love, she mourned for her alone, — not for remaining still a slave, for she never dreamed that it could be otherwise. By-and-by her master died also, and Laurine was left alone with her mistress; but the latter had never completely recovered from her little girl's death, and after the last misfortune she took to her bed, from which she never got up again. One day she called the young girl to her: "Laurine," said she, "I am going to my long home, and I wish to say a word to you. You have been faithful to me and to my child who is gone before me, and I could not meet her in the other world unless I had complied with her dying wish; for this reason I have left you free in my will. I don't know whether it is for your good, — I am afraid not, for no one will take care of you like a mistress; but as you have been a faithful slave, so I hope you will be a faithful freedwoman; and may God bless you! Pray for me fervently when I am gone."

The will was perfectly good, though if it had been otherwise, the heirs of the estate being people living in Europe, it was the interest of no one near to contest it, and so Laurine received the announcement of her freedom. She was thirteen when this happened. She had lost a kind mistress and a home, but she had gained that which gave her new life, new spirit, new thoughts, new powers, and self-respect. She felt like a bird escaped from a cage, not knowing what to do with herself, but bewildered with the joy. The world was all before her, with its strange vastness, with its toils and its dangers, its troubles and trials; but of these she knew little and cared less, she only felt to breathe more freely, and she knew she had none to obey, none to fear, none to flatter; and in her wayward fancy the first use she made of her liberty was to go off early in the morning to the woods, where she remained the whole day gathering flowers, picking berries, and watching the birds. As she often said afterwards, it was the happiest time of her life, and she would probably have settled down into an idle stroller, but her warm, loving heart stimulated her to exertion.

This is how it happened. As soon as her mistress was dead and the will made known, the estate was put up for sale by order of the heirs in Europe, and Mr. Cardon became the purchaser. Laurine was immediately turned off the estate by the manager, in company with a few more encumbrances, in particular an old man of the Koromantyn nation,[†] of whom we shall afterwards speak. Not that the young girl cared for being sent off: the forest abounded in fruit, of which she was fond; and for shelter she would contrive to steal into her mother's hut at night, when the white people had all retired to rest; and she cared for nothing else. But Laurine's heart had been accustomed to hold an object of love, her thoughts to own a point of concentration, and the void she now felt in both became painful to her. She had never inquired for her father, — no child of caste ever does, for, beyond the lighter complexion, which secretly but surely involves the grafting of European intellect on the warm strong feelings of Africa, it never is of any consequence from whom the Mulatto springs; and although such a slave points disgrace on the unnatural master who first sold him, and his unfeeling accomplice the master who holds him, yet no observation is ever made either by white man or black, for custom has sanctioned the sin. Laurine therefore never knew who was her father, nor ever asked; but of her mother she did think: she remembered the passionate love her mistress had borne for the child who was gone, and she longed to become, even she, the object of as much solicitude and affection. Now the Negro women are either passionately fond of their children, or they are hopelessly indifferent to them, and it was to the latter class that Laurine's mother belonged: she only looked coldly and vacantly upon the little girl as she came in and out, and admitted her to her cabin only as she admitted the cat, without care or notice, not even so much as to ask whether the child was hungry, or where she had been during the day. The slave had fallen to the condition of a brute; her maternal instinct, if indeed such had ever existed with her, had vanished with the calls of the infant, and she had come to look upon her offspring as an alien with whom she had nothing to do.

Thus Laurine, as yet a mere child, found herself all at once without a creature to belong to, to care for, or to love; all her little romance of affection had fled. Never did she look up to the white people with such admiration and respect; never did she consider the African race with such a sense of their low caste and hopeless inferiority. "If I was a white child," she would say to herself, "I should be loved, my mother would care for me; but then she is a Negro, and I am a desolate wretch," and with these reflections she often sobbed herself to sleep on the dry cocoanut leaves which she dragged in every night for a couch. But observing her mother more closely, she soon discovered that the Negro slave stood in more need of her child's aid, than the child of her mother's. Madelaine was one of those individuals in whom slavery had annihilated all power of thought, care, will, even self-preservation; she was by no means a rare instance, there were many like her even on the estate to which she belonged, and the late master had been obliged to think and act for these living automatons on the most trivial affairs. Listen to this all ye who advocate despotism! Listen to this, ye who argue the care of physical wants as that of supreme happiness, and see one of the effects of your system! He had to dole out their weekly rations meal by meal as to infants, — to attend to the daily covering of their bodies, — to watch over their cleanliness, and even to examine their persons, lest there should be some hidden sore, by which they would lazily allow themselves to be eaten up. Indeed every phase of slavery points a lesson to the wise of all people; and there are other nations besides the Negroes, who, if they but look, will see as in a mirror occasional reflections of their own condition. Madelaine, as a slave, knew nothing of sorrow; Laurine, free, became thoughtful and sad, and, though yet but a child, care sat heavily on her brow.

The estate being now transferred to Mr. Cardon, he placed Don Duro upon it as manager, and in the beginning, and before he came to know the peculiarities of each individual, he dealt out their weekly rations to each, *i.e.* two pounds of salt-fish† and two measures of cassava or tapioca;† and in naming this, it is as well we should be particular in explaining that each Negro had, besides this, a patch of ground, and one day in the week to cultivate it for himself.

One Monday evening, when Madelaine had received her portion at the muster-roll, and Laurine had stolen in as usual, the mother was eating the customary salt-fish quite raw, for she was too inert to set her pot boiling, or even to hold the cassava-flour† which accompanied it, without spilling the most of it on the ground. Poor Laurine was hungry, and she watched with eager eyes the wasted food, for she had been less fortunate that day in gathering wild fruit; but little did Madelaine care, and she saw her child stooping to pick up the rejected food with the indifference of a brute; and, in truth, Laurine was not long in discovering that her mother's was a hopeless case. Returning the next evening, she found her without anything to eat; she seemed indeed as if too lazy even to feel hunger, for, after picking up a few mangoes from under a tree, she lay down on her bed and shut her eyes to sleep. Laurine approached the bed: "Mother," she said, "have you had any dinner?" "Let me 'lone," was the cross reply. Laurine guessed she had not, so begging some plantains from a neighbouring hut, she put them on the fire, and in a little time she was able to produce some sort of a meal, which Madelaine took without offering a remark; and after having satisfied her appetite, she sat at the door of her hut to watch and laugh at any one who should happen to pass. Every day was a repetition of the last, till the next Monday, when rations were again given out, the same wastefulness was productive of the same want, and was met with the same apathy on the part of the brutified slave. At last Laurine began to wish for some other means of procuring food besides begging from the neighbours or wandering in the woods; she bethought herself of cultivating the little patch of ground which the custom of the Colonies had assigned to her mother, and though she worked mostly by moonlight, the neglected weed-covered ground soon became rich, and she was able to accompany the Negroes to the town market on Sundays, where it was usual for them to sell the produce of their gardens. The profits were so ample that she felt encouraged to continue, and, confiding the care of her mother to one of the slaves of the estate, she often took an odd turn in town, where she heard of work to do. In one of these journeys she was fortunate enough to meet with a pious, aged spinster, who took kindly to the little girl, and set her up with a small tray of needles and thread, etc., to sell; then she was pleased with her industry, and gradually helped her not only to support herself and mother, but to lay something by too.

It was not at once that Laurine conceived the idea of earning the freedom of her mother, — that idea suggested itself gradually. By a merciful dispensation of Providence, it is so ordained that the object we help becomes dear to us, and the more trouble we take, so also the greater love do we bestow. Laurine felt this; her automaton mother became dear to her exactly in proportion to her helplessness; she longed to be with her or to have a home for her. Then came confidential conversations with La Catalina, who informed her the law would protect her in the purchase of her mother's freedom if she could produce the legal amount, that is, five hundred piastres; and then followed an enthusiastic desire to obtain the boon, which for three years Laurine never once lost sight of. Such is her simple story, and such the motive of her persevering industry; and it was not mere labour she gave, it was the daily, hourly sacrifice of her own youthful, sociable inclinations, unpretendingly, unostentatiously, and almost unconsciously offered up on the shrine of filial affection.

CHAPTER IV.

Discomfiture

We left Laurine preparing for the business of the day. She had no sooner made herself ready than customers began rapidly to drop in, and in a few moments the little shop was crowded.

"Laurine, pearl of Sant' Iago, bring here a cup of mawbee[†] for a poor slave."

"Laurine, my humming-bird, some coffee for an old countryman."[†]

"O, Laurine, you help the sun to make the day bright; come, bless a friend with a look, and refresh him with a frothing cup of chocolate."[†]

These requests, gallantly worded in Negro patois,[†] soon however gave place to ruder and more peremptory commands, and the Negroes and coloured people, who are never permitted to eat or be seated in the presence of the higher race, fell back respectfully on the approach of their "superiors." Orders came in with such unusual rapidity, that Laurine, already agitated by the occurrences of the morning, now became almost distracted.

"La Catalina," she said, whispering anxiously to her companion, "I don't know what I am doing; pray come and help me. Santa Maria! there's Mr. Cardon and the Englishman and the manager, all coming in: may the Virgin help me! I am trembling all over."

La Catalina, always thoughtful and composed, readily left her department, — that of receiving the money and giving change, — to help her young friend, and, while the latter retired to her room to recover herself, came forward to serve the customers. The three gentlemen who had excited the alarm of Laurine now entered. The eldest was a tall, portly, handsome man, in the prime of life; the resolute expression of his eye, his imperious manner, and the overpowering loudness and volubility with which he spoke, indicated an arbitrary, irascible, and determined character. One of his companions, to judge from the freshness of his complexion, was a recent importation to the island; he was much younger, and appeared to be a man of unassuming and benevolent disposition. The other was of small stature, had a swarthy, Spanish face, and his manner showed what in Europe would be called utter ignorance of his place. The tallest gentleman entered first.

"Well, La Catalina, how do you do?"

The dame curtseyed.

"Where's Laurine?"

"She is busy inside, if you please, master, she can't come just yet."

The gentleman fired up. "What! you old baboon," he exclaimed, "do you think I shall be waited upon by you? Get back to your corner, and make way for the young one. I'll make her busy with me if she doesn't come quick. *Pardi!*[†] I am not going to have your wrinkled hands serving out coffee to me; just go and fetch her here at once, and make her bring me three cups of coffee all hot and frothing, do you hear?"

Poor Laurine was nervous enough already; but when she heard herself so roughly called for by the man whom above all others she disliked, she began to weep; though it was not so much the planter's overbearing manner, as the contemptuous familiarity with which he treated every coloured woman he approached, that caused our gentle maiden of Sant' Iago to tremble.

St. Hilaire Cardon sat down by one of the small tables in the shop, and waiting till his commands were obeyed, commenced drumming upon it as if his thoughts were busy and impatient. Don Duro, in the absence of anything better to do, threw himself into a chair, and with perfect *nonchalance* stretched out his legs like the open blades of a pair of scissors, and, with his head resting on the back of his chair, seemed to be making an attentive survey of the thatch. The European was the only one of the party who remained standing: he did so from choice, for there was an ample number of chairs and stools, but that position was more convenient for observing what was passing around him. "Strange!" thought he, as he looked at the Spaniard, "what odd customs prevail in these colonies, where a mere underling, a low ignorant servant like this, is allowed to sit down on equal terms with his master!"

"Dorset," said Mr. Cardon, suddenly stopping the movement of his fingers, "shall you buy any slaves this morning?"

"No," replied the other, "for, to say the truth, I cannot afford it. I have consented to go on board partly to gratify my curiosity, and partly because you say I may be of service to you in pointing out unhealthy subjects. But I assure you I am diffident of my own judgment: familiar as I may be with European forms of disease, the state of things here is new to me. I am afraid I shall only expose my ignorance."

"Bah!", said the other, "you know quite enough for me, — quite enough for the Colony: it is my belief the doctors who come out to practise were all of them only apothecary boys[†] in England, — nothing else, *parole d'honneur!*[†] Why, you are a treasure of learning here! Ask Doctor Pillstuff what his own name is in Latin, ha, ha! — and as to cures, what, as you say, can European doctors know of tropical diseases? the Indian women know more. Not that I would discourage you, not at all: I know you are a man of honour, and that is something in my eyes; it gives me confidence in what you say. I wish you would come and live on my estate, the Palm Grove, as a regularly engaged physician: I want you to find out the cause of a certain mortality among my Negroes."

"Not on the Palm Grove, my good Sir; I could not live away from my own place; but as my little property is next to yours, I can visit it every day if you like."

"Well, that will do: I forgot you lived so near: but you must do your best to find out what is the matter. I will give you the regular salary. *Sacre Dieu!*"[†] and the planter frowned and clinched his teeth, "I have had more losses this year than I can bear to think of: six Negroes died last week, and four the week previous; no man can stand this," and the angry planter rose, and in a fit of impatience kicked his chair to the other side of the shop; then stopping short, "Laurine," he called, "when are you coming with the coffee? do you want me to come after you? I will, if you don't make haste," he added, winking at the manager; then suddenly turning to another subject, "Dorset, so you won't buy any Negroes today because you have no money? It was my intention to offer you a loan, for it is a good cargo and the Negroes will go cheap; but, *parbleu!*[†] what do you think of this? I have not a dollar with me; I was actually obliged to borrow change from Don Duro here! I'll tell you what happened to me last night: all the money I took with me yesterday from town to pay Captain Hill cash down, all has disappeared! Some devil's dog got in while we were asleep, and carried it off, bag, box, and all! I'll find the fellow; I have sent the Alguazils[†] after him already."

"Señor," put in the manager in the midst of a yawn, "perhaps Quaco[†] is the thief: wouldn't it be well to flog him till he owns it?"

"I have flogged him already this morning; not that I think it was he, the black monkey — he cares no more for money than I care for his rags — but all Negroes know one another's tricks, and I would have flogged him till he told me something, only I wanted him with me this morning, and I couldn't afford to make him lame."

"It would be hardly fair to flog him on a mere suspicion," observed the stranger.

"I only wish I could find out the real thief," continued the planter in the same strain, "I declare I think I should kill him."

Mr. Dorset met the assertion with an incredulous smile, which the other observed.

"I would, I tell you. How dare any Negro steal into my room at night and touch my money, putting me to all this inconvenience! *Sacre!*[†] let me only catch him today, and we shall have a pickled Negro to show you tomorrow."

La Catalina here interrupted the conversation by bringing in the so oft-demanded refreshment; as she held it out however the cup happened to slip, the coffee poured in a stream upon the floor, and the china following after broke into a hundred pieces. A volley of curses burst from the lips of the angry planter, sufficient to have annihilated the premises had he been gifted with but half the powers supposed to have belonged to the enchanters of old.

In the midst of this scene a fine tall young Negro entered, whose black and shining face wore a good-natured, light-hearted expression.

"Ship come, Mas'r," he said.

"There, see how late I shall be! Curse the jade for spilling the coffee! can't you leave your smashes where they are, and go and fetch me some more, instead of standing there blubbering? And what are you meddling for, you black devil?" added he as he bestowed a violent kick on the lad, who was stretched upon the ground helping the dame to pick up her broken crockery. "What's the ugly racoon doing? get up, Sirrah! run and get the boat ready, if you don't want me to break a chair on your back."

"Es, Mas'r," said the lad, as he stood up with gestures indicative of pain, and rubbing the part assaulted; "whis boat, Mas'r?"

"The canoe, you dog, for us; and get the droguer[†] to bring the new Negroes back; and when you have got all ready, wait on the beach till I come. Off with you, Sirrah!"

Quaco did not wait for a repetition of the order, but was out of sight in an instant. His suspicious master went to the door to look after him, and at the same time made a telescope of his hand to survey some more distant object. "*Vive Dieu!*"[†] he exclaimed, almost dancing with impatience, "there is the ship coming in as fast as she can, and it will be impossible for me to get there in time for the first picking. That brown monkey knows I am in a hurry, and she does not come! I will teach her to make sport of me."

Whatever may have been the destructive intentions of the planter, they were all forgotten on the entrance of Laurine herself, the sight of whose pretty face and three large cups of coffee on a tray at once dispelled his ill-humour.

"Ha!" he exclaimed, advancing towards her as she placed the cups on the table, "you like to make yourself longed for, — eh, my pretty louis d'or?"[†]

Laurine's hands trembled as he spoke to her, — so much so indeed as to attract the notice of the manager, who, inane as he was, had sufficient quickness of observation where his passions were concerned.

"Mulatto girl," he said, leering at her, "do you know anything of Mr. Cardon's money that was stolen from him last night?"

"I, Sir!" exclaimed she, starting.

"Come, come now," said the planter, reproving the accuser, "she is too good a girl to be bothered. Now don't look so frightened! I will come back by-and-by, and you shall tell me all about it," and with a knowing wink he chucked her familiarly under the chin.

Laurine drew back in terror, and for very shame her eyes wandered to the crowd which had gathered before the door, where, to her great alarm, she saw Belfond, his eyes fixed sadly and reproachfully upon her. A faint cry rose to her lips, but she recollected herself in time; and Mr. Cardon, who had swallowed his coffee almost scalding hot, now paid his money, and with Gallic vivacity called to his companion to accompany him.

Fortunately for Laurine the haste of the gentlemen prevented any further remarks, and in a few moments they all left the shop. She then hurried to the door, and, straining her eyes, narrowly scrutinized every group at every turn and corner, and where people stood at doors or at ground-floor windows; and then her anxious gaze followed the three gentlemen, but nothing could she see of her lover, and, the throng of loungers growing more dense as it bore towards the beach, all further chance of seeing him was rendered hopeless. The crowd increased each moment, and continually grew more animated and varied. There were half-naked Caribs,[†] listlessly dragging forward their feet and gazing at some distant object, they knew not what; Negro-women with trays on their heads, pointing to the sea and uttering exclamations in tones of excitement and wonder; swarthy freedmen, hurrying on their carts, anxious to be employed in the expected disembarkation; and groups of Negroes, sluggishly moving among the boats, awaiting the commands of their masters, who strutted amidst the throng, conspicuous with their neat and snow-white clothing. From these the eye passed to the bay, where, upon a calm and crystal sea, the great object of the day's business, the long-expected slave smuggler, with her black and pointed hull, swelled on the view, and, with her white sails spread before the wind, glided swiftly into port. Craft of all kinds, — canoes,[†] droguers, rafters,[†] luggers,[†] — now pushed out from every point; and the animated scene of the beach was transferred with almost magical rapidity to the bosom of the sea.

CHAPTER V.

A Rash Move

As soon as the beach was deserted by the white men, Belfond, who had secreted himself behind some cottages, now emerged from his hiding-place and slowly walked to the shore. His heart was heavy, and he felt ready to do anything that would cause Laurine to repent of her refusal. In the ardour of his passion he had formed romantic schemes for the future, without ever dreaming of the difficulties in the way of their realization; now that his plans had failed, he felt disgusted with himself and even with life. Overwhelmed with disappointment, he wandered unconsciously to a distant part of the beach, which was wild and over-grown with brushwood; he walked with hurried and uncertain steps, and at times would stop suddenly and fix his eyes upon the sea, although in reality he saw not its billowy surface, but only the troubled visions of his own mind. By-and-by he came to a little bay formed by a graceful curve in the shore, ending in a headland beyond. It was a lovely spot, where the palm-tops waved above scented shrubs of mimosa,[†] and where the crimson flower of the wild shacshac[†] and the broad disc of the prickly pear[†] reflected their tints and forms in a clear rivulet, which, after mean-dering through the depths of the forest, as if formed solely to give life and coolness to its beautiful shades, here flowed calmly into the sea. Belfond paused in spite of his agitation, his features relaxed from their stern expression; for here he had often walked with Laurine at sunset, when the golden streaks of light shot along the stream; there, beneath yon bamboo, where its tall plumes waved over the path, they had often watched the shadows of the leaves moving on the moonlit ground, and listened to the music of the wind as it sang its eolian notes[†] amidst the hollow canes; and beyond was the wood where he had first beheld her and loved her as she was carolling blithely to the flowers she gathered. All these things rose to his mind, and the world and its hopes appeared vain and futile as a dream.

These reflections however were interrupted by the appearance of a canoe at a short distance from the shore, directing its course to the spot where he stood. Although it was single-handed, he would at any other time have prudently kept out of sight till he knew whether it contained a friend or a foe; but now, careless of himself, he stood in absent mood, fixedly awaiting its approach. Its occupant proved to be his friend Quaco, the same Negro lad who came to Mr. Cardon in Laurine's shop.

"How d'ye, countryman?" said the boatman as he rowed his skiff to land; for Belfond's mother having been a Koromantyn, he was often claimed as kin by the Negroes of that nation. "You no 'fraid they catch you?" asked the lad solicitously.

"Me!" said the Mulatto, "I don't care for anything."

The Negro opened his eyes; "Eh, me Gad, oh!" he exclaimed, and, resorting to the proverbs with which Negro converse abounds,[†] asked, "You Belfond not know *snake that would live has no business upon road,* eh?"

"I shan't stay here long, Quaco; I shall be off to Guiria[†] this evening and for ever: I shan't come back again."

"Eh hey!" exclaimed Quaco in great surprise; "and Laurine?"

"Oh, she won't care, we have parted for good;" then, as if to drive away the subject, he hurriedly stated that he hoped to enlist in the Bolivian army, where a coloured man had some chance of distinguishing himself. "You know," he said, "General Paez[†] is of caste blood himself, and so are many of the officers under him. I have a taste that way, Quaco, and I ought to be brave, coming of Koromantyn blood."

Quaco leaned upon his oar and fell into a deep reverie, — a very unusual thing with him, for he was generally communicative and full of animation; but the truth was, that a chord of the young Negro's heart had been touched by the remarks of his friend. Negro and slave as he was, he had long gazed upon Laurine with feelings of admiration almost amounting to worship. She moved before him like a very goddess, whose lustre held him entranced. He never dreamed however of approaching her; for, besides the distance which caste prejudice placed between the coloured girl and himself, — a prejudice almost as strong as that of the white people against the coloured, — he knew that Laurine's affections had been sought and won by another. He had so trained his feelings that they had settled into a quiet worship of Laurine, without admixture of any wish or thought of selfish nature. As he could never hope to obtain her for himself, his generous heart found gratification in friendship with the object of her love: hence an intimacy had sprung up between the two youths, — an intimacy however which met with no obstacle in their difference of colour, for unlike other young men of his class, who aped the supercilious airs displayed by their masters towards the Negroes, Belfond prided himself on never entertaining a prejudice which he so bitterly condemned in the white people.

As a pebble cast into a tranquil stream will throw into a mazy confusion the forms of the objects reflected from its bosom, so did the observations of Belfond disturb the thoughts of the Negro lad, and send them oscillating without rest or shape. He would have been more than human if there had not arisen in his mind some faint hope for himself, some half-formed inquiry "who knows?" and if some little castle in the air, ill-defined perhaps, yet brightly coloured, had not presented itself. He leaped out of the canoe, and eagerly offered his services, although well aware that a flogging would be the penalty for his neglect of his master's business. "Hey!" said he, "neber mind droguer now; me bring it by-and-by. Hey, go 'way! me sabey very well what for do."

Quaco was a remarkably good-natured fellow, and always very ready to help a friend, but just now he felt more than usually disposed to do so, and even went so far as to offer to Belfond the use of the canoe. "Master go to Palm Grove today," he said, "what he want with canoe, eh? he neber know nothing 't all 'bout he: go 'way! let me 'lone for do all ting."

Belfond felt no scruple in accepting the offer, and it was arranged between them that the canoe should be left on that part of the beach as if through forgetfulness, and that Belfond should wait till the evening, when he would be ready to make use of it.

"And when is our master likely to set out for the Palm Grove?" asked Belfond. "Do you think he is likely to buy many slaves today? for if he does so, it will keep him there some time. Have you overheard him say anything about it?"

"Ya, no!" was the answer; "no have no money this morning, ya hey! Master came down here so big! think to buy half that cargo — maybe all; so he bring down plenty money. But hey! last night one thief come in middle night, fine cleber thief, know too much, and took all. So master get up in the morning — box empty! Ya, ya, yah! go 'way! Then master say, Where's money, you all black debils? then talked too much, calls Quaco, flogs Quaco, and promises more flog every day till him find thief. Poor Negro broad back!† *Bird always says worm be thief.*"

Belfond bit his lip: the tide of good emotions which had left his heart now rushed back to their wonted place; and what a sense of right could not effect, even when appealed to by the lips of the loved one, sympathy for the troubles of a fellow-slave obtained.

"Quaco, I was the thief, you shall not suffer for my sins; my last act towards a faithful friend shall not be a bad turn: you shall take back the money before our master returns from the ship."

Quaco looked astonished: "What that? hey!" ejaculated he with that accented expression of surprise, and with those peculiar exclamations which the true African always uses: "yah! how you get in, eh?"

"I'll tell you, if you wish to know. From the news that you obtained by listening at our master's door, I guessed he must have brought money with him. I was determined to have it — no matter now for what use, — so last night, when they were all taking a walk by moonlight, I crept into the house, put the sleeping herb into every body's pillowcase, and then got under the bed. By-and-by they all came home. I saw master, where he put his keys and his box, for he looked at his money before he lay down, and in the dead of the night I took it all: no one heard me, — *sleep has no ears,* you know."

"Ya, ya, yah!" laughed Quaco till his eyes ran tears of joy and admiration; "that's the way! *grand talk not wise talk,* and master's tongue big too much: *fool lets dog eat his breakfast.* Buckra not always a sabey man,† — ya, ya, yah!"

"Quaco," said the Mulatto, interrupting him, "don't let us stop to laugh now: come with me down yonder, where I dropped the bag into the hollow of a mimosa-tree: come and help me take it out, and you shall put it on his bed or his table, or anywhere so that he may be sure to find it, and if he says anything about it, you can say, 'Master must have forgotten where he put it:' you shan't be flogged for me again, my poor Quaco."

"Hey, hey! what that? put back Buckra's money? hey cho, go 'way! *when fowls have teeth*, do you hear? You think me care for flog, — me Koromantyn? flog good for Koromantyn skin, — make me feel brave, for no care at all: Quaco back hard too much, go 'way! Come, countryman, don't be a fool now: if you go in a boat to Guiria, you'll want money; but if you want to throw away money, hearee to Quaco. See slave ship there? poor niggers there plenty: one of them a poor nigger girl: them tell me from ship's side, she Koromantyn king's child. Well, poor ting, — pretty black shining girl, white teeth, — poor ting never know worrok. Well now, you Belfond take that money, send somebody for buy her, so make her free."†

"Are there any coloured people there?"

"No much; some rich Mulattoes from Port Spain."

"Any that I know?"

"No sabey: wait here till I go see."

"No, I think I'll go and see myself."

"He! he!" again exclaimed Quaco, staring with surprise.

"Quaco, I feel today as if I did not care for anybody, white man or devil, and by the God of thunder I feel as if I could fight them both. I'll wager all the money that remains in the mimosa-tree, that I'll go to the vessel and leave it safe and sound and free as I am now."

Quaco grinned and giggled, but offered no opposition. He was a profound admirer of courage, and the nearer it approached to rashness, the more homage did he pay to its possessor. Now boldness was a trait in Belfond's character which had especially won his regard, and for this too did he love to claim him as countryman, for the Koromantyns are proverbially brave. There was besides a lurking idea in his mind, that if Belfond bought the pretty slave he might carry her off with him to Guiria (the Spanish mainland), and of course leave the field open to him, that he might try to gain Laurine for himself; but this, we ought to say, was but a faint and floating vision, which had assumed no shape in his mind:

he said however to himself, "Quaco loves, and loves, and loves, till love comes again, for doesn't sun shine, and shine, and shine, till earth shines again? But oh!" he added, recollecting himself, "sun never touches earth, he only touches sky: so hey! Quaco fool too much," and he quickly dismissed the thought. However, he accepted the wager.

The two young men now went earnestly to work. The droguer, for which Quaco was sent back, was got ready, the boatmen called to row it, and the commands of their master duly and properly delivered to them; nothing remained but to settle their own little private affairs respecting the canoe and the money. The latter was not all taken out: about as many doubloons as would suffice for the purchase of one slave were abstracted from the blue bag, and its remaining contents emptied into the hollow of the tree; the sum required was then put into the bag: this Belfond strapped round his waist with the belt which confined his knife, and concealed it with the folds of his cotton garment, for he wore no jacket or waistcoat. The rest of the money they left to chance for the present. "No one will think of looking into the hole of a mimosa-tree for money," said they; "and if any one should, and it is a Negro, we shan't grudge it."

The two boats now set off, — the heavy droguer to fetch back such slaves as should be purchased from the ship, the canoe to bring back the white gentlemen; and into the latter Belfond leaped, caring, as he declared, for not a thing or person upon earth.

In reality he had not much to fear. His master had not seen him for years, not since he had left him in France as valet to his son, who was then passing through the French University, and from whom the coloured youth had subsequently absconded, after picking up by stealth sufficient knowledge to render him for ever disgusted with slavery. Captain Hill, the master of the slave-ship, might, it is true, have recognized him, for it was he who caught him in the streets of Marseilles and brought him back to the Colonies; but he would be too much engaged that morning to think of other matters than the disposal of his goods; the young man also trusted much to his own altered appearance, to favour the chances of his safety.

"The only man I should have reason to fear," said Belfond, "is Higgins, the mate, if he is there still. The villain! I owe him a long account for the agonies he made me endure in the hold, and I suppose he owes me a grudge for my getting away so cleverly when he got drunk, and the Captain had left the ship to him, and they just in port — ha! ha! Well, we don't love one another."

"Hey!" said Quaco, "me knows that man. Hoh! last time he come to Port Spain, hoh! bad, bad too much!" and here, as if the lad was afraid even the waves should catch the import of his secret, he whispered something into Belfond's ear with a look of affright, and then touched a little amulet he wore about his neck, and muttered a prayer, which, as he had been taught by his mother, would preserve him from the power of the Obiah (the African witchcraft).[†]

"You don't mean to say he brings it to Fanty?"

Quaco nodded, and put his finger to his mouth to enjoin silence.

The coloured youth shook his head in silent astonishment; "Is there a God?" he said, curling his lips, as he went on pulling the oars; "ay, is there a God? that's the question; — to see a white man bringing Obiah stuff from the African coast and selling it for money to a runaway Obiah priest, who uses it to destroy white men! nothing but wickedness and confusion!"

"Hush! hush, hush!" said Quaco earnestly.

"Oh, I am desperate, Quaco! I don't care for anything. But never mind now, my dear fellow; here we are approaching the ship. I see they are very busy: plenty of customers! how crowded they are! Now quickly under the vessel, or they will be looking at me. That's it: now for it!"

CHAPTER VI.

The Slave Market. — A Rencontre

In spite of the crowd on board, which obstructed the view from below, it was easy to perceive in what part of the vessel the sale was going on, from the direction in which the people were looking, and also from a signal on the forecastle. The signal was not a flag, nor yet a written notice, but simply a Negro raised somewhat above the surrounding multitude; a female it was too, made to stand on a hogshead against the foremast, to which she was chained. Poor creature! she was the flower of the whole cargo, the healthiest and most comely, and was put in this conspicuous place, not only as a favourable specimen of the commodities offered for sale, but also that she might fetch a high price on account of her appearance; and truly her rounded yet delicate proportions might have served as a model for the finest sculpture, and were not the less striking for being set off by a skin black as ebony and shining as polished marble. Her dress was completely African, if that could be called a dress which consisted only of a strip of dark blue cotton folded round her person, then passed above her left shoulder, to be knotted in front at the waist, and thence falling down as a skirt. A single string of red beads confined the close curled hair which covered her small and well-turned head; beads of the same colour also adorned her neck, arms, and ankles: these were her only ornaments. She looked picturesque, standing there in her gay and primitive costume, her head leaning gently against the mast, which she held embracing for support, her eyes closed, and her full but well-formed lips slightly parted, the effect of faintness and exhaustion. Her companions in misfortune were none of them shackled as she was, but all had the same blue cotton scarfs twisted round their loins; the women decorated with beads of showy colours, and the men with their hair cut out in various shapes, as circles, squares, triangles, and crescents. With all these adornments however, the slaves presented a spectacle which, to say the least, was pitiable and disgusting: the horrors of the middle passage,[†] the effects of scarce and unwholesome diet, and diseases engendered by a crowded hold, were all too evident. The best of them were thin as spectres; some were covered with loathsome ulcers and marks of deformity, the consequence of long-continued crippled postures; and all were calculated rather to appal the beholder than to induce the most unwary to venture a speculation on their miserable lives. They had been hastily arranged in lots, according to the value set upon them by the Captain, but, from not clearly understanding his wishes, or perhaps from other motives, many had strayed from the places assigned to them. The Mandingos, Foulahs, and Mozambiques,[†] known by their more regular features, stood obediently enough in front. The effeminate race of Loango,[†] distinguished by certain raised figures in the form of dice all over their bodies, and by their long pointed teeth,[†] which appeared at every motion of their lips, reclined listlessly on the boards. The stupid-looking Eboes, Quaquas, and Mokos[†] crouched despondingly behind the coops and lumber; while the Koromantyns, with tattooed cheeks and fearless brow, looked on in dogged silence, as the multitudes continued to gather on the deck.

Meantime the confusion around them was great, and the noise increased. Voices of every pitch, from the hoarse bass of the rude Corsican,[†] passing through the various tones of Englishmen, Germans, French, Spaniards, Italians, and Danes, to the whining drawl[†] of the Creole,[†] were all trilling, twittering, chattering, and sputtering their several claims to the attention of the Captain, who on this part was busy enough with giving commands to the men and treating with his customers.

"Here, lend a hand, one of you boys, and haul away that black devil from the bulwarks; he'll be food for the sharks if you don't look out. See that nigger wench to the leeside there; give her a shove for'ard, will you? I wonder what she is after. There is another abaft the coops. The nigger beasts! after all the work I have had in setting 'em square, to go drifting about in that way! Take the rope-end to 'em if they won't move! The devil! give it to those nigger men laying on the boards there: make 'em stand up here near!" and then the bluff commander of the schooner "Venus" composed his features to a less troubled expression, as he turned to his favourite customer and exclaimed —

"Why, St. Hilary Cardon, my friend, right glad I am to see you. Look at this sight of niggers: by Jove, I've shoals enough to supply half-a-dozen estates if you have 'em. Now an't they jolly goods as ever you come in hail of? Come, now you shall have your choice."

The coffee-planter nodded and crossed his arms on his breast, while he slowly stepped here, stooped there, or bent aside, whispering to his manager or nudging his friend to call his attention to the human articles displayed for his approval.

"And see here," continued the Captain, approaching the foremast; "look up there, Cardon," and he pointed to the object we have before noticed, he speaking the while with considerable emphasis. "This here, I say, is a prize bit: just look what a Venus she is! *the soul*, as I call her, of my vessel, — ha! ha! — but isn't she a perfect beauty in a black skin as ever you set eyes upon?"

Mr. Cardon directed his eyes upwards and seemed to muse, but did not take the bait, and was about to turn his back to the mast, when the confusion on board rose to such a height as to interrupt further negotiation. The multitude, too densely crowded on a small deck, were all jostling together, and complaining in no very gentle terms; but louder than the hoarse murmurs and manifold grumbling of the discontented crew, and than all the gabbling din, was heard the whining nasal voice of a young Martinique planter, drawling out in Colonial patois† —

"Quo faire Mulâtres ca venir oti bequés yé? Insolents, yo ca pousser mo par derrière! Sortiz là, mo dire ous, Mulâtres effrontés, sacres pendus!" (How come Mulattoes here among white people? the insolent wretches are pushing me behind. Be off, you impudent Mulattoes! And then followed an oath which may as well remain untranslated.)

"I beg pardon a thousand times. I am humbly sorry!" was the conciliating apology of the offender, uttered in the same dialect, but in a voice peculiarly sweet and well modulated: it was that of our Mulatto. Even in the midst of his haughty masters, Belfond stood well and handsome;

and though his garments were cast loosely and negligently about his brawny shoulders, and his glossy raven hair hung in wild ringlets about his face and neck, yet there was something about him strikingly superior to the generality of his caste. He had none of that humble, cringing appearance, stamped upon them by their low condition. His proud dark eyes were full of meaning, his bearing was dignified and such indeed as would have challenged respect had he been a white man, but this, in one of his outcast race, testified of a rebellious spirit, and consequently conveyed an insult to every white man who looked upon him.

To understand the scene which followed, it is necessary that the reader should be made acquainted with the condition of the class of people who come under the denomination Mulattoes — a term usually employed to designate the free coloured population, the offspring of white and black parents. The laws of the various Colonies, however much they differed on other matters, according to the constitution of their several governments, all agreed at least on one point — they were all framed to keep down the mongrel race. And even where legislation was more lenient, the social customs of the white population became only the more oppressive, and the unhappy wretches were persecuted with such unrelenting severity as entirely destroyed their self-respect and prevented even the wish to rise. More than twenty years have elapsed since the events of this story, and nineteen have passed since the emancipation in the English Colonies, but prejudice against colour prevails there still. This prejudice is the bulwark of slavery in the Southern States of America; and in the Northern States, which claim to be the head-quarters of liberty, as well as in the French and English colonies, it forms the barrier to real freedom.

But let us pass now to the period of slavery in the British Colonies, when those laws were in force which laid the foundation of the still existing tyranny of society. Never did the Jews, even in the times of Richard and John,[†] labour under more grinding oppression than did the much-injured Mulattoes in our own boasted era of civilization. They were forbidden by law to stand covered or to remain sitting in the presence of a white person, to dress like him, to bear witness against him in a court of law, to resist when assaulted by him, to answer him in terms implying equality, or even to repose after death within the same place of burial. Volumes might be written on the restrictions to which they were subject;

but we think enough has been said for our present purpose, and we hasten to resume the thread of our narrative.

"What is that yellow devil saying?" inquired a gentleman near. "What brings Mulattoes here?"

"Out with them!" cried several voices at once, among which Don Duro's harsh tones were loudest. "Drive out the Mulattoes."

"I suppose," observed a facetious customer, "they are come to buy their mothers. I saw a Mulatto a little while back buy his own grandmother for a slave."[†] This announcement excited much laughter among the company, and probably our Mulatto might have been forgotten, for the southerns[†] are as variable as they are impetuous; but Mr. Cardon, who was always proud and authoritative, turned on the offender, and called out domineeringly, in much the same tone as he would have used in speaking to a dog,

"Get out, there!"

In this there really was nothing unusual. It was Mr. Cardon's way of addressing people of colour, and he had a hundred times bestowed upon them much more substantial marks of his displeasure for smaller offences; but in the behaviour of the Mulatto there was something unusual. Stung with rage and jealousy, he forgot his position as a man of caste, and with unexampled audacity stood erect before the white man without stirring an inch. The Captain saw in a moment what would be the consequence, and, being little inclined either to encourage a brawl on deck to the injury of his sale, or to drive away the Mulattoes, whose presence he had rather invited on account of their reputed wealth, he interposed to make peace.

"Easy now, easy!" he said, coming forward, "he is a harmless fellow, and the Mulattoes will stand back in a minute. I say, holloa, you yellowskin, just wear a little aft there until I have time to treat with you."

The young man thus addressed moved in the direction indicated, and took his place at the side of the vessel, to which all those of his class then on board were fast making their way amid the jeers of the white people. What the feelings of the Mulatto were it is hard to say, but the scornful expression of his face at this moment gave to his features such a striking resemblance to the proud planter himself as to cause many a smile and a whisper among the bystanders. Mr. Cardon did not perceive this, but he saw something else which provoked his displeasure: he caught the Mulatto's eye fixed upon him with that keen, steady, proud air, which tells of anger and rebellion in the soul. At any other time the planter would have visited even this faint shadow of resistance with immediate punishment; but his thoughts were engrossed with the business on hand, and, not choosing to prolong an interruption which had already annoyed him enough, he contented himself with threatening to throw the offender overboard if he did not take care. Having thus relieved his mind, he was about to make his way back to the foremast, when a voice reached him from the direction of the coloured man, and the words "Do so!" fell distinctly upon his ears. The planter turned round quick as lightning: he could hardly believe his senses, for, from the expression of the Mulatto's face, it was evident that he was the speaker. What audacity!

"Oh, *mon Dieu!*" cried Belfond's affrighted companions, shrinking from his side. The whole deck was in commotion.

"The wretch is mad!" vociferated the white men; "let him be seized and secured in the hold."

"Captain! Captain! if you don't take hold of him, we'll do it ourselves."

Mr. Cardon was already preparing to do so. Snatching a stick, a good stout one, from his neighbour, he rushed forward, and aimed such a heavy blow at the offender's head as must have killed him, had not the young man, dexterous and strong, grasped the weapon as it was falling, and held it fast, regarding the planter with a smile of most provoking composure, almost of contempt.

Who shall describe the fury of the white man, and his frantic attempts to disengage the stick from the hands of the Mulatto? Like a madman, he twisted, and pulled, and struggled. The *prestige* of caste kept the Mulatto from retaliation, though he powerfully resisted, and the planter, watching his opportunity, with a sudden and powerful jerk pitched him over the bulwarks. If this had happened in England, or even to a white man in the Colonies, what cries and calls for help would have announced the event! but here, where the consequence of a deed of violence and cruelty affected only a free coloured man, or one who was supposed to be such, it was thought nothing of; and as the water was heard to splash below, Mr. Cardon coolly walked back to the forecastle, amidst a chorus of triumphant voices and clapping of hands, which testified the approbation of the spectators. No one thought of saving the life of the Mulatto.

CHAPTER VII.

Black Cattle Purchased

The uproar among the white people alarmed the Mulattoes. Each, knowing himself to be an object of hatred, and conceiving himself likely to be the next victim of their vengeance, pressed in terror against his comrades. Some stood upon the bulwarks ready to jump into the boats, others crouched amidst their companions' feet, and a few, more hardy than the rest, begged the white men's pardon, and with ignoble humility craved permission to pass to the gangway and leave the deck.

"Get away with you," cried the white people, kicking them on the shins, as Mulatto after Mulatto passed timidly and hurriedly off. But in the midst of this movement a cry was heard, "A Negro overboard!" New confusion! not derision or insult now, but hurry and solicitude. "Whose?" cried several voices at once. "Cardon's," was the reply, and the master was at his post in a moment, eagerly giving orders for proper assistance: and how cheerfully and quickly did the sailors obey!

It chanced that on the off-side of the ship a canoe had been brought round from beside the gangway, — probably to afford the idle Negro who sat within it a better opportunity of observing the proceedings on board; but Quaco (for it was he) had brought the canoe too near, just below the spot where the contest took place above; and as the Mulatto fell, his body came in contact with the gunwale of the boat, which immediately dipped and capsized.

"Here, one of you sailors!" shouted Mr. Cardon impatiently; "*Sacre, Diable!*† why don't you make haste? he'll be drowned."

His anxiety was not disregarded: "How much will you give me for diving," said one of the men.

"*Sacre!* whatever is fair: where's the use of talking, Higgins, when the fellow is drowning?"

Instantly the mate was in the water, and, encouraged by the interest manifested by the crowd of spectators, he soon brought the Negro to the surface. His reappearance was the signal for cheers, for he had saved property from destruction; he had rendered a great service. And very edifying was the sympathy shown to the Negro: with what tenderness he was stretched in one of the boats brought round to receive him, rum put to his nostrils and poured down his throat, and his body rubbed by a dozen hands! At length signs of life began to appear: he sneezed, spluttered, kicked: perhaps he had pretended to be worse than he really was, but this the white men could not tell, and the master, between satisfaction at his recovery and wrath at the accident, thundered forth in his usual style, "*Sacre, Diable!* 'tis that *maudit Mulâtre:*[†] he fell on my Negro on purpose to drown him, confound the rascal!"

While these things were going on, Mr. Dorset stood by in amazement. He was as yet too new in the Colonies to share in the prevailing notions concerning Negroes, or rightly to understand the position he himself held with regard to them, and the scene, so strange, so subversive of his European ideas of justice and humanity, bewildered him. Here were gentlemen whom he knew to be honourable and kind-hearted: Mr. Cardon himself was generous to a fault, often even magnanimous, in his own small sphere of despotic rule; and yet these gentlemen all abetted one another in a total disregard of the rights of a fellow-creature (he was thinking of the Mulatto), and more regard was paid to a condemned criminal in England; but, thought he, it must be a mistake, — the coloured man must by this time have climbed up the ship's side, or perhaps has gained a boat somewhere near. To assure himself of this, he approached some sailors who were looking over the bulwarks, and inquired what had become of the Mulatto. No one answered at first, — people were too busy, — till a louder and more eager question on his part roused the Manager, who stood near him, and who replied with coolness that the drowned man was "only a Mulatto."

With indignant surprise the Englishman looked round: the truth flashed upon him in a moment. "Merciful heaven!" he cried, "make way there;" and tearing off his jacket he prepared to leap into the water; but the Captain tapped him on the shoulder.

"You need not trouble yourself, my good Sir," he said with a smile, "the fellow is swimming to shore as fast as he can;" and pointing forwards to a speck which was visible on the sea, he added, "There! don't you see him? you would have something to do to catch the rascal now. I watched him come up about a cable's length off: a brave swimmer, by Jove; never saw a better." And having delivered himself of this remark, the Captain put his hands in his pocket.

He did not however return to his business, but stood there with his eyes rivetted on the sea. Higgins came up with a look of intelligence.

"I know what you're after, Sir," he said to the Captain.

"You do, by Jove?" replied the other, turning quickly round and slapping his side: "it is he, then?"

"Himself, Sir, true as the needle,"[†] said the mate.

"Who?" asked a dozen voices.

"What's the matter?" inquired Mr. Cardon.

"What's the matter?" repeated the Captain; "are you so blind that you don't know your own slave? The Mulatto I picked up for you in the port of Marseilles."

Mr. Cardon turned pale with passion. By some movement of anger his foot struck against something, and he stumbled; but instead of looking to see what it was, he violently kicked it forwards, — which, to the surprise of every one, occasioned a loud jingling as of large coins of money. His next neighbour picked it up for him.

"*De par tous les diables!*"[†] exclaimed the planter as he beheld it: "the bag of doubloons stolen out of my box last night!"

"By Jove, then," interrupted the Captain, "the thief was your own Mulatto slave, for I heard something fall when you were thrashing him, and I was just going to see what it was. Come Cardon," continued the Captain, as he looked through his glass, "you won't lose him: the fellow, I see, is just setting foot on land safe and sound. By Jove, he is waving his hand at us," saying which, the rough seaman leaned back to give vent to his boisterous mirth.

Mr. Cardon bit his lip till the blood started, and was about to turn away in disgust, when Higgins came to him.

"Now," said he, "will you give me ten dollars if I catch him for you, besides ten more I expect for saving that boy, — will you, Mr. Cardon?"

"*Sacre tonnerre!*[†] don't pester me with your English money-worship."

"Mr. Cardon, no one but me can catch that fellow for you, — but me, I tell you: there's no bushrangers about here, nor alguazils, and if there was, I can do business in that line better than either, I'll vouch. Now you need not be thinking of how he got away from our vessel, for I was not on board, I tell you. Can a man be in two places at once? He would never have found the use of his legs so soon if I had not had business on shore that night. Ask the Captain there how I chained him and tamed him down in the hold. When we first got him on board, Sir, there was no keeping the chains upon him: he broke two. He is the very devil! But I tamed him, I tell you, and by the time we reached the port he looked like — like —"

"The leanest of these, I suppose," added Mr. Dorset, who had been listening attentively, and he pointed to some of the Negroes put up for sale.

"Pah!" said the Captain turning away, and putting his pipe to his mouth. "Whew! Señor," observed Don Duro, "I could tame him without that."

"Come now, Cardon," interrupted the Captain, "you had better leave him to Higgins: you can pay him for this and for saving the Negro when you pay me. I'll go bail he will bring you that cove before three days are over; he has the eye of an Indian for tracing a runaway.[†] I remember once, when I brought a cargo of slaves round to Granada, I sold a lot to a heavy planter down there, and he sent 'em off directly to his estate; but the devils no sooner got scent of the woods than they tied up the overseer that had the care of 'em, and cut away to the mountains. Higgins laid a wager that day he would capture every one of 'em before the morrow, and, by Jove, the fellow was as good as his word, for the black thieves were exhibited in the market-place next morning, cut up with the whip like so many crimped cod.[†] But won't you come and look at those articles of mine? I would rather sell 'em to you than to anybody else, and you can pay me when you like, I'm not particular; I'll give you such bargains as will make up for twenty such fellows as the one that got away. Come here!"

Mr. Cardon followed moodily.

"Well now," continued the Captain, "I suppose you don't care for that 'ere Wenus;[†] but here are some fine articles, I'll warrant!" and he dragged up one of the men from a sitting to a standing posture. "See this one; just look at his shoulders and his arms, did you ever see any like 'em? Why he'll clear you a forest in a week. I saw him felling wood myself on the river-side; he's a real Samson."

A shout of laughter met this vaunt, for the poor wretch, besides a lean, spare, weakly frame, presented to the beholders a set of features which marked him at once as belonging to the Eboe nation, the laziest and most useless of those imported from Africa.

"Now I tell you," said Mr. Cardon, "I am not going to be wheedled into carting a load of these unwholesome black bones off your deck; they may go to manure some other planter's land than mine. Pah! faugh! they smell of nothing but lamp-oil, horse-beans, and ulcers. I tell you I'm not going to be taken in so: you think I don't know how you rub them down and physic them before they come on shore, to hide their unhealthy looks."

"Come now, easy now! it's no use talking; you're as smart a man, and as keen in striking a bargain, as any I've ever dealt with; but goods is goods, and will spoil sometimes, particular when a ship has been tossed about by storms one half of the voyage and becalmed the other. You're a man of acute mind, and you should know that allowances must be made."

"It's the ugliest and most useless cargo I ever came on board to see."

"Odds, Sir! you do nothing but find fault. The time of year is bad for catching niggers on the Guinea coast;† and just look, Captain Gosmore set out at the same time with me for Cuba, — his cargo was all made up of niggers with clabba-yaws,† and their legs had guinea-worms† peeping out through the skin, you could see them moving, — and I'll wager he has made a fortune by his cargo. Niggers is getting scarce now, since the trade was got to be smuggling work, and the population on the plantations don't increase so as to provide against the scarce times."†

"You haven't a single available Negro: I wanted Quaquas or Foulahs."

"There's four of 'em there," said the Captain, kicking some who stood close to him, — not that he was a cruel man, not at all, but it was the way of treating Negroes.

The crowd of customers pressed so closely round that it became difficult to survey the slaves properly. This of course pleased the Captain all the better, as it served his purpose.

"I've got Koromantyns here, the finest fellows you could see."

"I don't like Koromantyns, they give too much trouble. And I see the marks of chains on their wrist and ankles: now slaves that are troublesome on board are just doubly so on land."

"Well now, by Jove, Mr. Cardon, you are hard to please. I have only one price for each of them, and I have given you the first picking, as I promised you last time; now, if you don't choose to take 'em, why, don't, that's all! others will." The Captain was provoked at Mr. Cardon's pertinacious depreciation of his cargo, — the more so, as he knew the planter's remarks would operate greatly against his sale, for Mr. Cardon's reputed wealth, together with his powerful mind and imperious temper, made him the most influential man in the Colony. Endeavouring therefore to meet his difficult customer, the Captain soon brought the bargaining to a close, and Mr. Cardon whispered to his friend to point out the best, "for," said he, "I must buy some, be they ever so bad." Some Koromantyns, Loangoes, and Eboes were indicated, and our planters selected eight of the first, seven of the second, and four of the last. "And now," said he to the Captain in conclusion, "you must throw into the bargain that Venus you have been praising so much, to make up a round number, or I will have nothing further to do with your goods."

"'Sdeath,[†] Sir, my Venus! my beauty! my prize slave, Gad! I think you will ask me for the ship next."

"Ship or no ship, Mr. Captain," vociferated Mr. Cardon, "I'm not to be trifled with, and you've been trying to do that ever since I have put my foot on board. Will you throw her into the bargain, or will you not? for I must be gone, — *sacre!*"

The Captain looked up and mused, and looked up again. "Well, you're a good pay, a brave purse, so as you give me money down."

"But I don't give you money down," interrupted the planter: "I find in this bag only a few doubloons of the large sum I brought down, whatever that cursed thief did with the rest."

A little circumstance happened here, which, though not connected with the story, will show the consideration our planter enjoyed in the Colony. A gentleman advanced from among the crowd, politely addressing himself to Mr. Cardon.

"Allow me, if you please, to pay the demand for you, as I don't care to make purchases this morning, and I have plenty of money by me at your service."

"Very well," said the other, neither surprised nor moved, "I am obliged to you." And while the Captain went hurriedly and petulantly to unchain the girl, Mr. Cardon procured writing materials, and indited a note of hand, which he presented to the lender. But this the gentleman immediately tore up. "Mr. Cardon's word," he said, "is enough, every one knows it is as good as gold: I only ask that he acknowledge, I can appreciate his honour." Mr. Cardon bowed proudly, and, passing off to the ship's side, he called Quaco to bring round the boats, and prepared to descend.

CHAPTER VIII.

How Government Servants Do Their Duty in the Colonies

The gentlemen took their seats in the canoe, and the droguer was brought alongside the vessel, to receive the slaves that had been purchased. In a few minutes they were all stowed in. The black young Venus, as the Captain called her, — she who had formed the signal at the foremast, — was the last sent down. As she was cautiously descending the ladder, some of the Negroes, those of the Koromantyn nation, rose to meet her with every token of respect, and one of them stooped fairly on all fours, to receive her foot upon his back, as she stepped from the ladder to the boat. Mr. Dorset pointed to the little scene with an expression of interest. "I should never have dreamt," he said, "that the Negroes had so much gallantry."

The planter, whose good humour was somewhat restored by the purchase he had made, turned quickly round. "Bah!" he said, looking at the Negroes, "that's nothing: I am used to that sort of work: it is not gallantry, how should they know anything about such a feeling, — the black things! The fact is, she was some grandee in Africa, so they will tell you, but I'll soon stripe that out of her."

Mr. Dorset was about to ask whether, from consideration for the habits she had been brought up to, he would not treat her with some indulgence, but was cut short by the impatient planter, who was taking a rapid though searching review of his goods, and directing his manager to make some alteration of their position in the boat.

"Don Duro," he said, addressing that worthy, who of course was in the droguer to attend to the goods, "do you have an eye to those Koromantyns, they are not to be trusted. And as for those Eboes, you must never look away from them till they get down to the estate: they will as likely as not throw themselves over the boat-side before you are aware of it. I would not trouble them now, Don Duro, they are just as well there, lying at the bottom of the boat: at all events, they are safe."

"I know, I know, Señor," replied the other, "I am up to all their ways, Señor: they will never catch me off my guard, Señor."

Mr. Cardon appeared satisfied with this, and taking his seat, he turned cheerfully to the Negroes at the oar.

"Now, Quaco! pull away, you rascal, and let us see what a good ducking does, and you shall have a holiday this afternoon, and perhaps a dance tomorrow night, as it is Saturday."

Quaco brightened up, and tucking his wet garments as high as they would go, he took the oar, and, with the other boatmen, set to work with all his might, beating time on the water to an animated song, which the rowers of the droguer took up alternately in a sort of chorus. The words — composed, as usual, for the occasion — were in some African language. Immediately on hearing this, the poor wretches who were crammed in the droguer started up with looks and gestures indicative of the wildest emotions. Some of them fell on their faces and wept aloud; others, unawed by the presence of the white gentlemen, laughed outright for joy; others again gibbered and gesticulated toward the canoe like a set of maniacs; while Quaco, who had caused all this commotion, only smiled, and continued his recitative as if nothing had happened.

"Oh, that's nothing out of the way," said the planter, observing surprise on the face of his European friend; "Quaco, who is a devil's imp if ever there was one, has been singing to them in his own language, and they have recognized it, and hail him, I suppose, as a countryman, perhaps as a relative, who knows? if we choose to grow romantic upon niggers."

"Is their language interesting! Is it worth learning?"

"What!" exclaimed St. Hilaire, "gibberish like that! *ma foi,* I think not."

"Do you know anything of it? did you ever pick up any words? I ask this, because I observe you have a rare facility in speaking languages."

"As for that, every West Indian has; our tongues are lithe and supple like our limbs, and in a colony like this, composed of people from almost every corner of the globe, we pick up languages in our childhood, as we do shells from the shore. But as for the African dialects, preserve me! I would not vulgarize my tongue with such sounds; besides, between you and me," he added, lowering his voice, "I would not trust them to teach me. A curious fellow came here from Europe some two years ago, wanting to write about Africa; so he came to my place, and set himself to learn Koromantyn from the Negroes, writing down the words as they taught him: they would assemble in a circle round him, and with the gravest and most solemn faces tell him the words he wanted. I told him then he was a fool, but he would not believe me. So by-and-by, when he had got his book full and thought himself learned, he travelled round to the other side of the island, and met some Koromantyn soldiers of the black regiment in *Bande de l'Est*.† Well, he began his conversation as he thought in pure African — not one of them could understand a word; he went to others — just the same; at last he found out that he had been befooled and made a dupe of, — a laughing-stock for the Negroes, just think! I had half a mind to give them all a round flogging, but the trick was so clever that I couldn't help laughing. Well," continued the planter after a pause, while he took off his straw hat to wipe his forehead, for it was growing hot, — "well, Dorset, what do you think of our bargain this morning?"

"I think," replied the other emphatically, "that you have made a woful and most unchristian bargain, unless indeed you mean to do without the services of these poor creatures, and send them to the hospital for a year; for in less than that time they will certainly not be fit for work: they are quite crippled, their constitutions are broken."

The planter at first looked earnestly and searchingly at his friend, but in another moment he appeared satisfied. "You little know, *mon ami*,"† he resumed, as he passed his handkerchief several times across his brow, and finally replaced his hat, — "you little know how quickly and comfortably and effectually these victims, as you would call them, recruit their strength. But you will soon learn, — soon learn: all in good time, *mon cher*."†

"Then again," quoth the European, "I am amazed at this Captain, at his boldness in venturing here: why the slave trade was done away with years ago. — in 1813,[†] if I am not mistaken."

"*Ce n'est rien, cela,*"[†] said the planter; "the prohibition only made the trade more exciting and interesting. People here see no more harm in illicit trade of this sort, than Londoners do in smuggling French gloves."

"I wonder they are not detected and punished."

"Detected!" exclaimed Mr. Cardon, placing his hands upon his sides: "you little know what colonies are. Why a place like this, so far from the seat of Government, scarcely feels its influence at all: the real kings are the officials sent over, and provided the offender has friends at our little Court to hush up and wink at his sins, he need never fear punishment, do what he may. As for abuses, — the unlawful meddling, the neglect of duty, and the unjust favouritism of these officials, — their name is Legion;[†] and who is to redress them? If the united remonstrances of the whole population cannot get a hearing at head-quarters across the ocean, be assured the sins of a favourite will never reach them."[†]

"Do you mean to say," asked the European, looking steadfastly at the planter, "that the Governor knows of this slaver coming in? Do any of the officials?"

"*Parole d'honneur,* I don't know, and I don't care," said Mr. Cardon, leaning somewhat aside; "as for myself, I know they won't meddle with me, not one of them: I am no friend of any of them either, but they all know it is as well to let me alone. For the rest, supposing there was some friend of any of the Government pack sinning here this morning, and the virtuous headman got scent of it, and took notice of it, to make a parade of his principles, *mon cher, — pardi!* a sum of money would soon stop his mouth. Ha! they are all alike — a parcel of mean, cowardly bullies. Now I will tell you a thing that happened but a short time ago: it will give you an idea of the lax way they do their work. A proclamation was issued in the name of the King, prohibiting the transfer of slaves from one Colony to another, under pain of forfeiture. There was a French widow lady residing here who had an estate on the Spanish main,[†] from which, before the proclamation came, she had brought seven or eight Negroes to Trinidad to hire out. Shortly after the new law came into force, the term for which she had hired out her slaves expired, when she very foolishly, and without consulting her friends, took them back to her estate, — during the night too. Having set them to work under her manager in Guiria, she returned here, thinking herself quite safe. Her maid betrayed her. She was sitting quietly one evening in her little home with her two daughters, young things of fifteen and seventeen years of age; an Alguazil stepped in, with a message, requesting her to come to a place that was mentioned, to speak on business with some of the authorities. She put on her bonnet, thinking to return in a little while, but, *pardi!* then and there she was walked off to prison. The Negroes in question were sent for at once and set free, together with the traitor, but the lady was kept in that prison for three long years, while her girls were left to the mercy of the world. Although I had not hitherto known her, yet I went to see her, as many others did, to express my sympathy for her misfortunes; my wife offered to take the two girls, but somebody had been beforehand on the same errand. I found the lady with a bed on the floor in a corner of her room, and one chair, — that was all. I don't know how she fared with regard to food. She was let out at last on the remonstrance of some one who had interest in our puny Court. I must say, by the way, what I suppose will please you, that the Negroes of the Island showed themselves to have a respectable amount of feeling on the occasion. They looked coldly on the traitor, and pitied the lady much; they even made a song of condolence, with a rather pretty chorus, to the effect that she

'Lies buried in the depths of the prison gloom
The damps beneath, above, around,
Till the fungus grows rank o'er her living tomb.'[†]

Well, contrast this severe expression of His Excellency's most virtuous indignation with the affair of the Barbadians, which happened but a short time ago. In the face of the proclamation and of many other stringent orders, — such as arrive here as fast as the mails[†] can bring them, — a ship comes into Port Spain, in broad daylight, with a cargo of young female slaves from that overpeopled colony, the island of Barbadoes.[†] Received by the Captain of the Port, passed by the Protector of Slaves,[†] numbered and named by the Registrar,[†] these slaves were offered for sale, and the inhabitants, foolishly trusting that all was right, made purchases, each according to his means and requirements. Months elapsed, and many of these Barbadians were transferred from owner to owner through several hands, and still nothing was said by the officials; when it occurred to them, for some reason unknown to any but themselves, that the Captain of the Port, the Protector of Slaves, and the Registrar of Slaves were wrong, so instantly they had all the Barbadians called together and set free. Do you think the officials were punished? — not they! they fattened, and the inhabitants were flayed. This is but a poor sample of what they do, and I might fill volumes with accounts of their misdemeanours and tyranny. I hate them and despise them."

"But this man, this Captain Hill!" said Mr. Dorset, as soon as he could get in a word.

"Ah, well, this man. *Oui, revenons à nos moutons.*† This man will carry on the trade till our men in office find it expedient to trumpet forth their virtue, and then all at once they will sacrifice him to their interests. I don't say myself that I very much approve of this trade, for I hate cruelty to animals; *mais que voulez-vous?*† we must have slaves to work, and the young Negroes die so fast in childhood and in infancy of one thing or another, that the Negro population would soon die out altogether if we didn't find some means of renewing it."

"But how comes this?" persistingly asked Mr. Dorset. "Are you sure the Negro children are taken care of, and that there is no mismanagement or unsuitability of climate or of their condition perhaps," he added doubtingly.

Mr. Cardon mused awhile, — then began to whistle, — and then, after another pause, said — "I must confess I don't understand it myself, for certainly the children of the free coloured population don't show the same decrease. I have often thought of this before, but have never been able to account for it. I have often suspected neglect of the young things, and for this reason I would never have a rearing-house, like so many other planters: I let the mothers stay from the field to nurse their own babies. In my opinion the birth of Negro children is more loss than gain.† In Cuba, now, they understand this very well, and many of the estates are manned with men only, with not a woman near them."

"How dreadful!" muttered Mr. Dorset.

"Captain Hill," continued the other, with scarcely a pause, "drives a fine trade there, I know; and I know moreover that he ventures his worst

articles here, for fear some day he should be caught, and his cargo for-
feited. Higgins is an excellent help to him."

"You did not seem to encourage him much in his kind offers,"
observed Mr. Dorset.

"No, but he will bring me that runaway villain nevertheless, just as he
said; but I don't care to encourage him. I hate him for his sneaking,
treacherous way: he will do anything for money, — he will cringe, fawn,
bully, or betray, if you only pay him for it. I never knew him do a common piece of civility without asking to be paid."

The breeze which had wafted the ship gaily towards the shore had
now lulled into a perfect repose, and the ripples had given place to a
smoothness like glass. The boats, as they glided along the unruffled surface, were reflected by the still water as in a mirror, and their shadows
met and mingled below with the tall corallines[†] and fucus,[†] which showed
clearly and beautifully through the crystal fluid; brilliant shells rested
like fruit upon the submarine branches, and glittering fish passed in and
out, like fairy forms gliding into their hidden bowers; and shadow and
substance, — the real and the unreal, — were blended in one magical picture. The broad expanse of azure above was unbroken by a single cloud.
Nature was clothed in the most gorgeous of her robes: the scene was
one which might have rivalled the beauty of Eden. So thought Mr.
Dorset, as he looked around, and watched the boats returning from the
ship, each bearing its group of exiles to their hopeless doom. And the
cadenced songs of the rowers, answering from boat to boat, sounded
mellow, melancholy, and wild, as the voice of music always does when
it comes from the sea. By-and-by the gentlemen landed, and joined a
group of planters, who stood on the beach, talking over the various incidents of the morning's sale, while the heavier craft were bringing up their
respective loads of goods.

Mr. Cardon's purchases were the first to come, and the manager, who
considered that his jurisdiction commenced from the moment the
Negroes were consigned to his care, accordingly took the place of his
master (though master he never acknowledged him), and issued his commands with lordly severity.

"*Párate, perro!*"[†] he roughly called, trilling his *r*'s with wrath; "stop
there, dog of a slave, and near to the right there, where the waggon

stands, and make haste to drag out those niggers sprawling at the bottom of the boat."

"Berry well, Massa," stammered the sable boatman as he threw out
one leg upon the sands; "but dem Eboe, me no sabey wharra for do wid
'em; dem da sleep, me tink, — no lika for moob!"[†]

"*Por Dios santo,*[†] make them move, or I'll make you!" vociferated the
manager.

Hereupon the boatmen, exercising on the wretched Eboes the same
tyranny which the white men were wont to practise on themselves,
snatched up the oars, and commenced bullying and tormenting the
desponding exiles till they forced them to rise and follow their more
lively companions, who were already filing off to dry land, glad per-
chance of any change that delivered them from the horrors of the ship.

CHAPTER IX.

Wrath and Retaliation

We may pass over our planter's return from the ship. Like other planters, he swore and bellowed at his slaves, and called them dogs and lazy "niggers;" and like other slaveholders, he carefully provided for the safety of his new slaves, ordering them to be rubbed down with citron-juice and rum to destroy the infection of the hold, and some spirituous drink to be given to revive them, well knowing how much his future wealth depended on their condition. As to the miscreant who had bearded him with such audacity at the sale, he had no hope of ever reducing him to submission and order; he therefore gave instructions for his capture and punishment, at the same time uttering execrations and threats of annihilation against the unhappy wretch, if ever he happened to come within reach of him: this done to his satisfaction, our coffee-planter mounted his horse, and in company with Mr. Dorset set off for the Palm Grove Estate.

A few words concerning Mr. Cardon. He was by no means what would generally be termed a hard master: he fed, clothed, and housed his Negroes well; he had a hospital for the sick, and a nursery to rear the little ones, with a *Mammy* to superintend it, and he took a pride in seeing his Negroes in good condition. He had also his fits of kindness and indulgence, and was often familiar with his slaves, mixing unreservedly with their conversation, and laughing at their remarks; yet, even when in his gentlest mood, there was always something lordly and contemptuous in his manner, a sarcastic mockery in his merriest joke, which never failed to keep them down. He was a clever man, and wonderfully successful in the management of his Negroes; he had been known to strike at the root of their prejudices, when they affected his interests, with rare sagacity. Once, for example, he had speculated somewhat largely in a very unpromising set of Negroes of the Eboe nation. These Eboes are a desponding people, and frequently commit suicide at the first opportunity, from a belief that when dead they will immediately return to their own far country. Contrary to our planter's orders, they had for some reason or other been stowed away for the night in a garret, and in the garret lay some old forgotten ropes. When the morning came, the greater number of the unhappy wretches were found hanging dead and stiff from the rafters. Mr. Cardon's tact was shown in the plan he adopted to save the remaining ones. He stalked in amongst them with an angry countenance, and addressing an Eboe interpreter, "Tell your accursed countrymen," he said in threatening tones, "that if I find one more of them hanged, I shall hang you all in a row, and myself at the head of you; and if I don't follow you to your country with this whip, by ———!" and he cracked it till the hills resounded again. No Negro was ever found hanged on his estate after that.

It was with a view of applying a remedy to some such disorder in another form among his Negroes that he had induced Mr. Dorset to accompany him to the Palm Grove Estate. This gentleman had gone through a regular course of study as surgeon[†] in England, (a most rare qualification in the medical men of the Colonies,) and Mr. Cardon thought highly of his professional ability.

"I know very well what is thinning the ranks of my Negroes," he said, "still I would have your opinion upon it, and would stop it if possible by some new remedy, more efficient than the one hitherto applied."

For some time they journeyed on without much conversation, each occupied with his own thoughts. At last Mr. Cardon suddenly turned full on his companion.

"I am going to speak seriously to you," he said, "and to ask you a serious and important favour, Mr. Dorset. You tell me you don't allow flogging on your estate; well, that is as you like: but if I should find it necessary to use coercion on mine, I insist upon requesting you not to interfere, either by look, word, or gesture."

"What!" exclaimed the other, "may I not intercede for a culprit?"

"No! no! not on my estate, not on any sensible planter's estate: the Negroes must never dream their master's mercy could be greater."

Another interval of silence ensued, even longer than the first; to break through the awkwardness of which, and to divert his companion's thoughts into a pleasanter channel, the planter now inquired gaily, how he was getting on with his affairs. "The last time I saw you in town, you were just sending a dozen wheelbarrows to your estate: what were they for? how did they answer?"

"Hem!" replied Mr. Dorset slowly, and coughing lightly as he spoke, "I suppose I must confess to a failure. I got them to save the women: I couldn't bear to see them carrying such heavy loads on their heads."[†]

Mr. Cardon burst into a fit of laughter.

"Well, in spite of all I could say," continued the Englishman, "they would persist in hoisting them on their heads; and whenever I expostulated, they only answered by twirling the wheel as it dangled over their faces, and calling it a 'cleber ting.' "

As may be supposed, this announcement in no degree abated the coffee-planter's merriment, the boisterousness of which somewhat wounded the *amour propre* of our novice; but he smiled placidly, and rode on.

"And what brought you," asked Mr. Cardon, stopping abruptly, — "you, a most tender-hearted, Negro-loving man, all the way from free, noble, moral England, to live among us cruel, miscreant slave-holders, to be a slaveholder yourself?"

"Simply this," replied the other quietly, "because I was left this little property which lies next to your estate, and as we were not rich, the obvious course was to come here and live upon it. I assure you, with the competition and ignorant prejudices of society in London, a young medical man must wait long for practice, and I had not capital enough to sustain me while waiting for the accidents of fortune. For the rest, I never entirely went with the public in running down the system of slavery, for I am inclined to consider it a means permitted by Providence to bring the inhabitants of a vast and unknown region into more immediate and direct communication with the children of enlightened Europe, and by this means to civilize the savages. It remains for me to do my part, by showing kindness, patience, and gentle teaching."

"And so you thought you would make your fortune by treating these Negroes of yours as you would your valet in your aristocratic country?

Bravo! success to you! and tell me, how do you get them to work on your no-flogging system? Are you never treated with long rows of Negroes on a fine morning, when they have a mind for a holiday, their foreheads bandaged up, their eyes nearly closed, and their tongues all the colours of the rainbow, with complaints of 'head he da hut he;' 'heart he da bong he;' 'kin he da burn all ober'?"[†]

Mr. Dorset stooped over his horse's head and coaxed it down with the whip, but made no reply.

"Were it not that I see you to be a single-hearted[†] man, Dorset, I would leave you to your mistakes, and your fate. *Pardi,* I pity you!"

"Hem! thank you," observed the other drily.

"No offence!" cried Mr. Cardon, beating down the luxuriant boughs which obstructed his way; "every one is liable to mistakes, and the noise and fuss that are just now made in England concerning this slavery are enough to blind wiser heads than yours, *mon ami.* I grant you would be right if the Negro were a creature on an equal footing with the white man in point of common intellect; but he is not — he is far beneath us."

Mr. Dorset objected that he was in the habit of speaking with his own Negroes every day, and he had always discovered in their conversation proofs of the same powers of mind, the same reasoning faculties, the same feelings as those of white people, only not cultivated.

"Bah! bah!" cried the other impatiently, "you don't know what you are saying, *mon ami.* In the first place, did you never observe the form and style of the Negro's face, and did it never suggest a baboon to you? I can show you, on the very estate we are going to, some of the Moco nation[†] so like the ourang-outang[†] as to startle one: you would not have me consider those as equal to Europeans, would you? I tell you moreover the mind of the Negro is not the same as ours: it can't calculate, it can't combine the various faculties, it can't reflect; it has its will, its memory, its understanding, like the brutes, and little more. Now see here: yesterday morning I had a great many reasons for coming down to this slave-market, and I also had a great many reasons for staying away; I weighed the two, — the balance fell in favour of the market, and you beheld me there. But the mind of the Negro cannot admit of many motives at the same time: one is all he can entertain, and the impulse and action follow one another as the report of a pistol on the flash. What is that but brute-like? Therefore next to the brute I place the Negro, and his race must bow before the intelligent whites."

Mr. Dorset elevated his eyebrows. "And do you mean to aver," he said, "that the colour of the skin is a sign of the low condition of the brain?"

"I do!" exclaimed the other with a force of tone that betrayed his positive mind; "I do! no doubt about it! everywhere throughout the world you see it: look at the lazy Hindoos, the stupid Egyptians, the worthless Red Indians, — all!"

"Mr. Cardon, did you ever read the history of Egypt? We read even in the Bible that its people were the most civilized on the globe; and elsewhere we find that during one period the fair-haired race were subject and slaves to the Egyptians, and that the prejudice of caste was as strong in the Thebaid[†] against the white people, as it is with us now against the Negroes. Remember that where the rod ruled once, it may rule again."

"Pooh! bah! tut, tut, tut!" cried the other, "*qu'est-ce que c'est que ça?*[†] what old woman's story is that? — a parcel of nonsense propagated by the Jews. I tell you, *mon ami,* there are men in the world who burn to make their influence felt: their vanity is a thorn which goads them on to disturb society; so having nothing else at hand, they must rake up old women's stories, and set themselves up as saviours of a people. Now, supposing I admitted, for the sake of argument, that the Negro was on a level with us, still he has only a certain number of hours of labour, just sufficient to season his life and make him healthy: he is well clothed, well fed, well housed, well nursed in illness, well taken care of in old age; this is enough for him. But the poor in England, look at them; work, work, work, night and day without rest, upon starvation fare, and all for the aggrandisement of some mighty Nabob,[†] manufacturer or middleman generally; was man made for this? I ask you. Have you ever visited the manufacturing towns in free, glorious England, Sir? I have, — *pardienne,* I have! I have travelled a good deal, and looked about me a good deal. Did you ever visit the courts and alleys of the greatest city in the world — immortal London? *Sacre!*"

"But, Sir! but, Sir!" interrupted Mr. Dorset, roused from his usual tranquil manner, "you forget they are free: a crust and freedom, surely!"

"They are slaves," cried the other with vehemence, as he pounded his saddle, "they are slaves, like my Negroes."

Mr. Dorset fairly wheeled himself round in his saddle, and gazed at his companion in amazement; he began to doubt the soundness of the planter's mind.

"Slaves!" continued the other; "what else are they? what does it matter whether it is the whip of leather that drives one man to work for his brother man, or the whip of starvation? The seat of pain is the same, the rest is all imagination. Did you ever go among the people who give you potatoes and pave your streets, who fight your battles and man your ships, — the Irish peasants? I should be ashamed, Sir, to see the lowest dog in the Colonies housed and fed and treated like them. Did you ever visit the mines? I should be ashamed, Sir, to treat my dog like some of those underground wretches. There is not a luxury you enjoy, I tell you, but is purchased by a thousand liberties, a thousand lives. And your legislators and aristocrats, and all your moneyed men! We at least have our slaves always in our company, playing with our children, taking part in our joys; but our brother slaveholders of England — 'Faugh!' say they, 'keep those squalid beasts from our sublime presence: we like to take their life-blood, but we really must ignore the horrors of the slaughterhouse.' Oh that I could write! I sometimes think I shall write. I remember once, when travelling through England, I sat on the outside of a coach; the man who sat next me was crying: at first I thought he had taken a drop too much, but a closer view satisfied me it was veritable, heartfelt sobbing. I felt for the man, and opened conversation with him: he was a servant to a baronet in the neighbourhood. '*The curse he gave me,*' said the man, '*just on account of a mistake, goes deep into me, till I feel like good for nothing. If I leave him, he will call me impudent, and hinder me from getting a place; and I can't talk, none of the poor can, we haven't words like those who are scholars, we can only feel, and be silent, and cry.*' Yes, I said, it would be like fighting with a little rusty wire against an enemy armed with a sharp-pointed sword. That's right, brother slaveholders of England, do as we do, *chers frères!*[†] Whenever you educate the poor, they will cut your throats; when we educate our slaves, they will do the same. *Sacre Mulâtre!* to think of his insolence on board the ship today! to think of all I did for him, — sent him to France to attend on my own son! *Le chien!*[†] he would cut my throat for it tomorrow; though I am — what was I going to say? *Sacre Mulâtre!*"

Mr. Cardon had it all his own way: it was useless for Mr. Dorset to oppose a remark, before the vehemence, the power, the eloquence of expression and gesture, which eminently belonged to the planter.

"Prejudice of caste? — *parbleu!* they have none, — oh no! And pray what is that stand-off reserve which keeps so effectual a barrier between the moneyed man and the pauper, — the noble and the trader, — the master and the servant? Why you know right well that you would rather die than shake hands before company with the footman who waits at your table, though he may have saved your life in the morning."

"Sir! Mr. Cardon!"

"Bah! I am not speaking personally, I tell you; I only say *you,* because I have no one else to say it to; you stand for the English nation, and you must listen to me. How do you treat your servants? Why, as if they had been created merely for your convenience and pleasure. You give them wages scarcely adequate to provide them with the decent clothing you require them to appear in. You take the health and the strength of their youth; and how do you reward them in their old age? Do you pension them and support them, as we do *our* old Negroes? No! you leave them to rot. What feeds the abominations of the English streets at night? Servants out of place,† sempstresses,† and others who have no future before them. Who prey upon them? Why, I tell you, the most licentious estate of the most licentious planter never presented one-hundredth of the nightly horrors of one street of your Babylon. Oh no! there is no slave-hunting, nor slave-dealing, nor slave-buying, nor slave-murdering in dear moral England! and that among not these half brute baboons, but just among God's loveliest creatures — women, sent among us to lead us to heaven. Pray where are your saints,† your excessively virtuous saints, that they suffer these things to be?"

Mr. Dorset laid his hand upon his arm to stop him, but it would not do, the planter's ire was up.

"Moral England!" continued he, "*pardienne!* Yes, the saints! they sent a ranting set of Methodist preachers down here: I kicked them off the estate, every one of them, — the murder-preaching set!"†

"Oh! oh!"

"You may say 'oh!' but it is so. The boasted Christian spirit of the Protestant form! that is laughable too. In our Church,† at least once a week the master and the slave kneel on a perfect equality before our God. Our priests are bound to ignore any difference between them, and they do so. How is it with the Protestants — eh? I will take a bishop going to the cathedral of his diocese on a holy sabbath. Will he imitate the humility of his divine Master only just a little? Will he go on foot only for this one day? Not he! on wheels he will drive, surrounded by the pomps and vanities of the very devil. And his wife and daughters, will they lay aside their silks and satins just for a few hours this one day, and join the poor in humility of garb and humility of prayer? No! behold them surrounded with rails, *noli me tangere* fashion,[†] to keep them from contact with those loathsome bestialities, the poor. And the sermon, mind you, all the while runs on humility! yes, in fine, hard, grand words, which the poor are never taught to understand; but they understand the meaning of the pomp and the carriage, the silk and the satin, the rails, and the stand-off looks, and they understand that humility is a Christian virtue intended only for the poor, to teach them meekly to bend their neck for the rich to set their foot upon them. Let me tell you that were I ever so much inclined to the Reformed religion, I should be ashamed to bring my Negroes to attend in your churches. Such devotion to pomps and vanities! such lack of devotion to God! Pah! disgusting humbug![†] — a word invented by the English for the English, and befitting them alone: you can't translate it into French nor German, no, nor Italian nor Spanish, nor any other tongue. Cursed be the day I put faith in their proclamations and promises, and was fool enough to settle in any Colony belonging to them. At any events, we planters are no humbugs. Fate has placed the whip in our hands, — a whip we call it, fearlessly and openly, and as a whip we use it. The moneyed men of England have a whip too, and use it too; but they sneak and snuffle, and put on a sanctified face, and tell their victims that the blows they give are so many blessed proofs of freedom."

What more he would have added is not known, for so intent upon his subject was he, that he had come unwarily into too close contact with the overhanging branches of the trees, and a bough laden with oranges struck him full in the face. "*Sacre!*" was of course the word, as he beat and struck at the offending branch, till the other, coming to the rescue, set him free.

"There now!" observed the Englishman in his good-humoured way, "you have annihilated all the branches of the trees, and all the aristocrats, to your heart's content, so let us take breath, and refresh ourselves with this delicious fruit. How luxuriant! how beautiful! I must pluck some," he said, filling his pockets and those of his companion. "There! while you were scolding head-quarters in England, my horses' hoofs have been trampling and squeezing the most luscious little oranges scattered about the road. Methinks that in the midst of such a glorious nature one could not well be very unhappy."

The planter took to whistling, and they continued on their way for some time without speaking.

Mr. Dorset was still in the fresh years of youth; he had tasted care, but not enough to dry up the strictures of his companion, he was inclined to attribute much to acerbity of temper, probably produced by crosses and disappointments, and he felt disposed to bear with him good-naturedly on that account, trusting to time, opportunity, and well-timed argument, to bring him round to a milder *régime* with his slaves. The day was surpassingly bright and beautiful; and as he gazed on the wild and gorgeous banks on either side with delight and curiosity, he discovered that not a leaf on tree or shrub, not a blade of grass, was like anything that grew in his own England, — vegetation was on so large, so varied, so rich a scale. Sometimes it was difficult to tell which was bird and which was flower, so brightly and confusedly were they mingled. Now his eyes followed the blue bird[†] till it was lost in a thousand mazes, or the oriole[†] and perroquet[†] perched on the tree-top like some brilliant flower; then they would rest on a tuft of blooming shrubs, — the macata,[†] the red hibiscus,[†] the oleander,[†] and the African rose,[†] — through whose closely twined branches the papaw[†] shot up its silvery column, with its crown of leaves and pendent racemes of odoriferous lilies, and hundreds of humming-birds, all poised on their glittering wings, were sipping nectar from every cup; further on, the slim mimosa was seen hanging its delicate fringes among the thick and solid leaves of the aloe[†] and cactus, and flowering lianas twined their wreaths from bough to bough, flinging odours to the wind, and grace over the wild confusion of the woods.

The sun had passed the zenith, and the heat, though oppressive in the towns, was here in the country tempered by a light breeze laden with perfume. Gradually the little birds grew silent in the woods, the wild beasts resorted to their lairs, and nothing was heard but the sighing of the wind among the leaves, and the faint bubbling of a woodland fountain, at which the horses stopped to drink. The sun shone with all the splendour of a southern mid-day, and the heat and stillness weighed on the senses with the quieting and dreamy influence of night. Even Mr. Cardon was content to smoke his cigar without offering to interrupt the contemplations of his more romantic friend. The horses, having satisfied their thirst, tossed their heads and snorted; the water dripped from their nostrils, and, after pawing the ground, they took the way unbidden towards the abode of their masters. The travellers proceeded beneath shady trees, fanned by mid-day breezes, and lulled to soothing reflections by the faint sweet sounds of reposing nature. By-and-by amidst all this stillness there arose, gently and sweetly at first, then swelling on the ear, the song of the Negroes, keeping time to their work. The Palm Grove Estate was in view. One voice seemed to lead in a sort of recitative, then the whole gang would join in chorus, and end the stanza: such is the true metre and spirit of African song.

Mr. Cardon seemed to lend a keen ear to the music, and once, when his companion addressed some question to him, he put up his finger in token of silence: "Hush!" he said, "listen."

> Oh! to beguile the labour of the day,
> And drown the sigh that struggles on its way,
> We'll cheat the white man as we creep along,
> *Chorus,*   With tune of merry song,
>   Though plaintive of our wrong.

> Ah! little would he care like us to toil,
> For ever turning this detested soil:
> To us the harvest yields no joy or gain,
> *Chorus,*   But only brings us pain,
>   The eating of our chain.

> The sea! that mirror of the heavenly vault —
> Is it the tears of slaves that make it salt,
> When vainly wishing they had early died,

Chorus,   And o'er the vessel's side
             They lean, their tears to hide?

When angry Heaven its airy cistern locks,
And with a drought the expectant planter mocks,
The whip's deep marks upon our shoulders grow,
Chorus,   And our tears like rivers flow,
             To enrich the soil below.

Our homes, our wives and children, what are they,
But the white man's mockery, victim, prey?
And how can we on such our love bestow?
Chorus,   A Negro's heart must know
             No feeling but of woe.

The white man's voice, 'tis angry, loud, and hoarse;
His frightful grasp, it has a hellish force;
And how can slaves escape his censuring eye,
Chorus,   But like the serpent sly,
             And with a coward's lie?

Yet, oh! when every fond emotion's still'd,
That ever once our own free bosoms fill'd,
And Slavery's breath has o'er our spirit pass'd,
Chorus,   Simoom from Obiah cast,
             With deadening poison blast.

Yet like the green Oasis in the waste,
One feeling still as fresh and rich and chaste,
Erect amid our soul's wide barren sand,
Chorus,   The love of fatherland,
             Will blooming take its stand.

Thus when a Negro stranger we shall meet,
And find in him a countryman to greet,
A bond all woven in deep mysteries,
Chorus,   By spirits in the skies,
             Will bind us in its ties.[†]

"Some white man, I swear, has been teaching them that song: that is no Negro language notion; I have only caught the last words though," muttered Mr. Cardon. "Fools! fools! they have heard I am bringing home some fresh arrivals. *Les maudits!*[†] they will sing anything but what I want them. See here, Dorset, here is something for you to learn."

The Englishman, who had somewhat lagged behind, now quickened his horse's pace, till he came to the planter's side.

"Here," continued the planter, "is some of the blessedness of slave-holding, — a confusion in the chaining, you will admit. Some years ago I took my family to live in the town, and of necessity left the management of the estate to my steward; but this did not quite please my Negroes: they liked their master better, they said: then how do you suppose they showed their love? Now, I am a man who likes to be absolute and have his way, but in this case the Negroes had theirs, *de par tous les diables!* — they instantly took to the poisoning work."[†]

"Good God!" cried the other with a look of horror, "what is that?"

"They began with the mules; then the horses, cows, poultry, all went, till I began to fear worse; so I came down and listened to their songs, for the laws of society here forbid one white man to listen to any complaint against another. So, as I was telling you, I listened to their songs, found out what they wanted, and yielded."

"God bless me! but this is the most dreadful thing I have heard yet: I hope you found out the offender, and brought him to trial."

"Brought him to trial! and suppose I did, and the wretch was condemned to be hanged, who would pay me for the loss, eh? No, thank you! when I want a Negro to be hanged, I hang him myself. But, *pardi!* in this case I knew them to be all concerned in it, every one of them, so I had nothing to do but to give in."

"What a horrible state of things!" exclaimed the other, drawing a long breath.

"Ay, but there is worse coming. This murdering work, or Obiah, as they call it, has been going on again upon my estate now for the last two years, — not only my cattle gone scores and scores of times over, but my best and choicest Negroes, till I am almost tired of renewing the gangs[†] by fresh purchases. If I could only find out the sorcerer, or Obiah man,[†] as they call him, I would hang him up on the very first tree; but the

Negroes are made to take such hellish, heathenish oaths, never to reveal how, when, where, and by whom the poison is administered, that it becomes hopeless to attempt finding out the criminals."

"Is there, then, no way of tracing it? Methinks *I* could."

"No; the poison is too subtle: neither taste, smell, nor appearance betrays its presence; and when you consider that noxious herbs spring up everywhere beneath the Negroes' tread, you will begin to understand what a tremendous power they have in their hands."

"Well, well!" exclaimed the other with an expression of amazement, "at least for this there never was a parallel in England."

"You forget the Whiteboyism[†] in Ireland, and the diabolical murders which could never be found out: can't you recognize something of the same sort here? This is the only thing that makes me suspect Negro slavery to be a crime. Every system that sets might over right has everywhere the same result, and it often makes me dream that there really is some glimmering of humanity in the Negro. Dorset," he continued, "I once had three daughters and a son; I loved them as all southerns love their children — better than my life. I accumulated wealth to establish them early according to their hearts' desire; and, that I might see them happy, I travelled with them all over Europe, and brought them home, my three daughters first. Long as I had been gathering my wealth, — and God knows I have gone through hard trials enough to earn it, — I would have given it all to save my cherubs, and gladly have begun the world anew for their sakes. First went my girls, — my three beautiful girls: I saw them gradually and gently fading away before my eyes, and then in a few more months they were laid side by side in their quiet graves. My son! my brave, bold boy! I had left him behind me in France: that Mulatto dog was with him, or I should have laid the crime at his door. Well, my son returned, and married a poor but lovely girl: both gone, one after the other! nothing left me now but their little infant to take care of. If I could save that one innocent head! — it is all I have left in the world to take care of or love. Sometimes I feel almost broken-hearted."

Mr. Dorset did not immediately address him. Whatever had been his opinion of his friend's hardness of character, he knew now that he had suffered; and a suffering creature, in Mr. Dorset's eye, had always a claim to sympathy.

"Can't you,"he said after a considerable pause, — "can't you form any idea as to the cause of it?"

"Oh! how do I know? perhaps, if I were inclined to listen to the Overseer's gabble, I might suspect the woman Coraly."

"Upon what grounds?"

"He says he heard her swear on the dead body of her child to wreak vengeance on the family."

"But that is strange: what could it be for? — flogged perhaps?" said Mr. Dorset inquiringly.

"Flogged? *Pardi,* flogged indeed? she no more cares for a flogging than you would for the touch of a feather; I have seen the woman myself undergo a flogging that many a Negro man could never outlive. I have seen the blue welts rise like network upon her back, and when you thought she had fainted, she would suddenly jump upon her legs, and turning a pair of fiend's eyes upon you, would say, 'Tankee, Mas'r!' and walk unconcernedly away."

"God bless my soul!" devoutly exclaimed the Englishman, horrified at the tale, but too much interested in the issue to remark upon it yet; "but I can't help thinking, from what I know of the feudal submission of the Negro, that it must be some unusual wrong that has worked her up to vengeance: you ought to inquire into it."

"I tell you, you might do your very utmost with that woman, and she would not care. I have locked her up in the stocks[†] myself, and she would scream all night, just to prevent the family from sleeping, and be none the worse for it next morning. But I'll tell you what seems to have been the cause: she was impudent to her mistress one day, and her infant was taken from her as a punishment, and locked up; the squalling brat took convulsions and died, and since that hour the very devil seems to have taken possession of the woman."

Our Englishman looked very grave. "Mr. Cardon," he said at length, "you are a man of intellect and feeling, and are reputed to be a man of honour and principle too: how can you reconcile to your feelings as a man, — excuse me, Sir, — to flog a helpless woman, to take away her infant from her, and lock it up? Oh, Sir! it is cruel work. You have talked a long time, with loud and bitter severity, on the social condition of England, but, thank God, at least we have not such cruelties as these to answer for: we don't carry barbarity quite so far as flogging a woman."

"Ho!" cried the planter with the least possible expression of levity, "chivalry! is it chivalry you are boasting of? English chivalry, — that's good! Now I acknowledge to considering the Negro but one degree removed from the brute, and I act accordingly. I should as soon think it a breach of the laws of chivalry to beat the mare I ride upon, as to flog an impudent Negress, — just the same. For the rest, where's the odds? You know the seat of pain is in the brain: well, what matters whether pain is excited on the back, when we call it flogging, or in the stomach, when we call it starving, — it is all imagination. But I tell you, Dorset, not to plume yourself quite so quick. We planters venerate the very name of woman — mind, not a Negro woman, — but such as God has given her to us, fair, good, and beautiful, — an embodied angel, to refine our souls and lead us up to Heaven. We show it in our desire to establish our sons early, according to their heart's desire, not for *money,* but for *love.* We are content, for this, to reduce our establishments as our children grow up, and give our sons sufficient to begin the world with, and to our daughters dowries to enable their lovers, if poor, to do the same. But what do your canting, moral parents in England? Would they reduce their establishments, to enable their sons to marry? No! but under the pretext of *prudence,* they grind their sons down to celibacy, till they are driven to profligacy. In the meantime, where has outraged nature taken refuge? In a boiling, seething lake of corruption."

"Sir!"

"*Oui, Monsieur,*† a lake, into which is thrown *pêle-mêle*† the fair, the innocent, the trusting, the loving of God's holiest creatures. After that, talk to me of chivalry indeed! where is yours? Fallen like a needle into the sea of abomination which overflows the streets of your Babylon. Go, take a pitchfork, and rake it out if you can and when you show it to me, I will give you my head."

"Mr. Cardon, these are grave accusations; there is scarcely anything more ungenerous than a sweeping censure. Just prove to me that the Negro is not a human being, has not a soul to answer for, has not a heart to feel, has not a claim to that salvation which our Saviour died to obtain; else I must deny your right to argue in this way."

"As for your women," interrupted the planter, perfectly unmindful of the remark, for he had got on his favourite subject again, — "as for your women, in spite of my respect for the sex, I don't know what to make of them. The mission of women from God is to sanctify our lives, and keep us brutes to what is right; but *your* women are so tainted with the hypocrisy of your Babylon, that to mention its corruption to them is an insult, — much more to expect them to correct it, poor innocent dears! Yes, they have suffered their work idly to pile up to such a height, that their souls may fly up to Heaven now, for any good they do; they are only in our way. *Fi donc! allez!*[†] it is vain to speak; I see that you yourself, my friend, are so walled-in with a stone wall of prejudices, that you cannot even understand me. Well, no matter, for here is my domicile. *Mais que diable!*"[†] he exclaimed, stooping low over his horse's head, and looking attentively on the ground, "what is all this?"

And in truth the road presented a strange appearance: it was strewn with broken eggshells, hair and feathers matted together with pitch[†] and red powder and sulphur intermixed; further, from the overhanging boughs of the trees depended rows of eggs from a string, and, on rising suddenly to an upright position, Mr. Cardon's hat struck against one of them, which instantly burst, and covered his coat with a grey dry power. The travellers both gazed at the strange accident; but in Mr. Dorset's face it was simple curiosity, while on the planter's brow there was care and anxiety. Neither of them spoke however till they reached the house, which they now approached at a smart pace.

CHAPTER X.

The Muster Roll

Troops of wild, half-naked domestics came out to welcome their master, with dips meant for curtseys, a wide display of white teeth, a rolling of white eyes, and a chattering of gibberish, to which the planter responded by a rap on the head of one, then of another, that stood in his way; while the pantomimic gestures of the sable youth and their sidelong glances at one another, as they discovered the powdered and stained coat of their master, may better be imagined than described. There were some children among them too, young things eight or ten years old; but these kept behind, — not on account of their entire nakedness, for that gave no more offence than the nakedness of the cattle in the field, but in order to be out of the reach of their master's whip, for they read danger on his contracted brow.

The gentlemen dismounted before an open door leading through a veranda to the sitting-room of the house, for, according to the hospitable custom of the Colonies, neither closed doors nor cautious porters ever impeded the entrance of strangers to any but a prison. The dwelling was low, formed entirely of wood, even to the walls, which were also shingled on the outside; and the naked beams and flooring of the garret formed the only ceiling to the rooms of the ground-floor. The partitions were neither painted nor papered, but wainscoted with fine cedar;[†] and the uncarpeted floor, of narrow planks of the pitch-pine,[†] just freshly scoured with sour oranges,[†] was white as new wood, and fragrant as the forest grove. The windows had no curtains, but were guarded with frames of green gauze, instead of glass, to soften the midday glare; a huge crystal chandelier hung from the centre beam; and the furniture consisted of chairs, surcharged with heavy carving and broadly gilt, and an enormous looking-glass, hung obliquely from the wall, so as to reflect the floor and everything in the room at a falling angle. Between the windows, on one side of the room, was a stately sideboard, with all the glass furniture of the house laid out upon it; among which we must not forget to mention the sangaree-bowls,[†] and several beautiful cylinders, used for shading the candles from the wind and night-moths,[†] for the windows are never entirely closed. This was the saloon, or hall, as it is called in the Colonies.[†]

Passing through this, the gentlemen entered an inner apartment, where a table in the middle, laid for dinner, at once showed the use of the room. The cloth was white as snow, the silver plentiful, the dishes and plates of the finest porcelain, from which a goodly row of female attendants, decked out with glittering necklaces, chintz skirts, and Madras coifs, were brushing away the flies with the aid of orange-branches and peacock-feathers. The mistress herself, a very fat, tall woman, with a languid look and sickly bilious complexion, was seated at the window, habited in a loose wrapper of white muslin, surmounted by a black silk scarf (she was in mourning); while on a cool Indian mat[†] on the floor lay an infant asleep on a silken pillow, a Negro girl watching by its side. To this little object Mr. Cardon, after the usual salutations to his wife, directed his eyes on entering the room, and with affectionate pride he subdued his voice, and invited his friend to approach and take a peep. "Is he not the picture of peace?" he said, kneeling to look closer at him, and with fond solicitude fanning away the flies. "Look here, Dorset, he is the image of my poor son;" and further to show the expanse of its brow, he ventured to slip up the cap which had fallen over its cheek; but the huge fingers of the grandpapa were too awkward for so delicate a task, and several sounds of "hush!" from the other end of the room warned him to desist, just as a bunch of glossy curls burst from beneath the border, so black as to draw forth an exclamation of wonder from the Englishman. It was, upon the whole, a beautiful child, — not like the blonde and fair creations of northern fancy, but a little being in whose soft contour, though still marked with the helplessness of childhood, there dwelt many a promise of strength and stormy passion. He was about a year old.

"Whist!† whist!" whispered the lady of the house, "leave the little creature to sleep, and do the honours of the house to your friend; you must both of you be hungry, the dinner has been waiting for some time."

He was not long in obeying; the infant was in the meantime removed to another apartment. After a short absence, to recompose their dress, the gentlemen took their places, and for awhile nothing was heard but the rattling of knives and plates. I scarcely know whether my readers expect a description of the dinner: it consisted, in the first place, like that of most planters, of a soup made from the *Arum maculatum,* and called calaloo;† there was also wild venison,† stewed turtle,† fricasseed iguana,† and, to crown all, a dish of the famous grugru worm,† for this is the grand dainty with old West Indians. Mr. Dorset shook his head when offered some, and looked away; but Mr. Cardon assured him that his dislike arose from fancy and custom, nothing more, and that he himself was not less surprised and disgusted, when he first went to Europe, at the sight of stewed snakes (eels) and raw meat.

When the first demands of appetite were satisfied, conversation began; at first in a general way, and afterwards on the more interesting particulars of home. Mr. Cardon inquired of his wife how the estate had gone on in his absence. She replied that things had gone on pretty well; that she had spent the day mostly in the hospital, attending to the sick, to the number of whom they would soon, by the overseer's report, have to add the Negro Anamoa.

"Well, that is no loss," observed the planter; "I was always sorry for that purchase. Dorset, I must show him to you; he is one of the Koromantyns, the only African nation, by the bye, for which I have a respect: they are brave, bold, and proud, and though I hate them for the trouble they give me, I am almost inclined to allow that there is something human in them," he added, smiling. Then, after a pause resuming, "As for this wretch, he was a prince in his own country, had his harem and his palace; he came to me just fresh after his capture, and, what do you think? at first he actually refused to work! I think I have cut that out of him though; and his countrymen in the field used to beg to do his task, but I have cut that out of them too, though I sometimes suspect they

do his work by stealth. Well, how is Coraly?" he inquired, again addressing his wife.

"Oh!" cried the lady, "never speak to me about that woman, I am a
martyr to her. I am the victim of my Negroes. You promised to sell her
away to a distance: why don't you, St. Hilaire?"

"*Ma bonne amie,*† I would give her for three stampees,† if I could get
any one to take her. I think I have struck bargains for that woman half-
a-dozen times, if not more; but just as everything is concluded and she
is delivered to her new master, she tells him she is good for nothing, can't
work, can do nothing but spoil the Negroes and other wickedness; so of
course I am obliged to take her back. However, Angélique, don't fret, I'll
send her away over the sea, and get rid of her that way, for she is a curse
upon me."

Madame Angélique Cardon sighed deeply, and Mr. Dorset, remembering all she must have suffered, felt compassion for her. Dessert was
served, and showed the usual amount of delicious fruit — pine-apples,
mangoes, bananas, balatas, sappodillas, etc., followed by confections
and jellies, which Negro cooks so well understand. Dinner was about to
conclude, when a sudden confusion arose at the upper end of the table,
and half-uttered cries and sundry dips on the part of the Negro girls
announced a domestic punishment; while the patient Madame
Angélique, who had found a soiled plate set before her instead of a clean
one, smashed it on the head of the sable attendant.

"Never fear!" exclaimed Mr. Cardon, observing the attention of his
guest directed that way, "I assure you their heads are very hard."

A loud cracking of the whip put a stop to further remark: it was a
signal for the muster-roll; and our planter invited his friend forth to an
open lawn at the back of the house, where the Negroes were standing
in a circle, each with a bundle of grass on the ground before him. The
names were soon called, and they then commenced repeating the
Vesper prayers in response to the Overseer, who stood a little apart,
leaning against a mango-tree, his arms folded on his chest. Prayers
opened with the salutation of the angel to Mary,† which the Negroes
repeated so unintelligibly as to call forth a remark from the Englishman
expressive of regret that they were not taught to understand what they
said.

"Hopeless, *mon ami!* quite hopeless!" replied the planter; "you might as soon teach donkeys to speak. All that one can hope for is to inspire them with a religious awe once a day, and that is a great deal. Some of these Negroes were christened about a dozen years back; I had just bought them, and my good wife, having very romantic ideas on the subject, took them in hand, and made a duty of teaching them."

"I am glad to hear that," exclaimed Mr. Dorset; "so it was not she who took the woman's infant from her?"

"My wife," continued the planter without attending to the question, "spent days in teaching those savages, and we had a priest here to perform the ceremony in a little pavilion attached to the house, which we always use for religious service; I will show it to you. But the good Father neither spoke nor understood a word of the Negro patois; perhaps he would have thought it desecration of his subject to give his sermon in it if he could; be that as it may, he held forth in courtly French on the blessings of Christianity and the horrors of heathenism, and he concluded with 'My friends, will you become the children of God?' Now my wife had taken particular pains to instruct them as to the way they should answer the priest whenever he put a question to them; but the poor devils, addressed in a language they could not understand, had puzzled away their brains until startled by the question, and then they stood completely stupefied. 'Will you become the children of God?' again asked the priest kindly and encouragingly; when one fellow, that young black racoon you saw with me this morning —"

"Do you mean the one you called Quaco, who fell into the water?"

"The same; he was a lad of about sixteen or seventeen, apt and rash; he called out, at a venture, 'Non, mon Père!' Instantly the rest of the gang took it up, and the pavilion resounded with a round chorus of 'Non, mon Père!' The poor priest was taken aback: 'What!' he cried, 'do you wish to become the children of the Devil?' and Quaco, taking the lead, and thinking to correct the error, the pavilion again resounded with 'Oui, mon Père!' Out strided our impetuous pastor; he would have nothing more to do with such incorrigible heathens, he said; and it was with difficulty that, suppressing our laughter, we could pacify his anger and bring him back. So you see it is quite hopeless."

During all this time the Englishman had full time and opportunity to note the groups before him. First of all there was Bretton, overseer of the Palm Grove Estate, — a man with a small head and an immense visage, very sallow and much freckled; he had long bare jaws, and features in which a certain expression of low malice contended for mastery over the habitual indolent cast of his countenance. His dress differed from that of Mr. Cardon in being entirely of check-linen;[†] it was very loose, in many places thin and much torn. He had no stockings to cover his slipshod feet, and his large coarse straw hat hung slouching on his head, more from custom than with a view to ward it from the sun, for he stood in the shade. Mr. Dorset remarked that he did not remove it when the gentlemen approached, but merely nodded. This want of manners was partly owing to that footing of equality on which the meanest white person stands with the proudest and richest of his own colour in the Colonies, for it is to their interest that they should so uphold one another; but mostly perhaps this want of common civility belonged to the character and habits of the man himself, who had fallen too low to entertain any feeling of respect for a superior. He approximated closely to the savages whom he drove, without sharing one of their virtues; he was content to adopt the primitive habits of the African Negro, was equally destitute of the stimulus of ambition, and equally forswore the trammels of decorum and self-respect.

For one thing however he was remarkable — no one had ever seen him under the influence of anger. Offences which often sent the master raving, only made him laugh. His favourite pastime was first to provoke some unfortunate slave, and then, laughing at any impotent show of resentment, to punish the wretch with the wanton ingenuity of a mean nature: this formed the highest exercise of his intellect. Such was the individual who was leaning against the mango-tree. Having made his sign of recognition to Mr. Cardon, as related above, and gazed vacantly at the visitor, he turned away his head to speak to some of the Negroes assembled.

These were all barefooted, — not from poverty, so much as from a custom suited to the climate. The men were naked to the waist, and wore short trowsers; sometimes these were dispensed with, and a short apron adopted instead. Most of them bore on their shoulder their several implements of labour, viz. a bill,[†] a hoe, and a spade, on which were hung a pair of wooden clogs, a gourd[†] for holding water, a calabash[†] to eat from, and a blue osnaburg[†] mantle; a few carried a basketful of coffee-berries[†] slung in front of them, as specimens for Mr. Cardon's inspection, as the full season of coffee-gathering was not yet come. The women were similarly laden; they also were barefooted and bare-shouldered, and distinguished from the men by having a kerchief twisted round their heads, and an ample skirt, whose folds, tucked up under their right arm, formed no ungraceful drapery about them. There was little to distinguish one nation from another, and whatever peculiarities had marked them in their childhood had now merged into one general character of careless, hopeless apathy.

Some of the slaves, as in the case of Madelaine, had not a thought beyond that of following the orders they received; their covering fell literally in tatters from their bodies, and common decency, such as even Negroes understand it, was disregarded. Others again looked sickly, yellow in hue, and drooping in their gait, as, for example, a remarkably well-built Negroman, to whom the other slaves seemed to look up with respect; — very slight indeed were the tokens of it, sometimes only enough to raise a suspicion, as, when bending under the load of his basket of coffee-berries, a young woman took it from him, and ran forward to show it to their master, asking his approval of the crop. He might have been forty-five, he looked sixty.

"Old crooked-backed thief!" said the Overseer with a drawling nasal twang as he pointed to him, and obliquely addressing the planter, "he pretends he is dying — it's all pretence; the lazy baboon, he does not like the work!"

"Won't work, eh?" exclaimed the planter; "don't like it yet, eh? maybe you will learn to like it when I take the whip to you myself."

The old man raised his head, and gave his master a look of defiance, while a smile of contempt and something like mournful resignation slowly crept about his shrivelled lips; but this momentary feeling of courage, slight as it was, soon passed away, and he pointed appealingly to his legs: they were greatly swollen, and the skin all cracked.

Mr. Dorset, in his capacity of medical adviser, advanced to feel the old man's pulse: he examined his tongue, his eyes, his skin, and particularly his legs; one of the Negromen taking advantage of the opportunity to relieve him of his implements.

"Well?" said Mr. Cardon inquiringly.

After a pause, and a renewal of the examination, the other replied, "Send him to the hospital immediately."

"Get along with you, you good-for-nothing old racoon," said his master roughly; then added, "Go to your mistress." He always said this when he felt pity.

The Overseer began to laugh, — it was something between a sneer and a chuckle, — but he was too lazy to utter more till urged by Mr. Cardon. "Hey!" he then drawled forth, "he takes something to make them legs swell; he don't like the work."

"*He hab Obiah 'pon him,*"† answered some one in the assembly. The voice came from a woman resting sulkily against the wall of one of the outbuildings near. She was the healthiest-looking of the whole set, and seemed to have spirit and impudence enough for ten gangs; though standing apart, Mr. Dorset's examination of the Negroes seemed to interest her in no small degree, while with a keen, attentive eye, and an odd expression of contempt and curiosity, she watched every one of his movements.

"Come, Coraly," said her master, "come here, you Negro-woman, we know one another of old; tell me now, and quickly, what you mean by Obiah."

The woman was erect in a moment, and with undaunted familiarity she spoke out.

"Me, Master! what nigger sabey (know), when white man not sabey?"

"I'll make you tell me."

"Me, Master!" she said, pointing to herself with emphasis.

"Or I'll take your grounds from you."†

"Hey hey!" she cried, stammering and stuttering her broken English with that childish accent which all, both white and black, adopt when speaking a foreign language they have never mastered; "hey! hey! well, me starve, — who lose nigger? not Coraly; who then care?"

"Coraly," said her master, fixing his eye significantly upon her, "I want to speak with you; come up to the house by-and-by."

"Master," continued the woman, "neber ask Coraly nothing, Coraly no sabey nothing; *no pick my mouth* (do not cross-question me), nothing there; but s'pose me savey, s'pose me tell master, what good to Coraly? bring back a my piccaninny, hey? did master cry for Coraly piccaninny? Master, you 'member Mulatto Belfond's mammy? she loved master plenty, too much; she saved master's life two times: did that save her flog? no! dead saved her from flog."[†]

She was interrupted by a nasal chuckle from the Overseer, for which she darted upon him a look not entirely conscious of impotence.

Mr. Dorset was at this time busy examining a lad of about fourteen, whose countenance bespoke incurable imbecility. Coraly advanced close up to him.

"Fine slabe, Master," she observed ironically; "that oberseer good too much; cleber man! he wanted to make this nigger-boy cleber too, so one time he flog him ebery morning 'fore he open his eye, 'nother time make him walk on four feet like a cat, then he tie him up like a dog, so maked him bark when people pass. So now Alibo, dis nigger-boy, is a fine cleber dog; put him under your bed, Master, a thief neber come to take your money again, he is a fine cleber nigger-boy."[†]

The Overseer did not attempt to deny the account, but treating the story with that eternal laugh upon his lips which often rendered him so provoking, he asked Mr. Cardon whether it was not a good invention for punishing the boy who had poisoned the house-dog; upon which Coraly smiled contemptuously, perhaps because she knew it was a falsehood.

But now the eyes of the assembled Negroes turned in the direction of the road whence the noise of the great travelling waggon was heard creaking heavily on its wheels as it came slowly up the avenue, and Mr. Cardon, turning indoors, beckoned to his friend to follow. "We will look at them from the house," he whispered; "the meeting of the old and new Negroes is very amusing; but we must not stay here, or our presence will be a restraint, and then they are not half so comical."

The Negroes, considering themselves dismissed for the day, now left the grass-plot, and old and young, men and women, all started off to meet the new comers.

CHAPTER XI.

Black Cattle Broken In. —
Effect of the Cowskin

There was one slave who had not joined the curious throng, — Anamoa, the Koromantyn. At first he stood straining his eyes to see the inmates of the waggon; then, as if seized with a sudden pang, he tottered away in the opposite direction, till he came to a large stone, when, overcome perhaps with exhaustion, he sat down and covered his face with his hands. And now the rumbling waggon stops, the travellers alight, and immediately a clamour ensues which defies description. The cry of joy, the warm greeting of love, the wailing of grief, the deep murmur of disappointment on the part of those who found none but strange faces, and the muttered yearnings of childless mothers anxious to adopt the young strangers, all offered a scene of tumult perfectly bewildering. Then a loud voice was heard above the rest, and Quaco, his sable face beaming with delight, led forth the savage beauty, the young Talima, by the hand. The noise subsided, the crowd gave way as he passed, and with the whole assembly in his train he sought Anamoa, who was sitting upon the stone. The old Negro looked up, a scream rent the air, and Talima, throwing herself upon his neck, sank fainting at his feet. It was his child, his long-lost African child, whom he thought his old eyes were never again to behold. What were his feelings? Were they as keen, as bitter, as those of a white man placed under the same circumstances? Indeed I cannot say: the higher reasoning of the white man might render his feelings more continually tormenting, the deeper passions of the Negro might render his the keener, — perhaps yes, perhaps no; but this is certain — nature was there within him, degraded, injured nature, and the old man wept long and bitterly as he pressed his child to his breast. The other Negroes, who had gathered round, though all so noisy before, were now hushed, and spoke in whispers; even the little ones pressed closer to their mothers' side in silence, so sympathizing is the heart of the Negro.

The scene caused great merriment in the large house, the white people looking out through the jalousies[†] and enjoying it each after his own fashion, — all but Madame Angélique Cardon, who was busy playing with the infant on the floor, while young Beneba, the nurse, though burning to join her companions, was kept dancing to amuse it. Mr. Cardon stood with his hands on his sides, contemplating the scene as one might a comedy. The Englishman, leaning forward on the window-sill, looked on with that interest which he might be supposed to take in the manifested emotions of beings whom he still considered human. Don Duro, the manager, who had come riding behind the waggon to see that the goods arrived safe, was sitting, nothing moved, and smoking, very comfortably on a chair, with his legs resting on the window-ledge; while the Overseer, with a low mocking laugh peculiar to himself, seemed unable to restrain his curiosity, for he soon left the company of the white people, to mix with the Negroes. Behold him now hovering round one group of women, then another, pulling their skirts, slapping their shoulders, or whipping off and flinging away their head-gear: he was very facetious at times. The young and good-looking girls shook him off with impatient disgust, the older and more prudent females moved out of his way, and the aged, who had learned something from experience, attempted a feeble response to his jokes. Thus disturbed, the Negroes, who hate the presence of white people in their leisure hours, — for, say they, *"white man's eye burns the Negro"* — made a movement towards their huts, which were about half a mile distant, and visible from the great house, looking like a rustic village embowered in trees.

The Negroes on their way formed a circle round the old man and his daughter, as if to shield them from the white men's observation; but Bretton somehow managed to work his way into their midst, and as they passed, his playful humour prompted him to attack the young African with one of his lowest and most unfeeling tricks. Anamoa forgot himself:

he had just recovered his child; his feelings had come back to him fresh and free, as when last he had parted from her; he, her natural friend and protector, forgot the loss of his rights, of his health, of his strength, when he saw her insulted; his ebbing spirit boiled up again, his feeble arm was nerved to vigour, and with one blow he felled the Overseer to the ground.

I have known a captain to be snoring in his hammock, wrapt in a sleep which not all the loud quarrelling of the passengers or the tramping of the cabin-boys could disturb: something went wrong on board, and in an instant the captain awoke, jumped from his hammock, and was upon the deck, — warned by what? some mysterious movement of the vessel, which he perceived as it were by instinct, even in his sleep. So it was with our planter: from the position in which he stood, and the manner in which the Negroes had crowded round old Anamoa, it was impossible he could see what had gone forward; but something warned him of danger, and before many seconds he stood in judgement on his recreant[†] slave. A word had explained the blow, but no word was either asked or spoken concerning the provocation of this blow, though, if it had been, it would only have excited laughter; but the Overseer was not hurt, not he! there he sat on the ground, laughing with that low malicious laugh, most spiteful when least noisy.

At sight of their master the circle opened, and the Negroes drew back terrified; and yet Mr. Cardon was merciful: he did not order the culprit's hand to be burnt, as was usually done for a similar offence in Martinique, St. Lucia, and elsewhere; he only ordered "the miserable brute" to be bound and flogged till not an atom of the flesh on his back remained whole. "*Sacre Dieu!* he would teach him to touch a white man: he would stand by to see it done himself!" The culprit was dragged forward, his body stripped, and bound to a ladder, in such a manner that the fore part of his person should be preserved from the action of the whip. While these preparations were going forward, Bretton, who liked nothing better than a scene of this kind, had seized the whip, and was diligently wetting it in a puddle near, to which he had crawled, — he was too lazy to stand up.

Mr. Dorset at first remained indoors, from a feeling of delicacy and reluctance to witness any domestic confusion; but when he saw them tie that tottering, feeble, sick old man to the whipping-ladder, the instinct of his benevolent nature induced him to join Mr. Cardon, though without any idea of interfering. His face contracted with nervous anxiety; he approached nearer and nearer, and then a remark from some bystander induced him to look round at the Overseer. He well understood what the man was doing — wetting the whip, that it might carry off flesh with every stroke: impelled by indignation, he tore the whip from the wretch's hands.

"No interference!" whispered a voice in his ear, "or you may witness scenes you won't like: believe me, let things be."

"I am not interfering," cried the young colonist; "but didn't you see what that — what the Overseer was doing? Don't you see plainly that the decrepit old Negro can't outlive it?"

"*Pardi!* he had strength to commit the sacrilege of touching a white man, so let him serve as an example."

Mr. Dorset yielded the whip into the planter's hand. But among the Negroes assembled a whisper began to circulate, which soon increased to an audible murmur, and those of the Koromantyn nation came forward and knelt in a suppliant attitude before Mr. Dorset. "You good heart, Massa; *do beg for he, — he old! he sick! he shame!*"

"Back with you, you dogs!" thundered their master, leaving no time to his friend to reply to their request; "*back with you!*" and before the uplifted whip, the sign of their degradation, the suppliants sprang upon their feet and took refuge timidly behind their companions. The whip has always a magical effect in taming men and reducing them to brutes.

But to the young Talima its power was yet unknown. During the foregoing scene she had remained completely bewildered. Her father, at whose word she had seen men fly, whose arm had felled lions in her own country, — her proud, fearless father, — she could not conceive why he had so unresistingly submitted to be thus dealt with by those white men, unless perhaps it was part of some mystic ceremony; but when she caught from the word of her companions some idea of the truth, it was piteous to see how she seized the cords with which they were binding her father, and, her eyes streaming with tears, sobbed forth her distress in her own unintelligible but earnest language. Bretton dragged her away; again and again she broke loose from his brutal hold.

"Can't you hold her down?" asked the master, grown impatient at the overseer's imbecility. Bretton, in compliance, pinned the young slave to the ground with his knee, laughing all the while at her vain cries for assistance.

The whip was now handed to the driver.[†] The driver is the Negro whose task is to flog the other Negroes: he is always chosen for this honourable post on account of his steadiness and obedience. The present driver belonged to the Mandingo nation, a sly, cowardly, treacherous race, made ten times worse by being reduced to slavery; but this by the way, it has nothing particular to do with my story. The cowskin was raised, and whistled as it fell, measuring the old man's back. He did not utter a word; but Talima's screams were fearful, to stop which Bretton took off his shoe and stuffed it into her mouth.

"Lend a hand here," exclaimed Don Duro, "the Negro is throwing back his head;" for the manager had joined in by this time, and he was ever anxious to show off to Mr. Cardon his knowledge of the Negroes' way. "Come, some one, light a piece of wood, and bring it here."

The temptation was too great for Bretton to resist, so giving up the charge of his prisoner to some of the slaves who stood nearest, he pressed forward to offer his services, for a new and more exciting pastime: and what was that? simply to raise the ladder, and place it resting against the tree, then to hold a burning torch before the victim's face, in order to divert him from suicidal intentions, — in short, from swallowing his tongue, — a practice often resorted to by African slaves when their lives become unbearable. In the midst of the confusion however Talima had again sprung forward, and, with her arms clinging fast about her father's neck, she endeavoured to shield him by interposing her person between him and the whip. Bretton tried to pull her away with one hand only, for he did not like to let go the torch with the other; but here the incensed planter stopped him.

"*Corbleu!*[†] leave her alone," said he; "since she likes it, let her have it."

"Cardon! Cardon!" exclaimed Mr. Dorset, unable any longer to contain himself; "have you no flesh and blood in you, that you have so little mercy for those unfortunate beings?"

"I'll double the number of stripes for that!" cried the planter, frowning.

"But the girl, — she has done nothing."

"Nothing? well! I tell you she likes the flogging, or she would not put herself in the way of it. Strike away at her, driver, and let her have it well; when she has fainted, we'll go on with her daddy."

The cowskin descended again with a broad sweep, not upon the old man, but upon his unoffending child, and a blue welt rose high across the polished shoulders of the innocent victim.

"God of mercy!" exclaimed Mr. Dorset, horror-struck at the sight, "this place is cursed, let me hurry from it!" and he rushed precipitately from the scene, — he scarcely knew whither. He had strided into and through the house, up the palm-lined walk, and through the gate to the high-road, before he recovered himself sufficiently to think where he was going. It was evening; the sun had just set, and earth for a moment was bathed in splendour, giving response to the departing glance of the light-giving god; then twilight came, and already the curtains of darkness were drawing close around. It is thus that night comes on in those countries, with the rapid, passionate character of all changes within the tropics. As Mr. Dorset slowly made his way along the road, many a sad and painful reflection came to his mind. The old fable of selling one's soul to Satan for wealth seemed to be realized before his view. He looked at the rich coffee-grounds which bordered the road, and in imagination he saw on each crimson fruit the warm droppings of human blood. His eye turned from them to the soil on which he trod; he thought he read there dire inscriptions of cruelty and wrong.

"O God!" he exclaimed aloud, "and is this the amusement of planters? are these the scenes which must in time become palatable even to me? England! my beloved country!" — but here he stopped, for a host of strange misgivings came crowding on his mind. The conversation he had had with Mr. Cardon in the morning — the things the planter had said — his retaliating accusations, could they be well founded? — were things so bad at home? Was the heart-rending misery so often witnessed there among the lower order, was it indeed inflicted on them by the upper classes? "Or," said he, "am I groping for truth in vain? Am I striving and vainly struggling against a wall of prejudice, as high as that which imprisons the feelings and reason of Cardon himself? Then, so is nature one universal working of cruelty, one echoing cry throughout the globe, of one creature preying upon another, man feeding on the vitals of his fellow-man. O Almighty God, show us thy mercy! make manifest thy providence!" He sighed deeply, and the sound of the evening breeze, passing lightly among the boughs of the forest, seemed to him an echo to the melancholy tenor of his thoughts.

CHAPTER XII.

The Obiah Priest

The mountains which rose at the back of the village were clothed, like all the Trinidad heights, with thick forests old as the flood. There was one however, not so high as the rest on which the woods were somewhat thinner; its lower part was mainly covered with a comparatively scanty brushwood, but half-way up this gave place to a dense thicket of nux-vomica, palma-christi, the branched calaloo, poisonous shrubs of the cockroach-apple,[†] and many other noxious bushes, all crowded so closely together as to be almost impenetrable. Nature, so beautiful and enchanting elsewhere on the mountains, here assumed a most repulsive aspect: dark, dismal blossoms, huge, misshapen fruits, and glossy leaves almost black with venomous sap, were mingled with thorns, long, pointed, and protruding, like spears of ugly gnomes; while a rank smell of unwholesome vegetation rendered the atmosphere around unpleasant and difficult to breathe. The chance traveller, hewing his way in these unfrequented parts, would turn aside to seek more practicable subjects for his hatchet, and the wild animals, the free tenants of the forest, would avoid it, as by an instinct given them by nature; yet through the tangled bushes that formed these melancholy shades, ever and anon there peeped the shrivelled face of an old Negro, listening, spying, watching, as if for the approach of some one. Sometimes, in his eagerness, he would half expose himself to view, and then might be seen strange appendages — snakes hanging and coiling about him, caressing him.

At the foot of the mountain, just commencing the ascent, there was one who did not dream of such a spy. Belfond had taken this direction from sheer absence of mind: he knew it would be dangerous to loiter about the village, as he might soon be recognized; he therefore betook himself to the first opening or semblance of a path into the forest, thinking to return at night to the mimosa-tree for the rest of the money, and start with it to Guiria in any boat he could lay hold of.

Belfond had formed no particular plan for himself, but the world was all before him. Experience, it is true, had given him some hard lessons, but with youth, vigour, health, and that fillip to his spirits derived from having foiled the planter, how could he despond? Besides, his was a proud heart, which could not, would not bend before a disappointment, and he now sought to drown regret in the exciting dreams of ambition. He would not allow his thoughts to revert to Laurine for a moment, but sought to keep them in check by amusing himself with anything haphazard. He drew a knife from his belt, and commenced trying his arm upon the strongest trees, and then pulled away by main force the tough lianas which looped and knotted them together. Then he climbed a tree, the tallest he could discover, and mounting from branch to branch with a dexterity which long experience alone can give, he stood on the very top, to watch the slave-ship from which he had been driven. His keen eye could even detect the movements of the people. He saw the Koromantyn girl taken down from the foremast, and recognizing his master's boats putting off immediately after, he judged by whom she had been bought. "But this is nothing to me," said he, "only I must get down now, unless I choose to be perched up here all day; for should I get down but to eat a piece of bread while those people are walking about, they will catch me."

He quickly descended, and plunged into the thicket, going heedlessly on, until the pathway became fainter and fainter and was at last entirely obliterated, so that not even his practised eye could detect a trace among the impenetrable woods now thickening before him. Some confused recollection of the place kept him hesitating ere he turned back, when he was startled by the low snarling of a dog, and almost at the same time a wizen fiendish face peeped out from the thickest part of the copse. He knew it well; it belonged to the being whom, after his master and Higgins, he disliked most in the world, — the Negro sorcerer, the Obiah man. It is true his dislike for them was not the same: his feeling towards

the first was unmixed hatred, but here it was a loathing disgust. Fanty
however had a claim upon him, for he was his mother's brother,[†] and the
only being upon earth to whom he could claim kindred.

Here, Reader, I find myself in some difficulty; for in relating the conversation which took place, if I give it in the precise words and language
in which it was uttered you could not understand it or, if you could, the
clipped and broken manner in which the Negroes connect the words of
a language to them so foreign as their masters', would make that appear
childish and ridiculous which was neither the one nor the other in its pur-
port. So with your leave I will transcribe it into as fair English as my
vocabulary permits.

Seconds passed, and minutes too, and still that fiendish visage and
Belfond were eyeing one another. This seemed to amuse the wizard, for
he laughed with a strange noise, — a sort of snarl, like that of his dog.
Immediately after, and with the shrill quivering tones of fretful age, he
said, using the similes and proverbs of Negro dialect, "*Flying deer hath
lion near:* who pursues now? And are the cayman's eyes sore, that the
turtle has come out of the water? — you are wet, I see. 'Tis well, dark
sky looks out for the tardy sun, for it knows it must come at last: I have
been watching for you; come in."

Belfond obeyed, the bushes giving way as he pressed them. An open
space, with a sheltering mango-tree, was the sorcerer's parlour; his sleep-
ing-room was a cave, from the roof-edge of which there hung number-
less amulets, such as bags of all sizes, egg-shells, deer's horns,[†] and
parrots' beaks; his companions were an American dog bald of hair,[†] and
three snakes, which came hissing and rearing towards the stranger, when
a growl from the sorcerer sent them back to their hiding-place.

"Sit down," said the Negro, bringing out a stool from the interior,
and setting it down with force.

Belfond seated himself, and looked moodily on the ground, wondering
how on earth he should get out of this malencontre.[†] The wizard went
back to his cave, and remained there some time, — so long that Belfond
began to look round him with a view to beat a retreat; but he was not
quick enough — his kinsman was upon him before he could stir.

"Here," he said, "is something you are to do for me; you must go
down yonder over the mountain, where your master lives."

"I have no call to the Palm Grove now, Daddy Fanty," which was the name this priest of dark science went by; for the Negroes number among their virtues a Spartan respect for old age: the old men go ever by the title of either Daddy or Uncle, as the old women by that of either Mammy or Aunty.

"You will have to call there for me; you must give this to Beneba."

Belfond looked at the old Negro's outstretched hand; it held a tube of bamboo-cane, closed up at either end with a cork.

"This," continued the Obiah man, "is a soft paste, which Beneba must rub into the baby's clothes every morning, and down its back after it is washed."

Belfond recoiled with horror: "It is Obiah! it is Obiah! — take it away."

The sorcerer's arm stiffened as it fell to his side, his eyes glared, his jaws quivered with evil meaning.

"Don't give that to me," said Belfond hoarsely.

The Negro's eyes were still upon him, while a low, nasal, snarling murmur gradually and slowly shaped itself into words: "You mule!† you fawn on the white man! you traitor, who would deny that your mother was a Negro —"

"Stop there!" cried Belfond, "you dare not say that in earnest; you know well how I have loved my mother's people, you know well what I have done for them. Who gathered the Maroons† up in the mountain yonder? Who taught them to till the ground, to lay up stores, to do without white people and their markets? Who taught them songs, and order, and courage? Who would have raised the glorious standard of liberty for them, — liberty and freedom, like America, like France, — and have made them a people among the nations of the earth, had they but listened to me and gathered round me like men, brave, bold, generous? But no! they would not, could not believe me: they must be murderers like you, and go, like sneaking cowards at midnight, to set fire to the white man's house, and murder him as he escaped from the flames. I am not a man to do that; I wouldn't head such warfare, no, not to save a thousand lives if I had them; nor will I now be your minion, and bewitch infants with Obiah; go, send your snakes to do that work, not me."

"You fawn on the white man!" continued the Negro, "you would save him, as your mother did."

"My mother!" said Belfond, "I know she loved my master, and I have not much to thank her for in that, and I know too what she got for it."

The Negro uttered a sharp snarl of exultation.

"Yes, I know she betrayed the secrets of her people when they were plotting an insurrection, and his would have been the first murder they had begun with: yes, and another time she spilled the poisoned coffee when he was about to drink it. Yes —"

"Your father!" growled the Negro, gnashing his teeth.

"Yes, my father! curse the word, I wish it stuck in my throat; I know all, and will tell you all, that you may know how deeply these things lie here," he said, pointing to his breast. "My father pampered her and brought her up to a gentle living, and I was scarcely born when he brought a wife home. Well, it was all in the regular course of things; but my mistress took a hatred to my mother, and, placing me with an old mammy to rear, sent my mother to work in the field, though she begged on her knees, crying and appealing for the sake of God to let her nurse her child just a little longer; and my mother could not dig fast enough, so they flogged her, and then she pined and died, — yes, by good luck for her."

"Not so Coraly," muttered the sorcerer, nodding.

"No, I know that; I know they met with tougher flesh in that woman; but I am not revengeful, and my mistress is subdued enough now: you ought to be content."

"But I am not content, and the little boy must go next."

"I will have nothing to do with murdering babes, I tell you," said Belfond, raising his voice.

"Then I will get someone else to do it for me soon enough," said the Negro, filling up with a low growl each pause as he spoke; "but for my dead sister, I would loathe you for a coward, a mule, a mongrel, a fawning lover of the cotton-face, a contemner of the true and the black. Look there," he said, pointing scornfully to the golden hue of Belfond's hand, "Koromantyns' blood has grown muddy there; and with a muddy heart, you mule, you love the whites that kick you; you writhe, and twist, and turn, and then you lick the foot that does it: the Obiah curse be on you and everything you love! I will get somebody else to do it."

Belfond did not resent the anger of his kinsman; his thoughts were busy on something else. "Poor little child!" he mentally exclaimed, "before God he stands as near to me as this murdering priest. Once, when by stealth I visited the Palm Grove, and met Beneba and her charge in the savannah, the innocent baby smiled on me, and opened its arms to come to me, as if I was its father. Poor little babe! I will not have it hurt: I will practise a deceit: God help me, that I cannot do the slightest good without treachery and cunning."

With this he turned upon the old Negro a calm, clear eye; but the tone of his voice was mournful, as he said aloud, "Daddy Fanty, I have thought better of it; I will take the Wanga oath;[†] the old commands the young."

The Dagoman[†] did not speak; he stood looking at him steadfastly.

"Yes," continued the youth, "give it to me; what am I to tell Beneba?"

The Obiah priest, still suspicious, squatted himself down on a log of wood opposite, and rested his chin upon his elbows to peer into the young man's face.

"Come, give it to me," said Belfond, stretching forth his hand, "you may trust me, I am half Koromantyn; I swear by the Obiah Wanga I am true; give it to me, I will drink the Wanga and obey."

The Negro, upon this, rose up and went into the cave.

"No matter," thought Belfond, "if I must, I must; and what if it is stuff to kill me and I die? an hour sooner or an hour later will matter to no one," he added with a sigh, "and life is but a curse to me; but if I can save the little child, he at least is a treasure to many, and his life will be precious to him by-and-by, since he can enjoy it. Yes, and the child *shall* live!"

The Negro now returned, holding a bottle, a small phial, and a mug. Into the mug he poured something from the bottle — it was rum; from the phial he scooped out with a slender stick some black stuff — it was the Obiah; and then he added water, and mixed them all: it was the drink of secresy, the Wanga, which should punish him who violated the promise given.

"Now," said he, "drink it off while I give you the words: now repeat with me:—

Obiah's power, Obiah's spell,
Pains of earth and pangs of hell,
Alight on him who dares rebel
        Against the Obiah's law!

And toads' and serpents' tongues shall lick
His flesh, which dead men's teeth shall pick,
And worms shall creep in numbers thick
        O'er him who breaks the law!

And Obiah's secrets you shall keep,
And in its magic you shall steep,
Till comes your turn in death to sleep,
        For such is Obiah's law!

Very well! drink! come, off with it!"

"Ugh!" said Belfond, draining the mug, "it is the most nauseous draught I ever took."

The old man's eyes twinkled: he had often before urged his nephew to take the Wanga without succeeding, but now he considered him his own, and in his withered heart there arose a sort of spurious affection for the young man. "There!" he said, "though I see you have spilt some, I am at ease now; *the dog is strong with his own.* Where were you going this morning?"

"I was simply waiting for the night, to go off to Guiria, but of course I will put aside that idea in favour of the Palm Grove; give me the box."

"Belfond," said the Negro, "never can you try the sea without my leave, but I will speak of this anon. Here is the bamboo box: Beneba has her instructions from me already; here is her own antidote in this small bag, give it to her, she knows how to make ptisane† of it: she must give it also to the mistress, according to my instructions, which she has already. And here is an Obiah bag for the master; it is to be sewed up in his pillow before tonight: when he puts his head down, the egg will burst within the pillow."

"And who," asked Belfond, looking up at the Negro with much curiosity, — "who of all these is to die first? Is it the child, or the master?"

"Master is not to die at all!" cried the sorcerer at the top of his cracked voice; "he is to get blind, and then — by-and-by — go mad! mad! mad! And Mistress, she can't marry, and she shan't die; and he shall go mad! mad! mad!" said the Negro, uttering a yell of exultation such as fiends send forth at thoughts of destruction.

"Whist! whist!" said Belfond; "prudence, Daddy Fanty! don't you know how many white men are near? *Mountains have ears as well as tongues.*"

"Ay," replied the other, recollecting himself, "*sleep should be light with him who eats the tiger's young one.* I forgot myself; but tell me, son of my dead sister, wherefore were you about to try the sea? Why seek the water when dry land has soft blossoms for your feet? though, were it otherwise, a brave man's foot fears not even a thorn."

"I am no coward," repeated the young man proudly, "I fly no danger, I am ready to meet it now as ever."

"Then, O my son, have you tried the cutlass? Know you how it cuts the cotton-skin flesh? or do you love the white man too much to try?"

"I have said before," returned the young man, rising angrily to his feet, "that I will fight the white man in a fair way, — man to man, and sword to sword, — as the brave do."

"Poor fool!' said the sorcerer quietly, fixing his eyes upon him: "know you the power which gives the white man sway over the Negroes?"

"Certainly! undoubtedly! it is knowledge: I have been in their country, and I ought to know it."

"Knowledge?" continued the other in the same calm tone, "yes, Obiah-knowledge; and would you have the Negroes wield cutlass in the broad day against the white man's Obiah, which works in his head all night? But let Negro cutlass cross white man's cutlass, and Negro Obiah cross white man's Obiah, and I will say for once it is fair; but this they will not do, Belfond, — they steep their guns and cutlasses in their Obiah, and then they kill you. Poor fool, Belfond! you won't believe old Fanty. My son," he added almost affectionately, "it is only Obiah and cunning and sly ways that will enable the Negroes to put their foot upon the high ground; use the Obiah, my child; be wise, and then you will get to look the white man in the face. The white man's Obiah is weak before the Negro's Obiah, if all would only use it: the Negro's Obiah commands life and death; fire, water, birds, and brutes, all obey the Negro's Obiah. Did you see such power as that with the white man?"

"Daddy Fanty, these things affect life, it is true, and your fame the vales repeat to the mountains, but let your power do good, not evil; your Obiah is no real friend to the Negroes: he is no friend who kills his friend."

"Yes, yes!" said the old man, with an emphatic motion of the head and with slow and measured words, "friend and true! For the Spirit of Death that serves me, whither does it take the Negroes? — through the Obiah power it takes them to Africa's shores, free! free! free! where no slave-hunter nor slave-chains can reach them. But hist!"

They both listened, the young man standing erect, but grave and attentive; the crippled form and shrivelled face of the old man were bent anxiously forward, looking down towards the valley.

"I hear shoes down the mountain," observed Belfond.

"Yes," said the old man with solicitude; "there, son of my forefathers, they come; but stay a moment yet," and he led him on a few yards, where the thorny bushes seemed best to forbid approach: "stay behind here, lest any one should come unawares." Then leaving him for a little, he returned to his gloomy cave, and brought back a string with an amulet depending from it, and throwing it about the young man's neck, he said —

"There! not a Negro yonder, or anywhere, shall dare betray you; seek the white man ever so briskly, ever so cunningly, for harm shuns this. Accompong, the African Great Spirit, has looked upon it; Assarci, the God of mercy, the Mediator, has blessed it; Obboney, the God of evil, fears it.[†] The sun light thy path, my son, and thy shadow fall upon him who seeks thee! for by the rising of my gall it is a white man who comes."

So saying, the old Negro turned abruptly from the bushes, leaving his nephew to thread his way through the maze.

CHAPTER XIII.

The Visit of an Enemy

Leaving our young traveller to make his way through the dense thicket with the usual ease of a forester, let us look in at the old Dagoman, to see whom he receives, and upon what errand. It was no unusual thing with him to receive a visit, but his visitors were rarely white people: his retreat, although the approaches to it were so dismal and forbidding, was sought by slaves from far and near; the discontented, the angry, the revengeful, the despairing, the wronged, all came to him for relief.

"The estate has been left in charge of a manager we dislike, give us a spell to bring back our master," said one; and the Dagoman would mix his dose, and mortality among the cattle would commence.

"Our master is going to Europe," would another complain; "I love him, and yet he leaves me behind, give me a spell to keep him with us;" and three horses would expire that night. "Our master has understood, he has given in," would the party say on the next visit; "give us an antidote for the other animals we have commenced dosing;" and, true enough, no further mortality would be seen there.

"The situation of our grounds displeases us," declared a messenger from a distant estate, "they are on the side of a steep hill, and unpleasant for us to cultivate; give us something that will show our discontent to our master." This messenger came but once; the Negro songs at fieldwork revealed the cause which brought the odious visitor — the Obiah spell, or let me speak in plainer words, the poisoning work; the master wisely granted what was wanted, and it went away.

As may easily be supposed, our Negro sorcerer made a fair living by this work. He was one of the old and useless who had been turned off the Palm Grove Estate when Don Duro Harding took the management of it. This however was done without the knowledge or approval of Mr. Cardon: he had always been given to understand that these slaves had run away, and were not worth attempting to recapture. Old Fanty, driven abroad to shift for himself in his old age and crippled condition, turned sorcerer and poisoner to maintain himself. The trade he chose was a lucrative one; people said he had amassed an immense deal of money.

The old Negro adopted various contrivances for making himself feared: one of these was the choice of strange pets. The companions of his life were three snakes, the largest of their kinds, and an American dog entirely destitute of hair. Of the reptiles, one was an aboma,[†] or boa-constrictor, fourteen feet long, which he called by the name of Mottle. Another was a horse-whip snake,[†] green, and tapering finely off to the tail, not in reality a dangerous kind, but feared by the Negroes from a superstitious belief that it whips to death any stray Negro it can seize; this the sorcerer named Cowskin.[†] The third was a coral snake,[†] the most venomous reptile of the Colonies, figured throughout its length with alternate rings of red and deepest black; this he called Vixen. These creatures wound themselves about the wizard's neck and arms, caressing him and obeying him, and guarding his gloomy domicile with their various noises of alarm and anger. How he had tamed them no one knew; the Negroes, over whose minds he had acquired an absolute dominion, considered his control over them as part and parcel of his divining power. The native Spaniards, however, or Spanish Indians I should rather say, would hint at the wonderful properties of a pretty little climbing plant, the *Mikania Guaco*, the juice of which, taken internally as tea, and inoculated into various parts of the body, acts as an effectual antidote to the bites of the most venomous serpents.[†] Its virtues, they will tell you, were discovered by a Spaniard who accidently witnessed the fighting of two serpents. The combat was deadly, and ended with the apparent death of one of them; but no sooner had the victor gone his way, than the wounded one crawled slowly and with difficulty to the bushes near, and choosing from among them the leaves of a climber, he recovered thereupon marvellously, and in a little time also went his way. The Spaniard with curiosity remarked and examined the plant, to which botanists have since given the name above mentioned. With the juice and leaves of this the sorcerer was supposed to have inoculated himself; or he may probably have extracted the reptiles' fangs by wrapping his hand in thick leather, presenting it to the serpent's mouth, and then dexterously withdrawing it, when the fangs, driven deep into the leather, would come away with it. Be that as it may, to the horror and awe of all who visited the sorcerer, there were the snakes, perfectly obedient to this word, and to him at least perfectly harmless. They knew him well, and came at his call, each according to its name — Mottle, Cowskin, and Vixen. As may be supposed, he was attached to them, — perhaps because he knew they were the only creatures on earth who cared for him.

With a considerable degree of agitation, the old Negro, just as he had parted from Belfond, and before he had had time to advance many steps, heard the loud yelping of his dog; then a confused noise of angry snarling and yells of pain, as if wild beasts were worrying his favourite to death; then a pistol-shot, and repeated blows as of a cutlass, — all within his domicile, and he but a few yards off! "Evil betide these limbs," he cried, "that I can't move quicker, and there is mischief at work in my home!" The first thought that came to his mind was that somebody had betrayed him, and that the bushrangers had come to catch him; second thoughts convinced him he was wrong. Stupid as the Negroes are supposed to be, they are wonderfully quick at calculating motives and fathoming the interest which prompts to an action, and Fanty was a man of experience. "I should be a dead weight to any white man," thought he; "they would have to feed me and house me, and I am too old and too deformed to work; they don't want me; they won't take me. But what can it be?"

He crept round amongst the bushes, peeped in slyly, very slyly; then there burst from him a shriek which made the very woods to ring, and he leaped forward and threw himself on the ground, — a proceeding which astonished the visitor so much that he started back. It was Higgins. Luckily the dogs were too busy in finishing their work to notice the entrance of the Negro, and of course after their master had commenced conversation with him the sagacious creatures did not molest him.

"Holloa!" cried Higgins, on perceiving the Dagoman, "you old baboon, is this where you live? Why I took it for the den of a runaway. Strike me dead, but this is luck! But harkye, crooked ape, what made you go away just now and leave me to be bitten by your d——d snakes, hell-dragons I should say? But I'm used to them, and I'll warrant I have laid them low; had it not been for the Captain's dogs here, which by good luck I borrowed, I should have been a pretty sight by this time."

The Dagoman made no reply, but, with his hands clasped above his head, exclaimed, "Eh, my Gad! my Gad! my Gad!"

"Can't you get up from there, for a black deformity as you are?" exclaimed Higgins; "I have no time to lose in keeping watch over your wailings; I've got other fish to fry, I can tell you. But last time I saw you, and 'twas down in that there village, you told me you wanted a box of Obiah; so here it is, old cripple, I got it on the coast of Guinea. Come, have done with your ———— swaying, and speak to me," he said, pushing him with his foot.

During all this speech the Dagoman had remained on his haunches, bending backwards and forwards, the very image of despair; but the contact of the white man's foot roused up all the spirit he had ever possessed. "Go off with you, cotton-face murderer!" cried he, striking back the proffered hand. "Obiah? me no Obiah. You have killed all I loved in the world: curse your hand!"

Higgins made a feint to laugh, though he felt more inclined to storm; but he wanted to see first how much money he could get out of the Negro by fair means.

"You and your snakes, old black Jumbee[†] —! but I've got no time to be jawing about a madman's fancies; just you fork out the dollars. Come, just look now, there are all sorts of things there, and, by Jericho and Neptune, the more Negroes you poison the better, — the better I'll be. I mean to turn trader myself, and bring contraband goods[†] to the coast; so go on, ugly old shrivelled nigger, poison their sooty blood as quick as you can. Come, get up, and get me the dollars."

"I'll give you nothing," said the Negro, "devil yourself, and fiend!"

"You speak so to me, do you? my Jo, you won't find it much to your profit; but we'll see!" and he fairly lifted the old man from his sitting posture to his feet, adding, with a threat worded not in the holiest of terms,

"If you don't now, this minute, fork out those doubloons,[†] — and you shall give me three, — I will set the dogs upon you. Come, Bull! Fangs!" chirping to the dogs, "just come here."

The old Negro, somewhat recalled to his senses, eyed the dogs and began to quake; particularly when he recollected how well trained to such work were the dogs kept by the white men, and how defenceless he stood, with his dead favourites strewn upon the ground before him. "I've got no money," he said doggedly.

"You have," said the sailor with a terrible oath; "and if you don't make haste, I'll make you give out more than you like."

"And where is a wretched old Negro like me to get money? Do you see me in the towns? Do you see me working, or trafficking, or selling? Would you squeeze blood out of a stone?"

"I'll squeeze blood out of you in very quick time, and teach you how to say 'Master' too, when you speak to me," said Higgins; and pulling forth a strong rope from the depths of his pocket, he proceeded to tie the old man in spite of his groans and remonstrances, while the two dogs kept snarling and showing their teeth, as if impatient to begin their proper task. But Higgins, entertaining some indistinct fear that the body of the Dagoman, if bitten, would bewitch the dogs, warned them off eagerly.

"Get away, Fangs, I tell you! Off, Bull, and keep your tusks for other game. Come! Whew!" and he enticed them away after him as he went into the cave to rummage; but what this cave contained daylight had never yet betrayed, and Higgins felt the want of a candle.

"Come, you ugly beast," he said, returning, "tell me quick, where is the tinder-box[†] and candle?"

"A poor, miserable old man, a wretched, helpless Negro never has a candle, Master; he goes to bed by twilight, and he rises with the dawn."

Higgins entered the cave again, but soon returned with a roar of pain. "A scorpion![†] oh! sent by the devil to bite me!" he roared, as he came forth, holding out his hand to look at the place, and writhing with the pain.

Inwardly the Negro chuckled; outwardly he broke out into protestations of innocence, for he knew that the rencontre[†] would be visited on him.

"Hold your foul tongue, will you!' cried the sailor, seating himself, the burning agony of his hand almost taking away his breath; "let me but get a little ease — oh, the pain! — and I'll serve you out."

His hand began to swell visibly; from the one puncture had oozed a drop of pink water, and around it, in a broad rim, was a livid purplish hue, which told how venomous had been the bite. Raging with pain he leaped up.

"I'll not bear this! Get me the money, you shrivelled bat, at once, if you wish to live another hour."

"How, Master," asked the Negro, in a meeker tone, — "how can I get what you want when I'm tied up in this way?"

"True! wait; but with this hand I can't manage," he said, as though thinking aloud; "I'll cut them!" So saying, he took the cutlass he had laid down, and without scruple cut flesh and rope together.

"Oh, Master!" yelled the Negro, "mercy! mercy! I'll get you some money! I have a little: I'll get it. Mercy!"

"Then get it, old vampire, and at once," growled the sailor, grappling the crippled form of the Negro and dashing him forwards; "give money, quick!" and approaching him again, he kicked him till he rolled over and over again; "get up, and bring me the money, and if it is not a handsome bagful, I will dash your brains out against the walls of this very cave, and leave the dogs to bury you."

The sorcerer knew he had no resource: his Obiah failed him here; it could do nothing against the sudden action of superior physical force upon a sickly, feckless, powerless old man as he was. He was glad enough therefore to get up, when, followed by the white man, he crawled all trembling to the foot of a mango-tree, and digging some little way down with a spade which he took from the forking of the branches, he uncovered to the astonished gaze of Higgins a bag of considerable weight, which the sailor instantly grasped with a hungry eagerness, forgetting for a moment, in the joy of possession, the agony he endured in his hand. It was heavier than he expected, and he had to use main force to lift it, and still greater efforts to heave it over his shoulder.

"Is this all you've got, — eh, black rascal?"

"Oh, Master, search all over here, I haven't a stampee to buy myself a bit of cassava for supper."

The sailor did not deem it convenient to press further; the bag, he felt, was as much as he could conveniently carry or conceal; he allowed himself therefore to appear lenient, and made as much of it as he could.

"You old ugly baboon devil, I know you have got another hoard, but I'll let you off this time on one condition. There's a runaway —"

The necromancer† grinned dismally.

"Don't be showing me your ugly teeth, old bat, but up, and help me to catch him."

"Me, Master? me?" exclaimed the Negro piteously, "with old legs like these? Turtle walks faster much than old Fanty."

"Do you think I wanted you to run after him, you drivelling old beast? No; but use your Obiah, and set a trap to catch him."

"Master, who do you want?"

"You know very well; it's the runaway Mulatto they call Belfond: he's about here, I know, for the dogs led me this way, and I daresay you know it too. Come, set your Obiah quick, or by all the storms —"

"Yes, Master," he replied, his feeble limbs shivering with suppressed rage. "Come tomorrow night to the Palm Grove Estate, and there you shall meet me, and have all that you want."

"You'll go there, you devil! Now, if you don't, I'll light a match between every finger and toe of your body and smear it with sulphur over a fire. What o'clock?"

"Cross down," replied the old man, pointing to the southern sky, where that beautiful constellation is known to sparkle.†

The sailor then called away the dogs, who were playing about the cave at French and English† with the mangled remains of the creatures they had killed, and, shifting his bag of money with some difficulty to an easy position for carrying, he went away, but moaning with pain. The sorcerer noted this: his face brightened with savage joy, his teeth ground with fierce pleasure; he followed him.

"Master," he said in a hoarse, eager whisper, "I've got a bottle of cure for scorpion-bite."

Higgins turned round half-dubious, but did not refuse; and the Negro, hastening back as much as his legs would permit him, in another minute returned with a phial of spirits and a dead scorpion soaking in it,† — the most approved cure in the Colony for the bite of that reptile. Higgins was too well used to the fawning, crouching habit of slaves, who will too often best serve when most ill-used, and he did not suspect evil here. He did not withdraw his hand when the Negro anointed it; he did not even shrink when the warm blood dribbling from the wounds of the old man mingled with the liquor poured over his own; nor did he even recoil when the Negro, as he thus busied himself, displayed at the end of each bony finger, nails of a hideous length, containing inside them rolls of something like soiled wax. He suffered him to anoint, to rub, and to bind his hand with a strip of banana-leaf. This done, he walked off, threatening with a tremendous oath that failure at the Palm Grove the next evening would beget a flogging by no means comfortable to the bones of old Fanty.

The old Negro watched him from within the bushes for a long time; then, when he thought himself fairly released from the presence of the white man, he sat upon the ground to look at his wounds, which he bound up with what rags his den afforded. He longed to give vent to his rage, but he prudently looked out from the bushes first, then he listened well up and down, waiting to discover the direction his enemy took. At last, feeling satisfied with what he learned, then, and not till then, did he examine the ruin which Higgins had left behind.

"Oh, my Gad! my Gad! oh!" exclaimed the Negro; "Feto! my poor Feto! he can't hear me, he can't see me; never will he wake me in the morning again; never come with me to chase the game; never love me, never keep with me! All lonely Fanty! My money gone! but that is little. Oh, my poor little Feto, my faithful dog! My mottled beauty, even little Vixen here," he said, taking up the remains of the coral snake, "all gone! only friends I had. My poor little Feto, could you not bark, you brute, to tell me the enemy was coming? Obboney take you, cursed cotton-face! pain be your food! but you have got something: these nails — they smeared you, and you shall come to our feast, — yes, for a spectacle of death! Rack be your bed, Fetish horrors your dying dream, and shape of chained baboon your heaven to come! Achch!" he said, as he lifted his arms to Heaven, shivering with revenge, "Achch!"

CHAPTER XIV.

Chasing Game. — Not Over-pleasant Reflections for the Game in Question

Well, was the fugitive caught? is our next question. We shall see. He heard the noise in his uncle's domicile as he stood a little way off amongst the bushes, and, in spite of the danger he incurred, he paused to listen; he heard the old man's cries, and instinctively made a movement to go and help him, but the voice of Higgins addressing his uncle, and the latter answering soon after, convinced him that the sorcerer had received no material bodily injury. He knew the voice of Higgins well, and he also knew what the man was capable of. Seeking a pitch-pine tree, on account of its strong smell, as most likely to prevent the dogs from scenting him, he quickly climbed up it to take a view of what was passing. He trembled with rage as he saw that conscienceless sailor bullying and kicking the defenceless old Negro, and he would have given worlds to have had a stone to hurl at his head; or, as he thought to himself, if he could but rush in and settle all old accounts! but the dogs — they get scent so quickly, and fly at one's throat before one can see them or hear them: and prudence held him back. He remained in the tree long enough to see and to smile at what happened to the sailor in the cave; but he felt it was best to take care of himself now, for Higgins, two dogs, pistols, a cutlass, and a rope, when all in company, boded no good to the runaway. Using a well-known Negro proverb,[†] which singularly enough is found among the Negroes as well as the Spaniards, he said to himself, "*When I see my neighbour's beard on fire, let me water my own; and when the storm rolls large stones down the mountain, let the calabash mind itself,* as Daddy Fanty says, so I had better be off."

His purpose was to travel quickly on till he came to a river, for he knew that if he could cross it the dogs would lose scent, and even if they were close upon him he might then climb a tree and be safe. But there was no stream in the neighbourhood. The pinguin,[†] with its broad leaves formed to retain the water, was abundant here, as was also the "travellers' fountain,"[†] a climber well known in the Colonies as affording an abundant supply of crystal water from its stalk when cut, and both these plants grow only where springs are scarce. But Belfond, though no frequenter of this particular mountain, was nevertheless aware that some springs were to be found near the top; he therefore directed his course thither instead of taking, as he at first intended, a direct course to the Palm Grove.

Higgins meanwhile had left the cave and its precincts, possessor of a bag of money much larger and heavier than he had ever dared to hope for. He at first felt a little bewildered, for the good reason that he did not know where to keep it. "Bring it to the ship?" he said, "that would never do! By all that's holy, I wouldn't trust one soul of them! Captain Hill himself would be the first to take it."

And even supposing it would be safe in the ship, still a difficulty arose, what account could he give of coming by such a hoard? His only plan would be to bury it somewhere in the woods, until he could decide what was best to be done. This moreover was an easy and a safe plan: he might bury it within three yards of the path, even while a wayfarer was passing, and provided he made no noise it would never be known, so dense is the underwood in the forests of Trinidad. But while he was yet cutting through the tangled network of grass and herbs to get at the ground, Bull and Fangs began barking like mad things, and making every possible sign to the sailor that there was game in the wind. Higgins understood in a moment, and covering his bag with herbage, not forgetting to mark well the place, he left it and sprang forward, cutting his way before him as he went.

Belfond was also cutting his way higher up the mountain; but as the trees and bushes were much thicker than towards the bottom, it was not to be expected he could go on very fast, and he had not nearly come to the mountain-top when he heard the dogs crying on his track. Now was the time when all his sagacity was needed! No one in Europe can form an idea of the difficulty of making way amid the pathless forests of the tropics: Belfond was accustomed to it, and in this lay his only safety. By the impatient yelping of the dogs, still far behind, he judged that Higgins was making no very great speed; but the dogs advanced, now bounding over the bushes, now creeping beneath; sometimes falling on a mass of branches solid as a wall, and being almost buried; sometimes getting nearly strangled by the interwoven creepers, through which they pushed; but still they gained fast upon him, and nothing remained for him but to get up into a tree and save himself from them.

Soon they came, clamouring furiously, while Higgins from afar was shouting with all his might to encourage them. Belfond, looking round from the high bough to which he had climbed, espied a considerable patch of the *Mauritia aculeata*† growing thickly clustered, and mingled with smaller thorny bushes, which served to fill up the gaps. This plant is near akin, if I remember well, to the yucca, or Adam's needle, but much taller, and the spines at the end of the leaves are much stronger and longer; it covers miles in the centre of the island, where there is little rising ground, but is rarely seen on mountains; here however, by good fortune, it grew luxuriantly. Just in the centre of this thicket were rotten stumps of a group of palms, which had sprung originally, as they sometimes do, from an undivided bunch of nuts. These palms, growing all so close together, had been blasted by the lightning, and had gradually rotted to the ground. Upon this space Belfond fixed his eye; but the leap was hazardous, not only from the height at which he stood, but also from the difficulty of taking a spring, both on account of his narrow footing and of the crooked position he was obliged to maintain under so many overhanging boughs; but it was his only safety now.

Meantime Higgins was approaching, and the dogs, still barking with fury, made violent efforts to get at him. Moments grew precious; Belfond tried another bough, which, though more slender, yet promised better, from standing more apart. He had no sooner rested his weight upon it than it broke beneath him, and he slipped within five yards of the dogs: dexterously however he grasped a bough, climbed up like a monkey to his former perch, and recommenced searching for a convenient place to leap from. Unfortunately, in his rapid march, Belfond had made a sort of path for Higgins, who, having once discovered it, followed it up rapidly. He was now within a few yards of the tree, unable as yet to see the runaway by reason of the thickness of the foliage, but by the motion of a particular point he could guess very well where his game was hiding. Presently, as he drew near, he discovered, thirty feet up a tree, the figure of a man making his way to the end of a bough. As he approached the end, the leaves became less and less dense, and the figure stood out: Higgins recognized him, and the woods re-echoed with his shouts of triumph.

"Hem!" thought Belfond, "curse not the cayman's mother till you have crossed the river;" and coolly and collectedly, amidst the looping lianas which threatened to entangle him in mid air, he took his aim, and leaped fairly into the middle of the thicket. Higgins, as he saw the feat, for a moment remained thunderstruck, but he took courage again.

"On, Fangs! at him, Bull! catch him, my boys!" and the dogs began to leap and bark furiously, but in vain; the bushes were eight feet high, and four to ten thick all round: at every point, in every direction, long wicked spears crossed and recrossed one another, or the spaces were filled up with smaller bushes equally stinging. The dogs leaped up again and again, and each time they recoiled with shriller cries of pain; then they snivelled at the ground, and at length one of them insinuated his body in beneath, dragging himself along on his stomach. At last he disappeared, and, to the oaths and shouts of Higgins, the other followed. Both were now out of sight.

Belfond, from within, was not unaware of his danger: his fine quick ear had detected the new movement, and with his eye fixed upon the place he perched himself upon the rotten trunk, which sank beneath his weight, all alive with wood-ants;[†] this however he did not mind. He held his knife ready, and just as the dog's head appeared from under the lowest leaves he struck it on the back, — it never barked again; the other dog followed, — it was harder to manage, and gave one dismal yell as it yielded its life.

Higgins now had some misgivings. "Bull! Fangs! at him! at him!" shouted he from without. All silence. "Dogs! devil! at him, I say!" Not a word anywhere. Then he fired his remaining pistol straight in the direction where he had seen the man leap; from hill to hill the sound reverberated, and then died away into perfect silence.

He now set about to reconnoitre; he hewed his way round and round the thicket, examined every side, but everywhere an impassable barrier was presented; he struck at the leaves, but they only blunted his knife. He attempted to reload his pistols, but even this he could not do now; he could not close his fingers, so huge and stiff had they become with the swelling. He tried to climb the tree: with great difficulty he managed the first bough, just high enough to catch sight of Belfond crouched down on the palm stumps, safe, bold, and daring.

Their eyes met; they did not speak, the war between them was too deadly. Higgins took a long and close survey of the place, and having concluded, greatly to his satisfaction, that it was impossible for Belfond to get out, — in short, as he said afterwards, that he was as safely lodged as in the town gaol, — he descended and went away.

Belfond's acute ear detected the direction taken by his enemy. He cleared a small space on the ground, put his ear down to listen, and discovered that he was gone towards the village, where he supposed he would try to get a reinforcement.

"Now is my time!" cried he, "now for dear life!" and leaping up he seized a whole bundle of lianas in his hand, dragged them to their utmost length, twisted them rapidly into a rope, and swung away, climbing the lianas like a squirrel, till he reached a bough; he caught hold, pulled himself up, and was again safe from the jaws of death.

No time was now to be lost. Belfond sped on his way briskly, nor did he stop till he got upon his proper track, which led across the valleys to the Palm Grove. Here he had to tarry a while, to satisfy the cravings of hunger; and so many wild fruit-trees hung their offerings within his reach, that it were a marvel if he resisted. With his ear always on the alert, he sat down and enjoyed his repast. But soon, when the physique was easy, came reflection, none to him of the pleasantest. Then he got up again from sheer agitation, and, as he walked along, broke forth into mournful soliloquy.

"Pretty wretch, indeed, I am, — sneered at by my mother's people, — hunted like a wild cat by my father's! No Pariah was ever worse than I am. What business have I to do right, I should like to know? The

Negroes would spit at me, and call me fool; the white people would kick me, and call me mule; and so they go on. Why should I care if that little child dies? If he lived, what then? he would grow up to hate me, because I, his uncle, would not be his slave; and he would catch me, and crush me, and chain me down to the hoe. And why should I care if my master goes mad? he would then give up hunting me down, and perhaps he would leave Laurine alone. Pah! what do I care about Laurine?

> Our homes, our wives and children, what are they,
> But the white man's mockery, victim, prey?
> And how can we on such our love bestow?
> The coloured race must know
> No feeling but of woe!†

"Little did I think, when I taught them that song, how soon and bitterly it would apply to myself. Let me see, — hideous stuff! Ha! hellish fiend, I am not in your power yet: you did not see how cleverly I slipped the liquid down my clothes. Ay, there my master served me: in trying to drown me he got my clothes wet, — so well soaked that my trick was easy. Well, it almost deserves another good turn. I would prefer death to that horrid drink; I would rather have my master's hate than that old sorcerer's love. Hem! I am to give Beneba this bag to sew up in his pillow: it will make him blind, and then mad. And this paste is for the child: it loves Beneba very much; I saw it cling to her when it would not go to her mistress, and when they little dreamed I was so near, carrying messages backwards and forwards for Laurine. No matter! and in the midst the little thing smiles and frolics and caresses Beneba. She is to anoint it with this fatal Obiah paste, and the child will sicken, and pine away, and cling the closer to Beneba, crying to her to save its little life; and I am to be the medium of this behest!

"There!" he exclaimed, dashing it against a tree, "that is the way I obey your hellish law; and there goes the Obiah-bag along with it! and so you may keep your senses, proud Cardon, father and master to me! O God, what a lot is ours! debarred of the common ties which bind the offspring of the brute; and why? because I have had education enough to wish to be better and greater. What a curse is education to our race! Without it I might have sat down in my uncle's company, and enjoyed his clever tricks and evil witchcraft; I should have gained power among the Negroes from our relationship. Without education I should have settled down to slavery; my master mayhap would have loved me and treated me with confidence; how happy should I have been! Without education I should not have known how degraded is my existence; I should have had no ambitious dreams, no yearnings, no aspirations after good and great things; I should have been content. Education, then, is a crime with the slave; it condemns him to the penalty of an eternal rack. Where, then, is God's justice? where is his goodness, his providential care, since he awards such terrible punishment to the coloured man for those very aspirations which form part of his nature? There is no God, — no, this world is one mass of confusion upon confusion; no Providence; no reward for creatures here below, but the gratification of the tiger when he feeds on the life-blood of his victim."

With this he relapsed into silence, while nature around softly, whisperingly answered him, with her eternal hymn of harmony throughout all space. Gradually came the hour of sunset; the light departed, and night set in. Beautiful, wonderful is night, as it hangs over the tropics! The moon had not yet risen, but the stars shone full and clear with tropical lustre, while the larger planets cast a sensible shadow on the ground; and fire-flies by millions were dancing in and out through the trees and over the savannahs, and in every nook and corner, like young stars let loose to have a holiday upon the earth. Now, like telescopic star-dust, they converge and gather to a ball; then, like a busting rocket, they fly away in all directions; here streaming to some point of attraction, or moving in and out in a maze of gambols. The air was alive and bright with them, and they seemed to go before our traveller like fairy guides, to cheer and light his path. Then came the moon — the bright, pure, majestic moon, — such a moon as a northern country never saw. Rising on her throne of light, she glided along her star-strewn path like a spirit of peace keeping watch over the slumbers of earth, hushing to rest all angry sounds, even in the heart of man. Her strong full light was not that of life, but of repose; so strong was it, that as the beams came pouring through the loop-holes of the trees, they seemed like solid bands; so still, that the patterned shadows of the leaves upon the ground seemed to move by enchantment; and the clouds, pillowy, fleecy, streaky, bore up the queen of night through ether of the deepest, clearest blue. The discord in Belfond's heart was resolving itself into the rich, grand tones of nature's eternal music. Gradually the impious theme died away from his thoughts; his feelings were lulled by the influence of the scene; and by the time he reached the Grove his mind had gained repose, disturbed only by the gentler and more generous emotions, like the undulations on still water produced by the soft evening breeze.

As he passed, he saw light in Mr. Cardon's house, but he did not approach; he bent his steps rather to the Negro-huts, to which he was readily guided by that peculiar distant murmur of voices, occasionally broken by a wild, startling exclamation, which characterizes the leisure moments of the Negroes.

The first hut he passed was Madelaine's: a pang shot across his heart, for here he had always hitherto stopped; however, it did not matter now, for it was dark; the door was open, but nobody was there. Next to that came Coraly's; that was dark and empty too, and so were all the others near; they looked deserted. He took a short cut across the gardens, to the Koromantyn side; here were crowds, and sentinels outside challenged him, but speaking the password, the crowd opened, and he entered the largest hut of the Negro village.

CHAPTER XV.

A Peep at the Hospital

There was a low murmur of many voices at the door, and within a subdued whispering among a semicircle of Negroes, sitting crowded on the floor, round a sort of bed, in a corner of the room, where lay the Negro Prince of Fantyn,[†] now slave on the Palm Grove Estate, ill, speechless, fainting unto dea th. I must tell how he came there.

St. Hilaire Cardon was cruel only by fits and starts, and upon extreme occasions like the present: now that he was left to himself, and no longer provoked by the resistance of the culprit, or the interference of an equal, he did not care to carry further a punishment which he probably considered had already reached the maximum of what was needed, when the girl first, and, some ten or fifteen minutes afterwards, the old man, were pronounced insensible. He ordered them both to the hospital immediately, with injunctions that they should be attended to properly.

Now it happened that Talima had fainted at the third stroke, less perhaps from physical pain than from fright and the shock her mind had received: but when, on her being removed, the cowskin was applied with double severity to the old man, broken, ill, and feeble as he was, yet was he a long time before nature entirely succumbed. St. Hilaire himself had rarely seen a Negro endure so much, and his big heart was moved, as it was always moved when he saw any of the lower animals writhing with pain.

"Take him away!" he said, after looking at the old man awhile, "Bretton, leave him alone; Quaco!"

"'Es, Mas'r."

"I say, take him away! *Sacre!* don't stand there rubbing your head, Sirrah: take him up very quietly, do you hear? and give him to the nurse."

"Señor," interrupted the Manager, "it's of no use wasting care on him; in any case he could not live another week."

"Silence! and let me talk, will you?" said the Master impatiently; and addressing himself again to Quaco, he gave various directions for care to be taken of the patient, and then, like an autocrat, he betook himself from the field of slaughter to his own quiet abode, where, upon soft cushions, he sought, reclining, that repose of body and mind which he so much needed after the disagreeable commotions of the day.

Meanwhile Quaco and two or three others moved the Negro gently off the ladder to a sheet which they passed underneath, so as to enable them to carry him without altering his position; and in that guise, very gently and very carefully, they bore him to the hospital, where they as quietly laid him on the floor. For once Quaco did not speak, but looked intently at his burden when he laid it down; while the nurse, coming forward, looked as intently on the wretch she was to tend. "Eh, me Gad, oh!" she exclaimed, "where de use? dis no man's body — dis chopped fles. Eh, me Gad, oh!" and she put her hands to her face.

At this moment appeared at the door the sneering visage of the Overseer, with that semi-laugh upon it which only fiends can wear in the presence of cruelty. "Here, old baboon," said he, speaking to the nurse, "here's a citron and some salt and pepper; squeeze the juice in, and then rub the pepper and salt into him, it will soon revive him."

"Mas'r," said the nurse, "no use curin wid dat cure; de man neber go trouble nobody no more;" and she turned away, to busy herself in getting materials for a bed.

Bretton, nothing baulked, looked at the unfortunate patient, touched him with his foot, tried to turn him, then stooped down, and pulling away the strips of clothes which had been lashed deep into the flesh, he began powdering in the contents of his paper. A groan of agony from the wretched man told of awakening sensibility. The nurse turned round in an instant, and flew to the spot, jerking away the Overseer's hand with impatience: "Hey! Mas'r Bretton, what you meddle for? Go mind you business; leave to nigger nurse de tings what belong to hospital; wha' for buckra (white man) meddle for?"

Thus pushed away, the Overseer responded with a kick and a sneer even louder than before. He never cursed — his passions were not deep enough to require that — but he would sometimes call names, where he thought they would carry a sting most keenly; and so he did now, though I scorn to transcribe them.

"Mas'r," said the nurse, with tolerable unconcern, "jus look up dere."

He lifted his eyes; it was Coraly, looking in at the window, and fixing upon him a pair of eyes like those of a snake when it seeks to fascinate its prey.[†] The Overseer quailed under that steady gaze. This Negro woman had the power of cowing him at all times, simply by addressing herself to that superstition which ever becomes the portion of those who give themselves up unrestrainedly to cruelty, even if originally brave, — how much more, if low beings like Bretton! With an effort to shake off what he still had sense enough to be ashamed of, he contracted his lips convulsively, and asked her with dogged assumption what she wanted.

"Mas'r Bretton," she replied, "let dat nigger 'lone; no touch 'em, me tell you."

"You nigger spice you, do you think I mind you?" he said, leaning backwards from his heels on to his hands; for when once down he never cared to rise immediately, but would pinch, and gall, and pull down the Negroes near him, even more effectually than if he were standing.

"Bery well, Mas'r," said Coraly, "no mind me; perhaps you no mind sleep tonight?"

"What should hinder me from sleeping, you black monkey?"

"Oh, notin 't all, notin 't all, notin; only jus don't touch dat nigger, dat's all. Me see Jumbee now at he head," said Coraly, fixing her dark glaring eyes upon the patient.

Involuntarily the Overseer started aside, and was on his feet quick enough this time; "I'm going for the cowskin for you," he said, with his finger up; and with this excuse he lazily dragged along his slipshod feet, and disappeared in the gloom.

Any one who could have remained near the hospital unperceived would have been struck with the jeering laughter with which the two Negro women saw the Overseer departing, and the mocking, jibing tones of their remarks, as the nurse pulled bandage after bandage from her store-box; but she had something else to think about too. "Here, you piccaninny,"[†] she said to one of the children playing in front of the door, "go climb da banana-tree yonder, and bring me from de top dere dat nice young leaf for dis poor nigger, — quick!" and the girl ran. Then to another, "Here you, take dis here calabash, bring me water, clear — clear!" and this one was off as quickly. The nurse did not attempt to move her patient yet, but fixed a pillow under his head, and then sat on the floor beside him, looking at him with eyes full of sorrow and pity. She saw Don Duro Harding at a little distance, and called to him to come.

"Mas'r," said the nurse, as he drew near with a cigarillo in his mouth, "me no know wha' for do: so many niggers sick, dere no bed for dis here; do go beg Missis come here, please mas'r, do, for God's sake!"

"*Perra maldita!*"[†] exclaimed the Manager in his mother tongue, breaking into a fit of impatience, "where's the use of taking up the room with a thing like this? Send him to one of the Negro-huts, let him die there; don't you know very well that even if he got well of this, still he would never be any good? he can't work, he's diseased."

"But, Mas'r Duro," urged the nurse, "it's our master self sent him here."[†]

"Don Hilario does not manage his own affairs at all, it's my business to manage them for him, so do you do as I bid you;" and off went this hard man, very indignant at having been bored for such a nuisance.

"Me Gad, oh! me Gad, oh!" exclaimed the nurse, in utter despair, "what me go do?"

"Come, sissy,[†] never mind," said Coraly, coming round to the door; and then she called smartly to Quaco, who had retired some little distance to avoid the Overseer, whom he hated, as did every Negro on the estate.

Both Quaco and Coraly were for removing the patient, as the Manager had ordered; but the nurse, who understood the need of poor patients better than they did, persisted in wanting her mistress, — she must have ointments and linen, and ever so many things besides; and then, she said, when she had made him "little comfortable," they might remove him when they liked.

Quaco was deputed as ambassador, and meanwhile, as the Negro lasses had returned with what they had been sent for, Coraly and the nurse moistened the lips of the sufferer, and, by degrees, got him to take water by spoonfuls. And then it was piteous to hear him moan, — not a loud moan, but a low, hollow, prolonged voice of pain, — and then again it died away, and the sufferer either slept or fainted.

Madame Angélique came at last, listlessly and slowly, and followed by a troop of black girls, whose duty it was to attend upon her footsteps, to pick up the briars from her path, and otherwise to watch lest her foot should strike against a stone.

It was her custom to visit the hospital once a day, generally in the morning, and she rarely refused a second visit when summoned by the nurse. In truth this was her good point: there are none so entirely given up to evil influences as not to have some little corner of refuge in their hearts, where the nature they received from above may abide in safety, — a bright spot, like a lonely star in the midst of darkness, — the soil for seed of future salvation, — the last hope of fallen man.

She approached languidly, put one foot upon the threshold of the door, handed the ointment and linen to the nurse, and then stopped, as if fatigued with the exertion.

"Tankee, Missis, tankee! do look here, Missis, do, please. All beds full: what for me do, for put dis poor nigger somewhere for rest? No bed 't all, nowhere. I give mine a'ready to one of dem sick niggers: I sleep 'pon de ground all night; so now there's no bed nowhere."

"Where's the Negro girl that was flogged this evening?" demanded the mistress.

"Oh, Missis! she's just down upon the floor inside there, fast asleep."

"I want to see her," said Angélique; "your master bought her expressly for me, and you must wake her up."

"Yes, Missis, — directly, Missis; but you see dis poor nigger wants a bed, — he bery bad, Missis, bery bad!" and the woman fidgeted about the patient, purposely uncovered the wounds she was dressing, commented on the difficulty of removing him, and went very near commiseration for the pain he must endure, — words in nowise pleasant to the lady, who knew very well what the man was punished for: so she cast a look of indifference upon him, and passed in the same slow way to the inner wards of the hospital. Coraly, I should have said, had gone away before she came up, for there existed between this slave and her mistress an instinctive dislike to meet; it was more than hatred, it was the bitter recollection which the presence of each revived in the mind of the other, of injury inflicted, mingled with an indistinct sense of injuries yet pending.

The hospital on this estate was in good order: it was a well-appointed, well-arranged building, with everything provided that was necessary, — in short, such a one as a rich man might be supposed to have; while among the poorer class of planters the hospital was simply a larger Negro-hut. Here were three wards, for the women, the men, and the children; from the latter however, there being no sick children just now, the beds had been removed to the other wards, while the tables, chairs, and other necessary moveables were brought into this. Madame Angélique passed on, while the groans of the sick arose on every side as she appeared, not altogether from pain, but as much from a childish manoeuvre to win attention and indulgence. To do the lady justice, she had a good deal to endure from them. Sometimes, from an obstinate indifference to their cure, proceeding probably from a lively sense of their value to their owner, they would throw away their medicine, or obtain from some of the stray Negroes lounging outside, some unwholesome fruit, which would entirely throw them back; or would act as did the head cooper,[†] who was at this time lying ill at the furthest end of the room, and whose case I will relate.

He had exhibited symptoms of swelling in the legs and general emaciation for some time past, with a pain in his left side, for which his mistress had that morning ordered a blister to be put on his back. She now inquired its success.

"Joloff, how is the blister?"

"Bery bad, Missis! bery bad!" he replied in a half-suffocated voice.

"Has Mammy dressed it yet?"

"No, Missis."

"Has she looked at it?"

"No, Missis."

She felt his pulse: he had a great deal of fever, and was really very ill.

"Hem! Mammy, come here. Joloff, turn on your side."

The patient was lying rather upon his back. A groan, as if his soul were departing, accompanied the efforts he made to move; in short, he declared he could not stir, the pain was so great.

"Come, Mammy, help me; what are you doing? Leave what you are doing there, and come directly to me."

The nurse had been dressing the wounds of Anamoa, from which she now, with lingering reluctance, moved away at the summons of her mistress.

"Mammy, help me to turn this man."

Groans most dreadful, as if he were on the rack, ensued, and the whole of his weight met the efforts of the mistress and the nurse. They were obliged to give it up.

"But," said the lady, "his blister must be dressed, and now I am here I will see it done. Call somebody to help us; Quaco was here just now, call him."

The nurse went out, but not a soul was in the way: everybody seemed to have disappeared like magic, except the troop of young lasses outside, who would only giggle and fuss, and do nothing if called upon to help. One of them was sent to call the Manager to assist, and, as by an afterthought, the lady rose to follow: perhaps she suspected some trick, as with a step very different in speed from her slow progress before, she tripped after her messenger, delivered her own behest, and returned, bringing the Manager with her, in no very good humour at having been disturbed from his evening lounge in a well-swung hammock. In his powerful grasp the patient was effectually turned; his groans went for nothing now, and he was made to lie on his face, to allow of examination. The bandage was raised a little, then a great deal, then loosened entirely.

"*Juste ciel!*"[†] exclaimed the mistress, "there's no blister here at all! Light a candle, and bring it here;" for it was rapidly growing dark.

The nurse searched up and down, here and there, through the bed and through the room, the man groaning piteously all the time; but not till the Manager happened to put his head out of the nearest window was the plaster found, — on the ground, where it had been thrown by the patient.

Madame Angélique, so faint and ill and feeble before, now acquired energy all at once. Her rage burst uncontrolled upon the unfortunate nurse, and shrilly, snappishly, overpoweringly, she reproached her with neglect. Why did she not watch him? why did she not tie his hands, or fasten him down on his back? It must be done now forthwith, as soon as the blister had been replaced, and the bandages properly fixed; to witness which Angélique sat down, fanning herself the while with her lacebordered scented handkerchief, quite overcome with her manifold exertions of muscle, nerve, and voice.

Meanwhile Don Duro's keen eyes were wandering about the room for something to vent his spleen upon. Mammy however had been careful: she was a capital nurse, and had often detected and cured disease in the absence of the doctor; not always, however.

"I sent in some of the new niggers, where are they?" gruffly demanded the Manager.

"Down yander, Mas'r, a toder room; dey no bad enough for want bed, so me put 'em in de piccaninny ward. One of dem hab guinea-worm."

The lady being still too much exhausted to move, the Manager took a candle, and went alone to see this guinea-worm;[†] — a thing somewhat like the first string of a violin, which inserts itself between the skin and flesh of the patient, in which it occasionally perforates a hole, and peeps out to take a view of the world without. Mammy had done her duty: she had pertinaciously watched from the moment she first detected it, had caught the head, fastened it gently to a card, and then awaited a further protrusion, to wind off its length; for if this be not carefully done, and the worm break, the leg will mortify, and the Negro be lost. There was clearly no fault to find here.

Further on, among the sore cripples gathered gibbering on the floor, was one with hideous sores all over his body. By means of black ointment and plaisters these had been covered and concealed by the Captain at the sale; but when rubbed and cleaned by Mammy and her assistants, the hideous truth revealed itself, as the Manager held the candle near, and started back with horror.

"Nigger-wench!" he hoarsely called, as he retreated backwards into the first ward, heaping upon her head every curse and every oath that fumed from hell, "the clabba-yaws[†] are in there!"

This disease is an aggravated species of small-pox, which occasionally rages within the tropics in Africa, and for which a species of inoculation is sometimes práctised on children.

"*Perra!*" he roared; "how is it you never told me of that?"

"Hey, Mas'r," said the nurse with undaunted effrontery, "da's wha' me tell you over and over, and beg you so hard for call Missis."

"You didn't, you nigger! it was for the old black beast that lies stretched on the floor there."

"I never said notin 't all 'bout 'em," said the woman doggedly; "me beg you call Missis 'count of dem clabba-yaws."

"Don't let me hear you say that again!" growled the Manager, gracing his commands with a kick, as she stood sulkily with her back to him; it was a spiteful, strong kick, which made the woman stagger, and maybe hurt her too, for she turned round quick upon him. A year before she would have borne it all patiently as needs be, but she had heard reports from town which had worked her up to courage; besides which, she was conscious of tripping on the score of truth, and was put upon her mettle to defend herself; she retorted accordingly.

"Wha' binness you hab for come here meddle for? I go tell Mas'r 'pon you! I go ask Mas'r wha' binness you have for cuss me."

"*Qu'est-ce que c'est?*" shrilly drawled Madame Angélique; "do you talk of appealing to your master, and I here? what new thing is this, you impudent woman-monkey?"

"Me no monkey!" replied the nurse in the same angry tone; "me take care your niggers; me no sleep night and day, mindin sick nigger: monkey never do dat; and you let da man tand dere for cuss me, — you tink me love cuss?"†

The Manager, blazing with wrath, was about to seize her, but Madame Angélique stayed him with a gesture; and while he made his retreat by the door, as he always prudently did when punishment was taken out of his hands, the lady, taking off her slipper, then and there, in the ward, with the sick groaning around her, belaboured the nurse to her heart's content, about the head, from right to left, upon the ears, upon the face, upon the forehead. There really was nothing very extraordinary in this, — it is a thing of daily and hourly occurrence: slavery begets a host of petty vices in the slaves, which are ever provoking the slaveholder; and he gets into the habit of recklessly using his irresponsible power in punishing the provocation. But this woman had latterly grown impudent. "Tankee, Missis!" she cried at every blow, "da wha' you give me? tankee, Missis!" till Madame Angélique's arm was fairly tired, and then she gave the woman one last hard blow, pushed her violently forward, saying, "There!" and hurried away all fussed and heated and angry, stumbling over the wretched Anamoa, who still lay senseless on the floor at the entrance. And so the bed was forgotten.

Madame Angélique, followed by her sable attendants, panted and puffed on her way home, longing to throw herself on her bed to rest, and feeling ready to fling a chair at the first unlucky wight who should disturb her.

CHAPTER XVI.

The Young African's Story. —
Quaco Also Relates His Adventures

Return we to the hospital. The bed of course never came; Mammy gathered up her coif, blubbered awhile longer, and at length grumbled herself into something like composure, and then, as if by magic, the Negroes who had disappeared now came crowding again about the windows and the door, commiserating and commenting in rapid and vehement language. Mammy's kind heart however was with the poor Negro who still lay upon the floor untended. She set to earnestly now; "Neber mind de buckra," she said to Quaco, who came in to volunteer assistance, "we do bery well widout 'em;" and when the patient's broad wounds were all dressed and "made tidy," as she said, the strongest of the Negroes raised him between them on a sheet, and gently bore him away to a hut, which the former occupant had vacated for him because it stood by the sacred cotton-tree — the Fetish tree of the estate.[†] The Negro-women made a collection of petticoats amongst themselves, and formed a bed of tolerable softness in a corner, and then they laid him gently down. Life was fast ebbing away, but they did not know it yet; they thought he only slept, exhausted from loss of blood.

"Now," said Mammy, when everything was arranged to her satisfaction, "da gal Talima, wha' dem call 'em, must come for watch 'em daddy: me must tand in da hospital for watch dem clabba-yaws." So adjusting her coif anew, and rubbing herself into order, she approached the place where the young girl lay fast asleep, unconscious of what had been passing around her. "Poor gal!" said Mammy, holding the candle close to her face, "da boddersome Missis been want for wake 'em up, jus for see wha' kind o' gal she be; now Mammy must wake 'em up for she see wha' kind a daddy she hab. Poor ting! sorry for wake 'em." After a considerable amount of shaking, the girl awoke, with the motion of the ship still in her head, bewildered enough, but not overcome, and she was soon made to understand where she was to go, and for what purpose. Mammy then helped her up, and with her strong arm fairly carried her into her new abode, where a couch of fresh-gathered, well-picked cocoa-nut leaves, spread by the side of her father's bed, awaited her.

It is a custom among the Negroes, and to some extent even among the Creole white people too, when a person is sick, for friends to gather round him in proportion as he is liked and respected. It never occurs to them that the unfortunate patient requires rest and quiet; all they think of is the pleasure it must give him to receive so many testimonies of solicitude. Accordingly the hut was crowded, and conversation, prompted by curiosity concerning the various events of the day, became eager and earnest. The whispering increased, and, in subdued tones, questions, comments, narratives, and exclamations passed rapidly from one to another among the company. There was no subject however in which they felt deeper interest than in the fate of the Negro-girl Talima, and therefore, while the sick Anamoa slept, she was called upon to relate the events which had brought her among them. She consented. The listeners quickly arranged themselves in a semicircle, and then, in the strange, sweet, rolling utterance and emphatic idiom of the Koromantyn language,[†] she commenced; her audience, like a company of story-telling Arabs, greeting every new incident with appropriate expressions of sympathy, — moaning, sighing, barbarous exclamations of surprise, or words of dislike and execration.[†] Her story has been thus interpreted to me by one of her companions.

"That old man, who lies there so defenceless," began the maiden, waving her hand with dignity towards him, — "he, so lately trampled underfoot and degraded before you, — he, whose tottering form would have obtained mercy from the worst cannibals of Africa, — that broken defenceless old man but a few years ago was strong, his form was erect, his brow was high, his arms made the tigers tremble in their lairs, his voice called thousands of men before him, for he was Lord of Fantyn, the most powerful kingdom of the Koromantyn district."

The narrator paused, when, by a simultaneous movement, every hand in the company was raised, and every head was bent low, in token of reverence and honour.

"Most of you here have heard," continued the young girl, "how vast was his palace and his household; his children numbered by tens and tens, but I was the loved one of all, because the orphaned image of his favourite wife, and I loved my father with the strength and the warmth of an African heart. Our town, Anamaboe,[†] was not then, as it is now, crowded with white men, residing there in tall and handsome houses; it was a simple African village, with low houses shaded by thick trees; at the head was an extensive court, and scented groves concealed the place where I spent my happy childhood."

Here again she was interrupted with words of commiseration and pity. She scarcely paused, but continued:

"I divided my day thus: from sunrise till noon, while my father was with his men, I strayed with my handmaids over the savannahs near the harem,[†] where we gathered flowers, or sat quietly in the fragrant groves, fashioning ornaments with parrot-feathers for the warriors of my father's band; from the height of the day till the cool evening I watched for my father's voice, for he would often call me to him to give him counsel in times of trouble; or, in peace, I would mount the steed by his side, and scour the forest after the lion, the quagga,[†] the zebra, and the antelope."

A murmur of applause ran through the assembly, while some few sobbed aloud at the recollection of pleasures they were never more to enjoy.

"Years rolled on, and the time came when suitors presented themselves to woo. A young warrior, son of a chief whose domains bordered on those of my father, proposed an alliance, and, according to the custom of our country, he brought spices, gold-dust, elephants' teeth, and that which you know is the most valued amongst us, heaps of salt, as gifts corresponding to the boon required. The affair, my friends, was nearly adjusted; we were allowed to meet, we were betrothed. Oh, groves of Fantyn, showering down blossoms upon our heads! oh, perfume of flowers, filling the air with bliss as we breathed! — gone, like the smiles of happy dreams! Friends, this prospect was soon destroyed. By whom? Listen! — the white man!"

"Obboney!" (evil spirit,) cried the assembly, waving mournfully from side to side.

"The white man who dwelt in the large settlement down by the beach was my father's friend. I hated him from the beginning, for I saw treachery in his cold cotton-face; but he spoke so sweet that my father would not suffer any one to say a word against him. The white man heard of the projected union with a frown; he was indignant: 'What!' said he, 'are those the gifts they bring for the most beautiful daughter of the great Anamoa, — so few and so mean? It proves the rumour true, that Anamoa is mocked and despised by the young man's sire.' My father repelled the charge, but he remembered the words, and they sank festering in his heart.

"It was at the chase of the zebra that he and Liguena quarrelled. My father by right aimed first; but his horse stumbling at the moment, he failed; Liguena, close by his side, brought the animal down, and, unconscious of any feeling save respect, he shouted as he gained the prize, and laughingly seized it. My father conceived it was in mockery, — the mockery which the white man had so repeatedly and strongly warned him of: words of defiance, provocation, and insult roused Liguena to reply, and then he was told to go, never to return. Rage and passion consumed his heart; he did not even seek an interview with me, but gathered up his presents and called his attendants at once. The white man was on the watch, and, as he set forth homewards, sent him a secret message of condolence. 'Make war,' he said; 'we will furnish you with arms and powder, and all we ask in return is that you give us the prisoners you take: let us have them as slaves.' Liguena listened to the white man's whispers, promised all that was asked, received the necessary arms, and war commenced. Anamoa flew to the white man; 'Liguena,' he said, 'is crossing my borders; I have no arms, you are my friend, help me.' And now was the crocodile made manifest. The white man wept at the treatment of my father: it was injuring himself, he said, to injure his friend. 'Make war, make war; we will furnish arms and powder, and all we ask in return is the prisoners you shall make; give us slaves.' "

The speaker was here forced to pause, such was the prolonged and oft-repeated hiss of disgust that ran through the assembly. She resumed:

"At first my father worsted the intruders, and Liguena showed some inclination for an amicable understanding; but the white man would still come about my father by night as well as by day, far into the heart of his kingdom, as well as near the sea-coast; he advised him to push forward into the enemy's country. Friends, behold the horrible success of war! for we are strong-feeling, earnest people, our hearts are not the stones that fill the white people's bosoms; our rage, like our love, is a burning fire, either to warm and foster, or to consume; and my father was as brave as he was skilful in the art of war. And now see the happy villages, with the smoke curling from every roof; hear the sweet voices of the mothers calling to their children at play; — that is in the morning. Look there again by-and-by: the cottages are empty, people fly in terror, flames enwrap the towns till the clouds seem red-hot, blood flows like rivers in the streets. The fair fields are spoiled, the corn is gone, and then follow famine and despair, pestilence and death. Those were the tracks of my father's footsteps; and in the mellow evening, when the slaughter was over and the hour invited to pastime and rest, there, where the young mothers sang and the children played, my father's band would collect skulls by thousands, and under the shade of the palm-tree select the best for throwing the ball, or drinking palm-wine.

"My father would have returned now, but the white man had sent him messages to urge him on with false hopes and promises; but he had ventured too far already; he was betrayed by the very messenger who brought him advice: he was taken, not to meet the brave man's death, but to be sold to the very white man who had pretended to be his friend — who had encouraged the quarrel — who had furnished arms for the contest. I never saw him again in Fantyn, and the dark treason was only revealed to me this day, when, after moons and moons of separation, we have met."

"Ay!" cried the assembled Negroes, in deep pity for the girl, "a story most sad! it makes our hearts ache, it brings the tears to our eyes."

"Meanwhile these transactions were carefully concealed from the black Court of Anamaboe; village after village had been taken on the frontiers. The towns were occupied by the enemy, and each day brought fresh news of his approach. I had a brother at the Court, but scarcely old enough to undertake the defence of the place. I did my best; I rallied the men, I kept them for a time steadily at their posts. The enemy came at last — the attack commenced. Hemmed in on all sides, I sent to the white man in my father's name for aid; it was promised to us, and given to the invaders outside. Then came horrors and carnage! Friends, I saw the flames hissing on the blood as it ran; screams of women, cries of children, moans of the old, rose on all sides; it was a fine harvest for the slave-dealing white man, and ships were just in port to take away those who were captured."

"Oh! yah!" again sighed the Negroes, "the treason is great with the white man! why should we be more just?"

"I had now done all that a woman could do, and I knew there was nothing left me but to escape. I threw a cotton veil about me, and, amidst the widespread confusion, fled to the gate. At one and the same moment I stumbled on the dead body of my brother and fell into the arms of — Liguena! Softened in a moment was his eye, subdued was that hoarse and passionate voice, and he clasped me in an agony of shame and remorse. 'Come with me, O maiden! I little thought to find you so near the groves of Anamaboe: they told me you had long, long ago gone far away with another. Yet, O Talima, I will save you yet; I will bring you where, for my sake, they will shelter you and take care of you.' Liguena led me rapidly through the fitfully glaring night, and I found myself entering the settlement of my father's friend, the white man. Instantly I saw the treason; I clung to Liguena, I wept, I begged him to take me away, but he was blind — blind like my poor father. He soothed me, rallied me, coaxed me; he promised me on the Fetish tree they were sincere, and he tore himself from me but for a little while, to stay the slaughter of the harem. I mounted on the window to see him go: I waved my veil by the light of the fires, I knew I should never see him more. Oh, Liguena! he who trusts to the fidelity of the white man is a fool, and I was the cause of the misfortune by which you learned it. Before I well knew where I was, the manacles were about my wrists and ankles; for the wind was fair, and the tide served, so was I borne to the ship directly, and the groves of Fantyn faded from my view for ever."

Talima ended; and unheeding the sympathy which each and all lavishly bestowed, she drooped her head mournfully upon her hands to weep; then she rose and looked at her father, but he still slept, and, reluctant to disturb him, she finally settled herself, reclining on her bed of leaves.

"Poor, poor Talima!" murmured the whole assembly compassionately, "God help thee! Hands that never worked must dig the ground now; no rest, no safety, no comfort for any; and her eyes will have to ache yet for what she will see her father suffer."

"I remember well," quoth Quaco, "Seeing him mounted on his favourite animal, a beautiful zebra: these creatures are hard to tame, and fierce, and white men and Negroes crowded to see him. Oh, brave sight! All dressed in gold and scarlet mountings, a crown of long parrot-feathers on his brow, and mounted on a zebra which none but he dared to touch! brave, grand king! I was young then, quite a boy."

"Oh, hey!" exclaimed the company, now excited to a story-telling mood, "Quaco, you tell us all about Koromantyn land, and how you came here."

"Me!" said the lad with ready gesture, "nothing much about me; but if all you can hear, Quaco can talk." Then placing himself beside Talima, the better to engage the attention of his hearers, he addressed them, in language which I thus translate.

"Countrymen, we can't go back to Koromantyn-land, but we can call Koromantyn-land to us, and times back and things done; for these belong to us — Master can't touch then, never! for *thought has no master.* We can love them, and tell them over, and share them, country-men; and though Quaco's tale is nothing beside poor Talima's, yet he can cut up his little crust, and, like all good niggers, share what he has got.

"My daddy belonged to King Anamoa; he was one of the guards about the Court. Brave man he was, but very old. War came, — not the war that sent Talima here, but another one long before, — and slaves must be sold to buy arms; war pressed very hard, and the white man pressed very hard too for slaves. Then my daddy, who loved the king, said, 'I am too old now to hold the sword or fire the gun, my hand trembles; sell me, O Anamoa, and get arms, or all Fantyn will fall into the enemy's hands: see, they are already at the borders.' King Anamoa was troubled at the thought, but the old guardsman would have it so, and he joined the gang of slaves and put the chain himself about his foot. I followed to the beach, for my mother's tears had sorely moved me, and I went to see what would become of my daddy.

"The white man examined the slaves, and it came to my daddy's turn to be looked at. 'This man is old,' said the slave-dealer, 'he can't work, he is not worth feeding;' and then it came into my head how they would starve my daddy because he could not work, and my mother's cries went to my heart. I went to the white man: 'Take Quaco,' I said, 'he can work well, so let my poor daddy go home.' The white men laughed at me; then they said, 'Come in the boat, to speak to the captain about it.' So Quaco jumped in, and sat by the side of daddy, comforting him. But when I came to the ship, the captain said, 'You fine young nigger devil, you must stay to keep your daddy company.' So they put chains upon my legs, and drove me below into the hold with the others. Then I shed a few tears for my poor mother's sorrow; but, thinking I could help my daddy when they put him to hard work, I said to him, 'Never mind, some day we shall run away and go back to Fantyn.' But my daddy's heart was full; he held up his hand, and showed me the big sea, and the ship going very fast. By-and-by we began to feel very hot, and to look about for a cool place to sit. Oh, it was like the *fourmis chasseurs*[†] in a rat-hole, — Negroes, Negroes, Negroes, piled here, piled there, standing on one another's feet, pushing for place to lie, unable to breathe, unable to sleep, the place smelt so bad; we longed to die.

"After seven days, the captain made us all come up to dance. We could not dance, — there was no music, and we were sick and sad; so then they brought the big whip to make the music, and they lashed us till the sickness was forgotten, and we danced sadly for an hour — many had fainted in trying. When we went down again, the place had been cleaned of the great dirt, and scoured, for it was wet still; but we lay down one at top of another, not caring, and we slept heavily and long. After that, a storm came — a great storm — and we all laughed and shouted to the wind, because we thought it would take us away; but it stopped. Then it happened that the ship did not move at all for a long, long time.

"They used to give us horse-beans and lamp-oil, but by-and-by we had not much of even this; and though the sick died by tens, still our meals got smaller and smaller — there was not enough provision for us; we used to scramble for it, and fight, and often the weak got none. One day the captain came down, and looked about him, choosing the old, the sickly, and the weak: my poor daddy was one, and I never saw him again, only by-and-by one of the Negroes looked through the one little window, and the sharks were playing about, opening their big mouths for more. Ohe me! that's the way my daddy went. I thought of my mother, and my heart was full."

Here a pause ensued for some minutes, to permit of the usual comments and expressions of sympathy, and then Quaco with his natural briskness plucked up again cheerfully and resumed.

"I have not told you how I came here; listen to this: all white men are not brave like Koromantyns, as you shall hear. When the ship came to land, I was sold; my first master was old Mr. Lamarre, who lived down at the wharf there in Port Spain; he wanted to make money, so he got a lot of cottons very cheap, and filled a little ship to go and sell them down in Angostura[†] yonder, and goes on board with them, taking me. The captain was a Peon,[†] with heavy looks; he set his dark eye upon master, and just when we came into the big waters of the Orinoco, what does the captain do, but he and the mate take me and fling me flop into the river. Quaco was not going to die so soon if he could help it, so I swam about the ship while they were fastening down master: but one of the men caught sight of me, so he shoved me off as I was catching hold; 'You nigger devil,' says he, 'I will chop your hand off, if you come here again.' So I swam another way, and climbed up the banks of the biggest island. The ship had gone off out of sight by this time, and hey! my friends, when I looked about me, there was master all naked, tied to a cocoanut tree hand and foot, trembling, and crying, and begging to Quaco," — and here the narrator mimicked to the life the beseeching tones of the white man, while the audience gave lively testimony of their enjoyment.

" 'Oh, Quaco! dear, good Quaco! pity me; you so kind heart, Quaco! untie these cords, and as soon as I get to Trinidad I will make you free.'

"Hey, Master, said I, buckra never keeps promise to poor nigger.

" 'May the lightning of heaven strike me dead if I don't,' says my master.

"So I pitied the white man, and when I had done laughing, I untied the cords and let him go.

" 'Now,' says master, 'dear Quaco, I am very hungry; get me something to eat.'

"Hey, Master! nothing here for nobody.

" 'Quaco, let's look for something.' So we went about to look. But in a minute master again calls, and says, 'Quaco! oh dear, Quaco! a wild beast has been here; look at its foot-marks.'

"No, Master; no wild beast, that's a man's foot.

" 'Quaco! Quaco! that's worse; Indians here eat people; let us run!'

"We were going along a wood of cocoanut-trees, I following my master, and he trembling and running. Somebody called to us; we looked about everywhere; nobody to be seen, though the voice was quite near. Something made me look up: what do I see but a lot of naked Indians they call *Warahoons*,[†] all on the tree-tops, in little houses like, and eating their dinner. '*Comer?*' said they, holding out a piece of raw fish. I knew they meant the Spanish word for *eat,* and that they wanted to give us something; but my master understood *come here,* so he catches hold of me all shivering. 'Oh, Quaco! dear, good Quaco! they are calling me, to kill me and eat me!' Hey, countrymen! I could have pushed him, I was so ashamed of him for a mean coward; but he was my master, so I was obliged only to look up at the Indians and laugh. I ate the fish they threw me, and my master, seeing me talk with them so free, was soon glad to take what they gave — raw and dried fish, and fern-roots, — which he ate faster than I did. Soon the Warahoons began to talk to him too. 'Come and live with us,' they said, 'and be free, like us; not slaves to clothes and to money, as you are. We are free, — we never work, we live as we like; we bask in the sun, we swim in the water, we sleep in the shade, we are happy.' But master shook his head; he wanted to go back to Trinidad, he said, so he asked them to sell him a boat, and row it to Port Spain, which, against their inclination and with much grumbling, they did, and Quaco went in it of course: master could not do without 'dear, good Quaco!' When we got to Port Spain, and master had done paying those Warahoons with a few bad cutlasses, Quaco said, 'Now, Master, there's lightning in the clouds you swore by; won't you make me free?' 'You black devil!' said he, 'after all my losses, to want such a thing! go and do your work, till I make money out of you,' and the next day he sold me to the Palm Grove. Hey! I am not sorry, — Master

Cardon is a master, and not a coward: Koromantyn would like to fight with him; Koromantyn don't mind his chain so much; but for that other — whew! hi! hey! yah!" and Quaco's concluding interjections were repeated in chorus by the whole assembly.

Admonished of their too energetic voices by the watchful Talima, who feared they would wake her father, they instantly subdued their tones, calling nevertheless for another story, for, like a toast, it must go round. Madelaine was squatting loungingly in a corner, and they cast their eyes upon her.

"You are oldest here now," said they, "we begin to call you Mammy Madelaine for respect;† give us lessons from your experience; tell us your adventures with the white man, and how, when a girl, you managed your rags. Where were you then, Mammy Madelaine? How were you when Laurine was born? — tell us."

Thus challenged, the automaton woman sat up, and uttering one of her wild heedless laughs, she drew her coif† tighter about her head, gathered her rags closer about her, and, after much pressing, related her history.

CHAPTER XVII.

Madelaine Shows That She Has Had
Much to Embitter Her Life

"Niggers all!" cried old Madelaine in tolerable English, "you want to know, and maybe I shall tell you. No! I was not always this way: when I was a young girl, I was a hard-working, loving thing, what the white people call a good girl — what, in truth, is *a fool*. Ants befooled me; death made me wise."

"Hey! hey! yah!" laughed the whole assembly; but Quaco, wag as he sometimes was, possessed the African virtues, and leaning across from his seat, he rapped the young ones on the head, reminding them of Madelaine's age, and enjoining them to hold a respectful tongue in their heads before her.

"Now, Mammy Madelaine," he said, "tell now, please, was that *four-mis chasseurs,* or *blessing of God,* what white people call, swarming your cabin, eating up all centipedes, scorpions, and ugly creatures that come for hurt you?"

The old woman shook her head; it was not those, she said.

"Was that parasol-ants, every one with a tribute-leaf in 'em mouth, marching to give 'em to two-headed snake in 'em nest?"[†]

"No, nor that; it was the small red ant,[1] that some of you may remember in Africa; the slaveships brought them over to this side of the sea:[†] they were the things that made a fool of me. You shall hear," said old Madelaine, speaking in her native tongue; "where shall I begin! When I

---

1. *Formica omnivora.*

was a little child I belonged to the Congo nation,[†] — honest, fine people, as the world knows. I used to see the white men come ashore; our people mistrusted them, would not speak to them, and kept away. Then the white men laid their goods down, and went away. So by-and-by our people came and looked at the goods, and as they liked them, they took them, and laid money down instead, and went away again: so you see how the white men trusted us. By-and-by these same white men found me playing in a field, so caught me up, put me in a bag, and ran away with me; that's all I know about it. The ship brought me to Granada, to old Mr. Perrin, father of the one who came here and laid out the Palm Grove Estate. I was brought up in the house, to play with the young ladies. Missis was always pleased with me, and as I grew up, she would give me the care of many things. I had the care of the cows, the sheep, and the fowls; I took care of everything then, it gave me pleasure. I liked the creatures; they all knew me, and each of them had a name which it answered to. I kept them clean and well fed; they were never troubled with toads or snakes, and they were very thriving. Sometimes the insects would get into the coops, but then I soon drove them out with burning green wood. Once upon a time the ants got in, and I was obliged to burn shavings on the ground for two or three days together, and I thought then there would be no more; but you shall hear how they made us leave Granada.

"One morning I went to the fowl-house, to see after some chickens just hatched. As I walked, I felt my poor bare feet stung all over — the ground was covered with ants; I could not go on, so I went to the carpenter's workshop to get a plank to walk upon, and I set it down from the door of the fowl-house to the coops; but the hens were off their nests, dancing and screaming as hens will do when they are stung, and the little chickens, when I looked at them, were all dead; the nests were covered with ants. I called to one of the women to come and help me, and between us we took out all the hens, picked off the ants, and got tobacco-plants, which we left burning on the ground. It was late now: I took my pail and went to milk the cows for breakfast. On my way I looked in at the sheep, there had been a sick one among them I wanted to see. Hey ho! my friends, it was dead! covered with ants thick upon it, so that you could not make out what the living heap could be till you brushed them off like a piece of thick crust. I did not stay then: I called to the cowboy to take away the sheep, and I went to get the milk. As soon as I had done, I made all haste to take it to the house, for by this time breakfast should be ready. I found Missis very cross: the breakfast was spoiled with the ants, the coffee was full of them, so were the cassava-cakes; and the syrup, which the white people use instead of sugar, was a mess of them. I had my tale to tell, and the family had nothing to drink but the milk I brought in. But the worst of all was the bread: wherever you cut it, there were ants inside; when you put a piece in your mouth, ants stuck to your tongue and stung it. We spent the whole of that day, we house-servants, pouring boiling water over the boards of every room and into every hole; and I stole out in the afternoon to look at the fowl-house, which I cleaned and smoked, and then strewed the ground with chopped tobacco-leaves. I felt so tired that night with having worked hard all day, that I had only time to throw myself on my mat and I was instantly asleep.

"Next morning I woke early, and then I went to the fowl-house again. Oh, it was worse now! the hens were all dying, the bigger chickens were dead already, and the new-laid eggs were bored through and swarming inside. As to the ground, I could not find a spot to walk upon, and no sooner had I put the plank down than I had to sweep it again, it swarmed so. I heard Missis's voice calling already, though it was so early; she was very cross, — every body was cross, — ants were everywhere. The nurse of the hospital was at one door, crying out that ants were swarming in the beds of the sick; the cook was at another door, grumbling that the kitchen was all swarming with ants in every corner; and before any of us had a bit of breakfast, there we were, busy, busy, all busy, — some scraping the meat, some sweeping the shelves, some scalding the vegetables, some straining the syrup, some trying to clean the flour; but no use, no, not a bit! The dinner was ant-soup, ant-stew, ant-fricassee, and ant-pudding, — ants everywhere, ants in everything. After dinner the same business over again, and we were obliged besides to put every pot and kettle down, even to the frying-pan, to boil water in, for flooding the kitchen flags and walls, and the vessels not being enough for this, some of the Negroes were sent to borrow more pots from the estates near us. No sooner were these gone, than messengers arrived on the same errand from the very places Missis had sent to. We stared, I can tell you, when we heard those estates were just like ours, overrun with ants. By-and-by our Negroes came back with stories still worse: in one place the cattle were eaten up alive in the night; in another place a sick mule was found eaten in spots to the bone, though he was not yet dead; and we soon fared no better ourselves, — the next day nothing could be got for the Master's dinner but some fried plantains and omelettes; and some of the field niggers were kept about the house, to sweep the paths and pour hot water wherever they appeared. There was now something to see: such running here and there from the house to the kitchen and back again! such talking! such work!

"When night came we were all of us troubled to think how we should keep the bread fit to eat. Some of us thought to place jugs standing in basins or tubs of water, and on the top of the jugs to put dishes and plates with the bread and anything else that wanted keeping. Then we placed all these in a row, and giving a last scald to the floors of the different rooms, we thought we might go to bed, for it was very late; and I laid myself down as usual at the foot of the young ladies' bed on the floor, and soon fell asleep. This did not last long: I soon started up out of my sleep with the stings of ants, they were all over me. I got up, and went to the lamp to pick them off me, — a hard thing to do, as I found, for no matter how you brushed them off, the heads always remained behind stuck in your skin. But just when I had begun this work, there I heard one of the young ladies calling to me that her bed had ants in it, and the next minute both young ladies were on the floor, crying out for help. Soon after, the whole family was up, — Missis and all the servants, for the same cause: nobody could sleep, and we were obliged to bring large calabashes, into which we lifted the bed-posts, and then filled the vessels with water. Of course we brushed and picked the beds until they were cleared. Missis allowed me to take the old hammock, and hang it up for me to sleep in, and I felt nothing more till daybreak.

"It was now the fourth morning since the ant-swarming began, and everything had been tried to stop it, but no sooner was I up than I found them in more plenty than ever. The fowl-house was a great moving mass of them. The cattle were covered with them, and dying; and when dead their bones were laid quite bare and white in one hour after. In the fields, the coffee-berries, at that time nearly ripe, were all eaten dry on the bush.

The Negroes could no longer dig without shoes; Master had to get a pair for every one of them. Everybody now began to be frightened, — white people, Mulatto people, niggers: all Granada was running with ants, no house was free; no window, no door, no box or keyhole, but they went in and out like a stream. The paths were thick with them, in some places they were stopped up with hills of living ants. There were more and more every day. They took to eating something more than people's victuals: they ate silk, Master's black coats, Missis's stuff table-covers, then glue, then the horsehair from off the sofa and chairs, and all the shoes, and the saddles and leather. When these were all gone, what did they do but begin to eat the young ladies' linen, the cotton petticoats, the muslin frocks, paper, wood, — yes, and brass!

"Green vegetables now got very dear; soon there were none. The leaves of the trees were eaten up, the grass was eaten up; the sugar-canes had all disappeared long before, because they were sweet; every one said we should die of hunger. The ants grew bold and impudent: they got to the sick, we could not help them, for, if we did, we soon got covered ourselves; they told me that the eyes of one infant were eaten out while it lay asleep. People slept in hammocks now, some one always sitting up to watch in every house, daubing the ropes with castor-oil every now and then. Master took it into his head to draw a thick ring of chalk round the pegs which held his hammock, but it had to be done over and over again so often, because of the ants running over it so fast, that castor-oil on the ropes was found to be the best plan after all. It was so hard to get enough of it; we had to work now all day at getting the oil out of the castor-bush seeds, or we should not have had enough, for everybody was wanting it.

"The field niggers were all called from their regular labours, and all day you might see them pounding the ants on the roads and about the houses, or pouring boiling water over them. But no sooner had the scalding water made heaps of dead ants, than heaps of living ants came crawling over them, just as if no scalding had been. Poisoned meat was thrown amongst them: then it was a sight too see how the ants got mad and ate one another up! but this was of no use either, there were only more of them instead of less! Another thing was done now: great fires were lit up to burn them; all night these fires were kept burning, and you might have thought the whole of Granada was in a blaze. But not a bit of use was it; the ants would come pouring over the burned heaps and put out the fires. The rivers did not stop them; you might see them making bridges over one another's bodies, and passing over the widest rivers. At last you could not even sit down and rest for any time, and my work all day was sweep, sweep, sweep, sweep, round the chairs wherever Missis or the young ladies were sitting.

"You might now see plantations left without master or nigger: the masters had run away to other countries, and the poor slaves roamed about looking for food, and for some place where they might sleep. You might now see fields all moving with ants, only here and there were the whitened bones of the cattle they had eaten; or at the doors of the houses you might hear the groans of the sick being devoured by the ants, which it was dangerous to disturb. No work now! no buying or selling! no dancing! no singing! no one in the markets, no one in the streets.

"Well, niggers, the Governor made a proclamation, offering a reward of twenty thousand dollars to any one who should find out a way of stopping the plague: it did not make much talk, people were too down-hearted to think much about it, for everything had been tried already, and the cleverest people had all left Granada before the plague got to the worst. But for me, a poor little Negro girl, I found out something — I found out that though these ants would crawl over the sweet potatoes, still they would pass them by, and not eat them; and for some time I had been supporting Master's family with gathering sweet potatoes. I did not think anything about it at first, till the poor niggers who were left without a master would come begging at the door. I used to get up early in the morning and pick the sweet potatoes, and heap them into the little nigger-huts to give away when any poor hungry creature came. The storehouse I had already filled for the family, I and some of the other niggers, and we were still keeping it full; but at last so many of the begging niggers came to us, that I got afraid I should have no more to give them soon, and something put it into my head to go and tell the Governor about the sweet potatoes I had found out. I could not go myself, but I sent a young nigger, Paul, that I loved, and in a few days the Governor sent for Master and for me, and he and some of the gentlemen there talked to Master to sign a paper to give me free, — so said I, curtseying, let me marry Paul, and I will stay and work for Master till he dies, — and this they put in the paper. I asked to let me marry Paul, because I always saw that, when white people got married, no one ever took them from one another; and I thought if I married Paul nobody would take me from my husband, nor my husband from me. So we were married that day.

"Niggers! now all of you listen," continued the old woman, "for I have something more to say. The plague, as the Governor called these ants, was worse than ever; we could not plant sweet potatoes fast enough, and we began to look down, and think we must die of starvation at last, when, one day, the sky darkened all at once, and before we had time to stop up the windows and stop up the crevices, crash went the trees, roar went the thunder, whiz came the lightning, and the houses rocked like mad! My mistress called us all to prayers, and there we were, huddling together, and praying to God, not knowing but we were just about to die; but the storm passed, and when we looked out, oh! to hear us shout, and cry, and laugh! — for the plague was gone. Nothing was to be seen of it but a few wet heaps of dead ants, here and there, up against the houses or on the roads, — the rain had carried all the rest away. Now the church-bells rang with thanks, and Granada looked glad and hoped for better times.[2]

"But my poor master had suffered too much; the plantation was destroyed, — the ants had not left a leaf of tree or grass, the storm had not left a field level; he had to borrow money to plant it all afresh, and to feed the Negroes and the family till the coffee should grow. Poor old master! we worked hard for him, for we pitied him, he looked so ill and heartbroken; and he had always been good to us, — he did not beat much, and when he spoke to us it was more fatherlike. But those coffee-walks[†] he worked so hard upon — for he worked with us himself — he did not live to see them come into bloom; before the buds came out, he was in his grave.

"I haven't spoken to you yet about young master, — he was not in Granada all this time, and he came from over the sea to take the estate. He was a sickly sort of man, very yellow, and he brought a wife with him. I should have told you, the young ladies had married, one gone one way,

---

2. The plague here described took place in 1780.[†]

and one another; and for me, I still lived with my old missis, because of Paul.

"I had two children, Felix and Anne; now, niggers, all of you, put all your hearts together, and all the love you have for one thing and another, and it would not come up to the one big love I had for my two children; they were free, you know, because I, their mother, was free, — that is the law in Granada. Well, niggers! all at once, young master said we must leave Granada and go to Trinidad, where people were rolling in gold, that's what he said; and says he to me, 'You may come too, for I must bring with me all my niggers, and Paul too.' I did not half like the thought, for my old missis had just died, and somehow I did not like the young ones: young master was cross, and was for working the niggers hard, and the missis made me work in the house after old missis was dead, just as if I was a slave. But Paul was going, so I swallowed the thought, and I packed up my little box and went, Master paying the passage. Then Master bought all this land covered with big bushes and old trees, and he wanted to clear it, so says he to me, 'Madelaine, you must work in the field now, and help to clear the land.' 'Master,' I answered, 'I can't cut down your trees, I have got my children to mind at home;' so up with his fist and he knocks me to the ground; 'that will teach you,' he says, 'to talk to me that way: when you married a slave you made yourself a slave, and we are in another country here, and that old d———d Governor in Granada can't meddle.'

"Well, it is no use talking much about those times: I was obliged to leave my little hut, and go with the other niggers to fell the trees: Paul of course used to keep near me, and that kept up my heart a bit. But the very first week, my little Anne tumbled down the sawpit and broke her leg; Master would not let me stay at home to nurse her, and the little thing, so used to my love and care, she died. It was very hard for me; I used to put my head on Paul's shoulder and cry myself to sleep every night, for I could not lie down.

"One day Master went to town and took Paul with him, — he told me he must make a coachman of Paul, he was such a fine young fellow; he said this to throw dust in my eyes, so that I should not make a noise — and they went. Paul never came back, and the niggers that pitied me got news that Master wanted money, and had sold him. Oh! oh! I did not cry

— I could not cry, I got sick, my heart turned within me; I did not eat for days and days, and then I began to want to eat earth;[†] I used to take it up by little bits at first, after that I used to stuff my mouth with it all day. My master was not long before he found it out, because my look was bloated, my face grew yellow, and he had other ways of knowing besides. He set the overseer to watch me; but he could not watch me so close, but that I would fill my mouth the moment he turned his head. He put me in the stocks, and kept me there on the sitting bench for one whole day without even drink, and then they brought me dinner, — pah! I could not touch a bit. So they tied my hands behind my back, and let me out so: well, in a little time the overseer found me lying on the ground on my face, licking up the earth with my tongue. The next thing they did, was to get an iron mask,[†] and put it on me: they thought they would cure me now; but they soon caught me putting the earth up between the mask and my chin, — ho! did not they rage?

"But it is of no use for niggers to kick against the white people — I found that. Listen to what they did: they took my dear little boy Felix; they brought him to the field, where I was with the other niggers clearing bushes; they stripped me, made me lie down on the ground on my face, and, giving one great lash to the child just for a taste, they put the cowskin into his hand, and made him flog me! I did not look at the child myself when I stood up, but I knew that the niggers looked dark upon him, and he had run away to hide himself. The child did not come home for his supper, he did not come home to sleep, nor all night; next morning they found him drowned in the pond. Well, oh, niggers! this gave me another turn. Paul was gone, my two children were gone, freedom was gone: what should I care for more? The sickness left me, and from that day I became the Madelaine that I am now. What should I care about Laurine for? — she is not Paul's child. Hey! and they will soon make a slave of her too. What am I? — I am not my own slave, I am my master's slave; then let him take care of me, let him feed me, let him clothe me, let him watch me, — that is his business, his look-out. I don't care at all, *for notin' nor nobody.*" And, relapsing into the wild half-idiocy usual to her, poor old Madelaine flung herself back against the wall, and gave a wide gaping laugh at her own folly in youth, to have ever cared for anything.

CHAPTER XVIII.

Belfond's Story

The loud expressions of sympathy which Madelaine's recital called forth were interrupted by the entrance of a new comer. The Negroes all looked up, smiled, opened their arms, and uttered exclamations of welcome; for who better loved, trusted, and respected, than Belfond, the coloured man? It was now, who should make room for him? — who should find him a place? — who should get him supper and make him comfortable? — and that one felt proud who could do anything for him. While he was eating, they entertained him with accounts of all that had passed, and when he had finished, he in turn had much to recount, — not about his visit to his uncle, that he kept to himself, — but about his escape from the ship and from Higgins. This amused the company so well that they one and all pressed him to tell them his history.

In relating his adventures, however, unlike his darker comrades, he did not tell all that had passed in his mind. He knew that their understandings, unawakened to anything above the little affairs of their brute condition, could never comprehend the tumults of his own struggling heart, or the strange feelings which had grown up in him. He was silent, therefore, on many things, and only told such as would interest them, and such as, he hoped, would give them new ideas, and tend to raise them to know themselves, and the masters before whom they crouched. He loved sympathy too, and in his gloomiest moods the warm friendship of the Negroes had often acted beneficially upon him, — had taken him out of himself, and, for a time at least, would make him forget the gnawing doubts which preyed upon his very vitals. To fill up the blanks of his tale, it will be necessary that I should take up the recital, and tell for him those facts connected with his early life which will serve to throw light on the workings of a mind fortunately not entirely bent by his condition to evil.

Born on his master's estate, and called upon from early childhood to pander to the caprices and submit to the tyranny of the white children, he became early an adept in all those vices which slavery burns into the soul of man; and if, in the practice of falsehood, flattery, and theft, he showed himself a greater adept than his fellow-slaves on the estate, it was not that nature had found him more inclined to those vices, but simply because he was more clever than they. With the same amount of talent, on a freer, happier soil, he might have been morally, and perhaps, too, intellectually great; but under the evil influence of his condition, his best and highest faculties only served to give strength to the vices he contracted.

Thus he throve, till the time arrived when his master considered it necessary to think of education for his children. It was the custom, and a beneficial one, among the planters, to send their children to Europe for two, or five, or more years, to complete their studies. Up to that time the children were much indulged; and in those days of colonial pride and ostentation, it was considered as a thing of course to send a slave to wait upon the young student during the toilsome period of his learning; and we may easily imagine the pomp with which the young West Indian paraded the streets with his slave behind him, like an autocrat with his one subject.

On Belfond, the visit to Europe had a great effect. It was ruinous to him as a slave, for it awakened within him feelings suitable only to a free man: it raised his mind above the level of the brutes, roused his energies, elevated his thoughts, and taught him self-respect, — all which only sowed the seeds of discontent and unhappiness.

It would have been a curious study for the philosopher, to follow the mind of this young slave, as his faculties gradually emerged from the prison in which they had hitherto been bound. At first, he could not comprehend why he was not despised and kicked on account of his complexion, and how it was that white servants admitted him among them. It puzzled him still more to detect and understand the differences which the white race mark out among themselves. He was shocked at their avarice, their hardness of heart, their inhospitality, and he would say to his brother slaves, "These white people, in their own country, have no kindness for their stricken brothers. When did the poor African leave the storm-driven traveller without a shelter, or without a share of what little he may have? We make the wanderer welcome, we are proud of such a guest; but the white man shuts his door to the hungry, and gives the leavings of his meal to his dogs sooner than to the wretch who has no bed but the wet stones of that cold country — no food but the refuse he may pick up in the gutter. Oh, comrades! their hearts are like their land, — cold, hard, and barren; they have no virtues, not even respect for old age." But that which most excited his curiosity was the power of reading; in speaking of it to the Negroes, he described the print as a white ground with black patterns laid thick upon it, which patterns spoke to the eye as the voice to the ear; he explained a book as the bridge of ideas from one man's mind to another, — the permanent stamp of passing thought, — the indelible footsteps of speech.

In a few years St. Hilaire Cardon paid a visit to Europe, and, with his children, travelled over its various countries, Belfond of course accompanying them; and when his master returned to the Colonies, he was left with the son and heir, who had now entered one of the French colleges, to complete his education. This gave still greater facilities to the young slave for improving his intellect. Now, for the first time, he heard of Toussaint L'Ouverture,[†] and the unfortunate Ogé of St. Domingo.[†] Revolutions of kingdoms, the march of freedom, and the equality of men, were subjects that soon became familiar to him. He awoke, as from a dream, to find himself one of the great human race — a creature endowed with a soul, animated by the breath of the Almighty; and it was with a mingled feeling of awe and astonishment that at last he took in the eternal truth, that the black man and the white man stand before God equal in his love, equal in his care, equal in his promise of a heavenly home; for before that time he had never thought of an after-life, save in some low condition, far, far behind the meanest white men. By stealth he learned to read and to write, and he extended his knowledge wherever books or conversation came in his way to favour it. Often, indeed, while his young master spent the night in pleasure-hunting,

Belfond stole out to hear lectures, or remained within to study, till of the two — the young master and his slave — the poor Mulatto was in reality the cleverer, and by far the better educated.

At length, by dint of search and reflection, Belfond thought he had succeeded in solving the mystery of that tremendous power which the white man holds over the black race. "It is knowledge," he said, addressing his comrades, — "knowledge gives wings to man; it carries him in mind above all grovelling things of earth; he looks down upon them, moves them, rules them, destroys them, or saves them, just at his own will and pleasure. Poor creeping, crawling things like us, he pounces down upon, like the condor of the Andes on the unprotected sheep. The only resource left us is to get the wings ourselves, and the way to grow them is to learn to read, — in short, the book-magic — the white man's secret — that which he so much dreads we should obtain." But it was an ill-omened state to which he had arrived: every day he was losing more and more of that apathy which makes slavery tolerable, while at the same time his condition as a slave necessarily prevented him from acquiring the virtues of the free. He had, it is true, floating notions of nobler aims; but those alone who have once been subject to bondage, can tell how blighting is its influence upon the soul, and how the constantly-repeated words of scorn and contempt wither up the best and dearest feelings of man. Even religion, — for, like all those of his race, he was inclined to devotion, — even religion was in its doctrine a dim, confused, incomprehensible page. He read the Ten Commandments: — Thou shalt love thy God: Thou shalt have no other gods but me, thou shalt not adore them nor serve them: Thou shalt keep holy the Sabbath-day: Honour thy father and thy mother: Thou shall not kill: Thou shalt not commit adultery: Thou shalt not steal, etc. And as he read, and strove to understand, it came upon him as a new thing, that profession and violation of the sacred word are too often one and the same with the haughty master, and that (as he graphically expressed himself afterwards) while the minister read one set of commandments from the altar, the whip cut another table upon his back: — Thou shalt love thy lawful master: Thou shalt yield submissively to his will, thou shalt not question his justice, thou shalt obey him in preference to thy Heavenly Father: Thou shalt keep holy every day by working for him: Thou shalt honour no father, thou hast no right to know of one; thou shalt honour no mother, for she has no care or training of thee: Thou shalt not steal thyself from thy master by flying from him, for thou belongest to him — thou, and thy soul with its highest faculties, and thy heart with its dearest treasures. What wonder, then, if his mind was confused between right and wrong — between his duties as a slave and his duties as a Christian — between the rights of his master and the rights of himself as a man? His mind was like the image of an Apollo defaced and broken up: the casual observer would pronounce it a worthless heap of misshapen stones; the student of Art alone would judge how beautiful the statue had originally been, and how cruel and wanton must have been the blows which deformed it.

The time came at length when the young master was recalled to his Colonial home, and the slave must return also. What! must he waste the remainder of his days in disgusting slave-work? — be compelled to labour in the field, and grovel with his fellow-brutes? Twice ten Christmas seasons and four more, as the Negroes are wont to say, had been counted since his birth; nine of them had been spent in the white man's country. He had remained too long; he had tasted freedom, and learned its value but too well. The bird born in imprisonment pecks the grain and sips the drink unconscious of the existence of any higher joy; but once let it use its wings, how soon will the bars which lately sheltered it, and the hand which fed it, become odious! — new feelings are aroused within it, its wild nature is awake and throbbing; it may see starvation before it in freedom, but even this is a paradise compared with what it must undergo amid the luxuries of a prison.

Belfond could no longer brook the idea of slavery; he loathed the very thought. He spent his nights in groans and tears, and his days in kneeling to his master's friends, frantically entreating that they would intercede for him, that he might stay. He would work, he said; he would send his earnings to his master, every sous;[†] he would exercise his talent; he should rise in the world, he was certain, and all should be for his master's glory, his master's profit, from his faithful, grateful slave. But in vain he pleaded. A few pitied him, but could do nothing; others treated his words as the ravings of a maniac; and he was desired to pack up his young master's things, and be ready to sail next morning. It was then that the demon tempted him, — the slave-nature worked within him, and despair framed an excuse: he rose in the night, took money, jewels, plate, all that he could lay hands upon, and stole away to the south, to the sea-port of Marseilles.

It was not then in France, as it was already in England, ordained that every slave on touching its soil should become free.[†] Captain Hill was just then taking in a cargo of olive-oil and figs, and having seen young Cardon in Paris with his valet, he recognized Belfond on the wharf, and watched him. The mate, Higgins, enticed him on board, seized upon him unawares, and threw him headlong into the hold, where he was instantly secured in chains. After a long and stormy passage, the vessel at length came in sight of Tobago, when the captain, having for some reason sailed into port there, went on shore to spend the night. The sailors of course made merry, rum circulated freely, and its fumes broke forth in song and revel. In a moment of inspiration, Higgins proposed to have up the slave, and make him dance for their amusement.

Belfond was no sooner brought upon deck than he saw at a glance the opportunity that presented itself; he did his best to please them, exposed his shrunken limbs for their jesting, and rattled his chains in a dismal dance to their hallooing. At length, one by one, they sank upon the deck, where they lay stretched like swine, and the general snoring warned Belfond that his time was come. He gathered his irons about him, seized the boat, and launched forth, without knowing whither his course would lead him. For more than two days he was upon the open sea; on the third day however he drew near land, and it proved to be his own beautiful island, the land of his birth, fair Trinidad. The Indians on the coast[†] were ready to help him strike off his fetters, and for awhile to afford him shelter. He remained a time with these good people, but, afraid of being discovered by the missionary of the district, he left them, and went forth to wander in the pathless forest, taking care to avoid the habitations of the white man; he afterwards assembled such of the Maroons as were inclined to a peaceful life, and they dwelt together in a forest village of their own building.

His tale of love is soon told. Laurine was as superior among the girls, as he among the young men, of the coloured class. He saw her — loved her, — it was a thing of course: his was a southern's passion, and with southern vehemence he wooed and won her heart. They were to have been married as soon as the maiden had earned sufficient to buy the freedom of her mother. But even here the evils of his condition pursued him: jealous of the girl he adored, and suspicious of all who approached her, precisely because he knew the extent of the danger to which she was exposed, he had too hastily taken umbrage at a refusal which, had his mind been only free from prejudice, would have won his admiration.

"For the rest," he said, in conclusion, while relating his adventures to the Negroes, "I have learned this, that I have a right to my own free-will, and to the exercise of my own free judgment, and I will use them while I have a leg to carry me and a head to guide me. So, hurrah for the woods! hurrah for justice — for life — for liberty!"

CHAPTER XIX.

The Slave's Burial. — Lights and Shadows of Savage Feeling

At the sound of Belfond's last word, — a word so dear to every human heart, — the dying Negro woke. The vital flame, which had sunk even to the socket, flamed up once more with a clear, bright, full light, ere it died away again for ever. Even before he spoke, the young Talima was on the alert to aid him in his efforts to rise: this he found very difficult, for he could not lie on his back, nor on either side; but, by the united assistance of the other Negroes, he was at length placed in a sitting posture, with his head resting on the shoulder of his child. Eagerly his sable friends crowded round him. They gave him water, bathed his temples, moistened his hands, and spoke words of comfort, such as poor slaves can utter who know what suffering is, and have nothing to give but the deep sympathy of their own hearts. Mammy of the hospital was then sent for: she came, with the fussy and important air which she was wont to assume amongst her fellow-slaves; but she had hardly looked at the sick man when her voice lowered.

"I knowed it," she said in a subdued tone; "I told ye all da same. Now, niggers, get all you want ready, for you'll have to bury him 'fore cross-down; he face tell dat; no comin' back from dat 'ere, no ways."

Anamoa looked up brightly on hearing these words, — to him as tidings of near relief. "Liberty!" he murmured, repeating to himself the word which had waked him, and which was one of the few he could pronounce in English, and a smile of joy came over his face. Talima, who had eagerly inquired the meaning of what the nurse had said, pressed her arms about her father with wild, uncontrollable distress. The pitying Negroes comforted her. "Courage!" cried they; "think, poor Talima, of the triumph that will soon be his! think of the freedom he will gain, and shed no tear, lest you spoil the glory of this hour."

But hush, Reader! give me a moment's patience before you breathe a word of doubt. It was not the triumph of Christ they spoke of, nor the glory of the coming kingdom of Heaven. They had never received tidings of the holy Gospel, to bring comfort to their souls, to give hope to their grieving hearts, — they were heathens. The unexplained prayers at muster-roll were as Latin to them; the word Jesus — that charm which lifts the veil of Heaven to the Christian soul — that tie which binds man, trembling, yet hopeful and joyful, to his God — was to these poor Negroes simply a hard word which they could scarcely pronounce. Yet God forsakes not even his lowliest creatures in the season of their trouble and pain, and truly hath he spoken, "Come all ye that are heavy laden, and I will give you rest;" and so it was even here. Over the dark untaught soul of the dying Negro hovered the pitying angel of mercy; and, wrapped in the African superstition that death bears the exile to his native place, came the dim foreshadowing of a better world — the promise of rest, of peace, of happiness for ever. There was no mourning, but encouraging words and cheering expressions; and many a message of love to their far-distant friends did these creatures whisper to the exile returning to his home. Sometimes they were interrupted by the sobs of Talima, which their chiding could not subdue, and here and there a hand was seen raised to a moistened eye; and the dying man sighed, grieving that he could not bear away his child with him.

Belfond was deeply moved by this touching scene. He was foremost in supporting the dying man, and it was chiefly on his arms that the burden rested, leaving as little weight as possible on Talima. But, even thus, her strength began to fail her, and the sympathizing Quaco gently shifted himself into her place. Anamoa's eyes grew brighter; the expression of his face was almost radiant. He seemed to gaze for awhile at something above the earth — at some joy beyond, which he was about to grasp; then looking round upon his friends, he made signs to them to draw near.

"Children," said he, "the Great Spirit calls me to him; he whose eye is the light-giving sun has ordained that, at the first ray of tomorrow's light, my spirit shall ride away to the region of my birth. Children, my last word — be true to one another! Truth, honesty, goodness to the tyrant, remember, O children, is treachery to yourselves. Children, may Assarci, the spirit of mercy, spread his golden wings over you! I am going." And all perceived the unmistakable signs that the hour was come.

In the midst of the varied activity of this strange busy world, what a sublime event is death! what a mysterious transformation! Revealed in its awful significance to the Christian, it is still to the heathen a bewildering change. Sometimes his instinct leads him close upon the truth; then away he wanders, his fancy peopling the unknown world with the strangest forms. The awful moment was now nigh; not a sound disturbed the stillness of the room. The women stayed their breathing; the men, as noiseless, stood up with instinctive respect in presence of the dread mystery. Anamoa breathed harder, then the sound grew fainter; a slight convulsive movement of the face, a shudder, a sigh, and all was over. The bands of life were rent asunder, and that poor Negro's soul, upon which the light had never shone, now stood trembling and heavy-laden before the great God who had created it, seeking the promised refuge of the weary and the oppressed.

No sooner had his head dropped lifeless upon the shoulder of Belfond, than the Negroes in wild excitement simultaneously shouted in triumph; they tossed their arms aloft, and sang a sort of paean, — wild, gladsome notes pealing in alternate measure through the still night; for that which brings deepest grief to the free, is the signal of joy to the slave.

Then gradually the women stole away, and after them the men, to make preparations for crowning the festival, the final deposit of earth within its mother earth. They wrapped the body in linen white as snow, and placed it on a table; then upon the head they put a gorgeous crown of parrot-feathers, such as the chief was wont to wear in Fantyn, and, as they came in, each addressed his spirit, believing it would hear them: "His spirit still remains with us," said they; "he will not leave us until sunrise, for so he said."

"The great Accompong," said one, in African dialect, as he approached with an armful of palm-leaves, which he placed one by one round the table, "has looked down from his high place. Assarci, in his mercy, has taken our fallen chief to a place where he will never suffer again."

"Thou wast brave," said another, bringing a branch of the sacred cotton-tree, which he placed between the hands of the dead; "thou wast mighty as the storm; but there are caves where the storm has no power, and the mighty chief of kingdoms has fallen into the pit of the traitor."

"Thou wast generous, O good Anamoa; thy kingly palace had room for the needy, shelter for the houseless, and food for the hungry."

"Thy people were happy under a sway gentle as the dew; thou wast kind to them as a father."

"Rest, O fallen king! exiles like thee, we shall remember thy dying words; we have gathered them up like golden treasure, and placed them deep within our hearts."

"Thy child's heart will we keep warm. The stumbling-stones will we roll away; the thorns will we pick up which encumber her path, — where we can, O Anamoa, for the promises of slaves are as barren land, and yield only briars."

"Hear us, O Anamoa, while yet thy spirit tarries; bear our messages to distant homes; say how we weep, and how we hope to join the loved ones again."

And a few wailings, but not many, closed the songs of those who brought offerings to the dead.

The room was decorated with savage yet graceful taste. Gigantic leaves of the cocoa-nut and tree-fern,† set upright upon their stalks, formed a canopy above, from which garlands of the blue and pink convolvulus,† and long chaplets of scarlet berries,† were looped and festooned in various lengths, while the choicest flowers covered the table, and fragrant leaves carpeted the ground. Bouquets too, tastefully arranged, were placed within the hands, upon the chest, and about the face of the dead.

Mammy of the hospital had left the hut, for the head cooper was very ill. He had been a clever, useful man, she knew therefore that it was of consequence she should be at her post. He groaned very much, and was always calling for water; Mammy had given him diluted lemon-juice for about the twelfth time, and was debating within herself whether she should risk another castigation for disturbing the slumbers of her mistress, by sending to the big house for a composing draught — when some one entered. Satan himself, with hoofs and horns, would have been to her a much more welcome guest, for it was Fanty, the Obiah priest. Mammy, whose kind heart found pleasure in her task, made it a boast that she had often carried Negroes through the most dangerous attacks without doctor or instructions; but she knew too well that Fanty, wherever he came, was the harbinger of sickness, decline, and death. But, for wealth or life, she would never have breathed a word to betray him, or have done aught against his will.

For a minute he stood still; he did not speak, nor did Mammy speak to him. He then went to the candle, and stretching out his bony, witchcraft-working fingers, with their long nails, he stooped as if to examine them minutely. Then he went close to the bed of each of the patients, looking at them and feeling them, and passed on till he came to the cooper. "You're thirsty," he said: "drink this;" and he held up a gourd, and supported the patient's head while he drank. Strange as it may appear, although the sick cooper knew that the draught was poison, and it is to be supposed he was born with as much inherent love of life, as other human beings, yet not a sign of hesitation did he manifest in taking it. Then the sorcerer smoothed his forehead, stroked his eyelids with his horrid claws, and forming circles of incantation round the bed with the right hand, as he muttered strange cabalistic words of some unknown language, he laid his left hand upon the patient's heart; Mammy, with her eyes fixed upon him in silence, standing motionless all the time like one entranced. He went out as quickly and as noiselessly as he had entered.

Meantime the preparations for the burial were still going on in the hut. Up to this time Belfond had been chief actor in the various decorations of the room; for, with his warm imagination and the keen poetic sensibility of his particular colour, he took pleasure in seizing the spirit of the strange festival. When everything had been arranged, he called Quaco aside, to fix with him on some spot where they might be certain the body would remain undisturbed.

"Dunno no such place," said the Negro lad; "sabannah hab rat, tree hab snake, and, worse nor all, white man's spade break da ground eberywhere: cutlass and rest neber live together."†

"How do you mean, Quaco?" asked Belfond, rather puzzled to know what his friend alluded to.

"Eh hey!" exclaimed the other, with the sharp, quick utterance peculiar to Negroes; "just hearee, you Belfond: you know dat tall bamboo-tree by the great sabannah, dere de grass is soft, de shade wide and cool, birds sing in de leaves, and at sundown we love to sit dere and talk. Time out o' mind poor Anamoa sit down dere when he weary, and talk 'bout far Africa to young people like me. Well, s'pose we bury him dere, — tomorrow-day massa Manager come past wid big dog, debil dog smells ground, scratches up, so whines, den massa Manager calls out, 'Niggers, come yere! somefin here! come, dig away, let me see;' so poor nigger 'bliged to dig till de spade dig up body, den massa Manager flog all round. Hey, Belfond, da neber do!"[†]

Belfond listened to his companion and mused. He looked at the calm, streaming moonlight, which traced fantastic forms in the deep shadows of the woods, and he wondered perhaps how far they would have to go to obtain rest, in a landscape which, at that hour at least, appeared all so peaceful. Unconsciously he looked in the direction of a small field in which it was customary to bury the slaves; Quaco, perceiving this, seized his arm eagerly.

"Mustn't go dere, no ways," said he; "bodies now'days tumbled in dere anyhow; too many niggers die now for hab quiet dat place. Last week, two buried together one sundown, — next morning all de ground scratched up, and two niggers gone!"

"Gone where, Quaco?"

"Gone back to Africa,[†] don't you know? — and it is a weary long walk."

Belfond laughed outright, — which nettled the other greatly, for, habitually good-humoured as the youth was, touch only ever so slightly on his superstitions, and directly he became irritable and impatient. It was in vain that Belfond suggested the interference of tiger-cats[†] or vultures:[†] the more said, the more angry the Negro became, for the love of the marvellous brooks no meddling of reason.

"Well," observed Belfond at last, after vainly trying to talk Quaco into common sense and equanimity, "this won't tell us where to bury the body. What shall we do?"

"I no speak no more: come here to dem new Koromantyns, and maybe dey'll someways tell what people do in Fantyn."

The group in question were sitting on the ground within the hut, talking and laughing in exceeding glee, like spectators, at a *fête*. When questioned by Quaco, they all stood up, and instantly went to the Fetish cotton-tree outside, and pointed to the sod beneath it.

Quaco, with a gesture of impatience, struck his forehead. "Fool!" he muttered to himself, "where Quaco head gone to — didn't tink o' dat afore?" then gaily resuming, "Come, you comrades, eberybody, come, let us dig. Now, Belfond," he said, looking at this friend, "dis 'ere cotton-tree belong to nigger, neber no white man disturb 'em here." Strange as it may appear, he spoke what he believed; for planters who violate the first rights of their fellow-creatures are usually found to respect the trees — often fruit-trees — of their slaves; — one anomaly among a thousand to be found in slave-holding society.

They proceeded to prepare for the burial; for, in tropical climates, a body may not be left more than three or four hours above ground. As the preparations were going on, Belfond said slyly in Quaco's ear, "Are you sure now that Anamoa would not rather be left above ground, to walk freely away to his own country?"

"He too sick!" roared the incorrigible Negro, frowning at what he considered his friend's stupidity, "and de way too long! we must bury him deep, so make him stay dere softly."

"But, my friend, how then can he ever get back to Africa?" persisted the other, laughing.

"Ah! you! cho!" exclaimed Quaco, nudging him impatiently with his elbows, as if he almost despaired of enlightening such idiocy; then turning again, "Don't you see?" he said, "When spirit finds he body 'bove ground, he takes body wid 'em. Now, what could spirit do wid body all cut up like dis 'ere? Go 'way!" and he went and fetched his spade, and, like a good sexton, commenced his work of digging the grave. "Eh, me Gad!" he went on, grunting to himself as the company left him one by one, "Somebody must come for help me here, — neber dig deep enough dis way."

A cold hand touched his shoulder: he turned, and lo! before him stood a figure dressed in white. Instantly the mind of the imaginative African beheld in it the form of the departed risen again. He staggered back with affright; "Eh, you!" he gasped with a quick utterance and an odd mixture of terror and solicitude; "go lie down again! you no fit for walk all dat way, me tell you."

"Hist, idiot! hold tight tongue in your head, will you? *Toad's cry betrays toad. Screams go through walls:* do you hear?"

Quaco instinctively clutched hold of his amulet, for he knew the voice of Fanty. "Me Gad, oh!" he whispered to himself, but he said not a word more. Fanty beckoned to him, and he followed into the hut.

As the sorcerer entered, the cheerful murmur of merry voices from those who were busy with the various arrangements for the burial dropped in a moment, as if under the influence of a spell. An undefined awe seized upon them, which was greatly increased by the old man's unusual appearance. His body, arms, and ankles were thickly bandaged round with linen all soiled with recent bleeding; "besides," said each to himself as he looked, "where are the snakes and the dog?" for never before, since he had assumed the priestly office, had he appeared without them.

"You fools!" exclaimed he, frowning, as he eyed them all round; "what noise! Far in the woods, a mile away, I heard you. Are walls deaf? Is the Master mad? Fools! keep your voice down: *lions should never roar near the hunter's tent,* do you hear?" then, perceiving the dead laid out, "And is that what you were going to bury under the Fetish tree?" he asked, turning slowly to Quaco, as he pointed to the body.

"Yes, Ta Fanty,"[†] meekly replied the youth.

"Not there! for if the tree belongs to niggers, don't you know the ground belongs to the white man, you fools? — no, not there, but under here!" cried Fanty, stamping upon the floor, "under here! And you, Talima," he added, as he drew her forward from the company, "you shall live here and watch the sacred dead, lest the white man's dog may come and smell it out."

Then the priest called for drink, and a large gourd, full of the refreshing mawbee, prepared from the seed of the *Mammea Sapota,*[†] was officiously presented him by Coraly; and, as this circulated, libations were poured on the ground in honour of Assarci, who, as well as being the God of mercy, was also the God of regeneration.[†]

"And now for an oath! a new oath!" cried the man of darkness, raising the fresh-filled bowl high in the air, "to a new oath! Mark that Belfond!" he said, pointing to the Mulatto, who was leaning against the door apart from the rest; "there is the son of my dead sister! the bloodthirsty cotton-faced tigers are seeking him. Let one of you dare betray him, dare neglect to shelter him, and, by the dread mysteries of Obi, he shall spin out eternity as the slave of the slave of the white baboon! Augh!" he hoarsely and vengefully drawled, "pass the bowl for the new oath!" and, amid stamps and violent gestures and imprecations of horrible import, the Negroes promised to lay down their lives before they would see one hair hurt which had ever grown on Belfond's head. Whereupon the old man opened his mouth again, and, as if to reward their ready obedience, with inspired looks and fiery eye he prophesied a visit from Higgins the night after the following, when he, the bushranger, he who hunted and hacked about the African worse than if he were a dog, "Here," he cried, "shall fall before the whole gang of you, a blackened corpse! Ach!" and the old man shook and gnashed his teeth in anticipation of his revenge. In breathless silence the Negroes listened and received their instructions, and when Fanty took a low stool and buried his face in his hands, they silently commenced digging; for while Fanty was present, they considered themselves under a leader whose will, not their own, should direct them.

The grave being dug, Fanty rose: this was the signal for burial. The women strewed the bottom of the pit with sweet-smelling flowers, and Fanty, with the help of Belfond and Quaco, lowered the body, wrapped in its swathing linen, and gently laid it on the perfumed bed.

"Now," said Fanty, "where are drums? where is the music?"

The instruments were procured: a portion of the hollow trunk of a tree covered over tight with calfskin was the drum, on which they struck with amazing celerity; a couple of African trumpets and short horns, and a rude sort of guitar, on which Fanty himself performed, completed the band; and they struck up triumphantly a hymn, composed long before by Belfond for some similar occasion. Belfond sang the recitative; the assembly joining in the chorus, accompanied by their savage music.

No more thou'lt watch the morning sun arise
With heavy heart and swimming eyes,
Nor send to Heaven thy unavailing cries

Chorus.   For one little moment's rest.
        Rest, Father! calmly rest.

Thou'rt now secure within thy quiet grave,
So, let thy tyrant Master rave!
He cannot blast the hope which cheers the slave,

Chorus.   When Death rings his solemn call,
        All hail! joy! brothers all.

For where's the wretch would for his fetters grieve?
A life in chains, who'd weep to leave?
No! Death is ever but a kind reprieve

Chorus.   To each poor degraded slave!
        But oh, thou! no longer slave!

Behold, aloft, in yon mysterious height,
The glorious host of sparking light!
Spirits they are who wait thy heavenward flight,

Chorus.   Where all men, all, are free, —
             Free! happy brother, free!

        They'll bear thee where the wild palm waves
        Its plumes above thy fathers' graves,
        Abodes where haply soon thy fellow-slaves

Chorus.   Will meet in the breezy air, —
             There in the breezy air.

        Where all day long our mothers sit forlorn
        By the rude huts where we were born,
        We'll fan, with perfumes of the rising morn,

Chorus.   Our own loved native groves —
             Own loved native groves.[†]

The women pressed round with their aprons laden with flowers. Talima came first, to fling in her offering; then others followed, and showers of blossoms soon hid the body from sight. Old Fanty then came forward, and was about to cast in the first clod, when . . .

Nay, but to make my narrative clear, I must crave permission to look back a little, and note what passed at the Master's house, where they supped and chatted and slept, unconscious and unmindful how in the slave-huts death was welcomed with that strange wild scene of revelry and music.

CHAPTER XX.

Conversation in the Great House. —
A Discovery and a Capture

On a downy couch, his head resting on cushions, and protected from the flies by smart young Negro lasses, who fanned them away with branches of lemon and cinnamon, — his feet rubbed by Beneba, because she had soft hands, — reclined the proud owner of the Palm Grove Estate. Sometimes Beneba, lulled by the silence and by the monotony of her task, would let her eyelids droop, and her head would nod: then her master would give her a kick, and, awakened to a sense of her transgression, the unlucky girl would recommence rubbing with renewed zeal and activity, to the suppressed giggles of the Negro girls at the upper end of the sofa. But neither the scented air, nor the cushions, nor the soft hands of Beneba could charm away the gloom which had settled on the planter's mind. Turn his thoughts whichever way he might, there would still arise before him that day's scene at the muster-roll, — Mr. Dorset, his looks of horror at the scourging, his words of pity for the rebel crew, and, to crown all, his words of disapproval openly and unreservedly spoken before the whole gang. In vain he pshawed and poohed and uttered a hundred Gallic *bahs!* expressive of his contempt for the whole affair: it would not do — he knew too well the danger of incurring the disapproval of a single individual of his own class and colour, while in the governing country public opinion against slavery was becoming every day more embittered. In sooth he found himself just now in no very easy position, and certainly in no very bland mood.

The scene of the young Negro girl striving to shield her father by the intervention of her own person, — which was ever recurring to his mind, — excited his sympathy, and something akin to regret came over him, when he thought of the stern necessity of crushing all self-respect in a stock so closely resembling — he did not exactly add *human beings* — but white people. While he was pondering these things, Don Duro entered. It was the custom of that worthy individual to come in about this hour to talk over the affairs of the estate, and smoke a cigarillo by way of company. St. Hilaire suffered him to sit down, and dismissed the girls in attendance, who hurried away in great delight, making sly grimaces to one another at the manager as they passed out.

Don Duro jerked his small person into a chair, and bending his quick, watchful, little black eyes upon the planter, as if seeking some point by which he might lay firm hold of his mind and steer it his own way, he commenced, in his usual ceremonious wording and unceremonious manner. "The Señor is tired?"

"What have you done with that old Negro?" asked St. Hilaire abruptly.

"Señor, I have left him to his fate," rejoined the manager; "it would never do for any of us to appear anxious about such a dog."

"Where is the girl?"

"In some of the Negro-houses, I daresay; but if the Señor wishes it, I can inquire: shall I send, and have her brought up here?"

"No! no!" replied the planter, turning away with evident ill-humour; "*Pardi!* can't I inquire after my own Negroes, without raising your officious suspicions?"

Don Duro was silent for a space. He was not a very good-tempered man himself, yet not altogether deficient in the power of self-control where his interests were concerned. He had long made up his mind to humour the impetuous planter, and so to exhibit devotion to the welfare of the family as to win his patron's confidence and gratitude; for he knew that if he could only once obtain these, it was by no means unlikely that the generous planter would make him a present of a share in the estate. These were his general plans; but he had a particular design in view this evening. He therefore allowed St. Hilaire's ill-humour to subside a little, and then very gently drew his attention to the affairs of the estate —

how the crop was gathering in — the labour done during the day — the diminished numbers of the Negroes — the increasing mortality — all the pains he had himself taken to preserve the black stock in health. Next he spoke of the hospital — told the story of the cooper and the mammy — of the new slaves and the clabba-yaws, and, without much respect for truth, he boasted of his care of them and how much he had done for the prevention of further infection. Nor did he omit the usual protestations of his extreme devotion to the interests of the family in general, and the happiness of his patron in particular.

At length, when he judged that he had brought the planter into tolerable good-humour, he drew a long breath and started the subject he had come upon, by asking his patron whether he had ever examined Laurine's papers, stating that he had reason to believe they were not drawn up in legal form, and therefore that the girl was as safely the property of St. Hilaire as Madelaine her mother. The bait did not take, — not even when he reminded him of what the girl was saving money for; nor when he related how he had seen her, early on the morning of the sale, in close and intimate conversation with the Mulatto, and was therefore amenable to the law for harbouring a runaway; nor even when he insinuated his belief that the girl had something to do with the Obiah. He read only silent contempt in his patron's face, and in his eye a slightly satirical, suspicious expression, as though doubtful of what all this tended to. But St. Hilaire, however lofty his mind, was not proof against the continuous attacks of this designing man, whose scheme was now to bring the planter gradually to recall to mind his recreant slave, — how he had defied him on board the slave ship, how he had escaped, and the probability that he had been the sole author of the poisoning. He hoped, by this means, to induce a sort of collateral wrath against Laurine, as abettor to those evil-doings, and thence to obtain his consent for arresting the girl and holding her prisoner on the estate.

Don Duro had already roused the proud planter into the desired state of anger and indignation, and was proposing the old plan of slashing the tendon-Achilles,[†] whenever the fellow was caught; by which means he would be crippled for life, and effectually rendered unable ever again to escape. But in the midst of these tokens of gradual success, the manager was interrupted by a very unusual visit at this time of night; for in rushed the Overseer, the image of horror, his hair standing fairly on end, while his goggle eyes threatened to fall from their sockets.

"What — what — what is the matter?" cried the planter and manager with one voice. But the Overseer only chattered with his teeth, and made a mumbling noise, which died away in his throat.

"Can't you answer me?" cried Mr. Cardon, taking him by the collar and shaking him, to call back his senses.

"I — I — I —" stammered he, staring deliriously round; "don't you hear them? Don't stop me! Run for your lives! They are coming to cut our throats!"

"Who? who?" demanded the planter with the greatest impatience.

"The Negroes! they're all up in rebellion!"

St. Hilaire listened; truly enough there were trumpets and horns, sounding notes of warlike triumph through the still night. Mr. Cardon was not a man to waste time in moments of emergency: he dashed away the Overseer, and in another moment he was equipped with arms, — musket, belt, knife, and cutlass — and giving arms to Don Duro, who received them somewhat trembling, though taking good care not to express any objection, he ordered the two to follow him. "Pooh! you infernal coward!" he cried to the Overseer, who was shivering and lagging behind, "come along! and if they but dare to touch a hair of your head, I'll soon settle them. Here, take your whip and these ropes, and come along: 'twould be dangerous to give you a gun;" which orders the chattering, trembling Overseer was fain to obey, for fear the Negroes might otherwise discover him alone and murder him.

Prudence suggested that they should gain on the Negroes by stealth, and reconnoitre. The noise in the Koromantyn hut was at its height, and to this point they directed their steps, selecting a path behind a thick mass of bushes. The warlike instruments and triumphant voices sounded loud and clear, and the party crept round to a place whence, through a badly closed window, they could see what was passing within, and St. Hilaire, imposing silence on his companions, looked on with curiosity and amazement. They were just lowering the dead body into a hole dug in the centre of the hut-floor. Strangers too were present. One tall young man stood with his back to the aperture through which the white men were watching: who could it be? The planter instinctively concentrated his attention upon him. The hymn commenced: he led, singing the recitative: at the very first sound of that voice Mr. Cardon started. Yet he waited till the song was over; then the party stole round, step by step, the Overseer getting ready his ropes, the Manager his whip; St. Hilaire himself was ready with his weapons, should he find it necessary to use them.

The doorway was so thickly crowded without and within, that it appeared impossible to enter without being seen; but with one push St. Hilaire stood in the middle of the hut. Before one of them had detected his presence, Belfond was on the ground, stunned with a blow from his master. "I say, you there, bring the ropes quick, before he comes to!" At this Don Duro came up, with the scared-looking Overseer holding fast to his coat, and the process of tying and securing the prisoner was soon got through.

St. Hilaire was still stooping down, fastening the last end of the rope, the Negroes standing off to the furthest distance, dropping off one by one through the door and window, when an apparition approached, at sight of which the Overseer roared for his life. A bent, dwarfish, demon-like figure, with glaring eyes, had fastened on the planter, and sent his vampire claws up through his hair; and when, with an oath of annihilation, the planter turned and caught hold of the arm, it was gone as soon as touched: so well was it smeared with oil and grease, that it slipped like an eel through his hands, and the figure disappeared. Troubled at a vision he could not account for, and although his reason was too sound to believe in supernatural visitations, still St. Hilaire felt uneasy, and unconsciously hurried over what yet remained to be done.

It was necessary to remove the prisoner, who was still senseless; on the Manager devolved the task of locking him up in the stocks. Then the place was well examined, and secured for the night; the watch-dog was chained near the door, and the Manager himself lay down ready dressed, to be on the alert at the least noise. The Overseer was charged to have the dead body taken up; and his fright having by this time evaporated, he could enjoy the delight of cracking his long terrible whip, and driving before him the sullen gangs, who were made to carry their dead chief to the appointed burial-hole of the estate. Mr. Cardon himself, leaving these several tasks to his employés, retired, — not to rest, but to pace up and down his room in trouble and restlessness until morning.

CHAPTER XXI.

Two Travellers of a Different Stamp

Nothing could be quieter than the village of Sant' Iago on the morning after the slave-sale; the merchants and planters had returned to their several homes, and the empty ship, leaving Higgins behind, had sailed away up the Orinoco, to take in a cargo of turtle and lamp-oil, for the grand port of Trinidad. Laurine was up with the grey light, and more alert than was her wont in getting through the little affairs of the morning. By-and-by she went towards the woods, to gather choice blossoms to make up into bouquets for the Port Spain market, a grand festal day being near at hand. The hedges, banks, and roadsides were covered with the gay adornings of the season, and all things seemed to smile; but the beauty of Nature only increased the sadness of her thoughts, and, sobbing and choking with grief, she was fain to turn back to her little home, and seek comfort in the society of her simple friend. Their little table was already laid: she sat down and tried to eat, but every morsel stuck half-way down, and she could only answer her friend's remarks with monosyllables, which it cost her a painful effort to utter without permitting her tears to start afresh. When the meal was ended, and everything neatly put away, she took up some needlework, and, seating herself at her little window, began to sing; Catalina, good soul, took a chair too, and amused herself with reckoning the gains of the morning over and over again. Suddenly Laurine's voice dropped: Catalina looked round, and saw the tears fast streaming down her face. The child is tired, thought she; and then immediately added aloud, "Laurine, you don't look as if you had slept last night, what is the matter? I am sure that work will kill you, you are for ever at it."

Laurine, with an effort to check her grief, answered briskly that she was "well, quite well," and standing up, she displayed her work to her companion. "Look here, good Catalina, — have I not managed this work nicely? It is a festal dress for La St. Jean:† look at these sleeves plaited in cross-barred patterns, and at these pockets edged with gay ribbon, — do you see how I have filled them with little pink cowries† from the shore, to jingle like money while the dancer moves. And I have gummed down the wings of the small gold-beetle† and of gay butterflies, and what pretty patterns they make! I have been a long time collecting them in this little cedar box, because the wood preserves them; and I expect a good price for this dress. I ought, I am sure, to be thankful to God for the number of good customers he bestows upon me."

"And above all, my child," said the dame, in a warning but affectionate tone, "never be proud or vain; always bear in mind the fate of the crabs on the day of creation."

"Oh, Catalina, pray tell me about it, it will do me good to listen to you."

"Well, my child," answered the aged spinster with a solemn face, "it is a deep lesson for youth. When creation began, it took four, five, six, seven days, and then God called all the animals together, to receive their heads: they assembled on a wide savannah, and the heads were handed to them by angels. All the animals stood there quiet, one here, another there, all modest and respectful, save the little crab, and she kept walking here and marching there, and showing off her pretty steps sideways and every way, for people to see, till, when she thought to ask for her head, the heap was gone — there was not one left. So you see what pride brings people to! The Holy Virgin protect you from such a sin, my child!"

"One could almost fancy," observed Laurine, "that some animal had taken up a head more than his share: was it the two-headed snake, I wonder?" she added innocently.

"I suppose it was, my child; and I have heard tell of another thing, — that the monkey, full of tricks, jumped in front, and just as the crowd reached the savannah, and with one spring he whipped up a human head, and skipped to the top of a palm-tree with it. The angel said, 'Come down, rascal!' He would not come, but threw down the head: it was then so dirty and bruised that man would not have it, and the angels were obliged to make him an entire new one; so monkeys have human heads, and remain thieves and vagabonds, to this day."

"Very true, good Catalina; and I just remember I have heard another story about those wonderful beginnings of all things: I heard it from Fanty, who is learned in African magic, he says —"

"Likely, likely," said the spinster, shaking her head, "and Fanty knows a great deal; but oh, my child, keep clear of that man: remember that religion forbids us to commune with evil-doers, lest we become so ourselves. Padre Martino says that Obiah is a crime, and everybody says that Fanty is an Obiah man. But, *Ave Maria! Santísimos Santos!*"† she exclaimed, crossing herself with great rapidity, and looking with horror towards the back door, "here is the man himself! I hope he didn't hear me."

Despite the good dame's advice, Laurine rose to bid him welcome; for was he not aged and infirm, she said to herself, and poor? — he was also near akin to her loved though too hasty and impetuous Belfond. As she opened the door however, she uttered a faint exclamation of terror. His face was bound up in blood-stained cloths, and one of his arms was in a sling. Before she had time to say a word he addressed her.

"Sorrow is on my old head," he exclaimed with a harsh and tremulous voice, "and Fanty will soon be laid far down under the grass. See!" he cried, holding up his wounded arm, "this is what poor old Fanty gets for helping others; but body-pain is nothing, — heart-pain! that's worse. Better had Belfond drunk the death-giving Obiah, and Fanty had laid his old head under the grass beside him, than that he should die by bits in the white man's dungeon."

Laurine did not utter a word: with her hands crossed upon her bosom, and the big drops standing on her brow, she gazed at the Negro, awaiting in terror the explanation of his words.

"*Ah!*" continued he, raising his voice to a shriller key, "*sorrow comes easy; trouble is cheap to get; years and money cannot send it away;*" saying which, he turned to go.

Laurine sprang after him: "Speak to me, Fanty!" she cried; "oh, tell me what has happened to him — to Belfond!"

The Negro eyed her for a moment keenly; then, as if moved by her entreaties, he edged himself to a low stool, and, squatting down upon it, related the facts which are already known to the reader.

During the colloquy, Catalina had joined them with eyes and mouth open to listen. As soon as she had heard enough to understand what was the matter, she suggested a remedy after her own fashion. "My child, we will speak to Padre Martino," she said; "he is a holy, pious man."

The Negro's wounded and disfigured visage became contorted into a hideous sneer, which so terrified the spinster as to prevent her from finishing her speech. "Away!" he cried, raising his bony hand; "away with white men's sorcerers (meaning priests)! *does not right hand wash left hand?* who ever heard one white man say another white man did wrong?"

"Fanty," said Laurine eagerly, "and you, good Catalina, leave it all to me; I will do it if I die. I will go to the Palm Grove, and beg mercy for him myself. It is but a few days ago that Madame Angélique herself wanted to coax me away from my shop to nurse the little child, because it loves me, and I play with it so merrily. I will say, Take life, take freedom, only let Belfond live."

"*Santísimos Virgen!*"† broke forth the pious spinster, throwing up her eyes and fingering her beads; "is it among the tempters you would go? Oh, my child, never go where the wicked are! stay here, and God will put it into our hearts to think of some way of saving him yet."

"Don't stop me!" said Laurine passionately, "for do something I will, — though I scarcely know what yet. I think I'll go to the Fountain Estate. Yes, that is it! Lead the way, Fanty; bring me to Mrs. Dorset's, she is kind and sweet, she will listen to me, she will pity my sorrow."

"My child," whispered La Catalina close to her ear, "will you go alone with that man?"

"God is with me," said the young girl, "he will take care of me;" and throwing her arms about her friend's neck, she wept long and bitterly.

"She is right for once," said Fanty. "Young girl, they are looking for you, to catch you and make a slave of you, and on the high road you must not go; but across the woods, to where those good people live, you are safer, so come at once, — old bones like mine have no business in the place of danger: come!" then, tearing herself from Catalina's embrace, she fled in haste with her companion. As she sped beside him, her spirits began to rise; her young heart prophesied success, and already she saw her lover at her feet, safe, free, grateful, and devoted for ever.

Unconsciously she quickened her pace, and glided on, unchecked by bush or thorn, till warned by the voice of her companion to stop.

"Old legs may fall and break," said the old man crossly, "who minds them?"

Laurine felt her error, and though her heart and wishes were bounding before her, she nevertheless stopped to help him, made him lean upon her, and talked kindly to him; and before her sweet influence his ill-humour soon vanished. The road they took was a shorter and much less frequented way than that taken by the two planters the day before. As they advanced, the country became wilder and more lonely, the hedges grew thicker and higher, till at length none but forest-trees flanked their path, their branches entwining so closely above as to obstruct the light of day, while the dark woodlands beyond resounded with the howlings of monkeys,[†] and the screaming of parrots, as they fled at the approach of man. Amid scenes like these, and with such a companion, we cannot wonder that the young girl's spirits in some degree reflected the gloom around her; but she was a hopeful creature, active, contented, looking always to the bright side of things, and finding cause for cheerfulness even under the darkest cloud.

They ascended a gentle slope, where the thick woods opened suddenly into a pleasant glade, and from the top the sea came in full view before them. The sun was just touching the western horizon; the rolling masses of purple and gold, which seemed to bear the fiery orb, were surmounted with streaks of delicate green, like glimpses of a distant fairy-land, and these again shaded softly away to the pure azure of the zenith. A crimson splendour clothed the valleys, and the outlines of the hills were softened by a transparent veil of delicate lilac. The sea, like a resplendent mirror of gold, reflected the tints of the sky above, and its burnished waves, laden with the glow, pressed on impatiently to the shore, as if unwilling to keep such treasures to themselves. Laurine clasped her hands, her knees touched the ground, and she prayed. Fanty looked at her, and drew aside, for there is a guardian spirit ever near the innocent and the earnest, which warns the wicked to keep aloof, and even the fiendish Obiah priest respected her devotions.

When she rose, the glory of the scene was already fading, and twilight was approaching. The change to darkness was rendered more sudden by those masses of clouds lately so bright and gorgeous; they were now moving heavily across the sky, which soon became quite overcast, and, in a few minutes more, rain descended in overwhelming torrents, like those which must have fallen when the great Flood began. Laurine clung to the nearest tree, lest she should be forced down the hill; she was of course soaked to the skin, but she thought more of the old, feeble, and wounded Negro than of herself, and tried to persuade him to keep under shelter with her. But he shook his head, and beckoned her onwards: "I knew of this," he said, "that is why old Fanty came this way. Just behind these trees, quite near us, is an Indian's hut. Forward! quick! and remember old Fanty's tongue can't twist to their Spanish words; young girl must talk for him."

The twanging sound of an old guitar, and the nasal, drawling, monotonous song of a Peon — *i.e.* half Indian, half Spaniard — was now heard above the roar of the descending rain, and by dint of strong efforts Laurine and her companion came to a good-sized low-roofed hut, the inmates of which seemed particularly busy and cheerful. There were a great many women and children, but only one man, — the Peon, who seemed to be the head of the family. There was no need of introduction: our travellers were strangers, and caught in the rain, — this was enough. The women wiped the best stools, set the pot to boil, and slung the hammock on the peg; by-and-by a small table was set in the middle, and a meal offered to the travellers, of which, according to savage etiquette, they must partake, or be considered enemies. When the repast was finished, Old Fanty, grunting with satisfaction, for it was a long time since he had eaten anything so savoury, ensconced himself on a low stool in a dark corner, took out his pipe, and began to smoke. Laurine joined the women at their work; they were busy in preparing cassava from the poisonous root of the far-famed manihot, in a shed adjoining the dwelling-room.

It was late in the evening when the women finished their work, and Laurine, fatigued with her long journey and her late vigils, slept soundly until morning, when the merry voices of the Indian children waked her. The rain had passed away, and nature awoke with renewed loveliness, giving forth fragrance with double profusion. The air was cool and invigorating, and a thousand birds were on the wing, chirping and warbling with gladness at the revival of daylight and serenity. The children were out too, laughing and shouting at one another, for they were earning their breakfast in true Indian fashion, by shooting at pieces of dried fish and tassa,[†] hung upon the tree-tops, as rewards for their skill.

Some chocolate was then prepared, and with this, together with large tempting cassava-cakes, Laurine and her guide made a comfortable breakfast. They had scarcely finished, when Old Fanty grumbled out his hurry to move, and in truth Laurine required no pressing. The Indians would fain have detained them, but the old Negro waved his hand in token of refusal, "For," said he to Laurine, whom he beckoned to interpret, "we must be away now; old feet such as mine, and soft-footed like you, are both slow."

"Then I will go with you a little way for company," said the Indian; "I am going towards Bande de l'Est, to my brothers and friends, bound for the Orinoco tomorrow morning at three by the bright moonlight: we are off on a hunting expedition along the banks, and *acuerdate bien*,"[†] he added, addressing Laurine, "if anything should happen to make a boat welcome, meet us by the Tamana river, on the sea-shore."[†]

This piece of intelligence seemed to afford pleasure to the Negro; he grunted, and nodded, and looked as pleased as with such features he could look. Then Laurine received the good wishes of the women, calmly, quietly expressed, in the manner of all Indians. The Peon called to Emanuel, his eldest son; and these two heaving on their shoulders a bundle of nets, cutlasses, and poles, the little party set off.

Old Fanty however did not seem to like the path which the Indian took and after awhile they parted, the Negro and the damsel continuing their journey alone. The late oppressive heat had been tempered by the last night's torrents, while the few hours' sunshine of that morning had been sufficient to suck up the sopping wet, leaving only enough moisture to make the ground cool and comfortable. They had not proceeded far, when the woods began to thin, the country grew more open, and a prospect soft and beautiful as any in those sunny climes presented itself to their view: the colours of the landscape grew richer; the verdure of the hill-sides and savannahs was lost in the overspreading hues of azure, scarlet, yellow, white, and purple; while in the cultivated hollow before them, the planter's house was seen peeping from amidst groves of palm and bowers of passion-flower, peaceful, happy, and beautiful, as a spot stolen from the gardens of Paradise. Here Fanty took his leave of the maiden. "Assarci look upon you!" said he; "Assarci guide you and bless you! For you never feared poor old Fanty, though everybody hates him and shuns him. Go! no harm shall come to you; though Fanty dies to get it, you and Belfond shall have happiness and freedom soon. Go tonight to Madelaine's hut; Fanty will be there too: white man will give no ear to Laurine's prayers, but Fanty will. Away! go!"

They parted, and Laurine sped on hopefully, and never once turned her eyes to look at the blooming temptations of the country, which at other times would have made her linger for hours on the road to cull them. She was already amidst plantain-walks,[†] where the fruit hung in large and heavy bunches, and in another moment she was skirting the cacao-walks[†] of the Fountain Estate, where the songs of the Negroes proclaimed them at work. Anxious to avoid them, lest they should detain her with their conversation, she crept along in concealment behind the trees.

The harvest had begun: companies of men, women, and children were dispersed among the trees, some stripping the boughs of their purple fruit, and dropping it into baskets beneath; others were seated in the shade, extracting the beans or nibs, which were cast into a large receiving basket, while song, joke, and laughter went round, to cheer them at their labour.

Leaving these on her right hand, Laurine soon approached the rude dwelling of the Fountain Estate. But rude as was the building, — no better indeed than a log-house in the backwoods of America, — it looked pretty, with its little garden, fenced all round with blossoming pomegranates,[†] and its trellised bower of granadilla[†] dropping bright-tinted flowers and ponderous fruit; and close by, on the edge of an abrupt descent, a natural fountain gushed forth, beneath the shade of huge native fruit-trees. It was from this pretty fountain that the estate took its name.

Laurine approached the house, and requested a girl to beg of her mistress that she would allow her to speak with her. In a few moments she was ushered into a room in which Mrs. Dorset was sitting, surrounded by half-a-dozen little sable attendants, whom she was teaching to sew. Laurine, as she entered, dropped a curtsey.

"Well," said Mrs. Dorset, "I am glad to see you, Laurine; what news?"

The poor girl attempted to reply, but her courage failed; and when her lips moved, her voice died away in upheaving sobs, as though her heart would burst its bonds.

Mrs. Dorset laid down her work, and in sweetest and most encouraging tones addressed her: "Tell me, my poor girl, what is the matter with you, and what can I do for you?"

Poor Laurine was quite at a loss how to tell her story; she had been dwelling, all the way she came, on the certain happy result of her petition, never once reflecting on the difficulty she might have in presenting it; but the kind words of the lady reassured her, and the recollection of the dungeon, and the captive within it, doomed to starvation, gave new energy to her mind.

"Please your mercy," she said, adopting the form of speech which the coloured people are taught to use in Spanish colonies, "there is a fellow-slave of my mother's on the Palm Grove Estate, who is in disgrace."

"On Mr. Cardon's estate, is it? What, the old man? or is it his daughter?"

"Please your mercy, it is neither of them; it is a runaway slave, who was caught the other night, and they are going to do something terrible with him."

"Is it your brother, Laurine?"

The young girl hung down her head, and her heart began to throb, while tears, — big, silent, burning tears — fell upon her apron as she grasped it in her trembling hands. With the quick instinct of a woman's heart, Mrs. Dorset guessed the truth at once, and, with equal delicacy, she refrained from asking any further questions, beyond the culprit's name.

"Please your mercy," replied Laurine, looking up through her tears, "it is a Mulatto slave, who years ago went to France to wait upon Mr. Cardon's son, who is now dead. He ran away, the evil spirit tempted him; please your mercy, I know it was a very wicked thing to do; but, if you will beg for him, please your mercy, he will be steady now. At all events, he is in the dungeon starving!"

"Starving?" exclaimed Mrs. Dorset, with a look of incredulity and surprise.

"He has been there since last night, your mercy; and Mr. Cardon declares he will make an example of him to all the runaways in the Colony, for he is spoiled and ruined for ever, he says. Yet I think, if your mercy would only beg for him this once —"

"Starved! Heaven preserve us! starved! — that must not be: and yet what is to be done? Shall I call my husband? — he left Mr. Cardon's last evening in anger for some other such demonstration of severity, — he won't go there again, I am sure. But why can't I go myself? Laurine, do you think your master would listen to me?"

"Surely, your mercy; he never refuses a lady."

"Then I will go;" and, tying on her bonnet in haste, she left the house, followed by Laurine, and set off for the Palm Grove Estate.

CHAPTER XXII.

Reprieve

When Mrs. Dorset and Laurine reached the Palm Grove, not a soul was to be seen: the place seemed deserted. Laurine proposed that, as the sitting-room was much exposed to the sun, the lady should rest awhile in Madame Angélique's room, while she went to reconnoitre. Mrs. Dorset entered, and took a chair. It was a long and somewhat narrow room, the floor of which was waxed and polished. A low French bed stood in a recess at the upper end; there were also a prie-dieu[†] and a couch covered with fine linen white as snow, a white marble table in the centre, a marble lavatoire,[†] a marble toilet-table, a large swing glass,[†] and a magnificent pillared wardrobe,[†] — all of rich and costly materials, giving an air of refinement and luxury to the room, which contrasted strongly with its homely construction. A door, which was now locked, formed a communication between this room and another.

Soon a sound reached the ear of the visitor, which at first she had not noticed, — that of a heavy footstep in the room adjoining, pacing up and down, backwards and forwards, without cessation. "At all events," thought she, "there is somebody within, and I had better look for Laurine." She rose, and moved towards the window, when she saw the young girl returning in company with Beneba, whom, after a good deal of searching, she had at last discovered, walking with the child in her arms under the trees. Beneba informed the lady that Madame Angélique was out making calls, and that the step in the next room must be that of her master, who had shut himself in his study since breakfast.

"Can't you tell him I wish to speak with him?" asked the lady.

Beneba looked scared at such a proposition: the whites of her eyes glistened, and her fat African mouth was puckered up like the drawn opening of a sack, while the baby, little amused by her dulness, threw itself, crowing and laughing, into the arms of Laurine.

"Do let your Master know I wish to speak with him!" reiterated Mrs. Dorset.

"Madame says you are to go and call Master," repeated Laurine, with an imploring expression. "Do go, dear Beneba!"

The girl muttered something between her teeth, then answered aloud that she would go to the kitchen, to tell Clora to look for Rosaly to send Quaco to speak to her master. Mrs. Dorset was obliged to submit to this roundabout arrangement, and composed herself to wait, while Laurine, her heart throbbing with anxiety, took the little laughing babe to her heart, and smiled through her gathering tears as the little hands gaily loosened her long tresses from the comb which confined them.

Their attention however was soon drawn to one of the remotest of the out-buildings, whence proceeded the sound of many voices, apparently in angry contention; and presently three or four Negroes, surrounding a taller man, came forth, the Manager and Overseer following close: they approached the house, and made for Mr. Cardon's study. Laurine looked as if her eyes would start from their sockets, and she put her hand to her heart to still its beating, for she recognized her lover, and saw by the Manager's look that his fate was sealed. The group entered Mr. Cardon's room by a side-door which opened into the courtyard. Laurine strove hard to catch a sound of what was passing within, but a stillness as of death ensued. Presently a stir was perceptible, and faintly, yet distinctly, there fell upon the ear the clank of chains and the ringing of iron instruments. Forgetting everything save her lover, Laurine dragged Mrs. Dorset to the closed door between the two rooms, and, with the baby pressed close to her bosom, she wildly battered against it. No notice was taken: who cared for her voice? She urged Mrs. Dorset to speak, and that tone and expression peculiar to white ladies produced its effect, — the door was opened by Mr. Cardon himself. His hat was on his head, but he doffed it in a moment, and assuming at once that courteousness to the sex which he never forgot, even under the most irritating circumstances, he advanced to lead his guest away to the saloon. But Laurine, with a cry of desperation, grasped Mrs. Dorset's arm and forcibly drew her into the study.

The floor was strewn with instruments of punishment, — manacles, ankle-rings, chains, and above all, a heavy bar of iron with a ring and padlock, for fastening round the neck of incorrigible fugitives. There were, besides, a cowhide on the table, and a knife. Mr. Cardon's face, as he returned to the room and looked towards the culprit, bore the dire expression of anger and despotic will. As for the slave, if there had been any hope of obtaining mercy by inducing submission, it vanished at the first glance; for what hope could be entertained of one on whose brow the pride of Lucifer sat enthroned? Nevertheless his appearance was one of extreme suffering: his hair was matted with gore, his clothes were torn and stained, his fine eyes were haggard and unearthly in their expression. Mrs. Dorset looked from him to his master imploringly. "I am come," she said, "to ask pardon for him, in the name of Him who forgave his enemies on the cross; as we seek mercy for ourselves from above, let us deal mercifully to those who offend us; forgive him, Mr. Cardon! I beg, I beseech, I implore you, forgive him!"

Before the planter had time to reply, two persons entered the room, one of whom went up directly to Mrs. Dorset.

"Anna, my dear, what can have induced you to come here? Did I not beg you would never come here? These are not scenes for you. Come away, I insist upon it. Mr. Cardon, I beg you will excuse the intrusion, we shall not trouble you long. Come, Anna, come!"

Mrs. Dorset replied by throwing her arms about her husband's neck, and looking up in his face, her eyes streaming with tears. Mr. Cardon politely advanced: "I am not one who would lightly refuse a lady's petition," he said; "let this wretch confess his crime, let him tell who it is that administers the Obiah to the slaves and destroys my property, and I will not touch a hair of his head."

Madame Angélique had thrown herself into an armchair, and was whining out most theatrically, "Oh, my children! Here at last is the monster who destroyed them. Alas, poor me!"

Don Duro thrust his hands into his pockets, and, looking profoundly wise, demanded that the prisoner should be made to tell where old Fanty was to be found, — "The crippled beast who ran away long ago, Señor:

people say he is an Obiah man, and I remember he is this dog's uncle. I tried," said the Manager, pointing to the culprit, — "I tried to make him confess it, and I thought to compel him by jamming the door on his arm: but he is a dog! — a pig!"

The Overseer stood sneering and leering with his goggle eyes, for he anticipated a feast for his malicious heart; while the little infant, which Madame Angélique had attempted to take, clung fast to Laurine, for it was repelled by the angry voice and anxious face of its granddame.

The planter looked at the child, and looked at Laurine. How could he help it? — she was so beautiful, — trembling from head to foot, her headgear off, and her silken hair sweeping in waving tresses almost to her feet, while through her long and moistened lashes there gleamed the fitful flashes of her anxiety and fear.

"And she too," exclaimed Don Duro, pointing to her, — "I swear she has something to do with it. I accuse her, Señor, of harbouring that runaway *demonio*, and of carrying messages and philtres for him backwards and forwards to this place. Make her confess it, Señor."

Laurine looked piteously round; she knew and felt her utter helplessness.

"*Allons donc!*"† said the planter, "we will look into that afterwards; she came here with Mrs. Dorset, and through respect for madame, we will let her be for the present; let us despatch this wretch first. Come, Sirrah, and before this lady, who condescends too much, in feeling for a black criminal like you, — come, render an account of yourself. These Negroes here, and every one on the estate, I am sure, are all longing for their release from your infernal machinations: I want no other proofs of your black deeds: speak, therefore, if you would hope to live another day."

"Oh, I am sure," cried Mrs. Dorset, with eager looks, as she disengaged herself from her husband and advanced a little in front, — "oh yes, he will speak, I know he will! Speak! — and Mr. Cardon will forgive you, he has promised it."

The prisoner was still silent, but, with the same stubborn, wild look, kept his eyes fixed on his master's face.

"Pah!" said Mr. Cardon, after pausing for awhile, "idle work this! Why I tell you, Madame, that were I to set him loose, he would give you a dose of Obiah the first thing, as a token of his gratitude. I know the dog! Ah, speak, dog! — open your mouth, dog! — or bark, you vicious cur! — or snarl, if you can't speak!"

With a long gasp the Mulatto lifted his fettered arm, laying bare as he did so a hideous wound, and looking upwards, as in appeal to eternal justice, he broke forth: — "Listen!" he cried: "he calls me dog! then dog let it be; dog, therefore, is my father! *Your* pardon? — I would not have it, I would throw it in your teeth if you gave it. Ay, beat me! bruise me! hack me! kill me! The same blood that flows in your veins, colours mine; in your conscience you know it. Ha! I laugh to scorn your laws and your systems; they cannot alter that great law which God has written in our natures, nor make you one whit less responsible to Him for my welfare, than for that of the white child you pampered and taught to trample upon me. How will you answer to God for this? My degradation, my sufferings, — they cry to Heaven for vengeance upon you. My life — that blessing which God placed in your hands to endow me with — you have turned to a curse: take it! drink it as it oozes with my blood — fit draught for your wine-cup! and remember, when you slumber at night, that every drop will turn to Obiah, — Obiah! do you hear me! — and shape into demons to people your dreams: that is my curse for you! Now do your worst with me — I am ready."

A breathless silence followed this audacious harangue: the words, the expression, the unparalleled boldness, had struck every one dumb with horror. Mr. Cardon convulsively grasped the knife, which lay on the table before him, and the two minions, the Manager and Overseer, roused by this movement, sprang upon the prisoner, dragged him to the floor, and like tempting demons held up his foot for the crippling operation — the cutting of the tendon.

But Laurine, in terror, had thrown herself at the planter's feet: "Master! Master! oh, merciful, kind Master! look at him, he is ill, — he is delirious, Master! He doesn't know what he says; let your anger fall upon me — I will suffer it all."

St. Hilaire, in his rage, spurned her from him; his hand flew up with fury. What stayed him? Was it a touch of his better nature? Was it the little child, which, frightened by the distress of its favourite playmate, chimed in with its cries as it strove to climb the grandfather's knees? Was it the pale, sweet, beseeching face of Mrs. Dorset? or pity for the humble thing which lay in crouching beauty at his feet, that made him pause before he struck? Or was it the consciousness that there stood behind him, watching every movement, a white man, hating and deprecating oppression? Or was it all these in quick succession? It were hard to tell; but, quick as the changes of the tropical skies, Mr. Cardon changed his purpose. He seemed to reflect a moment, then turned to Mrs. Dorset.

"Madame," he said, "out of courtesy to you, I will give him yet another chance. Let Laurine tell all she knows about the Obiah, and perhaps it may yet save him."

"Please your mercy, on my knees this hour," exclaimed the young girl, clasping his knees with vehemence, "here before Almighty God, — I know nothing about it, and Belfond is quite as innocent."

"On your oath, "asked Don Duro, "did you never carry messages, and bottles, and powders to the Negroes on the estate, under pretence of visiting your mother?"

"Never! never! never, Master!" replied Laurine.

"Do you mean to say," continued Don Duro, "that you never spoke to this young man, or never — ?"

Mr. Cardon interrupted him. "Laurine," he said, "if what you say is true, you will prove it to me by your submission to the orders I am going to give you. Your papers of freedom, Laurine, are reported to be incorrect and informal, and your name still remains uneffaced among the slaves mentioned in the bill of sale, as pertaining to the Palm Grove Estate. If that be true, you are to all intents and purposes part of this property, which I bought, and I require your services accordingly. Your shop and everything in it, you are aware, belong to me. I require you to remain here till I examine the registry and papers; and remember, that on your good behaviour and submission to my orders will depend the fate of that wretch," he said, pointing to Belfond; "and now, miscreant, go!"

"I will not have your pardon!" roared Belfond, hissing the words through his teeth, and wrestling with the men who held him.

"See to him, Don Duro," said Mr. Cardon, with authoritative composure, "and take him away, lest I be tempted further; secure him in the dungeon."

"Now, Madame," said St. Hilaire, coming forward and addressing Mrs. Dorset, "let us withdraw to the saloon;" and he courteously offered his arm to lead the way, leaving his wife to settle with Laurine as to the nature of her new duties. Mr. and Mrs. Dorset however were not inclined to stay longer, and Mr. Cardon was fain to accompany them part of the way home.

"I scarcely like," he said to the lady, as he walked by her side, "to part with you on such terms as these. I am sure, Madame, you set me down as an ogre."

"Not exactly that," replied the lady, with a sweet low voice.

"But something like it, I suppose," he added quickly; "and for what? for securing that demon — that — that — Madame! Madame! do you know what a tiger I should let loose in that wretch? The compounder, the administrator of Obiah! You surely would not wish such a thing: why, I should consider myself responsible to the whole Colony for the mischief that would ensue. His fame would soon spread throughout the island, and every Negro who imagined a complaint against his master, would go to him to buy his infernal help; particularly now, since all this hypocritical fuss about Emancipation has made the Negroes fancy themselves injured."

"But how can you tell it is he? for, after all, as far as I have been able to understand, there exists no proof against the unfortunate young man."

"You heard him yourself speak something like a confession of it, Madame."

"Nay, nay," replied the lady persuasively, "you would not take the ravings of delirium for a confession; — you are too humane, too just, Mr. Cardon. You had only to look at his face to know how ill he was; besides, it was a threat of future visions, not of past offences, remember. And after all, what is this Obiah, which I hear so often spoken of? — I cannot comprehend what it is."

"Madame," replied the planter with a heavy sigh, "it is the Negroes' power; they say it is witchcraft, I believe it to be poison. The country abounds with deadly herbs, of whose properties we are totally ignorant, but with which the Negroes are familiar; they mix them, stew them, distil them, and then make their Obiah compounds. They give them to us to breathe, in the form of fragrance, — to eat — to drink

— to touch; they make us take them through the pores of our skin, and we know nothing of it. The poison is either slow, and takes months to do its work — then the victim fades away, sinks without a trace of a cause to be discovered; at other times it is sudden — the victim foams at the mouth, reels, falls down, and dies. What can we do? We are at their mercy!"

"Strange!" ejaculated Mr. Dorset, who had not hitherto spoken; "have the bodies been properly examined?"

"I have said before, they have: no trace is ever found by doctor or chemist."

"Is there no suspicion as to what drugs they use?"

"We are not sure they do use drugs, or they use such as are too subtle for our detection. We know the Brinvilliers,[†] it is true: here it is," he said, plucking a corymb of small red and yellow flowers from the foot-path, and presenting it to the lady; "you see it grows everywhere underfoot; it yields a poison as deadly as it is subtle, and has received its name from a celebrated poisoner of the reign of Louis XIV, who is supposed to have used it in the composition of the *acqua toffana*[†] she used. We know also something of the deleterious properties of the root of the pommerose[†] and the cockroach apple; *mais sacre!* Madame, how limited is this poor knowledge to theirs! We are entirely at their mercy."

"In short," said Mr. Dorset, "irresponsible power in the master is parried with as terrible a weapon on the part of the slave."

"*Peste, oui!*[†] and, like an invisible demon, this Negro witchcraft crawls round the white man's domicile, seizing in its deadly grasp the fairest and sweetest: this is the Negro's injured innocence! *Corbleu!* the most arbitrary master trembles before that!"

"To speak plainer," resumed Mr. Dorset, "the very chain he has fastened round the foot of his slave, the Negro in his turn has locked by the other end round the neck of his master."

"Bah!" exclaimed the planter, "I am in no mood for arguing."

"Well, well," interrupted the lady, endeavouring to turn the conversation to a less irritating topic; "tell me, what are you going to do with that poor girl Laurine? Her lot seems to me very hard: for no fault that I can see, she is about to lose her earnings, her means of living, and her freedom."

"Say but the word, my good lady, and I will give her two shops, and her mother's freedom to boot; but I must first keep her on her good behaviour, and make her tell me what she knows about this Obiah, and that devil incarnate whom we suspect of compounding it: that was my motive for speaking as I did, and for detaining her; I never intended to carry out my threat, and I shall be the more inclined to let her go, because I suspect that fellow, my Manager, has his eye upon her."

"God help her!" sighed Mrs. Dorset.

"Is it possible," urged Mr. Dorset, "that you could find no easier and readier means of discovering the secret? why, methinks any Negro, for the promise of freedom —"

"Not one, I tell you, — not for gift, or promise, or threat; — not even when he is dying will he confess a word which might throw light on the cause or the means. I will tell you what I saw myself in the year 1822 in Martinique.† I went there on business, and remained long enough to witness the completion of the tragedy I am about to relate. The Obiah had spread its ravages to such a fearful extent, that a Court was instituted, to stay the progress of its crimes. The bloodthirsty Davoust was chosen to execute its decrees: he went about with two hatchets, — a large one for cutting off heads, a small one for cutting off hands, — summoning before him every Negro suspected; he then and there pronounced sentence, without hearing or appeal, and had such forthwith executed. Such terrific examples were intended to scare away the Obiah; but, like an evil genius, it only seemed to open still wider its dark and terrible wings over the island. Davoust became sanguinary with the practice of his office, and, weary of the too lenient execution with the hatchet, had sixteen of the most hardened Negroes caged up in the great Place Lamentin, and ordered them to be burned, one after the other. Twenty thousand slaves were called from all parts of the island, to witness the scene; a small drizzling rain fell the whole day, as though sent on purpose to render their deaths more slow and torturing; yet in the face of this not a word was uttered by the sixteen criminals, nor by the twenty thousand who looked on: they remained impenetrably silent. The square was like a black sea of human beings, silent, sullen, dogged. I saw them go away in the evening in the same gloomy mood, and during that night there was not an estate on the island where death from poison did not occur.

The evil was in no degree arrested, and, wearied out and conquered by the persevering horrors of Negro vengeance, the Court closed its sittings in 1827.[3] And these are the innocent lambs for whom all England is sighing at this moment! — for whom the ladies are weeping, — pardon, Madame, I speak only of the misguided fools in England, — and for whom the gentlemen are ready to draw their swords!"

During all this time Mr. Dorset and his lady had not offered a word of remark; the latter, it is true, had two or three times looked round with an expression of horror, and a stifled exclamation had risen to her lips; the former walked on with his hands behind him, his mild eyes somewhat closed, and his lips pressed gently together, as if all surprise had passed into settled dissatisfaction and regret. Thus they proceeded, leaving St. Hilaire to speak without interruption.

"It is for these reasons," he continued, "from knowing their obdurate hearts, that I cling to the hope of getting something out of Laurine. She is a good girl, and attends to her religion. I can just whisper a word to her confessor; he will visit her, and if she does know anything about this Obiah, he will make her come and tell me; that is my only hope. When this is done, Madame, I promise you to dismiss her well rewarded."

They had now reached the turning of the lane which led direct from the high road to the dwelling-house of the Fountain, and St. Hilaire paused to take his leave. His tone and manner were greatly changed since they had met before: the loud, authoritative voice was subdued; his manner, so bold and proud, was now almost gentle, and there was something sad in the expression of his dark, manly eye, which even his continued flow of conversation did not remove. Now, about to part from his companions, he took both their hands, and held them long within his own. "I have been talking about my Negroes," he said, "and my plans, and, seriously, I may never see them accomplished — I came with you this evening for an entirely different purpose: it is to you, dear lady, that I now address myself in particular; you add to all the charms of lovely woman, those of the mind and the heart; and I have something I wish to say to you, Mrs. Dorset: — should anything happen to me, will you

---

3. An account of these circumstances appeared in the Paris 'National' of November 9th, 1841.

promise to be a friend to my poor little Léonce? — he may stand in need of your kindness."

"My good Sir!" exclaimed the lady, startled by his earnestness, "why should you think of such a thing?"

"*Parbleu!* I cannot tell myself; but I feel strange this evening: whenever my thoughts go forward to the morrow, they fly back like stones thrown against the wall; I look forward, and all appears blank; something hangs over me, I am sure. It is useless trying to laugh me out of it; if that were possible, I should have done it myself. I only wish you to remember well my words to you this night; and," he added, shaking their hands again and again, while he turned from the lady to the gentleman, "remember as long as you live this my parting advice: — never interfere with another's affairs, or suffer another to interfere between you and your Negroes, for you do not know what mischief may come of it, nor where it will end. Suppose, now, you had children, and had plans of your own for governing them: severe as your rules might occasionally appear to a casual visitor, you would not like him to create a scene before them proclaiming you cruel, would you? No, *parbleu!* I am sure you would not. It would ruin your authority and the order of your establishment; it would destroy all respect for you in your children, and produce confusion in your household. *Eh bien!* so it is with those Negroes of mine. Yesterday morning they respected me as a sort of king, — a despot, maybe; but all kings are despots; — well, they will never respect me again: the *prestige* is gone which protected me, I feel it and know it; God only knows what hangs over me."

"If I thought such a thing," exclaimed Mr. Dorset quickly, "I should never forgive myself."

"Ah, *n'importe!*† I forgive you," said the planter hurriedly; "and now, Dorset, another thing I have to say to you in particular; if you had not come to me so unexpectedly this evening, I should have gone to you to say it — I had so intended. I wish to give you this paper; it is a formal acknowledgment of the money advanced to me by Pelham the other morning at the slave-market: you remember the circumstance; give it to him. I have mentioned the debt again in my will. I have left you, together with my brother-in-law, executors; let this debt be the first paid off, should I never see you again, for I would not have a word breathed against the name I leave to the little boy. So good-bye! adieu, adieu, Madame! Remember my poor Léonce!" and, waving his hands, he walked away quickly towards his home.

CHAPTER XXIII.

Presentiment of Death

St. Hilaire had nearly reached the avenue which led to his home. He was walking very fast, and looking up at the sky, absorbed in thought, when suddenly he was awakened from his reverie by a rough voice addressing him, "I say! holloa, Mr. Thing-a-me! holloa!" and a bulky figure came up the road, waddling and blowing; no longer with the fawning manner of the mate on board the brig 'Venus,' but with a triumphant, familiar manner, such as suited Higgins as the possessor of wealth. "Blow me!" continued he, "but you are a fast-sailing goer, my jo! and you are deaf, I should think, for I have been behind the hedge, bellowing my breath away to you. Odds, man! can't you stop a bit, and let a fellow know what's doing on your side of the world? I've got a bit of news for you."

The planter turned and stood erect, as the speaker advanced.

"Now, Mr. Cardon, don't be looking so proud at me; arn't I a white man, like yourself? I tell you, I'll bring your Mulatto slave to you before another day is out."

"He is found, and caught, and secured," was the concise reply.

"Is he though?" exclaimed the other, starting; "'sblood!† where did you get him?"

"Just here, in one of the Negro-huts; and without your help after all, you see."

"Zounds!† that's queer. How the devil did he get out of that 'ere thorny prison? He's the very devil! but he's caught, you say. Hem! but have you found the Obiah man — the real Obiah man? What will you give me if I find him for you? — it's the real Negro priest poisoner, who did all the ruin on your property, as true as I am here; and the word of Tim Higgins, Esquire, I hope, is as good as any of them there jackanapes what sets up for nobs[†] in Port Spain, and harn't as good a right to hold up their heads as me. Howsomedever, I'll bring him in tow tonight, all bound and chained for you; but first I must have a room, and the manager and overseer must hang up their hammocks by the side of mine, in case I should want help. Mind, I say, in case only; for my jobs is waluable to me, and I don't like meddlesome hands a-hauling of my nets. You mind, I haven't them dogs of the captain's with me, for you see they're never to be trusted when you want to keep a sly look-out; so you must let me have a shooting-gun. You needn't go sneering along that way, Mr. Cardon; I can tell you, white men needs keep a sharp look-out, when they has got those hell-hound Koromantyns to hove-to."

St. Hilaire heard no further, for they had now reached his own door; and as, according to the hospitable custom of the Colonies, a stranger, however disagreeable his manners, never enters a house in the country without meeting a generous and kindly welcome, this Higgins was freely admitted into the society of persons who, if in Europe, would hardly have allowed him to sweep their stables. St. Hilaire, after recommending his visitor to join his wife, who was taking chocolate in the sitting-room, left him, and retired to spend the evening in his own room, — not in writing or smoking, as was customary with him, but at his desk, looking over papers. He seemed to have spent many hours at this occupation at some previous part of the day, for he drew forth from a wardrobe sundry boxes of letters loosely thrown together, and a basket by his side was nearly filled with square scraps of torn letters. It was already late, and every one had gone to sleep before he locked his desk for the night. This done, and his papers arranged in their respective places, he went to look at his little grandson, the only being left him on earth, of all those on whom his hopes were once fixed. The child was sleeping in a small closet adjoining its grandmamma's room; it lay in a crib, softly cushioned, and all curtained with flowing net. He lifted the light drapery: sweetly, calmly the little innocent slumbered, with its plump hand beneath its cheek, which lay shaded with clusters of raven ringlets; and over that cherub face he bent, fervently to bless it, coaxing its smooth

forehead, and tenderly kissing it again and again. The child moved a little, then heaved a baby sigh as it recomposed itself to sleep, St. Hilaire
echoing the sound with a heavy, heavy heart; then he dropped the curtain again, and left it. He next retraced his steps, proceeding through
various intervening apartments to a small pavilion at the end of the
house, which was fitted up as a little chapel, where the priest celebrated
mass at such times as he was called to the Palm Grove to officiate.

St. Hilaire was not habitually a pious man; like most Frenchmen, he
usually left devotion to the ladies of his family, jocosely declaring that,
provided they were good, he was pretty certain of getting into heaven by
holding tight to their skirts at the gate. Tonight however, as he entered
the chapel, he made the sign of the cross, and knelt down to offer to
Heaven a short but earnest prayer for mercy. Then again he rose, and
passed through a side-door to an inner room used as a vestry.
Approaching the further wall, he drew aside a heavy silk curtain, which
hung from the ceiling nearly to the floor, and looped it over a peg on the
wall, so as entirely to uncover a full-length family picture: it was in the
best style of one of the great painters of the day, and was one of those
rare works of art which fix themselves on the memory when thousands
of contemporary scenes have faded away. The group consisted of four
figures: a girl about sixteen, pale-browed and pensive, was seated on a
rustic chair, and, with drooping eyelids, was tastefully arranging some
flowers which she held in her hand; at her feet was a sweet, intelligent,
dark-eyed Hebe,[†] whose lap was laden with flowers, some of which she
had selected, and was looking up and presenting them to her sister: a
third, a slender, smiling, ethereal-looking nymph, was seen tripping
towards them on the right, bringing garlands and branches of rose and
jasmine: behind these, to the left, stood a young man with his hand resting on the back of the chair, — his brow was serious, and his deep and
thoughtful eyes indicated much of the elements of good, yet in his young
and handsome face were visible traces of dissipation and European revels. St. Hilaire took a chair, and seated himself opposite the picture, fold-
ing his arms and gazing upon it with all the earnestness of his soul, —
for those were the portraits of his children.

The thoughts that were hurrying through his active brain paused
before the reminiscence that was rising, and the turbulent feelings that

were rushing and eddying through his heart, slackened their impetuous course, to group, unite, melt into one strong holy yearning after treasures received into the bosom of eternity. His whole mind seemed to gather itself up in contemplation of the objects before him. Moments — minutes fled; the great clock struck the quarter, the half-hour, the three-quarters, and still the father gazed, until nature imperceptibly merged into that state in which the soul, loosening as it were the ties which bind it to the earth, enjoys for awhile the liberty of spirits, and heedless of the boundaries of time and space, setting at nought the order of earthly things, it revels in the past, the present, and the future. He dreamed; and the magic of art, which had fixed the likenesses with a permanence denied to the originals, blending with the magic of fancy, the figures one by one stood out from the canvas alive. The downcast eyelids rose, revealing the sweet, soft, full orbs which they overshadowed. "Louise!" exclaimed the bewildered father, extending his arms to the resuscitated dead; but the exclamation died away on his lips, and his arms dropped again, as the transformation before him continued: the flowers drooped, faded, beckoned, fell; in their place, living eyes of Afric's children seemed to multiply unceasingly around, and each pair, with its respective expression of misery, became a voice, and shrieked its unutterable woe; and with that intuitive perception which belongs to the soul in dreams, the father knew that this was the eternal doom of his beloved for neglected opportunities of helping the fallen ones entrusted to her care. The face of the second turned itself towards him; alas! its Hebe expression of glee was gone, giving place to wan despair, for around her too those terrible moving eyes extended, coiling like the folds of a serpent, eating into her form, till nothing appeared but the face writhing with torture. Vainly the father struggled to get near them, to brush away those shrieking eyes, — he was immoveably fixed to his chair. And those types of ruined souls — he saw them extending on one side to his youngest, and on the other to his son — his eldest-born — the pride of his house; but here were mingled other forms from other climes — souls destroyed, not by omission, but commission; their shrieks were shooting like chains about his neck, about his person, and the father saw him dragged downwards — downwards — downwards. The strong frame of St. Hilaire was convulsed with horror, and he woke with a start — the effort he had made to save his son. He rubbed his eyes, spoke aloud, walked about the room, to free his mind from the fearful impressions it had received; then he went to the picture, and felt it all over, touching each figure in turn, to assure himself it was painted canvas. But human nature, encased though it be in iron, can bear only to a limited point. Exhausted with mental agony, and overwhelmed with the accumulated sorrows stirred up anew by his terrible dream, he sank upon his chair, and this strong, bold, wilful man wept like a little child. His head drooped upon his chest, the large cold drops stood upon his brow, his limbs shivered, the agonies of a hundred lives tortured him in that one short hour, — the despot was subdued, and he bowed before the power of Almighty God. Then did the angel of mercy, which is for ever hovering over the unfortunate, droop its wings over this suffering mortal, and touch him with its wand of peace; he slept, this time sinking into obliviousness and repose. A short time elapsed, and he half woke up with a strange consciousness of a coming change. There was a sound as of rushing floods, and a din of voices, which in vain he strove to understand. Then he woke up entirely, and found it was no dream, but a terrible reality. In a moment his mind was clear, and, heedless of the suffocation of the rolling smoke which was filling the rooms, he rushed from one apartment to another, till he came to the crib of the sleeping babe, — it was gone! He hurried forward to Madame Angélique's apartment; it was empty, only at the open window was Laurine, crying to him in agony — "Master! Master! fly for your life! I have the child; he is here, I have saved him. Fly; Master, they are seeking to murder you, — for God's sake, fly!" — and the flames, crackling through the dry wood of which the house was built, rolled swiftly along the walls to enclose him.

CHAPTER XXIV.

All Up in Rebellion

Let us now go back a few hours and see what was passing in the Negro-huts. It was Saturday, the day usually granted to the Negroes for cultivating their grounds; on this occasion however, excited by the events of the morning, they had left the fields early, and had retired to their huts to talk. They were now assembled in the one which had been apportioned to Talima, who lay stretched on a mat, resting her chin on her elbows, as she gazed admiringly at the antics of Quaco, who was setting the company in a roar by turning the white people into ridicule. The power of mimicry is strong in the Negro — with Quaco particularly so; and as he slouched along like the Overseer, or strutted like the Manager, the imitation was so like, yet so ridiculous a caricature, that the assembly were in fits. His critiques on the personal attractions of the white ladies were not less relished; and as the lad became more and more excited by the plaudits of his bearers, he detailed many a spicy anecdote of the white people in their own country, which Belfond had formerly related to him. Others again were grouped round Laurine, giving her sympathy and comfort; they wiped her eyes, threw their arms about her, kissed her forehead, and wept; then, in terms of warm affection, they gently urged her to come among those who longed to comfort her and divert her grief by friendly converse.

Very different was the temper of another individual who here interrupted the proceedings of the assembly, and at the sight of whom they looked cowed, huddling together in the corners. "A good-night to you, my children!" said Fanty as he entered: there was a general murmur of response; but all stood aloof, save Coraly, who immediately placed a stool for him, and offered a pipe. "Woman!" he cried, as he pushed the pipe aside, "*an empty bag cannot stand;*[†] give me to eat, and hot!" A fire was instantly made with dried twigs and branches, and a pot set to boil, while a round calabash was got ready, together with a long, narrow gourd, to serve as a spoon or scoop. The fumes rose savourily through the room, and, to judge by the relaxing expression of the sorcerer's face, were fast softening his heart; indeed, when the mess was ready and duly poured out, the old man ate as though he had not broken fast for three days before.

The meal over, Fanty returned the calabash, carefully wiped his lips, looked round at the company, and spoke. "Countrymen," he said, in his native tongue, "*when the head quarrels with the feet, the back must break.* The white men no longer stand together as they used; they must fall, and we children of Africa must rise. I come here tonight to tell you how the King of the white people has called us children; how two smaller tributary kings, Buxton and Wilberforce, have confessed to loving us, and to make war upon other white kings to make us free.[†] Time was, my countrymen, when the Negro might long for freedom till his mouth ran water like a river; now the thing will come before we know how to swallow it. Time was, countrymen, when *only the shoe could know whether the stocking had holes;* now the white man's shoe slips off, and the holes are bared to all Negroes' eyes. Did you mark the gentleman here the other day? — you see I know all that happens. What did he come here for? — just as a spy, to see whether Master flogged his Negroes. Time was, countrymen, when *cork-wood was not mahogany,* but now *wood is wood everywhere,* and the white man's back shall smart before he dares to do with us again as he likes."

Quaco had been listening attentively; he did not however share in the awe inspired by the presence of the sorcerer, but freely broke the silence, and advanced to argue. "Hey, Daddy Fanty," he exclaimed, "wharra talk so for? — *Grand talk neber wise talk,* and *eggs mustn't dance 'mong de stones.*[†] We know, Daddy, you be one sabey man, — but go 'way! Quaco always listening at master's door knows somefin too. Now, da white man come here toder day, — he be one foolish man, so white people call 'em."

"Neber mind!" murmured many voices; "he good heart to niggers, and *who throws kindness in de fire, will find 'em in de ashes:* he be good to niggers, niggers will be good to he."

"Cho!" exclaimed the lad, looking round contemptuously, "hold your mouth, and let me and Daddy Fanty talk. Me know bery well Massa Dorset no spy: he foolish man and good heart, dat's all: and as for free law, go 'way, dat neber come for nigger, nor for nigger children: *when cattle die, dem leave misery to 'em skin,* — dat's de way wi' poor niggers. Now, Daddy, you are a sabey man, so do jist tell us what for white man so grand, and nigger so low, hey?"†

Fanty gathered himself up, took the pipe from his mouth, and related a legend current among the Africans, which, put into clear language, runs thus: — When the Great Spirit, Accompong, made all things in the sky and on the earth, he made two men, — one in the day, and he was white, the other in the night, and he was black. The next day the Great Spirit called the white man and the nigger before him, that they might choose their future lot; and in one hand he held forth a calabash full of gold and perfumes, and in the other only a book. Foolish nigger took the calabash, and, with the gold, the fruit, and the rich things, he sat down under a palm-tree to sing. The white man took the book; then he washed himself, and looked about him; and the book taught him the secrets of all things, and he learned how to get the calabash, the gold, all the rich things, and lastly, the nigger himself. "So that is the way, countrymen, that the niggers got to be slaves, and the white men to be so great."

A groan went through the assembly; — "Oh, hey! is nigger neber to come right again? Oh! hey! oh! Didn't same spirit make the two?"

"Assarci," continued the old man, "he, the good spirit of regeneration, has long ago promised that the time shall come when the white man shall be glutted, and, in his feeble state, the calabash, the gold, and the rich things shall fall upon him and crush him. Then shall the Negro come and hold out his hand to his fallen brother, and shall lift him up, and together they will walk upon the earth in peace. That is what I have learned by the magic of my country; but, my children, I come here tonight, not for tales like these, nor yet to send you back to far bright Africa on the wings of death; I come to free that child of my dead sister, the Mulatto Belfond. The sun must not shine tomorrow, my children, before that boy is free;" and, with a shout, the old man stood upon his stool, and with outstretched arms and excited gestures called to the people before him to approach, for the administration of the Wanga Obiah oath of secresy, adherence, and obedience. They piled wood upon the ground before him, and the gathering flames shot upwards, as he uttered in his strange dialect the incantations of his craft: the whole group might have stood for a scene in the dark kingdom below.

Meantime, the object of Fanty's concern was lying quietly on the floor of his dungeon. This place had not been built expressly for the purpose of confinement; it was merely the lower part of the house, or, to speak more correctly, an enclosure formed by the foundation-walls, about four feet in height, on which rested the wooden superstructure of the family dwelling. It had formerly been used for stowing away barrels, boxes, old furniture, and wood; but as, of late years, rumours of rebellion had become rife, it had been found desirable, on large estates, to have a stronghold for securing unmanageable Negroes, and Don Duro had long ago ordered the lumber to be removed. Into this place Belfond had been thrust; his wrists and ankles were fettered, and secured by a chain to a ring in the wall, probably to prevent his reaching the door, which was not very strong. Belfond however was not inclined to give trouble now: from the moment he left his master's presence, he neither uttered a word nor attempted resistance, but, composedly and quietly sitting upon the ground, submitted at once to his fate. Here his tyrants left him; and the long afternoon passed, and the evening came and went, and then he wearily saw the night advance. He could hear the loud voice of his master, when he returned from his walk, and the detestable twanging tones of Higgins, which made his blood boil; then the shrill tones of his mistress, reprimanding some unfortunate delinquent of the household, or the sweet laughter of the little child. One by one these sounds died away, for night was come, bringing rest to all but him

He stretched himself upon the ground: it was damp and noisome, and huge rats scampered fearlessly over his body. He tried to sleep, but could not; his thoughts grew busy, and he seemed to live again amid scenes long since forgotten, dwelling with painful distinctness on the happy hours he had passed. Little incidents, which years of activity and adventure had blotted from his memory, came forth in lines of bold relief, with every little touch and shading fresh as though impressed but yesterday; then his days in France, his stealthy acquisition of knowledge, his intense delight when he effected his escape from his young master, — from which his thoughts passed to his second escape from Captain Hill's vessel to the wilds and woods of Trinidad, and, as a crown to all, the blissful moments he had spent with Laurine. But when he remembered how he had last beheld her, he groaned aloud and gnashed his teeth; he writhed upon the ground, and cried to Heaven in pity to strike him, an impotent worm, which could not even turn upon the foot that crushed him. "I am of a race accursed upon the earth," he cried; "what was life given me for? I did not ask it: I am alone in the world, useless and helpless, — no one cares for me, not a soul!" and then, by some train of emotions, his thoughts reverted to his mother. "Oh, my mother! African, black, humble as you were, you loved me! Where are you now? Does peace dwell where you are, my mother? does my voice reach you? do you sometimes look down upon me from your starry abode?" And, as if in answer, a light upon the ceiling caught his eye; he gazed at it, — it was the gentle green light of a little firefly;[†] but his heart hailed it as a signal from her he called upon, — a guardian spirit, come to watch over him, and bear him company in his solitude. Think not meanly of him, kind Reader, for this superstitious feeling; the stoutest heart will yield to such in times of deepest wretchedness, when the mind vainly seeks for comfort in common things, — when reason holds down her head defeated, and religion itself only serves to excite the imagination.

Here however his meditations were interrupted by the barking of the watch-dog; its fury seemed to increase, then it yelped, gave a dismal howl, and again all was silent. "Some thief," thought Belfond, "prowling about to carry off our master's things — cursed be the day I learned that ugly word, I can never unlearn it! Well, I don't blame the thief, why should I? I am a thief myself; I would not take a straw from my fellow-slave, but I have run away from my master, and carried off his capital vested in these bones and sinews. Poor limbs! bruised and torn, and, still worse, guided by a head most hopelessly rebellious! who will care to use their worthless labour again? I am to be murdered, as an example to the gangs, — a valuable example, if they will take it! Oh, Negroes! poor, degraded, crawling things, without spirit, without a wish to be free!"

Suddenly his reflections were cut short by an indescribable sensation of something extraordinary outside; there was a rushing, a smothered sound of footsteps, which his hearing, rendered keen by solitude, soon detected to be those of a multitude; then a smell of fire, and almost immediately after clouds of smoke came rolling through the crevices in suffocating thickness. The wretched prisoner crawled as near to the door as his chains would allow, and dismally, imploringly cried for help; but, remembering his condition, he checked himself: "They are burning me alive," thought he, "and they are doing it in the night, to avoid detection. Well! my sufferings will soon be over; what can it matter, an hour sooner, or an hour later? I will lay me down, and bid it welcome."

But the movement outside increased; a sound like the distant roar of the sea, now in whispers, now rising into louder murmur, starting into shrieks, rolling in hoarse remonstrance, burst upon his ear. The door of his dungeon was attacked; stones and hammers were striking wrathfully, the doorposts cracked, the door was wrenched open, and in the midst of flame, and heat, and smoke, dark figures hurriedly grasped the prisoner. They forgot that he was fettered; but, perceiving their mistake, a lantern was brought, the chains were knocked asunder, and in another moment Belfond was dragged into the air, — the free, fresh, blessed air of heaven!

Bewildered by the glare and the uproar, Belfond was at first unable to stand upon his feet; his eyes were blinded with the light, his head reeled, and he fell; and when he rose, he gazed upon the fire before him, and watched the rushing, gathering multitude with the air of a dreamer, bewildered and stupefied. With rage and fury the snake-like flames ascended; they but touched the dry roofing, and the thatch was in a blaze, and a waving column of dazzling fire rose high, making red the clouds above. The noise increased; there were cries of females and shrieks of alarm, savage screams of laughter, hoarse sounds of angry contention, and one mad roar of triumph: the Negroes had proclaimed an insurrection.

Amidst this tide of human voices there was one focus of deafening tumult; but, rising above it all, was the voice of St. Hilaire, furiously contending with his rebel slaves. The sound acted upon Belfond like an electric shock; his whole frame was nerved with instant vigour. Was it triumph? was it rage? was it vengeance? At first it was all of these, but, only for a moment effervescing, they quickly settled down into a holy compound of the heart's natural pleadings. Seeking the tyrant whom he knew to be his father, bruised, broken, wounded as he was, he rushed forward to defend him, knocking aside all who opposed his way. "Comrades! comrades! don't kill him for God's sake!" he cried, as the Negroes pressed closer and closer upon their master.

Cardon had already with his single arm laid Negro after Negro upon the ground, dealing blows from side to side with the butt-end of his gun; but as he caught the words of Belfond, — "You miscreant," he cried, "curse you! do you think I am to owe my life to you?" and with fearful strength aimed a deadly blow at his head. Before the words were ended, a hand had pushed Belfond beyond his reach — it was Fanty; and Cardon fell beneath the weight of a hundred blows.

It was now impossible to restrain the Negroes: they were maddened with the deed. It was in vain that Belfond shouted to them, reasoned with them, warned them; that he ran about from place to place, calling them to order, and to a concern for their own safety. They had given themselves up to the desperate delirium of their conscious guilt. Without plan, or chief, or immediate confederates in the island, these demented creatures rushed to destruction; and when the house fell with a tremendous crash, their cries of triumph reached for miles, like an alarm-bell to the plantations around, and, as the showers of sparks flew about, and the bright roaring blaze grew wilder and brighter with the fall of every crumbling beam, the whole formed a huge bonfire, round which these infuriated savages danced and exultingly shouted, like the raging spirits of the element itself. As to Fanty, he was entirely lost in the confusion. If chief there was, it must be Talima, the warlike daughter of Anamoa; for she had seized a horse, and with a torch in her hand was seen galloping off in the direction of the cane-fields, with a large detachment of the furious herd at her heels. But our hero did not follow; his heart was heavy: "He would not let me save him!" he kept repeating to himself, — "He would not let me save him!" and, weary and desponding, he turned to the Negro-huts to be alone. He was making his way thither, with his head down and his hands in his pockets, when somebody ran against him — it was Quaco. "Hey!" said the youth, recognizing him by the glare of the fire, "me been a look for you; me just hear alarm-bell 'pon de Fountain Estate; you better look sharp, Belfond!"

"I had better," was the reply; "a pretty business you have made of it! Better have left me where I was."

"Yah! hey! how you talk foolish!" exclaimed the youth. "Go, hide yourself, that's all! leave all de rest to we niggers. They neber go punish us all, — too many dollars lost, eh? Yah, go 'way!"

"My poor master, you have murdered him!" said Belfond, "and most likely mistress too."

"Hey!" put in Quaco, with kindling eyes, "Missis, manager, oberseer — all! and, what you tink, — Mas'r Higgins too, da white Obiah man! Yah! hey!" and he finished his sentence by acting in strong caricature a state of terror and a running for life, and then he leaped up and laughed with glee.

"Where is the little child?" interrupted Belfond.

Quaco grew serious immediately. "We had got 'em," he said, "and somebody mad nigger throwed 'em in de fire, when Laurine showed up and saved 'em, — then away, and nobody seen 'em since. Come, good-bye, Belfond! Da Talima be fine gal! let me go see what all of 'em be go down yonder!" and before Belfond could stop him, he was off.

CHAPTER XXV.

Escape

The Negroes on the Fountain Estate, although orderly and obedient to their master, yet, as was natural, displayed a good deal of restlessness. They kept out of sight of the white people as much as they could; but ever and anon young ones would cross the hedges, to hear and see what was going on, and there was questioning and commenting among the older heads, too nearly interested in the event to conceal it. Nor was there less anxiety at the house; for here the inmates of the Palm Grove had taken refuge, bringing with them their confusion and terror, and good Mrs. Dorset had a great deal to do. There was Madame Angélique fainting at every instant, and she had to be attended to and comforted. She was just recovering from one of these fits, when Laurine rushed in, bearing in her arms the little Léonce, thought to have been murdered by the infuriate Negroes. Placing the frightened babe, not with the grand-mamma, but on Mrs. Dorset's lap, and without waiting to give a word of explanation, Laurine fled as precipitately as she had entered. Eager and loving were the caresses the ladies bestowed upon the child, who was rendered tenfold more interesting by the mysterious way in which it had been recovered.

The anxiety of the ladies was great; Mrs. Dorset, especially, was anxious about her husband, who had gone to the Palm Grove at the very first signal of alarm. By good luck Don Duro happened to be in the way, looking for a strong place wherein to secure his prisoners. Yielding to the entreaties of the ladies, he mounted his horse, and went in the direction of the fire, which had now extended to some fields of sugar-cane on the outskirts of Mr. Cardon's estate. Thither now were the Negroes thronging, headed by the warlike daughter of Anamoa. Columns of rolling clouds were rising, with a trail of fire raging, roaring, streaming after him. All the neighbouring white people, for miles around, were galloping to lend assistance; the militia too were there, with their uniform and arms. There were hoarse voices swearing, mules tramping, water streaming, and black figures on foot, and white men on horseback, moving to and fro against the red glare, like demons in Pandemonium.[†]

Just on the path, as Don Duro was hurrying to the spot, stood a Negro woman, shouting and laughing at the scene; she showed so little sense of self-preservation as not to heed the coming horse, nor to get out of the way even when it was close upon her. With a terrible oath Don Duro led the animal trampling over her, and when the horse stumbled, he lashed the creature that lay writhing beneath the horse's hoofs. His brutal phrases however were cut short by the voice of Mr. Dorset, calling for help, and to this, of course, he immediately attended. Setting his horse at full gallop, he found that gentleman endeavouring, with great difficulty, to support a wounded white. The Manager alighted to lend assistance, but what was his horror when, by the light of his lantern, he recognized the objects before him! Higgins lay ghastly and dying, — not from any visible wound, but clinging round him, like a beast of prey, was the crippled body of the sorcerer Fanty. Faithful to his promise, the old Negro had sought the sailor, and then and there, in the midst of the confusion and terrors of the rebellion, regardless of the shots and the blows which assailed him on all sides, he had leaped upon him, and darting his long and poisoned nails into the ears of his enemy, he clung to him with a strength and pertinacity which no effort could overcome. It was a hideous spectacle: the old man's glassy eyes were wide open with a fixed stare, while a demoniac grin on his shrivelled lips showed the last working of his soul before it took its final leave of earth's trials and wrongs. It was impossible to disengage him, and Higgins cried piteously for water; but ere they could bring it, the words thickened in his throat, and, before many minutes, he lay a blackened, loathsome corpse, just as the sorcerer had foretold.

Leaving the gentlemen to settle between them as to the propriety and mode of burying these two, thus locked in the embrace of hate, we may direct our eyes another way, to a different scene.

Weary, disgusted, and desponding, Belfond had turned from the spot where St. Hilaire fell, and endeavoured to gain some place where he might be alone, and away from the tumult which his soul abhorred. He was thinking of his father; — "He would not let me save him," he repeated to himself; "He would not let me save him! — I, his own son, cursed even in that!" and with his head resting on his bosom, he bewailed his unhappy fate, and wept over the untimely death of one whom he would have loved had he been permitted. He had instinctively taken the direction of the Negro-huts, and had turned abstractedly to look at the progress of the fire, when he thought he heard the voice of one sobbing. He followed the sound to Madelaine's dark hut, where, not without a suspicion which at once awakened all his tenderest feelings, he found Laurine, like a frightened bird come back to the deserted nest for protection. In one moment all was forgiven, all was forgotten, for, at his soft, whispered call, she sought her lover's wing at once, and, throwing herself on his bosom, cried as if her heart would break. "Oh, Belfond, Belfond, help me! they trod my mother down, I saw her fall; I saw him, that terrible white man, trample upon her; — I heard her groans, and I heard the whip whistling as it lashed her, and she dying beneath the horse's feet!"

"Hush! my Laurine, hush!" replied her lover, "our trials are nearly over. Say, will you come with me now? or will you stay here, and give away your precious freedom, and more than freedom — all that makes you dear in my eyes, Laurine?"

"Take me! take me! I will go with you anywhere," said the maid, in smothered accents.

"Then God bless you! God bless the hour and the day that hears you say these blessed words, Laurine!" said the young man, touching the ground with his knee; "it is the dawn of brighter, holier times for me, — days that no cloud can ever wholly darken."

"Oh, Belfond!" whispered the young girl, throwing her arms about her lover's neck, "to hear you speak so is such a happiness for me! I was so wretched at hearing you deny the goodness of God."

"Ah, well, it was of no use preaching to me then; my heart would never acknowledge a God in any place where Laurine lived a slave; — but free! ah! heaven shines in every ray of light; the holy goodness which surrounds you will be to me a beacon light to lead me upwards. Oh, Laurine! did you but know the hell that worked within me while I saw the chains doubling and doubling about you, and I — impotent wretch! — unable to move a hand to save you!"

In such sweet converse they left the Palm Grove, and plunged into the woods beyond. The fires disappeared behind the dense foliage of the forest-trees, and the din of voices of the terrifying and the terrified died away behind the hills, which the lovers now rapidly traversed; and, as the wild thorns and prickly bushes thickened on the untrodden plain, Belfond was forced to carry the maiden, were it only to husband her strength for the long journey of flight before them. The night had deepened, and had spread her mantle in solemn majesty over those wild solitudes, when it occurred to Laurine to ask timidly, whither they were going, and whether her lover was taking her to the runaway camp.

"What! take you, my treasure, to the runaway camp? — nay, my brightest star! what was pleasant to think of, the other day, will hardly do for us now; but first set my mind at ease concerning one subject, — what has become of little Léonce?"

"I took the child," said the young girl, "and at first hurried off with him to my mother's hut, thinking to keep her quiet at home; but she was off with the rest, and no entreaties of mine could bring her back; and the poor little thing I had in my arms was so terrified, and clung to me with such a low piteous wail, that I bethought me to run on to the Fountain Estate, and there leave it, — and so I did. Then I fled as for my life, to try and get my mother home. I was just a few trees from her, when, oh, Belfond! Don Duro, galloping forward, trampled her down under his horse's feet; they killed her before my eyes! — my poor mother! — my poor helpless mother!" and the young girl hid her face in her hands. "And then, Belfond," she resumed, "when he rode away and left her, I went to carry her home, and the Overseer came on hallooing to me, and telling me to stop, or he would shoot me. How cruel, cruel, cruel they are!"

"Laurine," interrupted Belfond, "we won't stop to talk upon that point now, for I suppose we shall never quarrel about it again. You asked me where I was taking you: brighten up, my star, and I will tell you: there, beyond the sunny islands across the water, — there, where none are slaves, where Bolivar has given to all equal rights,† — there am I taking you, Laurine; where you can share my uprising, and bless me as I go; where our children will be a glory to us, and our union sanctified, and held sanctified by the people among whom we live; — there, Laurine, am I taking you. And first you shall teach me to be good, my sweet flower. It is many a year since I said a prayer, and you shall bless me; you will see how good I shall be when I feel I am free for ever! All I wanted was to feel myself something in this great, beautiful world, — something responsible to God. Do you see, Laurine, that fallen tree, lying prostrate on the ground! see the little twigs it sends shooting upwards — those are its endeavours to rise, but a power greater than all its force keeps it chained to the ground: such is the poor slave, and such are his impotent yearnings to rise. Believe me, blessed Laurine, the very spirit of rebellion I exhibited, my disgust and discontent, were but so many proofs of my worship of the Supreme."

Thus they journeyed, till, about two o'clock in the morning, they reached the eastern side of the island, where the Tamana joins its sparkling tide to the ocean, where the crescent forest of palms spreads its waving heads along the shore, and the Indian fishermen spread their nets in the shade. Belfond paused, and looked around him. "Here," he said, "they know me; they will not mind my waking them up; they will give me a canoe and provisions, and we shall be off." As he said, so it was done: the Indians asked but few questions, for they were used to helping the wretched fugitives who came that way, and such provisions as they possessed they freely gave to those who needed them.

Fortunately, some fishermen had their canoe ready to put out, and, glad of the company, they stowed in their provisions, intending, as they said, to make a good voyage of it, — up the Orinoco, for turtle-eggs and wild turkeys, to exchange at Port Spain for knives and fire-water. When all was ready, and Laurine comfortably seated, Belfond stood up a moment by her side, and looked back at the beautiful island he was leaving. "Farewell!" he said, waving his hand; "no spot on earth is more lovely than you. God might have chosen you for Eden when first he created man; angels might have lived among your gardens. What dreams of prosperity, of glory, have I not had about you, — all spoiled, corrupted, poisoned by the white man! Farewell, then, sweet island! the best I can wish you is that you may daily send forth slaves, flying, like myself, to be free!"

The Indian on the shore smoked his calumet[†] as he listened, and waved his hand in response to Belfond. Now the skiff[†] is off; and the moonlight dances brightly upon the waters, and the breeze rustles softly among the palm-leaves, and the surf breaks in gentle cadence on the beach, — the hymn of nature's joy, the mingled song of sea and forest.

CHAPTER XXVI.

Conclusion

My readers may perhaps wish to know something concerning the fate of the other personages who have figured in the preceding pages. Mr. Dorset demanded and obtained pardon for the Negroes of the Palm Grove Estate,[†] — the more easily, as the implication of guilt affected them all, and the circumstances of the times rendered it advisable to hush up all such evil examples; the planters therefore agreed among themselves to tell no more than they could help to their wives at home. Mr. Cardon's death was attributed to the fall of the roof of his house upon him as he was rushing about to put out the fire, which was stated to have originated accidentally; the misconduct of the Negroes was explained by the confusion which ensued, and, in courtesy to Mr. Dorset's pleading, they were let off, after a sound flogging to each. A few of them were knocked down to Mr. Dorset at the sale of the estate, which took place shortly after, and among these were Quaco, Talima, and Beneba. Coraly was quietly smuggled off to Martinique, and has never been heard of since. Madame Angélique Cardon in due time married the Manager, and, up to the year of the Emancipation Act,[†] the Palm Grove was a thriving estate. Léonce, the little child, was taken great care of, and was said to be fonder of being with Mr. and Mrs. Dorset than with his grandmamma. A certain love of rule displayed itself in his character at an early period. When we heard of him last, he was at school in New Orleans, whence he wrote word, that as soon as he was at liberty to act for himself, it was his intention to join the American army to put down the Texan "rebels."[†]

Some little time before the Emancipation Act, a slaver was seized off the coast of Trinidad. The slaves, mostly children, were apprenticed to various individuals in the island, and the gold-dust and ivory sent to England with great ostentation. It was whispered among many that this was Captain Hill and his smuggler again, but that his name and former dealings in the Colony were for obvious reasons suppressed. How far this was true, I know not; but it is believed he may still be found stealthily carrying on his trade across the Atlantic to Cuba, and he is considered on the whole a very prosperous man.

The Overseer I know nothing more about; no doubt he went the way of all such, and ended as he had begun — grovelling in everything that was low.

Enough has not yet been said, however, of our good friends, Mr. and Mrs. Dorset. They ought to have been prosperous, but they were not. With enthusiasm they commenced a system of teaching and reforming among their slaves, which on all occasions ended like the experiment of the wheelbarrows — in failure. On slaves that were African born they invariably succeeded in making some impression, but on Negroes born as slaves in the Colony, never; these were all hardened, cunning, and corrupt. A single voice, judiciously raised, may overthrow a system, but no single effort can counteract its effects. Mr. Dorset made the mistake of expecting that his individual action, through a small space of time, could efface the evils of an unrighteous influence which had been working for centuries upon a whole race. As he never allowed flogging, his slaves were of course the laziest among the lazy. "*Master*," they would say to him, "*when we dead, and we go in a heaven, we go sit down softly (idly)*," — that was their idea of supreme happiness. His crops, as may be imagined, were never good; and when the Emancipation Act was passed, the Fountain Estate, small as it was, had so many encumbrances that it was put up for sale, and Mr. Dorset, in a new country and without friends or relatives, fell into distress. But a little time after this the writer received a letter concerning him, which told of better prospects; it was to the following effect:—

"Some days ago I was called to the door to see two *vendors*; you remember what they are, — Negro-women with trays upon their heads, going from house to house with articles for sale. The first who accosted me was a pleasant-faced girl — she had fruit and vegetables; and, as she placed her heavy tray upon the floor for my inspection, I had a full view of the other vendor behind, a magnificent-looking creature, black and shining as Newcastle coal; strong, too, or she could never have borne upon her head such a ponderous heap of silks and cottons and laces as she soon prepared to display. 'What is your name?' said I to the first, 'for I don't recollect seeing you before among the vendors of the town.' 'It is only lately I have set up,' she said (they disdain to say Missis now), 'and my name is Beneba; I used to belong to the Palm Grove, and afterwards to the Fountain.' 'Oh,' said I, 'to Mr. Dorset; I am sorry to hear he is so poorly off.' Whereupon Beneba tossed back her head with a look of scorn; 'Not so poor,' she said, 'while they have got friends like us.' After a pause, and for the sake of saying something, I ventured a question as to where they were. 'In a nice house,' said Beneba proudly, 'and living like gentleman and lady, as they are, and we are working for them and for the little piccaninny that is born; all I get for my tray is for their living, and what Talima there behind me gets by her tray, and what her husband Quaco gets by the two carts he has got on the wharf, is to get a heap of money to set him up as merchant, for we all think he would not like to be always living this way; he would like to do for himself.' "

A few years afterwards an opening occurred in New York, and thither Mr. Dorset removed his family. His success was first marked by a remittance to his colonial friends; but the good creatures sent it back, alleging that the money advanced was a free gift, and should remain so; they would be well paid in hearing that he was rich and happy.

These are the actions and sentiments of a people whom the leading journalists of the day profess to consider too ridiculous and puerile to enlist the sympathy of so great a nation as England.[†] Well for us if we could find but one out of every hundred, as disinterested, as simple-minded, and as generous!

THE END.

ANNOTATIONS TO
The Slave Son

p. 95

Dedication to Anna Jameson: Best known as a feminist and art critic, Anna
Jameson was also an opponent of slavery. Her connection to Marcella Fanny
Wilkins is as yet unknown to us, but she acted as a mentor to many women
writers, and it may be that Wilkins asked her advice about publishing *The
Slave Son*. Interestingly, Jameson's travel memoir, *Winter Sketches and
Summer Rambles in Canada* (1838), contains a sympathetic account of the
difficulties faced by runaway slaves from the United States who had crossed
the border but were threatened with extradition on the pretext of having committed felonies.

p. 99

† **Wilberforce:** William Wilberforce (1759–1833), British member of Parliament
until 1825 and anti-slavery leader.

† **Mrs. Stowe's work:** *Uncle Tom's Cabin,* published in 1852, by Harriet Beecher
Stowe (1811–96). This was a widely read novel about American slavery
which did a great deal to advance the abolitionist cause within and beyond
the United States. (See discussion in the introduction to this volume.)

p. 100

† **caste:** A hereditary class, socially distinct, whose members inherit exclusive privileges or disabilities. Specifically in South America, applied to the several
"mixed breeds" among Europeans, Amerindians and Africans.

p. 101

† **simoom:** A hot, dry, suffocating sand-wind which sweeps across the African and
Asiatic deserts at intervals during the spring and summer; also known as
khamsin and *sirocco*.

† **Douglas:** Frederick Douglass (1817?–95), an American slave with a white father, escaped from slavery at the age of twenty-one to become a prominent abolitionist speaker and author. He is especially well known for his *Narrative of the Life of Frederick Douglass, an American Slave* (1845).

† **being horsewhipped for walking between two white ladies:** See discussion in the introduction to this volume.

† **eighteen years ago:** Slavery in the British colonies was abolished in two stages, during the period between 1834 and 1838.

p. 102

† **what the Irish were in the days of the penal laws:** Many Irish Catholics supported the cause of James II in 1688, when William and Mary ascended the British throne. In Ireland this "bloodless" revolution was a protracted and bloody struggle, ending only in 1691, and followed by a series of penal laws intended to destroy Catholic social and economic power. These restricted Catholic activity in everything from land ownership and participation in civil life to education. Unlike people of mixed race in British colonies, however, landed Irish Catholics had held a substantial amount of wealth, land and power before the penal laws – and could escape them by conforming to Protestantism. (See discussion in the introduction to this volume.)

p. 103

† **Mulattoes:** Persons of half-white European and half-black African descent.

† **Terzerons:** Persons of mixed descent, theoretically of three-quarters European parentage.

† **Quadroons:** Persons of half-mulatto and half-white European descent, considered "one-quarter African".

† *Capre:* A person of mixed descent, usually Amerindian and Spanish, with or without some African heritage; feminine *capresse*.

p. 104

† **generous and glorious nation:** Britain, which had abolished slavery.

† **"And let us pray, that come it may, and come it will for a' that, When man to man, through all the world, shall brothers be and a' that." Burns:** An altered quotation from the last stanza of Robert Burns's "Song 'For a' that and a' that' " (1795). Wilkins leaves out the middle of the stanza, quoting only the first two and last two lines: "Then let us pray that come it may / (As come it will for a' that) . . . That man to man the warld o'er / Shall brothers be for a' that". The song's most famous line – "A Man's a Man for a' that" – expresses its overall idea that the worth of "an honest man" has nothing to do with rank or wealth.

† **Legendary Art:** Anna Jameson published the first volume of her major work of art history, *Sacred and Legendary Art,* in 1848. The four-part project occupied her for the remainder of her life; the last part appeared posthumously, completed by her friend Lady Eastlake, in 1864.

† **Mr. Patten, the philanthropic Librarian of the Royal Dublin Society**: The precise connection between John Patten (1774–1864) and Wilkins has not been established, but in light of *The Slave Son*'s several references to Irish insurrectionary movements, it is notable that Patten was connected by marriage to Robert Emmet, executed for leading "Robert Emmet's Rebellion" in 1803. Patten himself was arrested after that rebellion, and charged with "treasonable practices", though he was later released. Despite his "treasonable" past, he later became librarian of the Royal Dublin Society, a post he held for twenty-two years. The Society was formed in 1783 to develop agriculture and the "useful arts" in Ireland.

p. 105

† **Orinoco**: A river in Venezuela, flowing about 1,500 miles (2,400 kilometres) from its source in the Parima plateau near the Brazilian border northwards to the Colombian border, then northeast across Venezuela into the Atlantic Ocean. The mouth of the river is a vast swampy delta, near the southern edge of the island of Trinidad.

p. 106

† **the island was suffered to remain as wild and uncultivated as when first proclaimed a Spanish conquest**: Trinidad was nominally Spanish from 1498 when Columbus "discovered" it, but formal possession and settlement only began in 1592, with the founding of San José de Oruña (St Joseph). Even then, Spanish settlement was minimal, and the island remained sparsely populated, with no prosperous plantations, up to the 1770s–80s.

† **Roume de St. Laurent**: Philippe-Rose Roume de St Laurent was a French planter born in Grenada in 1743, who came to Trinidad after the 1777 Spanish decree inviting foreign settlers. He became the foremost advocate for French immigration to Trinidad, and lobbied successfully for the 1783 Royal (Real) Cédula ("decree", rendered here "Schedule"), which promised land grants and other concessions to foreign Catholic settlers.

† **Granada**: The island of Grenada.

† **Royal Schedule**: The Royal Cédula of 1783.

† **Governor Don José Chacon**: José Maria Chacon was the last of the Spanish governors of Trinidad (1784–97). He implemented the provisions of the 1783 *Cédula de Población* opening up Trinidad to foreign settlement. In 1797, Chacon surrendered the island to Sir Ralph Abercromby, accepting the Articles of Capitulation ceding Trinidad to the British.

p. 107

† **piastres**: The *piastre* was the Spanish "dollar", the *peso duro* or *piece of eight*, widely used throughout Spanish America and other countries until the mid-nineteenth century.

† **Crown-land**: Land owned by the state.

p. 108

† **Indians**: Amerindians, the aboriginal inhabitants of Trinidad, probably from both the "Arawakan" and "Cariban" (Kalinago) groups, originally settled in the area between the Amazon and Orinoco rivers on the South American mainland.

p. 109

† **Regidor**: A government official under Spanish civil law, a kind of town councillor.

† **missionary**: A Spanish Catholic priest who governed the settlement along with the Regidor and was responsible for the conversion and spiritual welfare of the Indians.

† **not excepting China**: In fact, this experiment in Chinese immigration to Trinidad took place in 1806–7, long after Chacon's term of office ended.

p. 110

† **Home Government**: The British government.

† **Vespers**: The Catholic Church's evening prayer, one of the two main "hours" of the Daily Office.

p. 111

† **midcrop-time**: The period of harvesting sugar cane usually lasts from January to June.

† **Port Spain**: *Port-of-Spain*, now usually *Port of Spain*, the main seaport; it replaced the earlier Spanish capital of St Joseph.

† **south-east coast**: In the nineteenth century, a sparsely populated, inaccessible part of the island, with very few landing places.

† **Hidalgo**: Spanish nobleman, gentleman.

† **"Ave Maria!"**: "Hail Mary!"; a Latin exclamation expressing awe.

† *bargame Dios!*: "For God's sake!"; a Spanish exclamation of disbelief or annoyance.

† **white ants**: A general term for small termites, living in large ground or tree nests, most commonly applied to *Nasutitermes costalis, N. ephratae* and *Microcerotermes arboreus*. They often eat wood products such as furniture and books, which crumble into dust when the affected item is touched. Also known as *wood ants* (see p. 223).

p. 112

† **book-muslin**: A fine kind of muslin (delicately woven cotton fabrics used for ladies' dresses, curtains, and so on), owing its name to the book-like manner in which it is folded when sold by the piece.

† **"you can trim the muslin as the lady of our good Governor Chacon once did, – quilt it all over with fireflies within the squares."**: Governor Chacon was unmarried; in any case, this tale of decorating a dress with live fireflies was

apparently a romantic fantasy, though nonetheless repeated in subsequent novels set in Trinidad. (See discussion in the introduction to this volume.)

† *caramba*: A mild Spanish expletive.

† *niña Inglesa*: "an English girl" (Sp.)

† *mira!*: "Look!" (Sp.)

p. 113

† *"Santos mios!"*: "My saints!"; a Spanish exclamation of surprise.

p. 114

† **Orders in Council**: Laws issued from London regulating the treatment of slaves during the period of slave "amelioration", 1824–34. These laws were greatly resented by the slave owners.

† *Ahí,* **Señoras!**: "There, ladies!" (Sp.)

† **cowskin**: A long whip made of plaited leather strips.

† *"Sencilla!"*: "Simpleton!" (Sp.)

† **St. Hilaire Cardon**: The name (and character) probably derive from St Hilaire Bégorrat (1759–1851), a prominent Martinique-born French planter who settled in Trinidad in 1785, living on a sugar estate in Diego Martin. He was one of the island's largest slave owners, and a powerful defender of slavery. (See discussion in the introduction to this volume.)

p. 115

† *"Sencilla, qué locura es esto!"*: "Simpleton, what madness is this!" (Sp.)

† *demonios*: "devils" (Sp.)

† *traidores todos*: "all traitors" (Sp.)

† *borrachones todos*: "all drunkards" (Sp.)

† **Palm Grove**: Probably a fictional name, based on Orange Grove, the wealthiest sugar estate in Trinidad *c.*1832; this was owned by William H. Burnley (see also note to p. 322).

p. 116

† *de verdad, palabra de honor*: "Truly, word of honour" (Sp.)

† *Hombre*: "man" (Sp.)

p. 117

† *"Muy de verdad, Señora"*: "Truly, Madame." (Sp.)

† *vagamundo!*: "Vagabond!" (Sp.)

p. 119

† **tamarind**: *Tamarindus indica*, the tamarind tree. Pod fruits, juice and pulp used for sweets, beverages and flavouring. Known locally as *tambran/tambrand* and *imli/imri*.

† **coral**: Also "coral-tree", *Erythrina poeppigiana*, a tall tree widely used as a
    shade tree for cocoa and other crops, especially in higher areas. When in
    bloom, the orange-scarlet flowers are very conspicuous and the tree can be
    seen for miles. Usually known in Trinidad as *immortelle*, *mountain
    immortelle* and *madre del cacao*.
† **bignonia**: This probably refers to *Tabebuia serratifolia*, formerly *Bignonia serrat-
    ifolia*, the yellow poui, a tall deciduous tree, with showy masses of yellow
    flowers at intervals during the dry season. A single tree stands out from the
    surrounding vegetation and can be seen from a long distance off.
† **locust**: *Hymenaea courbaril*, a large native evergreen tree; the wood is hard,
    heavy, tough, close-grained, yellowish-brown when cut, darkening to reddish-
    brown with age, used for housing beams, furniture and wheel shafts.
† **cinnamon**: The inner bark of an East Indian tree, *Cinnamomum zeylanicum*,
    dried and used as a spice. Not generally cultivated in Trinidad.
† **indigo**: Plants of the genus *Indigofera*, from which a blue dye-stuff is made; not
    generally cultivated in Trinidad *c*.1832.
† **nuts of the cotton**: That is, the pods, containing useful fibre; cotton was an
    important crop in Trinidad in the 1780s–90s, but was little grown by the time
    of the novel's setting.
† **chocolate-bush**: *Theobroma* sp., the cacao or cocoa tree, from whose seeds
    cacao and chocolate are made. The young trees are delicate and are usually
    shaded by faster-growing plants or trees.
† **cane**: Sugar cane, *Saccharum officinarum*, a tall grass from which sugar is made,
    had been Trinidad's chief export crop since the 1790s.

p. 120
† **Sant' Iago**: As noted, a fictional name; there are numerous small villages and
    hamlets along the coast northwest of Port of Spain.
† **Madras shawl**: "Madras" is a name applied to large, brightly coloured plaid
    handkerchiefs or yard goods, originally of silk and cotton and later of cotton
    only, exported from Madras, India. These pieces were used as a head covering
    by Caribbean slave and free black women, especially in Trinidad and the
    French islands.
† **bodied skirt**: Most likely a skirt or petticoat combined with a short bodice or
    jacket stiffened with pieces of bone, wood or metal called stays. Designed to
    restrain and emphasize women's figures, stays were considered virtually essen-
    tial for respectable female dress.
† **cakes**: Made from fried grated cassava.

p. 121
† **reseda and roses, pinks and myrtle, sweetbriar and English daisies**: *Reseda* is the
    European mignonette, *Reseda odorata*, native to the Mediterranean. *Pinks* are
    species of *Dianthus*, having white, pink, red and variegated sweet-smelling

flowers, native to Eastern Europe. The common (European) *myrtle, Myrtus communis,* is a shrub with shiny evergreen leaves and white sweet-scented flowers; the myrtle was held sacred to Venus and used as an emblem of love. *Sweetbriar* refers to a rose, usually the eglantine, *Rosa rubinosa,* and other species having strong hooked prickles, single pink flowers and small aromatic leaves. *English daisies, Bellis perennis,* a favourite garden flower of Europe and the British Isles, have small flat flower-heads with yellow disk and white petals, closing in the evening.

† **Martinique patois:** The French Creole language; a creole language with mostly French-derived vocabulary but with grammar and phonology also derived partly from African and other languages. Varieties of this language have been or are spoken in numerous Caribbean territories (as well as elsewhere), with different dialects or varieties spoken in different areas, for example, St Lucia, French Guiana, Haiti. This was the most widely used language in Trinidad from the late eighteenth to early twentieth centuries. Usually known in Trinidad as *Patois* (formerly also *broken French* or *Negro French*; *creole French* usually referred to the Creole-influenced French spoken by local creoles of European descent) and *Patwa, Creole* or *Kwéyol* elsewhere.

† **reals:** A Spanish coin worth one-eighth of a peso, or five English pennies, used in Trinidad until the 1840s.

† **rose-apples:** The round, pale yellow, rose-scented fruit of the tree *Eugenia jambos,* native to Southeast Asia. Usually known locally as *pomme rose* (see p. 298).

† **balatas:** *Manilkara bidentata,* a very large native South American tree with heavy but easily worked wood. The fruit is an edible round berry with a brittle, yellow, outer wall, usually containing one or two dark brown seeds, and slightly gummy, milky-sweet yellow pulp.

† **sappodillas:** The fruit of *Manilkara zapota,* a native South American tree. The fruit is roundish, 2–3 inches (5–8 centimetres) in diameter, with brown, thin, slightly fuzzy skin and edible light brown sweet mealy flesh with a cinnamon-like flavour; usually having several brown or black, shiny oval flat seeds. Plant latex is used to make chewing gum.

p. 122

† **a little song of her own composing:** Apparently original with Wilkins. The beginning section sound like a vapid version of "lower" Protestant hymns; the second part ("I look on the earth . . ."), reminiscent of the well-known "Lord of the Dance", has Celtic influences, as well as some of the more insipid aspects of parlour music.

p. 124

† **ajoupa:** A small, thatched lean-to or hut, sometimes without walls, usually used as a temporary shelter for hunting or working in the fields. Also spelled *ajupa, joupa.*

† **forest palm**: Probably the carat palm, *Sabal mauritiiformis*, a fairly tall native palm, with large, drooping, fan-shaped, deeply cut leaves once used extensively for thatching roofs.

† **walls and doorway of cocoa-nut basket-work**: That is, in the manner of basketry made for gathering coconuts.

† **liana**: Vine, particularly the large, long, woody kind that hangs in loops from trees.

† **vampires**: *Desmodus rotundus rotundus*, the South American vampire bat. It attacks cattle and horses, and sometimes humans, making a small bite and lapping up blood that flows; its saliva delays coagulation of the blood. It can transmit diseases such as rabies, and secondary infection of the wound can occur. Major epidemics of rabies in Trinidad in 1925 and again in 1931–34 led to important research on cause and control of rabies.

† **cotton-tree . . . covered all over with those fly-mocking flowers**: Probably *Ceiba petandra*, the silk-cotton tree (see note to p. 238).

† **fairy-fringe . . . blue-winged blossom**: Unidentified plants, probably epiphytes or vines growing on the large tree.

† **great changeable rose**: Possibly the flowers of *Hibiscus tiliaceus* or *Thespesia populnea*.

† **great cactus**: Probably *Nopalea cochenillifera*, the most common large cactus in Trinidad, usually known as *rachette* or *prickly pear*, growing to 13 feet (4 metres) tall, with a trunk to 8 inches (20 centimetres) or more in diameter, sometimes with short spines. It has many branches of flat, fleshy, mucilaginous, oblong joints; these are eaten and the juice is used medicinally and as shampoo. (See also *prickly pear*, p. 142.)

† *four-o'clock*: *Mirabilis jalapa*, whose colourful tube-like flowers open late in the afternoon.

p. 125

† **maize**: "Indian maize" or "Indian corn", *Zea mays*, a cob and kernel grain originating in South America.

† **purple cassava**: Presumably a purplish-tinged variety of cassava (see below).

† **Angola pea**: Probably *Cajanus cajan*, the pigeon pea or congo pea, having four or five highly nutritious seeds per pod.

† **koosh-koosh**: *Dioscorea trifida*, a native South American vine. The edible tubers are pointed at the top where stem attaches; flesh white or light purple, very smooth, crisp and slippery; cooks very quickly. Usually spelled *cush-cush*.

† **sweet potato**: The edible tubers of the native South American vine *Ipomoea batatas*, usually having thin reddish skin and white flesh.

† **plantain**: Varieties of *Musa paradisica* with large, banana-like, somewhat angular, horn-shaped fruits, containing less sugar than bananas; cooked before being eaten.

† **cassava-bread**: A bread made from grated cooked cassava, *Manihot esculenta,* an important food source native to South America. The hard type is round, about ¼–½ inch (0.6–1.2 centimetres) thick, crispy, usually very large. Soft cassava bread is round, soft, flexible, very thin, smaller than hard cassava bread.

† **bush-rangers**: Militia men (volunteer amateur soldiers) searching for "maroons", runaway slaves in the forests.

p. 126

† **the fat of an aboma**: *Boa constrictor constrictor,* a large thick-bodied snake, locally named *macajuel.* Wilkins is spicing her story with elements found elsewhere, as the common name *aboma* is used in the Guianas, not Trinidad and Tobago, and there for the anaconda, not the boa constrictor. "Macajuel oil", rendered from the fatty tissue stored in the body cavity of large healthy snakes, at one time was – and perhaps still is – used as a rub for swollen and injured limbs and joints, and is still probably an ingredient for practising obeahmen and obeahwomen (Boos 2001).

† **beebeewood**: An unidentified tree.

† **royal palm**: *Roystonea regia,* a large and majestic introduced ornamental palm, used for avenue planting.

† **vonvon beetle**: *Rhynchophora palmarum,* a palm weevil; the larva is the edible *groo-groo worm* or *palmiste worm* (see note to p. 189).

p. 128

† **registry**: The Slave Registration Order (1812) made it mandatory for all slave owners in Trinidad to submit regular returns of their human property. Black or mixed-race individuals not listed on the registry as slaves could claim to be free.

p. 129

† **tressel-bed**: A portable or movable bed supported upon trestles, frameworks of upright pieces with diagonal braces; usually spelled *trestle-bed.*

p. 132

† **Koromantyn nation**: "Koromantyn" or "Coromantin" was a term used to refer to those slaves whose port of departure in Africa was the Dutch fort at Kormantin, in the Gold Coast. It came to be used for Akan peoples – Fante and Twi (Asante and Akuapem) – of what is today southern Ghana. This term has no modern usage in Africa.

p. 134

† **salt-fish**: Usually, imported dried salt codfish. It formed a substantial part of the food given to slaves and eaten by the poor.

† **tapioca**: An edible starch, made from the flour of the cassava tuber.

† **cassava-flour**: A crumbly, meal-like flour made from cassava; usually known locally as *farine*.

p. 136

† **mawbee**: A bitter liquid, sweetened for drinking, made from boiling pieces of the dried bark of *Colubrina arborescens,* a small tree. Usually spelled *mauby.*

† **countryman**: A fellow passenger from Africa; a person of the same country, region, ethnic or language group.

† **chocolate**: A hot beverage made of locally grown and processed cocoa, milk, and spices such as cinnamon and nutmeg. Also known locally as *creole chocolate, creole cocoa* and *cocoa tea.*

† **Negro patois**: Any local non-standard English, usually the English Creole language. Also known as *broken English, Negro English.*

p. 137

† *Pardi*: "Of course"; "Needless to say" (Fr.)

p. 138

† **apothecary boys**: A disparaging term for a person who prepared and sold drugs for medicinal purposes; at this time apothecaries often practised as general medical practitioners but were not considered physicians.

† *parole d'honneur*: "word of honour" (Fr.)

† *Sacre Dieu*: "Holy God" (Fr.)

† *parbleu*: "Needless to say"; "Of course!" (Fr.)

p. 139

† **Alguazils**: An alguazil was a police officer or constable under the Spanish system; used in Trinidad up to the 1840s.

† **Quaco**: From Twi (Ashanti) *Kwaku,* the day-name for a boy born on Wednesday.

† *Sacre!*: A mild French oath.

p. 140

† **droguer**: A seagoing, open-decked, single-masted coastal sailing barge, about 60 feet (18 metres) in length, used in the West Indies and especially associated with Trinidad.

† *Vive Dieu*: A mild French oath, approximately equivalent to "God alive!" or "My God!"

† **louis d'or**: A French gold coin.

p. 141

† **Caribs**: An indigenous people, widespread over areas of the Eastern Caribbean and South American mainland prior to European contact.

† **canoes**: A canoe was a small craft, a wooden dugout made from a single log, traditionally used by the indigenous Amerindians.

† **rafters**: A number of logs, planks, casks and so on, fastened together in the water, floated from one place to another by poling or pulling.

† **luggers**: A "lugger" is a small vessel with two or three masts, having four-cornered cut sails set fore and aft.

p. 142

† **mimosa**: *Samanea saman*, a very large native South American tree with an enormous spread of branches making an umbrella-shaped crown. The deeply cut leaflets and the pink and white, brush-like flowers resemble those of the Mimoseae family. The wood is dark and durable. Known locally as *samaan*.

† **shacshac**: Any of several herbaceous plants, usually *Crotolaria* sp., whose fruit pods rattle when dry. A *shac-shac* is a musical instrument, made from a hollowed gourd or similar fruit, partly filled with seeds or pebbles, attached to a stick handle and played by shaking.

† **prickly pear**: *Nopalea cochenillifera,* also known as *rachette,* growing to 13 feet (4 metres) tall, with a trunk to 8 inches (20 centimetres) or more in diameter, sometimes with short spines. It has many branches of edible flat, fleshy, mucilaginous, oblong joints; the juice is used medicinally and as shampoo.

p. 143

† **eolian notes**: Notes produced by the wind – Æolus being the Greek god of the wind – perhaps with reference to an Æolian harp, a stringed instrument designed to be sounded by the wind. The Æolian harp was especially popular during the Romantic movement in the late eighteenth and early nineteenth centuries, and it was often used as a metaphor for the creative mind acted upon by Nature or inspiration.

† **the proverbs with which Negro converse abounds**: See discussion in the introduction to this volume.

† **Guiria**: A city on the north coast of Venezuela, directly across the Serpent's Mouth in the Gulf of Paria; the Venezuelan port closest to Trinidad.

† **General Paez**: One of the leading generals in the South American Wars of Independence.

p. 145

† **"Ya, no! . . . Poor Negro broad back!"**: "Ya, no! . . . he has no money this morning, ya hey! Master came down here so big! he was thinking to buy half that cargo – maybe all; so he brought down plenty of money. But hey! last night a thief came in the middle of the night, a fine clever thief, knew a lot, and took all. So master got up in the morning – the box was empty! Ya, ya, yah! go away! Then master said, Where's the money, all you black devils? then talked a lot, called Quaco, flogged Quaco, and promised more flogging every day till he finds the thief. The poor Negro's broad back!"

† **"Buckra not always a sabey man"**: "The white man is not always a wise man."

p. 146

† "Hey, hey! what that? put back Buckra's money? . . . send somebody for buy
her, so make her free.": "Hey, hey! what's that? put back the white man's
money? hey cho, go away! *when fowls have teeth* [that is, never], do you
hear? Do you think I care about a flogging, – me, a Koromantyn? flogging is
good for Koromantyn skin, – it makes me feel brave, not to care at all:
Quaco's back is very hard, go away! Come, countryman, don't be a fool now:
if you go in a boat to Guiria, you'll want money; but if you want to throw
away money, listen to Quaco. See the slave ship there? there are plenty of
poor niggers there: one of them a poor nigger girl: they tell me from the ship's
side, she is a Koromantyn king's child. Well, poor thing, – a pretty black shining girl, white teeth, – the poor thing has never known work. Well now, you,
Belfond take that money, send somebody to buy her, and make her free."

p. 148

† Obiah (the African witchcraft): A folk system of magic and using supernatural
forces to bring about effects ranging from success in love or business to harm-
ing an enemy; based primarily on West African rituals but incorporating
Christian and other practices. Usually spelled *obeah*.

p. 150

† the middle passage: The infamous voyage on the slave ships from West Africa to
the ports of the Americas.

† Mandingos, Foulahs, and Mozambiques: "Mandingo" refers to various groups
who speak a northern Mande language; in terms of the enslaved, this most
likely referred to people from the Gambia. The Fula ethnic group extends
from Senegal and the Gambia as far east as Nigeria and Cameroun.
"Mozambiques" refers to the Bantu-speaking people who would have come
from the Mozambique region, for example, Makua. These terms continue to
be used in Africa.

† Loango: A baKongo kingdom and its port. Those who were shipped through
Loango might have come from a wide range of Bantu-speaking groups in the
interior of Central Africa.

† distinguished by certain raised figures in the form of dice all over their bodies,
and by their long pointed teeth: Elaborate scarification was practised by a
number of African peoples. Deep cuts are especially typical of some Congo
groups (present-day Zaire) and the Tiv people of the Benue Valley of Nigeria.
Unlike the identifying "tribal marks" of the Yoruba and Igbo, such marks
were often considered primarily decorative and changed over generations.

† Eboes, Quaquas, and Mokos: "Eboes", now usually spelled "Igbos", refers to a
major ethnic group in southeastern Nigeria, speakers of a Benue-Congo language. Quaquas may refer to speakers of Avikam, a Kwa language spoken in
Côte d'Ivoire, or to those captives shipped from the Gran Lahou region.
Mokos were individuals whose African point of departure was one of several

ports on the lower Cross River in the Bight of Biafra region of Nigeria; this
term does not seem to be used in Africa today.

† **Corsican**: Among the French settlers in Trinidad were several Corsicans; Corsica
had become part of France in the eighteenth century.

† **whining drawl**: See note for *Adolphus,* for p. 30.

† **Creole**: In its earliest sense, *creole* indicates being native to the Caribbean, that
is, born in the Caribbean but of foreign descent, in contrast to someone born
in Africa or Europe. Here, it refers to a locally born (white) person of
European descent.

p. 151

† **Colonial patois**: Here, the French Creole language referred to above as
Martinique patois (see note to p. 121).

p. 152

† **the times of Richard and John**: During the reigns of Richard I (1189–99) and
John (1199–1216), English Jews suffered from mounting discrimination and
persecution.

p. 153

† **"I saw a Mulatto a little while back buy his own grandmother for a slave."**: The
original publication ends this sentence with a question mark that might well
have been intended for an exclamation mark.

† **southerns**: Denizens of hot or tropical areas, considered by northerners to be
especially passionate, as well as indolent.

p. 156

† ***Sacre, Diable!***: A mild French oath, roughly "Holy God! The Devil!"

p. 157

† ***maudit Mulâtre***: "damned mulatto" (Fr.)

p. 158

† **true as the needle**: That is, a compass needle, which always points to the true
(magnetic) north.

† ***De par tous les diables!***: "By all the devils!" (Fr.)

p. 159

† ***Sacre tonnere!***: "Holy thunder!"; a mild French expletive.

† **the eye of an Indian for tracing a runaway**: The Amerindians' skills in forest
tracking and hunting made them sought after for recovering runaways and
maroons.

† **crimped cod**: To *crimp* is to cause the flesh of fish to contract and become firm
by gashing or cutting it before *rigor mortis* sets in.

† **Wenus:** That is, Venus. Though the v/w alternation is a well known feature of literary (cockney) dialect, there are no other examples of Captain Hill using such pronunciation, including this word. Higgins, however, later does say "waluable" (p. 304). Both are thus portrayed as not really being "well-bred".

p. 160

† **Guinea coast:** The term "Guinea" was used in many different ways; here it probably refers to the European name for a portion of the west coast of Africa, extending from present-day Sierra Leone to Benin.

† **clabba-yaws:** Yaws is an endemic tropical infectious disease caused by the organism *Treponema pertenue,* spread by direct contact with skin lesions or with contaminated objects. It produces aggregations of inflammatory cells, sometimes forming destructive and deforming lesions of the skin, bones and joints. *Crab-yaws,* here *clabba-yaws,* is a variety characterized by thickening of the tissue, fissuring and ulceration of the soles of the feet, and, less commonly, the palms of the hands.

† **guinea-worms:** Dracunculiasis is a pathological condition resulting from infection with the parasite *Dracunculus medinensis*; the adult worms are about 3 feet (1 metre) long, and are quite evident as they emerge slowly through the skin of their victims. "There is no drug suitable for effective mass treatment of dracunculiasis, and from time immemorial, the disease has been treated by slowly winding the emerging worm around a stick" (Hopkins 1993, 687–88). The larval form is spread by ingestion of an aquatic crustacean, and elimination of this disease depends on decontamination of water supplies.

† **"Niggers is getting scarce now, since the trade was got to be smuggling work, and the population on the plantations don't increase so as to provide against the scarce times.":** The British transatlantic slave trade had been abolished in 1807, so the scene described here involved illegal trading or smuggling. There were fewer births than deaths on the Caribbean slave plantations, and the slave populations declined steadily between 1807 and 1834, everywhere except Barbados and some of the very small non-sugar islands.

p. 161

† **'Sdeath:** An oath, "by God's death"; archaic by the early nineteenth century.

p. 165

† **black regiment in *Bande de l'Est*:** The *Bande de l'Est* is the eastern coast of Trinidad, especially Manzanilla, Mayaro and Guayaguayare. Demobilized soldiers of the West India regiment, mostly Africans, were settled in and around Manzanilla after 1815.

† ***mon ami*:** "my friend" (Fr.)

† ***mon cher*:** "my dear" (Fr.)

p. 166

† **why the slave trade was done away with years ago. – in 1813**: In fact, the British government made participation in the African slave trade illegal for "new" colonies like Trinidad in 1806, and in 1807 generally.

† *Ce n'est rien, cela*: "That is nothing." (Fr.)

† **their name is Legion**: A proverbial saying meaning "they are very numerous"; it derives from the biblical story of the Gerasene demoniac (Mark 5 and Luke 8). Asked by Jesus "What is your name?", the possessed man's demons answer, "My name is Legion; for we are many" (Mark 5:9).

† **you little know what colonies are . . . be assured the sins of a favourite will never reach them**: Cardon exaggerates the situation, but his picture of corrupt officials, conniving with slave owners who sabotaged laws to protect slaves and to prevent illegal transfers and sales of slaves, is essentially correct with regard to the period 1824–34.

† **Spanish main**: The northern coast of the mainland of Central and South America, especially Venezuela, as opposed to the islands of the Caribbean; usually *The Main*.

p. 167

† **'Lies buried in the depths of the prison gloom, / The damps beneath, above, around, / Till the fungus grows rank o'er her living tomb.'**: A source for this quotation has not been found, and it may be original with Wilkins.

† **the mails**: A vessel plying at regular intervals between two ports for the conveyance of mail, goods and passengers. By the nineteenth century, this was generally interchangeable with "packet". (See note to *Adolphus*, p. 74.)

† **a ship comes into Port Spain, in broad daylight, with a cargo of young female slaves from the overpeopled colony, the island of Barbadoes**: Illegal transfers of slaves from Barbados to Trinidad, where they fetched much higher prices, persisted right up to 1831–32 despite efforts to stop them.

† **Protector of Slaves**: An official appointed under the 1824 Amelioration Order in Council, to implement its provisions and generally act as the slaves' protector.

† **Registrar**: An official appointed under the 1812 Registration Order in Council, to implement the elaborate periodic registration of all the colony's slaves. One purpose of this was to check illegal purchases of slaves transferred from other colonies.

p. 168

† *Oui, revenons à nos moutons*: "Let us return to our subject"; literally, "to our sheep". (Fr.)

† *mais que voulez-vous?*: "But what do you want?"; that is, "What can one do?" (Fr.)

† **". . . certainly the children of the free coloured population don't show the same decrease . . . I have often suspected neglect of the young things, and for this reason I would never have a rearing-house, like so many other planters: I let**

the mothers stay from the field to nurse their own babies. In my opinion the birth of Negro children is more loss than gain . . .”: During the years between the abolition of the slave trade and emancipation (1807–34), planters were preoccupied with the steady decline in their slave populations. A *rearing house* was a place where slave babies were kept while their mothers worked in the fields. Cardon’s view that a birth was “more loss than gain”, though typical of planters before 1807, was probably unusual in the period in which the novel is set.

p. 169

† **corallines**: Seaweeds with hard coral-like joints.

† **fucus**: Seaweeds with flat leathery fronds.

† *Párate, perro*: “Stop, dog”; a derogatory command. (Sp.)

p. 170

† **“Berry well, Massa, but dem Eboe, me no sabey wharra for do wid ‘em; dem da sleep, me tink, – no lika for moob!”**: “Very well, Master, but those Ibos, I don’t know what to do with them; they are sleeping, I think, – they don’t like to move!”

† *Por Dios santo*: “For Holy God”; a plea. (Sp.)

p. 172

† **surgeon**: One who heals by manual or operative means, treating wounds, fractures, deformities or disorders by surgery, as opposed to a physician, who treats illnesses with physic, or medicines.

p. 173

† **“The last time I saw you in town, you were just sending a dozen wheelbarrows to your estate: what were they for? how did they answer?” . . . “I suppose I must confess to a failure. I got them to save the women: I couldn’t bear to see them carrying such heavy loads on their heads.”**: This “joke” was widely circulated to illustrate the slaves’ stupidity.

p. 174

† **‘head he da hut he;’ ‘heart he da bong he;’ ‘kin he da burn all ober’**: “His head is hurting him, his heart is binding him, his skin is burning all over.”

† **single-hearted**: Straightforward, honest, sincere.

† **Moco nation**: Mokos (see note to p. 149).

† **so like the ourang-outang**: Such comparisons of Africans to apes were a staple of European racism in the eighteenth and nineteenth centuries. Cardon’s views, though expressed very forcibly, are typical of contemporary slave owners.

p. 175

† **Thebaid**: The territory belonging to Egyptian or Boeotian Thebes.

† *qu’est-ce que c’est queça?*: “What is this?” (Fr.)

† **Nabob**: Indian prince; that is, a powerful and wealthy man.

p. 176

† *chers frères*: "dear brothers" (Fr.)

† *Le chien!*: "The dog!" (Fr.)

p. 177

† **Servants out of place**: Servants without a place of employment.

† **sempstresses**: Seamstresses; needlewomen.

† **saints**: The anti-slavery advocates, most of whom were evangelical Christians, were nicknamed "the Saints".

† **"Yes, the saints! they sent a ranting set of Methodist preachers down here: I kicked them off the estate, every one of them, – the murder-preaching set!"**: Methodist (and other nonconformist Protestant) missionaries were active among the slaves in the British colonies in the years before emancipation; many planters, like Cardon, were very hostile to them.

† **our Church**: Cardon, like most French Creoles, was a Roman Catholic.

p. 178

† *noli me tangere* **fashion**: *Noli me tangere*, a biblical Latin phrase meaning "touch me not" and taken from Christ's words to Mary Magdalen after the Resurrection (John 20:17), usually signifies a proud and stand-offish demeanour.

† **humbug**: A deception, fraud, sham; a person who practises deception, an impostor, a fraud.

p. 179

† **blue bird**: *Thraupis episcopus* (English *blue-grey tanager*), a bird, bright greyish blue with a patch of vivid violet blue on wings, that frequents open woodland and cultivated areas.

† **oriole**: *Icterus nigrogularis*, a strikingly bright black and yellow bird, length 8 inches (20 centimetres). The pendant nests are commonly seen in tall trees. Known locally most often as *cornbird*, but also as *cacique, carouge, common cornbird, golden oriole, Trinidad oriole* and *yellow oriole*.

† **perroquet**: Probably *Touit batavica* (English *lilac-tailed parrotlet* or *seven-coloured parrakeet*), a very small parrot, mostly green and black with yellow wing-band and lilac tail.

† **macata**: An unidentified plant.

† **red hibiscus**: The common red-flowered variety of *Hibiscus rosa-sinensis*, an introduced plant widely naturalized throughout the Caribbean.

† **oleander**: *Nerium oleander*, a poisonous evergreen shrub, native to India, having leathery lanceolate leaves, and cultivated for its ornamental red, pink or white flowers.

† **African rose**: An unidentified plant.

† **papaw**: *Carica papaya*, a small native South American tree, 10–30 feet (3–9 metres) tall, with a weak trunk 6–9 inches (15–23 centimetres) in diameter,

and a crown of large, deeply incised leaves. The round or ovoid fruit has yellow or orange skin when ripe, and a sweet edible orange or yellow flesh, with numerous round gelatinous black seeds.

† aloe: *Aloe vera,* a succulent plant having rosettes of long fleshy pointed erect leaves, 1–2 feet (0.3–0.6 metres) long, with short, widely spaced prickles along margins; the leaves and their juice are widely used medicinally. Known locally as *aloes.*

pp. 180–81

† **Oh! to beguile the labour of the day . . . Will bind us in its ties**: Apparently original by Wilkins, this recitative, with the tune formed around the rhythm of the spoken phrase, is reminiscent of Irish folk melodies.

p. 182

† *Les maudits*: "The accursed ones, wretched ones"; an expression of pity. (Fr.)

† **poisoning work**: French Creole planters in Trinidad were haunted by the fear that slave obeahmen and -women used their knowledge of poisons to kill livestock and humans. (See discussion in the introduction to this volume.)

† **gangs**: Groups of workers – slave, indentured or free – usually with a specific task.

† **Obiah man**: A person who practises *obeah*, witchcraft (also *obeahwoman* for female practitioners).

p. 183

† **Whiteboyism**: The "Whiteboys", one of several eighteenth- and nineteenth-century secret societies which developed in Ireland, derived their name from the coarse white linen overshirts they wore. "Whiteboyism" became a generic term for the activities of these secret groups, who protested the enclosure of common land, high rents and payment of tithes to the (Protestant) Church of Ireland by destroying property and terrorizing the countryside, provoking fears of insurrection and assassination. (See discussion in the introduction to this volume.)

p. 184

† **stocks**: A traditional English form of punishment, by which persons were fastened by hands and feet to a wooden structure and kept there for varying periods. The stocks were usually set up in a public place, in order to add shame to the confinement. It was often used to punish female slaves in the last years of slavery when flogging women was prohibited.

p. 185

† *Oui, monsieur*: "Yes, sir" (Fr.)

† *pêle-mêle*: "in a jumble, in disorder" (Fr.)

p. 186

† *Fi donc! Allez!*: "Fie, then! Go!"; a French expression of disdain or dismissal.

† *Mais, que diable!*: "But, what the devil!" (Fr.)

† **pitch**: Natural bituminous asphalt. The (Great) Pitch Lake, several hundred acres in area in southern Trinidad, is the largest natural deposit of asphalt in the world. At present, it is estimated to be about 250 feet (76 metres) in depth, but was previously considerably deeper. The lake was first described in writing by Sir Walter Raleigh in 1595, who used the pitch to caulk his ships. The area began to be seriously exploited commercially only towards the end of the nineteenth century. The surface of the pitch is quite soft, and was softer and more liquid before that time; therefore, it would have been possible to get stuck in the pitch while walking across it slowly. (The Pitch Lake also figures in *Warner Arundell,* especially chapter 30.)

p. 187

† **cedar**: *Cedrela odorata,* the Trinidad cedar, a large deciduous tree; the aromatic wood is used for cigar boxes, houses and furniture.

† **pitch-pine**: Several species of pine tree, most native to North America, having very resinous wood, source of turpentine and lumber.

† **sour oranges**: *Citrus aurantium,* a tree bearing round orange citrus fruit with bitter pulp; the peel is used for seasoning and candy. Known locally and elsewhere usually as *Seville orange.*

p. 188

† **sangaree-bowls**: Sangaree is a drink made of diluted, spiced wine.

† **night-moths**: That is, night-flying moths, as opposed to the usual day-flying butterflies, and the less common species of day-flying moths.

† **saloon, or hall, as it is called in the Colonies**: The main reception room of a house, more or less elegantly furnished, used for the reception of guests, banquets and so on. The local proverb *Braggin' ah hall, nutten ah chamber* describes someone whose actual circumstances or abilities do not live up to their own boasting.

† **Indian mat**: A floor mat woven from dried grass stalks or reeds, traditionally made by the indigenous people of Trinidad.

p. 189

† **"Whist!"**: "Be silent!" (now archaic or dialectal English).

† *Arum maculatum,* **and called calaloo**: Actually the leaves of *Colocasia esculenta,* the edible *dasheen* tuber (English *taro*). (*Arum maculatum* has a similar flower, but is a cool-weather European plant.) *Callaloo* is made from dark green leaves, usually dasheen, cooked with *ochro* (English *okra*), usually including coconut milk and crab or salt meat, and swizzled into a thick slimy soup.

† **venison:** *Mazama americana,* the *red* or *small brocket deer,* is a small reddish-brown deer, with small single horn-like antlers, occasionally with a small branch or "double horn", which are periodically shed. Frequently hunted for meat. Locally known as *deer* or *biche.*

† **turtle:** Several possible freshwater and marine species.

† **iguana:** *Iguana iguana,* a large, generally green, long-tailed lizard, with a spiny crest along mid-back. Its flesh is valued as for food by many people.

† **grugru worm:** The larva or grub of *Rynchophora palmarum,* a large palm weevil known as the *vonvon beetle* (see note to p. 126). They are found naturally in the decaying trunks of the palmiste tree, but may be attracted by any incision made in a healthy tree. "The eggs develop and produce the much appreciated 'gru-gru' worms, a highly palatable and *recherché* morsel for the gourmet. In order to procure a large supply of these worms, it is customary to fell the tree and make several incisions in the trunk. Within a period of 15 days, the larvae are hatched and fit for eating" (*Journal of the Field Naturalist Club,* February 1893: 149–50). Also spelled *groo-groo worm.*

p. 190

† *Ma bonne amie:* "My good friend." (Fr.)

† **stampees:** A *stampee* was the smallest silver coin used in Trinidad at this time; equal to a quarter of a *bitt,* or one sixteenth of a peso or dollar.

† **Prayers opened with the salutation of the angel to Mary:** The Ave Maria, or Hail Mary, based on the greeting of the Angel Gabriel to the Virgin Mary (Luke 1:28). Normally, vespers starts with psalms rather than with the Hail Mary.

p. 192

† **check-linen:** Linen patterned in checks, one of the cheapest fabrics available; like the other elements of Bretton's appearance, his cheap suit speaks to his "low" habits.

p. 193

† **bill:** From English *bill* or *billhook,* an implement for pruning, cutting wood, hedges and so on, having a long blade with a concave edge, often ending in a sharp hook, and a long or short wooden handle in line with the blade. Eventually replaced in Trinidad and Tobago by various styles of *cutlass.*

† **gourd for holding water:** A dried hollowed-out squash fruit (or small calabash), usually with a long neck (or added stick) used as a handle, traditionally used as a drinking vessel.

† **calabash:** A hollowed out and dried fruit of the calabash tree, *Crescentia cujete,* used as a bowl. The hard shells of the spherical fruits, cleaned of pulp, cut in half and dried, are used as containers and bowls.

† **osnaburg:** A kind of coarse linen originally made in Germany.

† **coffee-berries:** The ripe red fruits of the coffee tree containing seeds which are cleaned and roasted to make the coffee beverage.

p. 194

† **"He hab Obiah 'pon him"**: That is, he is suffering from an act of obeah, a spell.

† **"I'll take your grounds from you."**: Plantation slaves were allocated "provision grounds", plots of estate land that the slaves could use for growing food. They could consume or sell the produce; the threat to deprive Coraly of her grounds was therefore serious.

p. 195

† **"Master . . . neber ask Coraly nothing . . . dead saved her from flog."**: "Master . . . never ask Coraly anything, Coraly knows nothing; *don't pick my mouth* (do not cross-question me), there is nothing there; but suppose I did know, and suppose I told you, what good would that do me? would it bring back my child, hey? did you cry for my child? Master, you remember Mulatto Belfond's mother? she loved you a lot, very much; she saved your life two times: did that save her from flogging? no! death saved her from flogging."

† **"Fine slabe, Master that oberseer good too much . . . he is a fine cleber nigger-boy."**: "A fine slave, Master, that overseer is very good; a clever man! he wanted to make this nigger-boy clever too, so once he flogged him every morning before he opened his eyes, another time he made him walk on four feet like a cat, then he tied him up like a dog, and made him bark when people passed. So now Alibo, this nigger-boy, is a fine clever dog; put him under your bed, Master, a thief will never come to take your money again, he is a fine clever nigger-boy."

p. 197

† **jalousies**: Blinds or shutters on the outside of windows, made of wooden slats sloping upwards; they can be adjusted to be (partially) closed to exclude sun and rain or (partially) opened to admit air and light.

p. 198

† **recreant**: Cowardly; afraid.

p. 200

† **driver**: Generally, the male slave who supervised a work gang on a plantation.

† ***Corbleu!***: A mild French oath, roughly equivalent here to "Oh for God's sake!"

p. 203

† **nux-vomica, palma-christi, the branched calaloo, poisonous shrubs of the cockroach-apple**: *Nux-vomica*, the seed contained in the fruit of *Strychnos nux-vomica*, a non-native tree, from which strychnia poison is obtained. *Palma christi* is *Ricinus communis* (English *castor oil plant*), a tall shrub; seeds contain castor oil, used medicinally. The *branched calaloo* is probably a native inedible plant with large deeply cut leaves, such as *Philodendron* or *Monstera*. *Cockroach-apple* is not a local name, but probably refers either to the native

plants *physic nut* or the *manchineel*; the smell of the fruits is said to kill cockroaches. The former, *Jatropha curcas,* is a shrub or small tree; blackish seeds
contain toxin, used for medicine and *obeah.* The latter, *Hippomane
mancinella,* is a tree with small, spherical, green fruits; all parts of the tree
contain a copious white latex which has a blistering effect on skin.

p. 205

† **mother's brother**: In many West African societies, an individual's mother's
   brother (maternal uncle) traditionally has special responsibilities for that person.

† **deer's horns**: See note to p. 189.

† **an American dog bald of hair**: Probably the *Mexican hairless* or *Mexican crested
   dog,* a small dog without hair except for tufts on the head and tail.

† **malencontre**: Mishap; mischance.

p. 206

† **mule**: Mulatto; half-white.

† **Maroons**: Runaway slaves living in the forests or mountains of the Caribbean
   colonies, often in organized communities. (See discussion in the introduction.)

p. 208

† **Wanga oath**: A sacred oath administered by an obeahman on an African fetish
   or charm.

† **Dagoman**: Possibly a reference to "Dagomba", a Gur language spoken in
   Ghana.

p. 209

† **ptisane**: Originally a nourishing and slightly medicinal beverage made from bar-
   ley; now usually a hot infusion of medicinal herbs. Usually spelled *tisan(e).*

p. 211

† **"There! not a Negro yonder, or anywhere, shall dare betray you; seek the white
   man ever so briskly, ever so cunningly, for harm shuns this. Accompong, the
   African Great Spirit, has looked upon it; Assarci, the God of mercy, the
   Mediator, has blessed it; Obboney, the God of evil, fears it."**: Accompong,
   Assarci and Obboney are presumably deities of the "Koromantyn" (see note
   to p. 272). According to Bryan Edwards, almost certainly the source for this,
   Accompong was the Creator and Supreme Being; Assarci the God of the
   earth; and Obboney the author of all evil. (See Edwards 1793, 2: 66.)

p. 213

† **aboma**: See note to p. 126.

† **horse-whip snake**: *Oxybelis aeneus,* a long, extremely thin, ashy-grey or brown
   snake, with a scale colour pattern resembling a finely plaited leather whip. In

folk myth, it is incorrectly believed to use its tail as an instrument for flogging its antagonist, particularly attacking pregnant women.

† **Cowskin**: A plaited leather whip. See p. 114.

† **coral snake**: Either of two venomous snakes found in Trinidad, having red, black and white bands: *Micrurus lemniscatus diutius* (the larger of the two) and *M. circinalis*. Though coral snakes' neurotoxic venom can be fatal, they tend to be fairly docile during the daytime and can often be handled without any danger; as the jaws and fangs are very small, most bites are between the toes or fingers (Boos 2001).

† **little climbing plant, the *Mikania Guaco*, the juice of which, taken internally as tea, and inoculated into various parts of the body, acts as an effectual antidote to the bites of the most venomous serpents**: *Mikania micrantha*, a slender twining plant with arrowhead- or heart-shaped leaves; known locally as *guaco* or *waku*. The use of this plant's juice externally as a cure for snakebite in Trinidad was widely known (for example, De Verteuil 1858, 127).

p. 215

† **Jumbee**: A ghost, spirit of a dead person; of West African origin. Usually spelled *jumby* or *jumbie*.

† **contraband goods**: Slaves imported illegally from Africa or other colonies in the Americas.

p. 216

† **doubloon**: A Spanish gold coin used in Trinidad up to the 1840s, worth sixteen pesos or dollars.

† **tinder-box**: Before the invention of the match, the standard way to start a fire or strike a light was with flint, steel and tinder (light wood shavings, charred linen and the like). Flint and steel were struck sharply together, and the resulting spark ignited the tinder. Flint, steel and tinder were usually carried together in a small "tinder box".

† **scorpion**: The most commonly found scorpion in Trinidad is *Tityus trinitatis*, yellow-brown to dark brown or black, about 5 inches (13 centimetres) long with slender pincers, common in old houses, under leaves and in cane fields; the sting is painful, and mortality is about 4 per cent. Other species are generally smaller, rarer and less poisonous. The most common symptoms of scorpion sting are lacrimation, salivation, sphincter relaxation, muscular cramps, perspiration, vomiting and convulsions.

† **rencontre**: An encounter between two opposing forces; a battle, skirmish.

p. 218

† **necromancer**: Sorcerer; obeahman; also known locally as "negromancer".

† **"Cross down" replied the old man, pointing to the southern sky, where that beautiful constellation is known to sparkle**: This refers to the constellation

Crux, the Southern Cross, a small kite-shaped group of four stars – two of
which, Acrux and Becrux, are among the twenty brightest visible stars in the
sky; its long axis points directly towards the South Pole. Although not high
up, it is readily visible standing upright above the southern horizon, leaning
over to set, several hours later, to the southwest. At the latitude of Trinidad,
the Cross would rise at about 10:00 p.m. on 1 May, about 8:00 p.m. on 1
June. The designated time would therefore probably be between midnight and
2:00 a.m.

† **playing . . . at French and English**: That is, fighting, like these traditional battle-
field opponents.

† **phial of spirits and a dead scorpion soaking in it**: In addition to the traditional
ingestion of alcohol as an antidote to snakebite or scorpion sting, parts of the
snake or scorpion, especially the head or the horny tail or "sting", are steeped
in rum and kept handy as a stronger, partly magical, remedy. In fact, alcohol
speeds the spread and absorption of any injected venom.

p. 220

† **well-known Negro proverb . . . *When I see my neighbour's beard on fire, let me
water my own***: That is, take warning from what happens to others, and take
steps to prevent damage to yourself. This is still a widespread proverb in both
English and French Caribbean areas, for example, Jamaican "When you see
you neighbour beard ketch fire, tek water wet fe you."

p. 221

† **pinguin**: *Bromelia plumieri*, a ground bromeliad plant. The leaves are thick,
erect, narrow, strap-like, spiky, red-margined, covered with long, dark brown
scales and armed with very pronounced spines, arising from the base in a
spreading rosette. Since the plant often grows in clumps, the spiny leaves create an imposing barrier, sometimes used as fencing.

† **travellers' fountain**: *Uncaria tomentosa*, a woody vine with tetragonal stems
growing very long, forming a profusion of intertwining branches, climbing by
stout, triangular, hooked spines; known locally as *liane d'eau* and *croc-chien*.
In the valleys of the eastern Northern Range, these lianes "often grow across
rivers . . . and the tangle of vines with their hooked stipules are notorious for
sticking onto the clothes of passers-by . . . The mature stems are slashed and
the water which spurts out under high pressure is drunk by woodsmen,
hunters and hikers. The taste is brackish but sweet . . . The collection of the
water for use as medicine requires considerable effort since the water squirts
'up in the air' when the vine is cut" (Morean 1992, 29).

p. 222

† ***Mauritia aculeata***: An older scientific synonym for a palm tree not actually
found in Trinidad. The closely related M. *flexuosa*, a tall native palm, height
to 50 feet (15 metres), is found only in a few isolated areas in Trinidad, where

it is known as the *moriche palm*. It has large leaves, about 3 feet (1 metre) in diameter, and small spherical fruits borne in large pendulous bunches.

p. 223
† **wood-ants**: Termites. (See note to p. 111.)

p. 225
† **"Our homes, our wives and children, what are they? . . . No feeling but of woe!"**: Like the earlier song (see p. 122), this appears to be original with Wilkins.

p. 228
† **Fantyn**: Fante, one of the Akan peoples of present-day Ghana.

p. 230
† **a snake when it seeks to fascinate its prey**: This reflects the longstanding though false belief that the foetid breath "given off" by snakes – known as their "fascination" – paralysed prey.

p. 231
† **piccaninny**: A widespread contemporary term for child, usually a black or African child; usually *pickney* in Trinidad and Tobago. From Portuguese *pequenino* "very little one".
† ***Perra maldita***: "Damn bitch"; a strong Spanish insult.
† **"it's our master self sent him here"**: In the original *its*; normally this would be the emphatic English Creole form "is our master self . . .".
† **sissy**: Sister; term of address or reference to a close woman friend, mostly used by creoles of African descent.

p. 233
† **head cooper**: Slave artisan in charge of making barrels and hogsheads for storing sugar, molasses and rum.

p. 234
† ***Juste ciel!***: "Just Heavens"; a polite French oath.

p. 235
† **guinea-worm**: See note to p. 160.
† **clabba-yaws**: See note to p. 160.

p. 236
† **"Me no monkey . . . you tink me love cuss?"**: "I am no monkey! . . . I've taken care of your niggers; I don't sleep night and day, minding sick niggers: a mon-

key would never do that; and you let the man stand there to curse me, – you
think I love curses?"

p. 238

† **sacred cotton-tree – the Fetish tree of the estate:** *Ceiba pentandra,* the *silk cotton*
tree, an extremely large native tree, 100 feet (30 metres) tall or more, with
large horizontal branches; the trunk often has huge buttresses. The fruit pods,
3–4 inches (8–10 centimetres) long, are filled with seeds embedded in a silky
fibre formerly used for stuffing cushions, lifebelts and so on. (A shorter variety is the source of the floss known as *kapok.*) In folk belief, it is the home of
jumbies, soucouyants and other spirits, who come out from the roots at night;
it is generally avoided.

p. 239

† **Koromantyn language:** One of the languages of the Akan peoples of what is
today southern Ghana; that is, Fante and Twi.

† **her audience, like a company of story-telling Arabs, greeting every new incident
with appropriate expressions of sympathy, – moaning, sighing, barbarous
exclamations of surprise, or words of dislike and execration:** See discussion of
story-telling in the introduction to this volume.

p. 240

† **Anamaboe:** A city along the coast of what is now Ghana; this is in the Akan
region, specifically in the area peopled by speakers of Fante; now spelled
"Anomabu".

† **harem:** The women's part of a house or residential compound.

† **quagga:** A South African equine quadruped, similar to the zebra.

p. 245

† *fourmis chasseurs*: Hunter or army ants; *Eciton* sp., especially *E. burchelli,*
nomadic ants which periodically move in vast numbers from place to place.
They are highly aggressive, preying on animals much larger than themselves.

p. 246

† **Angostura:** A town in Venezuela, now Ciudad Bolívar.

† **Peon:** A free person of Spanish (Venezuelan) origin or descent – sometimes a
"mixed race" person of Amerindian, African and European descent – usually
a manual labourer in cocoa cultivation, woodcutter or hunter.

p. 247

† *Warahoons*: An Amerindian group mainly resident in the Orinoco delta; in the
past, they occasionally traded or resided in Trinidad. Also spelled *Guarahoon,
Guaraoon, Guarauno, Wallahoon, Warao* and *Yaruro.*

p. 248

† **Mammy Madelaine for respect:** "Mammy" was a respectful title used by slaves when speaking to older women.

p. 249

† **parasol-ants, every one with a tribute-leaf in 'em mouth, marching to give 'em to two-headed snake in 'em nest:** The leaf-cutter or parasol ants *Atta cephalotes* or *Acromyrmex octospinosus*, known locally as *bachac,* species of ant which cut leaves into pieces and carry them, on narrow but clearly visible trails, to underground nests in which a fungus is cultivated. The *two-head(ed) snake* is either of two non-venomous, snake-like, legless lizards, whose tail end resembles the head end. *Amphisbaena fuliginosa,* the spotted worm snake, is small, mottled black and white. *A. alba,* the red worm lizard, is larger and ranges from deep yellowish red-brown to pale cream in colour. They appear to be attracted by worms in the loose soil brought up by the ants. Known also as *bachac snake, double-head(ed) serpent, mother of the ants, serpent à deux têtes*; also *black and white coral, black and white two-head(ed) snake* (*A. alba*); and *spotted worm snake* (*A. fuliginosa*).

† **small red ant[1] [1]*Formica omnivora*:** Possibly *Solenopsis* spp., fire ants, small, reddish-brown ants with a painful sting.

p. 250

† **Congo nation:** The term "Congo" generally referred to any Bantu-speaking people from western Central Africa.

p. 255

† **coffee-walks:** An area planted with coffee trees, arranged in rows.

† **The plague here described took place in 1780:** Ant infestations in Grenada, Martinique and Guadeloupe in the late 1770s and early 1780s were said to be one of the reasons for French migration from these islands to Trinidad during this period.

p. 257

† **want to eat earth:** Probably a disorder resulting from malnutrition: "Dry beriberi's symptoms are remarkably similar to those of a mysterious illness of the slaves called the *mal d'estomac* in some islands and *hatiweri* or *cachexia Africana* in others. Physicians first thought that the lack of energy, breathlessness, and nerve problems including an unsteady, high-stepping gait . . . were caused by dirt eating; later investigators have suspected that the cause was hookworm disease. But . . . dry beriberi remains the best explanation for this particular ailment" (Kiple 1993, 501).

† **iron mask:** A metal device placed on the head of slaves to prevent dirt eating.

p. 260

† **Toussaint L'Ouverture:** The main leader of the Haitian Revolution up to 1802, when he was betrayed by the French General Leclerc and sent into exile in France on Napoleon's orders, dying in 1803 in a remote prison in the Jura mountains.

† **Ogé of St. Domingo:** Vincent Ogé, a free coloured leader in Ste Domingue (that is, St Domingo, present-day Haiti), led a revolt early in 1791 which was brutally suppressed, Ogé being executed. It was followed by the outbreak of the great slave rebellion in 1791.

p. 262

† **sous:** Cash, money; a *sou* is a French coin of low value, formerly the twentieth part of a *livre,* subsequently the five-*centime* piece.

p. 263

† **It was not then in France, as it was already in England, ordained that every slave on touching its soil should become free:** In England, the ruling of Chief Justice Mansfield in 1772 had established, not that every slave touching English soil was free but that a colonial slave in England could not be held in servitude there, nor returned to the colonies, against his or her will.

† **The Indians on the coast:** Amerindians living in the coastal missionary settlements.

p. 268

† **tree-fern:** A very large tropical fern, usually *Cyathea* or *Alsophila,* with an upright stem, growing to the size and form of a tree.

† **the blue and pink convolvulus:** Usually refers to *Convolvulus* sp., a number of plants having slender twining stems and trumpet-shaped flowers not native to Trinidad. This may refer to an imported ornamental or to a similar local plant.

† **long chaplets of scarlet berries:** A *chaplet* is a Catholic rosary. They were often made locally by stringing *crab('s) eyes,* the seeds of *Abrus precatorius,* a slender, somewhat woody vine, common on hedges and poles. The small ornamental oval seeds, bright scarlet with a black base, are poisonous if eaten.

p. 269

† **"Dunno no such place . . . cutlass and rest neber live together.":** "I don't know any such place . . . savannahs have rats, trees have snakes, and, worst of all, the white man's spade breaks the ground everywhere: a cutlass and rest never live together."

p. 270

† **"Eh hey! . . . Hey, Belfond, da neber do!":** "Eh hey! . . . just listen, you, Belfond: you know that tall bamboo-tree by the great savannah, there the grass is soft,

the shade wide and cool, birds sing in the leaves, and at sundown we love to
sit there and talk. Time out of mind poor Anamoa sat down there when he
was weary, and talked about faraway Africa to young people like me. Well,
suppose we bury him there, – tomorrow Master's Manager will come past
with a big dog, the devil dog smells the ground, scratches up, and whines,
then Master's Manager will call out, 'Niggers, come here! something is here!
come, dig away, let me see;' so the poor niggers are obliged to dig till the
spades dig up the body, then Master's Manager flogs everyone all round. Hey,
Belfond, that will never do!"

† **Gone back to Africa**: African slaves were thought to believe that in death they
flew back to their birthplace.

† **tiger-cats**: *Felis pardalis,* the ocelot, a small wild cat.

† **vultures**: *Coragyps atratus,* the black vulture, a large bird, length 25 inches (64
centimetres), wingspread 4½ feet (1.4 metres). A very common resident in
Trinidad; known locally as *cobo.*

p. 272

† **Ta Fanty**: According to Bryan Edwards (1793), "Ta" was a title of respect used
to an older man, from the "Koromantyn" word for father.

† **seed of the *Mammea Sapota***: The grated seeds of the *shapot* or *mamey sapote*
(*Calocarpum mammosum*) are used in the flavouring of cakes and other
sweetmeats.

† **libations were poured on the ground in honour of Assarci, who, as well as being
the God of mercy, was also the God of regeneration**: A widespread custom in
Africa. Again according to Edwards (1793, 2: 66), first fruits and libations
were offered to Assarci, the Koromantyn God of the Earth. Some Creoles of
African descent in Trinidad still pour the first few drops of a new bottle of
rum upon the ground.

pp. 274–75

† **No more thou'lt watch the morning sun arise . . . Our loved native groves**:
Apparently original.

p. 278

† **tendon-Achilles**: The tendon of the heel, the principal extensor of the foot.
Repeated runaways might be punished in this way to make them virtually
immobile. Such a punishment was illegal in Trinidad at the time during which
the novel is set.

p. 282

† **festal dress for La St. Jean**: St John the Evangelist, one of the Twelve Apostles;
his saint day is 27 December, but this probably refers to 6 May, the day of
observance of the Feast of St John before the Latin Gate.

† **little pink cowries**: *Cowry* refers to a number of small oval-shaped, porcelain-like marine shells, with a narrow opening on the underside as long as the shell; used as jewellery and money in parts of Africa and South Asia. However, these shells are not in fact found in Trinidad. If the author is referring to local shells, these would probably be the *chip-chip* or *butterfly shell*, *Donax denticulatus* or *D. striatus*, a small triangular bivalve mollusc shell, white with variably coloured bands, found in beach sand, especially on the eastern coast of Trinidad.

† **wings of the small gold-beetle**: Probably *Chrysomelid* sp. (English *leaf* or *tortoise beetle*), which lives on vines found in the Northern and Central Range; it has a beautiful gold colour and is used in South American jewellery.

p. 283

† *Santísimos Santos!*: "Holy Saints!"; a Spanish exclamation, here indicating hope of not having been heard.

p. 284

† *Santísima Virgen!*: "Most Holy Virgin!"; an exclamation of surprise and curiosity.

p. 285

† **howlings of monkeys**: This refers to *Alouatta seniculus insularis*, the native red howler monkey. Their very loud howling call can be heard in the forests at dusk and dawn. Also known as *howler, macaque rouge, red howler* and *red monkey*.

p. 287

† **tassa**: Strips of dried beef; also *tassaja*.

† *acuerdate bien*: "Remember well"; a Spanish warning or recommendation.

† **Tamana river, on the sea-shore**: Tamana is the name of the highest hill in Trinidad's Central Range, but no river of that name flows to the east coast.

p. 288

† **plantain-walks**: Rows of cultivated plantain "trees".

† **cacao-walks**: Rows of cocoa (cacao) trees.

† **pomegranates**: The fruit of the tree *Punica granatum*, a large roundish many-celled fruit, with a tough leathery rind of orange-red, containing many seeds each enclosed in a juicy reddish pulp. Native to northern Africa and western Asia; naturalized in warmer regions but never common in Trinidad.

† **granadilla**: *Passiflora quadrangularis*, a climbing plant and its large fruit; the thick, white flesh and greyish jelly seed covering is used for making ices and drinks. Also known as *barbadeen*.

p. 291

† **prie-dieu**: A low prayer stool on which one person kneels, in front of a shrine or small altar.

† **lavatoire**: Washbasin.

† **swing glass**: A mirror suspended on pivots.

† **wardrobe**: A movable closed cupboard, fitted with hooks or pegs and shelves or movable trays and drawers in which clothing is kept; usually bedroom furniture.

p. 294

† ***"Allons donc!"***: "Let's get on with it, then." (Fr.)

p. 298

† **Brinvilliers**: *Spigelia anthelmia,* an apparently very poisonous plant, with small lanceolate leaves readily blackening on injury or drying. The name commemorates a notorious poisoner, Marie de Brinvilliers, a French aristocrat, executed in 1676.

† *acqua toffana*: A poison, usually spelled *Aqua toffana.* "Madam Toffana of Siciliy had built a career based on poisoning in the seventeenth century. Her method was quite inventive. She rubbed arsenic into the joints of freshly slaughtered swine, removed the synovial fluid, and used it to make 'Aqua Toffana.' Ostensibly this potion was sold as an aid to improve the complexion by removing redness from cheeks. But if desired, it could also be used to remove spouses from conjugal beds. Permanently. As many as 600 people may have met their end in this fashion before Toffana was brought to justice and publicly strangled in 1709" (Schwarcz 2001, A13).

† **pommerose**: See note to p. 121, for *rose-apple.*

† *Peste, oui!*: "A plague, yes!"; a French expression of irritation.

p. 299

† **in the year 1822 in Martinique**: Fear of slaves poisoning livestock and human beings was especially pronounced in Martinique. There was an outbreak of poisoning by slaves in the Lamentin district of Martinique in 1822, and "special tribunals" were set up to try the accused poisoners. Also in 1822, a slave uprising in Martinique was brutally suppressed and seven slaves executed after a "trial" in the Royal Court; their right hands were cut off, they were decapitated and their bodies were exposed publicly before being "thrown to the vultures". In Trinidad itself, actual poisoning cases attributed to slave use of obeah or poison were infrequent or rare by the 1820s; the climate of fear referred to here more likely pertains to situations elsewhere in the Caribbean.

p. 301

† *n'importe!*: "It doesn't matter!" (Fr.)

p. 303

† **'sblood!**: An oath, "by God's blood"; like "'Sdeath" (p. 161) and "Zounds"
below, it had an archaic ring by this period.

† **Zounds!**: An oath, "by God's wounds".

p. 304

† **jackanapes what sets up for nobs**: That is, low-life rascals who try to pass for
gentlemen. Despite Higgins's protests, this description seems to suit him.
"Esquire" after one's name signified a claim to gentlemanly status.

p. 305

† **Hebe**: Greek goddess of youth, cupbearer to the gods, and wife of Hercules. A
"Hebe" usually means an adolescent girl in the prime of youth.

p. 309

† **an empty bag cannot stand**: That is, a hungry person cannot work; another
proverb widespread throughout the English and French Caribbean.

† **"the King of the white people has called us children; how two smaller tributary
kings, Buxton and Wilberforce, have confessed to loving us, and to make war
upon other white kings to make us free."**: This refers to the British government's policy, in the years before emancipation, of legislating for the protection and "amelioration" of colonial slaves, under pressure from the
anti-slavery movement. Sir Thomas Foxwell Buxton (1786–1845), a British
member of Parliament, took over parliamentary leadership of the abolitionist
campaign from Wilberforce (see note to p. 99) when the latter left the House
of Commons in 1825. Slaves recognized that they had some powerful allies in
Britain.

† **eggs mustn't dance 'mong de stones**: That is, not only are they not the same sort
but they could get hurt. In Trinidad this is usually rendered as "Egg have no
right at rockstone dance."

p. 310

† **"Cho! hold your mouth . . . nigger so low, hey?"**: "Cho! hold your mouth, and
let me and Daddy Fanty talk. I know very well that Master Dorset is not a
spy: he is a foolish man and has a good heart, that's all: and as for free law,
go away, that will never come for niggers, nor for niggers' children: *when
cattle die, they leave misery to their skin,* – that's the way with poor niggers.
Now, Daddy, you are a wise man, so just tell us why the white man is so
grand, and the nigger so low, hey?" This proverb refers to the use of cow skin
– more usually female goat skin – as the tops of drums, so that they are
beaten even after death. One local version is *Papa Goat dead he nuh lef nutten but Nanny goat dead she lef trouble gie she skin,* "When Billy Goat dies
he leaves nothing, but when Nanny goat dies she leaves trouble for her skin."

p. 312

† **gentle green light of a little firefly**: A small brown insect (*Lampyridae* sp.) with a luminous yellowish or greenish spot on the tip of the abdomen which blinks on and off as it flies at night. Often seen in gardens and around houses just after sunset. Usually known locally as *candlefly*.

p. 317

† **Pandemonium**: Literally, a meeting place for all the demons; coined by John Milton, the term appears in *Paradise Lost* (1667) as the name of "the high capitol / Of Satan and his peers" (I.756). By the mid-nineteenth century, it had lost much of its pejorative significance and often simply meant an unruly uproar. Nonetheless, by capitalizing it and using it to refer to a place, Wilkins re-emphasizes its original infernal connotations.

p. 320

† **where none are slave, where Bolivar has given to all equal rights**: Simón Bolívar, the Liberator, was the leader of the independence struggle in "Columbia" (modern Venezuela, Ecuador and Colombia). He and Francisco de Miranda proclaimed independence from Spain in 1811, but a disastrous defeat by Spanish troops, coupled with the Venezuelan earthquake of 1812, put an end to hopes for liberation until 1814. Eventually Bolívar secured Venezuelan independence in 1821, as part of a larger state, Gran Colombia. Slavery was not abolished in Venezuela until 1854. (See discussion in the introduction to this volume.)

p. 321

† **calumet**: An Amerindian tobacco pipe, with a clay or stone bowl and a long reed stem.

† **skiff**: A small seagoing boat, adapted for rowing and sailing, especially one attached to a ship and used for purposes of communication, transport or towing.

p. 322

† **Palm Grove Estate**: The original edition of the novel has – in this instance only – Orange Grove Estate, the real name of William H. Burnley's estate in Tacarigua, the wealthiest sugar estate in Trinidad *c.*1832.

† **Emancipation Act**: Passed by Parliament in 1833, it came into effect on 1 August 1834.

† **Texan "rebels"**: Texas joined the United States of America in 1845. Disputes about slavery and loyalty to the Union versus secession were the dominant issues in Texan politics in the early 1850s.

p. 324

† These are the actions and sentiments of a people whom the leading journalists of
the day profess to consider too ridiculous and puerile to enlist the sympathy
of so great a nation as England: The establishment press in England argued
that the public should not support the American abolitionist movement in its
campaigns against slavery in the southern states.

REFERENCES

Anthony, Michael. 1997. *A Historical Dictionary of Trinidad and Tobago.* Lanham, Md.: Scarecrow Press.

Beckles, Hilary. 1987. *Black Rebellion in Barbados: The Struggle Against Slavery: 1627–1838.* Bridgetown: Carib Research and Publications.

Berlin, Ira. 1974. *Slaves Without Masters: The Free Negro in the Antebellum South.* New York: Pantheon Books.

Bernstein, Iver. 1990. *The New York City Draft Riots: Their Significance in American Society and Politics in the Age of the Civil War.* New York: Oxford University Press.

Blight, David W. 1989. *Frederick Douglass' Civil War: Keeping Faith in Jubilee.* Baton Rouge: University of Louisiana Press.

Boos, Hans E.A. 2001. *The Snakes of Trinidad and Tobago.* Austin: University of Texas Press.

Booth, Michael R. 1965. *English Melodrama.* London: Herbert Jenkins.

Brand, Dionne. 1999. *At the Full and Change of the Moon.* New York: Grove Press.

Brathwaite, Kamau. 1973. *The Arrivants: A New World Trilogy.* London: Oxford University Press.

———. 1994. *Barabajan Poems: 1492–1992.* New York: Savacou North.

Brereton, Bridget. 1979. *Race Relations in Colonial Trinidad, 1870–1900.* Cambridge: Cambridge University Press.

———. 1981. *A History of Modern Trinidad, 1783–1962.* London: Heinemann.

———. 1983. "The Birthday of Our Race: A Social History of Emancipation Day in Trinidad, 1838–1888". In *Trade, Government and Society in Caribbean History, 1700–1920,* edited by Barry W. Higman, 69–83. Kingston: Heinemann Jamaica.

———. 1989. "Society and Culture in the Colonial Caribbean: The British and French West Indies, *c.*1870 to *c.*1980". In *The Modern Caribbean,* edited by Franklin W. Knight and Colin A. Palmer, 85–110. Chapel Hill: University of North Carolina Press.

———. 1992. "Searching for the Invisible Woman". Review article. *Slavery and Abolition* 13, no. 2: 86–96.

———. 1993. "Social Organisation and Class, Racial and Cultural Conflict in Nineteenth Century Trinidad". In *Trinidad Ethnicity,* edited by Kevin A. Yelvington, 33–55. Knoxville: University of Tennessee Press.

Brodber, Erna. 1988. *Myal.* London: New Beacon Books.

Campbell, Carl C. 1992. *Cedulants and Capitulants*. Port of Spain: Paria Publishing.

Carpentier, Alejo. 1969. *El reino de este mundo*. Barcelona: Editorial Seix Barral.

Chamoiseau, Patrick. 1998. *Texaco*. Translated by Rose-Myriam Rejouis and Val Vinokurov. New York: Vintage Books.

Chapman, M.J. 1833. *Barbadoes*. London.

Cobham, Rhonda. 2000. "Jekyll and Claude: The Erotics of Patronage in Claude McKay's *Banana Bottom*". In *Queer Diasporas*, edited by Cindy Patton and Benigno Sánchez Eppler, 122–53. Durham: Duke Univesity Press.

———. 2002. "Mwen na rien, Msieu: Jamaica Kincaid and the Problem of Creole Gnosis". *Callaloo* 25, no. 3 (summer): 868–909.

Course, A.G. 1962. *A Dictionary of Nautical Terms*. London: Arco Publications.

Crafts, Hannah. [c.1855–60] 2002. *The Bondwoman's Narrative*. Reprint, edited by Henry Louis Gates Jr. New York: Warner Books.

Cudjoe, Selwyn R., ed. 1999. *Michael Maxwell Philip: A Trinidad Patriot of the Nineteenth Century*. Wellesley: Calaloux Press.

Danticat, Edwidge. 1998. *The Farming of Bones*. Harmondsworth: Penguin.

Day, C.W. 1852. *Five Years' Residence in the West Indies*. 2 volumes. London: Colburn and Co.

De Lisser, H.G. 1919. *Revenge: A Tale of Old Jamaica*. Kingston: The Gleaner Co.

———. 1929. *The White Witch of Rose Hall*. London: Ernest Benn.

———. 1937. *Under the Sun: A Jamaican Comedy*. London: Ernest Benn.

———. 1952. *Psyche*. London: Ernest Benn.

———. 1953. *Morgan's Daughter*. London: Ernest Benn.

de Verteuil, Anthony. 1986. *Sylvester Devenish and the Irish in Nineteenth Century Trinidad*. Port of Spain: Paria Publications.

———. 1987. *Begorrat/Brunton: A History of Diego Martin, 1784–1884*. Port of Spain: Paria Publications.

———. 2000. *Great Estates of Trinidad*. Port of Spain: A. de Verteuil.

Dorland's Illustrated Medical Dictionary. 1994. Edited by Douglas M. Anderson. 26th edition. Philadelphia: W.B. Sanders.

Douglass, Frederick. [1845] 1993. *Narrative of the Life of Frederick Douglass, An American Slave. Written by Himself*. Reprint, edited by David W. Blight, Boston: Bedford Books.

———. 1996. *The Frederick Douglass Reader*. Edited by William L. Andrews. New York: Oxford University Press.

Edwards, Bryan. 1793. *The History, Civil and Commercial, of the British Colonies in the West Indies*. Vol. 2. London: J. Stockdale.

Fisher, Philip. 1985. *Hard Facts: Setting and Form in the American Novel*. New York: Oxford University Press.

Fitzhugh, George. [1857] 1960. *Cannibals All! Or Slaves without Masters*. Reprint, Cambridge: Harvard University Press.

Foner, Philip S., ed. 1950–55. *The Life and Writing of Frederick Douglass*. 5 vols. New York: International Publishers.

Fredrickson, George M. 1971. *The Black Image in the White Mind: The Debate on Afro-American Character and Destiny, 1817–1914*. New York: Harper and Row.

Gates Jr, Henry Louis. 1988. "The Trope of a New Negro and the Reconstruction of the Image of the Black". *Representations* 24 (Fall): 129–55.

Giles, Paul. 2001. "Narrative Reversals and Power Exchanges: Frederick Douglass and British Culture". *American Literature* 73 (Winter): 779–810.

Glissant, Edouard. 1981. *Monsieur Toussaint*. Translated by Joseph G. Foster and Barbara A. Franklin; edited by Juris Silenieks. Washington, DC: Three Continents Press.

Gomez, Michael. 1998. *Exchanging Our Country Marks: The Transformation of African Identities in the Colonial and Antebellum South*. Chapel Hill: University of North Carolina Press.

Gonzales, Anson. 1972. *Self-Discovery through Literature: Creative Writing in Trinidad and Tobago*. Trinidad: A. Gonzales.

Griffith, Julia, ed. 1853. *Autographs for Freedom*. Boston: Jewett.

Heath, Roy. 1979. *From the Heat of the Day*. London: Allison and Busby.

———. 1981a. *Genetha*. London: Allison and Busby.

———. 1981b. *One Generation*. London: Allison and Busby.

Hedrick, Joan. 1994. *Harriet Beecher Stowe: A Life*. New York: Oxford University Press.

Hentz, Caroline Lee. [1854] 1970. *The Planter's Northern Bride*. Reprint, with an introduction by Rhoda Coleman Ellison, Chapel Hill: University of North Carolina Press.

Higman, Barry W. 1984. *Slave Populations of the British Caribbean, 1807–34*. Baltimore: Johns Hopkins University Press.

Hopkins, Donald R. 1993. "Dracunculiasis". In *The Cambridge World History of Human Disease*, edited by Kenneth F. Kiple, 687–88. Cambridge: Cambridge University Press.

Hooker, J.R. 1975. *Henry Sylvester Williams: Imperial Pan-Africanist*. London: Rex Collings.

Ignatiev, Noel. 1995. *How the Irish Became White*. New York: Routledge.

Jacobs, Harriet. [1861] 1987. *Incidents in the Life of a Slave Girl*. Reprint, Cambridge: Harvard University Press.

James, C.L.R. [1935] 1971. *Minty Alley*. Reprint, London: New Beacon Books.

———. 1976. *The Black Jacobins*. In *A Time and a Season: Eight Caribbean Plays*, edited by Errol Hill. St Augustine, Trinidad: Extra-Mural Studies Unit, University of the West Indies.

———. [1963] 1983. *Beyond a Boundary*. London: Stanley Paul. Reprint, New York: Random House.

John, A.M. 1988. *The Plantation Slaves of Trinidad, 1783–1816*. Cambridge: Cambridge University Press.

Joseph, E.L. [1838] 2001. *Warner Arundell, the Adventures of a Creole*. London: Saunders and Otley. Reprint, edited by Lise Winer; introduction and annotations by Bridget Brereton, Rhonda Cobham, Mary Rimmer and Lise Winer, Kingston: University of the West Indies Press.

Kincaid, Jamaica. 1996. *The Autobiography of My Mother*. New York: Farrar, Straus and Giroux.

Kiple, Kenneth F. 1993. "Disease Ecologies of the Caribbean". In *The Cambridge World History of Human Disease*, edited by Kenneth F. Kiple, 497–504. Cambridge: Cambridge University Press.

Lalla, Barbara. 1996. *Defining Jamaican Fiction: Marronage and the Discourse of Survival*. Tuscaloosa: University of Alabama Press.

Lamming, George. 1953. *In the Castle of My Skin*. New York: McGraw Hill.

———. 1979. *Season of Adventure*. London: Allison and Busby.

Liberty Bell. 1839–58. Boston: Massachusetts Anti-Slavery Fair.

Lombardi, J. 1971. *The Decline and Abolition of Slavery in Venezuela, 1820–1854*. Westport: Greenwood Press.

Lovelace, Earl. 1996. *Salt*. Boston: Faber and Faber.

Martin Jr, Waldo E. 1984. *The Mind of Frederick Douglass*. Chapel Hill: University of North Carolina Press.

McFeely, Wiliiam S. 1991. *Frederick Douglass*. New York: W.W. Norton.

McKay, Claude. 1933. *Banana Bottom*. New York: Harper and Brothers.

McWatt, Mark, ed. 1985. *West Indian Literature and Its Social Context*. Cave Hill, Barbados: Department of English, University of the West Indies.

Mendes, Alfred H. [1934] 1984. *Pitch Lake: A Story from Trinidad*. Reprint, London: New Beacon Books.

Millette, James. 1970. *The Genesis of Crown Colony Government: Trinidad, 1783–1810*. Curepe, Trinidad: Moko Enterprises.

Mittelholzer, Edgar. 1952. *Children of Kaywana*. New York: John Day.

Morean, Francis. 1992. "Croc-chien: Life Water from the Forest". *Trinidad and Tobago Review*, April, 29.

Nugent, Maria. [1966] 2002. *Lady Nugent's Journal of Her Residence in Jamaica from 1801 to 1805*. Edited by Philip Wright. Reprint, Kingston: University of the West Indies Press.

Peterson, Carla. 1992. "Capitalism, Black (Under)Development, and the Production of the African-American Novel in the 1850s". *American Literary History* 4 (Winter): 559–83.

Philip, [Michel] Maxwell. [1854] 1997. *Emmanuel Appodocca, Or, Blighted Life: A Tale of the Buccaneers.* London: C.J. Skeet. Reprinted, Port of Spain: Mole Bros., 1893. Reprint, edited by Selwyn R. Cudjoe, Amherst: University of Massachusetts Press.

Philippe, Jean-Baptiste [Anonymous]. [1824] 1987. *An Address to the Rt Hon Earl Bathurst . . . By a Free Mulatto of the Island.* London: The Author. Reprinted as *A Free Mulatto,* Port of Spain: Paria Publications.

Phillips, Caryl. 1990. *Higher Ground: A Novel in Three Parts.* New York: Penguin.

Puri, Shalini. 2003. *The Caribbean Postcolonial: Equality, Post/Nationalism and Cultural Hybridity.* London: St Martin's Press.

Ramchand, Kenneth. [1970] 1983. *The West Indian Novel and Its Background.* Revised edition. London: Faber and Faber.

Reid, V.S. 1949. *New Day.* London: Alfred Knopf.

Roediger, David. 1991. *The Wages of Whiteness: Race and the Making of the American Working Class.* London: Verso.

Rousseau, Jean-Jacques. [1762] 1970. *Emile, or On Education.* Reprint, translated by Allan Bloom, New York: Basic Books.

Sander, Reinhard W. 1988. *The Trinidad Awakening: West Indian Literature of the Nineteen-Thirties.* New York: Greenwood Press.

———, ed. 1978. *From Trinidad: An Anthology of Early West Indian Writing.* London: Hodder and Stroughton.

Schwarcz, Joe. 2001. "Meet Our Old Friend Arsenic". *Gazette* [Montreal], 8 April, A13.

Segal, Daniel A. 1993. " 'Race' and 'Colour' in Pre-Independence Trinidad and Tobago". In *Trinidad Ethnicity,* edited by Kevin A. Yelvington, 81–115. Knoxville: University of Tennessee Press.

Senior, Olive. 1986. "Real Old Time T'ing". In *Summer Lightning and Other Stories,* 54–66. Harlow: Longman Caribbean.

Sommer, Doris. 1991. *Foundational Fictions: The National Romances of Latin America.* Berkeley: University of California Press.

Stowe, Harriet Beecher. 1839. "Trials of a Housekeeper". *Godey's Lady's Book* 18 (January): 6.

———. [1839] 1879. "Trials of a Housekeeper". In *The Mayflower and Miscellaneous Writings,* 98–105. Boston: Riverside Press.

———. [1852] 1981. *Uncle Tom's Cabin or, Life among the Lowly.* Boston: J.P. Jewett. Reprint, edited by Ann Douglas, New York: Penguin Books.

Thomas-Bailey, Melisse. 2001. "Samuel Carter and the *San Fernando Gazette*". Paper presented to the Conference on Henry Sylvester Williams, University of the West Indies, St Augustine, Trinidad.

Toussaint, Michael. 2000. "Afro-West Indians in Search of the Spanish Main". PhD dissertation, University of the West Indies, St Augustine, Trinidad.

———. 2001. "George Numa Dessources, the Numancians, and the Effort to Form a Colony in Eastern Venezuela, *c.*1850–54". Paper presented to the Thirty-third Conference of Caribbean Historians, University of the West Indies, St Augustine, Trinidad.

Walcott, Derek. 1969. "A Far Cry From Africa". In *In a Green Night*, 18. London: Jonathan Cape.

———. 1970. "What the Twilight Says: An Overture". In *Dream on Monkey Mountain and Other Plays*, 3–40. New York: Farrar Straus and Giroux.

———. 1990. *Omeros*. New York: Farrar Straus and Giroux.

———. 2002. *The Haitian Trilogy*. New York: Farrar Straus and Giroux.

Walker, David. [1831] 1995. *Appeal to the Coloured Citizens of the World, but in particular, and very expressly, to those of the United States of America*. Reprint, New York: Hill and Wang.

Walrond, Eric. 1926. *Tropic Death*. New York: Collier Books.

Winer, Lise. 1993. *Trinidad and Tobago*. Varieties of English Around the World, vol. 6. Amsterdam: John Benjamins.

Winer, Lise, and Mary Rimmer. 1994. "Language Varieties in Early Trinidadian Novels, 1838–1907". *English World-Wide* 15, no. 2: 225–48.

Wood, Donald. 1968. *Trinidad in Transition: The Years After Slavery*. London: Oxford University Press.

Young, Elizabeth. 1999. *Disarming the Nation: Women's Writing and the American Civil War*. Chicago: University of Chicago Press.